# RAVE REVIEWS FOR COLLEEN THOMPSON'S ROMANTIC SUSPENSE!

## HEAD ON

"Well written with realistic and appealing characters, *Head On* is a mesmerizing story that keeps readers guessing as the murderer draws closer and secrets are revealed. A compelling tale of romantic suspense, it is a strong, satisfying read."

—Romance Reviews Today

"*Head On* is packed with tension and hard-edge suspense. The story is unforgettable and weaves a rich tapestry of good and evil. Prepare yourself for an all-nighter. *Head On* really delivers. It's a great read."

—Fresh Fiction

"Thompson's novel is filled with realistic dialogue, compelling narrative and believable conflict. The multiple viewpoints add dimension to the plot, and the characterizations are very well done."

—*Romantic Times BOOKreviews*

## HEAT LIGHTNING

"Thompson has crafted a top-notch, thrilling romantic suspense."

—*New York Times* best-selling author Allison Brennan

"This nicely complicated tale has plenty of edge-of-your-seat suspense. The villain is quite violent and evil, and the mystery moves along at a good pace. The main characters' acceptance of certain traits the people in their lives possess is well developed...."

—*Romantic Times BOOKreviews*

# DANGER IN THE SHADOWS

"Is someone at the house?"

She didn't answer right away, but over the cell phone he recognized the sounds of movement, of the SUV's door closing. The dog fell quiet, so Jay could make out the jingling of keys and the chiming of the seat belt reminder.

"Dana, answer me right now." He tasted bile as a new thought shook him. "Is someone with you?"

As he shoved his feet into his boots, he heard her engine starting.

"No, I'm all right," she said. "He's gone."

"Who's gone?" he asked.

"I saw somebody outside. Couldn't see who it was, but I'm sure it was human."

"Shit." He should have brought her here with him, should have kept her safe. "How close?"

"I think he was right outside—I heard a footstep, but when Max barked, he ran to the salt flat. He was armed, I'm pretty sure. Rifle, shotgun—one of those with a long barrel. It was hard to get a good look. Max was going crazy, and when I looked back, the guy was gone."

Jay grabbed his keys, "I need you to check your rearview. Do you see anyone behind you?"

# COLLEEN THOMPSON

# THE SALT MAIDEN

LEISURE BOOKS     NEW YORK CITY

*To friendships rooted in the written word...*
*And all the Midwives who help bring them to the light.*

A LEISURE BOOK    ®

December 2007

Published by

Dorchester Publishing Co., Inc.
200 Madison Avenue
New York, NY 10016

ISBN 10: 0-8439-6017-5
ISBN 13: 978-0-8439-6017-4

The name "Leisure Books" and the stylized "L" with design are trademarks of Dorchester Publishing Co., Inc.

Printed in the United States of America.

10 9 8 7 6 5 4 3 2 1

Visit us on the web at www.dorchesterpub.com.

# ACKNOWLEDGMENTS

I owe a great debt to those who helped make *The Salt Maiden* a reality. First, I'd like to thank agent Helen Breitwieser and editor Alicia Condon for their enthusiasm from the start. But the story never would have made it past my office door without the help and encouragement of the merry band of talented fellow writers who served as my first readers. Thanks to Patricia Kay, Jo Anne Banker, and the members of my fabulous critique group, the Midwives: T. J. Bennett, Wanda Dionne, Joni Rodgers, Anna Slade, and (last but never least) Barbara Taylor Sissel.

Thanks, too, to my family: husband Michael Thompson and son Andrew, I appreciate the way you picked up the slack while I was chasing the deadline dragon, and I never would have gotten this idea without our amazing road trip adventures.

I would also like to say thank you to Sheri Ermis, R.N., who was immensely helpful with my medical questions. Any errors in the department are my own.

One final note: the location of Devil's Claw was a conglomerate of any number of desolate places I have visited, including tiny Mentone, Texas, in Loving County. Though I stayed as true as possible to the facts, the flora, and the fauna, I freely admit to taking a few geographic liberties where they better served the story.

# THE SALT
# MAIDEN

# *Chapter One*

*In the desert*
*I saw a creature, naked, bestial,*
*Who, squatting upon the ground,*
*Held his heart in his hands,*
*And ate of it. . . .*

—Stephen Crane,
"The Black Riders and Other Lines"

Long before the ancient Aztecs and Egyptians ever dreamed of making mummies, nature had perfected her technique. First take a corpse—a human's, for example—and protect it from the ravages of predators and weather. Then find a quick way to strip the body's tissues of all water content.

Dry winds do a fine job, providing the unfortunate's final resting place is cold enough to discourage hungry insects. But even in a hot locale—say the arid country of West Texas—certain natural compounds serve the purpose quite as well.

One of the most effective substances is common salt, including the white crystals surrounding a body in a cavern so far beneath the desert's surface, the coyotes and the turkey vultures never sense its presence. And neither do the searchers, whether they use horses, SUVs, or small planes in their hunt for one missing woman amid the hundreds of square miles where rattlesnakes outnumber humans and scorpions have outlasted every species since the dinosaurs.

Could she speak, our modern mummy might beg the searchers to look longer and look deeper. But, of course, she's been beyond that for some time.

\* \* \*

Dana Vanover stopped dead in the middle of the hallway of Texas Children's Hospital in Houston. Her head was already shaking as her mother turned.

"I'm not doing this," Dana told her. "I'm sorry for these people, Mom. Truly sorry their daughter's condition is so serious. But I don't want to get to know them. I don't want to feel . . ."

Her mother arched an elegantly sculpted blond brow and folded arms both tanned and toned from tennis. Her latest cosmetic procedures might have smoothed the lines from her face, but they did nothing to erase the disapproval. "Feel what, Dana? Sympathy for the only grandchild I'll have?"

Spinning on her heel, Dana stormed toward the elevator, her long strides easily outdistancing her mother's. The staccato *click-click* of high-heeled sandals trailed her.

"Please, Dana, let's not dwell on—" Isabel's voice rose to a squeak.

Dana turned in time to see her mother toppling forward and reacted reflexively to save her from a fall.

"You all right, Mom?" She scanned quickly, her gaze sliding from her mother's sleek blond pageboy haircut to the summery green-and-white dress.

"I . . . I'm fine," she said, then pointed down at the pretty pear green sandals to indicate a broken strap. "The price of vanity, I guess."

As she extricated herself from Dana's grip, her mother shuddered at the unexpected touch. Isabel Smith-Vanover Huffington tried to hide it, but Dana knew very well that she loathed all forms of physical contact, particularly those that took her by surprise. Dana had once heard whispers of abuse in her mother's childhood, but no one in the family was willing to discuss it.

Dana shook her head. "One day you're going to break your neck in those things."

"If I do, at least I won't be caught dead in those abominations you insist on wearing."

Dana frowned at her. "Right." But it wasn't the insult to her Birkenstocks that grated.

"Oh, for heaven's sake. You must know I was joking." Her mother took a deep breath, then reached for Dana's elbow. At the last instant she dropped her hand instead and kicked off the broken sandal, then bent to pick it up. "We've come this far. Please."

She bobbed along a step or two before Dana stopped again beside a brightly colored mural of cheerful cartoon animals.

"She's really not your grandchild, or my niece either. Angie saw to that when she put her up for adoption. Nikki belongs to the Harrisons. We were never even meant to know about her. And we never would have if she weren't in such bad shape."

Tears welled in her mother's green eyes. "They've asked for our help. To save that dear child's life."

Isabel had learned of the "dear child" only when a private investigator had landed on her doorstep three weeks earlier, yet here she stood, playing the queen of empathy, though she had never shown more than ill-disguised revulsion for her own two daughters' illnesses. Had Nikki Harrison and her parents really won Isabel over during her first, brief visit to the cancer center, or was she merely trying on the role of distraught grandmother to see how well it suited?

"We've both been tested," Dana told her, "and if the match had been good I would have gladly donated bone marrow for a transplant. But it's not a possibility, and I can't afford to get any more involved in this—"

"You used to be such a caring girl. And you still do so much good. For animals, at least."

Dana braced herself against the implication that she thought more about her canine and feline patients than about people. "I told you, I *am* sorry. But I can't bleed for everybody, Mom. I don't have the energy right now. I have a veterinary clinic operating at a loss, thanks to the time I took off after my surgery. And I still have a ton of wedding gifts to send back, along with some pretty damned awkward notes to go with them—"

"You haven't finished that *yet?*" Her mother's eyes shot wide. "Oh, Dana. It's been more than three months now. What on earth are people going to *think?*"

Dana didn't have an answer. She felt guilty enough without Isabel hammering the nail in deeper.

After passing a nurses' station, her mother paused to check the room numbers on a sign before she turned a corner. Still hobbling, she made careful progress while Dana followed in her wake, helpless as a leaf drawn by the current. But not as unprotesting.

"I'm sorry, Mom. Sorry *I* won't be giving you a grandchild. Sorry I haven't been able to write your friends to tell them, 'Here's your Waterford dust catcher back; thanks anyway. Alex, the rat bastard fiancé, thought the whole hysterectomy-at-thirty-one thing was too much of a downer.'" She wanted to deck the sniveling coward every time she thought about how he had dumped her by text message and then ducked the resulting shit storm with a quick transfer to the New York office of his brokerage firm. "And I'm especially sorry I can't get sucked into another of my big sister's dramas right now."

People were giving her a wide berth as she passed them: a frail-looking young mother towing a small boy by the hand, a round-faced woman in raspberry-bright scrubs pushing a cart of trays that stank of steamed broccoli and heart-healthy chicken. Poor, sick kids were going to love *that.*

"You're making a scene," her mother whispered as she hobbled. "And finding Angie is the least we can do to save that sweet child. When you see how hard her parents are praying for a miracle, how totally devoted they are to—"

Still following, Dana cut her off. "There's no guarantee Angie's going to be a match, even if we did know where to find her. She still hasn't cashed those checks, right?"

Dana and her sister each received a modest monthly stipend from a trust fund set up after their father's death. Neither would come into the full amount until she turned thirty-five. For Angie that was less than a year away. Then she'd be free to blow $2.4 million on her various addictions. Until then, however, she depended on the monthly payments. But Dana wasn't too worried just because Angie had put off cashing the last two mailed to her. It probably meant she'd drifted into a relationship with a man content to pay the bills for as long as the ride lasted. Or possibly she was so into one of her commissioned weavings that she'd temporarily forgotten about drugs—or even food. Or maybe she'd hooked up with some commune and given over all her cares to Jesus. Where Angie was concerned, almost anything could happen—except another rescue from her sister. That ship had sailed—and sunk—already.

"She hasn't cashed them," Isabel confirmed, "and when I called, the sheriff told me no one's seen her in at least two months. But she can't have gone far. He found her car out by the house where she was living. Apparently the engine's gone bad. Something about a cracked block, maybe?"

Dana felt the first frisson of unease then. "What about her loom?"

"He says as far as he can tell, all her things are still there. And I asked especially about the loom."

*It's not my problem, not my problem, not my problem.* Dana repeated the words until they blended like a mantra. Angie had sworn at her for rushing to the rescue the last time, had skipped out of town and vanished the time before that. *And if I have to fight with her now, on top of everything else . . .* Dana rubbed her temples, but she couldn't hold back her concern.

Troubled though she might be, Angie wouldn't leave her loom behind. Not that one thing, not ever. Once, during a rare calm visit while Angie was in rehab, she had described it to Dana as her only constant: the shuttle that married the varied strands of warp to weft and wove scant snatches of peace out of her chaos. She could become almost poetic when she talked about it. Angelina Morningstar, she called her weaver self, the artist. Other people called her that, too, and during her more stable periods, "Angelina" made good money selling work inspired by years of cultural anthropology courses that had never quite translated into a degree.

"Maybe you should fly out there and check on her." Dana's suggestion slipped out before she could stop herself, though she already suspected it was a lost cause.

Her mother paused before a closed door. "Heaven knows I'd like to. But you know very well she'll head for the hills if she hears I'm within a hundred miles. Besides, Jerome has put his foot down this time."

Although her mother's husband of six years loved nothing more than seeing his name listed among the big-time benefactors of well-publicized charitable endeavors, the real estate developer had never approved of his wife "enabling" Angie's irresponsible behavior. But Dana suspected Isabel was using him as an excuse, that she would far rather send her younger daughter as an emissary and throw money at the trouble than risk yet another heartbreak. It was tough to fault her mother, since Dana wished that she could do the same thing, wished that the buck didn't always stop, inevitably, with her.

"I'm *not* doing it this time," she insisted. "And I'm not going to make the Harrison family's tragedy mine."

Her mother raised her knuckles toward the door and paused to give her a look from the intersection of Shrewd and Appraising. "Come inside for just a minute. We'll need to wash and put on masks and gowns. Then we can meet the Harrisons. Do that much for me, and I swear I'll never bring up this subject again."

*Not my problem, not my problem, not my problem,* went the mantra. But the moment Nikki Harrison looked up at her through Angie's brown eyes, Dana's resolution shattered, along with her vow to stay out of her sister's life and get her own on track.

# *Chapter Two*

*Sobriety sucks. It hurts like hell.*

*It makes my mouth taste shitty and my eyes feel like they're melt-ing and my brain buzz like a drunk bee. It makes me remember.*

*But I can fucking do it this time. No rehab, no support group, no clueless little sister taking time out from the Perfect Life to make me feel like such a screwup.*

*Just the desert this time. The desert and the loom.*

> —Entry one (undated)
> Angie's sobriety journal

*Friday, June 22, 5:27 P.M.*
*98 Degrees Fahrenheit*

"How far would you go . . ." As Dana Vanover's convertible bumped along the rutted caliche road, she whispered the first line of the childhood game she'd played so many times with Angie. For years they'd finished it with questions spun from girlish fancy.

"*How far would you go . . . to spend a Saturday in detention with all the members of The Breakfast Club?*"

"*. . . to sing on MTV with Cyndi Lauper?*"

"*How about for a date with Luke Skywalker—or better yet, Han Solo?*"

But as the girls grew into women, Angie's questions took on an intensity that made her younger sister shiver. "*You keep saying you love animals so much, but how far would you go to save them? What about giving Mom's mink coat a decent burial—or are you too afraid of getting into trouble?*"

When Dana had refused, Angie had gone ahead and done it, the first hint that when it came to limits she meant to spend a lifetime testing hers. On that occasion her actions ended up getting her sent for the summer to some kind of wilderness survival camp for troubled teens, the first of many such sabbaticals away from home to "straighten her out."

"So how far did you go this time," Dana asked her missing sister, "to run away from everyone who ever loved you?"

As she peered across a flat expanse dotted with thorny scrub brush—and absolutely nothing else—she caught her first sight of the answer to her question: *the dead center of nowhere*.

As Devil's Claw appeared on the horizon, she was stunned by the miserable huddle of buildings that had the nerve to call itself a town—the *only* town—in Rimrock County. Named for a hard-luck weed whose seeds, according to the Internet, clung to passersby for dear life, Devil's Claw looked as if it was barely hanging on.

"This surely can't be all of it," she muttered as she drove past the beige two-story courthouse and stared at what couldn't amount to much more than a few dozen peeling wood-frame structures. She'd read in an article she called up in *Texas Monthly*'s online archives that there were only a couple of dozen residents. Roughly twice that number lived in widely scattered shelters all around the area, bringing up the total population to around seventy-five, which made it the least-populated county in the United States.

But reading it was one thing and seeing it another. In the withering heat she didn't see a sign of life. Not a person, not a stray dog, not a single green leaf. What in God's name could have led Angie to this hellhole?

Since she ran out of town long before she ran out of questions, Dana turned the car around and headed back to the courthouse, where a single vehicle, a dusty station wagon, lingered. She frowned, recalling that the sheriff had told her on the phone he'd meet her here in his Suburban. But she had arrived a half hour earlier than she'd expected.

Her gaze drifted to a flicker of movement across the street

as someone adjusted the crooked blinds covering the window of a boxcar-sized white building. The Broken Spur Café, according to the hand-lettered sign above the door.

Her stomach growled for something fresher than the energy bar in her purse. Something crisp and leafy, she dared to hope. After setting the brake and shutting off the BMW, she climbed out into the searing sunlight. This would be as good a time as any to get her first glimpse of the locals. She needed a good stretch, too, after her eight-and-a-half-hour drive from Houston.

She opened a grease-stained door, and the only two men inside abruptly stopped their conversation. The first, a wiry, short man with a thatch of snowy hair and a stained apron, gestured toward her with his spatula from behind the counter.

"You're here about your sister," he said, while the second rasped, "Damned interferin' hippie, that girl. Glad to see the last of her."

Something in the voice told Dana that the customer seated at the counter in front of a pack of Camels and a half-eaten burger was actually a woman, not a man, in spite of the Clark Kent glasses and the short gray hair combed back straight and flat against her skull. The faded jeans and T-shirt offered no confirmation either, since their owner had no curves to fill them.

Stunned by their abruptness, Dana demanded, "How do you know why I'm here, and what do you know about my sister?"

"I know we've got one shot at this salt dome project," said the woman, "and your *sister's* done her damnedest to queer the deal for us. So as far as I'm concerned, good riddance to bad rubbish."

Five minutes later Dana was back out in her idling car again, having been told, "We don't serve a damned thing 'green and meat-free' in the Broken Spur," by Abe Hooks, the owner of the area's sole restaurant, gas pump, and store.

"Pompous redneck," she grumbled. She had half a mind to sic her mother on him to teach him the finer points of condescension.

As if on cue, there was a ringing from the seat beside her. Bracing herself, Dana pushed a button to answer the satellite telephone her mother had rented after learning that regular cell phone reception here was spotty at best. Unthinkable that Dana should stray beyond the range of her influence.

"You're there?" her mother asked. "Did you find out anything?"

"Not much," Dana admitted, "but I haven't met the sheriff yet."

"You tell him he'd better hurry. You tell him we're not losing that poor child."

"You mean Nikki." Dana had noticed that her mother never said the name, as if the *idea* of a cancer-stricken granddaughter appealed more than the individual.

"Of course I mean her. Who else? I swear, I haven't slept a wink in days. I'm too afraid that if I close my eyes, the phone will ring, and—"

"I understand, Mom." Dana had heard it in her nightmares, the call that would tell her she was already too late. Though Nikki was holding her own so far, germs had a way of slipping past even the most thorough precautions. "Has there been any change yet?"

"Nothing that I've heard about."

In the background Dana caught the bright clink of ice cubes and the more muted coos of doves. Evidence enough that her mother was unwinding with her usual "happy-hour" vodka tonic as she lay beneath her vine-draped trellis, her painted toenails pointed toward a bright blue pool.

Though she hated vodka tonics, Dana's mouth watered at the thought of her mother's backyard paradise in the River Oaks neighborhood of Houston. As her eyes scanned dust-beige bleakness, she struggled to recall cool turquoise framed by greenery and the sweet fragrance of the pale pink blooms of Isabel's specially imported honeysuckle.

"I know it must be tough there waiting," Dana allowed. "But maybe you'll feel better hearing that I'll be dining on filet d'Power Bar this evening. And sleeping heaven knows where."

The nearest hotel was back in Pecos, and the thought of adding yet another hour to the nine hours she had already spent on the road depressed her. Was it possible that someone here rented rooms?

"Just try to think of this as an adventure, Dana. Let's keep this about Nikki, dear, not you."

Resentment prickled. Though she had been away from home only a day, Dana already missed Lynette, her fellow veterinarian and business partner, along with her Welsh corgis, Ben and Jerry. She missed the ice cream, too, along with the prospect of a big, crisp salad, a long shower, and a longer sleep in her own bed.

Movement caught her eye, a dust cloud rising in the distance and drifting steadily toward the courthouse along the rutted desert road. Other than a roadrunner chasing after something—a lizard, maybe—it was the only activity in town. Though she felt certain unseen eyes were watching from the few buildings in range, not another person stirred. Even the pair of stunted trees and the courthouse lawn had withered in the heat.

"I'd better go. The sheriff's coming. I'll call you if there's anything new."

"You be sure and mention my suggestions," Isabel urged her.

Dana had a clear vision of herself hiking far out into the desert and dropping the expensive phone. Then her mother could sit beside her pool and issue her "suggestions" to the creosote and tarbush, though she'd probably prefer the nodding pump jacks.

"That sheriff needs to understand we're serious—you aren't going anywhere until you have your sister." Isabel took the same tone she did when calling the landscape company to complain that the oleanders weren't clipped to her standards. "Tell him you're staying put until he gets off his tail and finds her."

"I've talked to him on the phone a couple of times, and he's been out seriously looking for days and days—since I explained how much that loom meant to her and what's at stake if we don't find her." Or, at least, he'd *told* Dana he'd been searching. Now that she'd been treated to a taste of Devil's Claw hospitality, she began to have her doubts. Especially since she'd learned that Angie had stirred up hard feelings around town.

Not wanting to worry her mother over it, Dana focused on the positive. "Sheriff Eversole says he's questioned practically everybody in the county, and he even got a search plane out here. I wouldn't exactly call that sitting on his—"

"Maybe you should let him know the Huffingtons can be *extremely* generous when we're grateful. I'm sure an elected official in a place like that could find some use for a sizable . . . *contribution* to his next campaign."

"I'm a little confused," said Dana. "Which is it you want? The browbeating or the bribery? Because I want to make sure we're on the same page here."

"You don't need to be sarcastic. I just can't stop thinking about that precious child."

Her mother's statement nudged at something huddled, dark and ugly, in a place Dana didn't want to look. A thirty-one-year-old woman had no business being jealous of a sick girl, no business wondering why the same mother who had made her believe she needed to be perfect would love *this* child without reservation.

Dana told herself she should be happy her mother had progressed. But instead of saying so, she snapped, "And what about your daughter?" The daughter who couldn't come close to meeting Isabel's exacting standards.

"Of course I worry about Angie. But as she's reminded us

so many times, she is a grown woman. A grown woman who has turned her back on everything I've tried to do." Pain lanced through her mother's words, pain that she had every right to, considering the way Angie had treated her each time she attempted—however misguidedly—to help.

"I know. I know, Mom. Sorry." As Dana looked past an unpainted leaning house and straight out to the horizon, her anger leached away. "It's just . . . you wouldn't believe the distances out here, how far it is from everything we take for granted. What if she *is* lost somewhere in this country?"

But even as Dana reminded her mother of the danger to Angie, her mind wandered to the undersized six-year-old at the center of so much medical equipment. On the day they'd met, Nikki Harrison had been pale and sweaty after a round of vomiting from chemo. Her gaze, though, was so clear and bright and present that the sight froze Dana's breath inside her lungs. In that moment the little girl *was* Angie, the way she had once looked.

*How far would you go to get her back?*

"I'll bet we'll find out anytime that your sister's been holed up with some man or other." Bitterness sounded in Isabel's voice. "Until the money runs out and the party's over."

Dana stared at the silhouette of the white Suburban floating toward her on a shimmering cushion of heat waves. "I don't think they do a whole lot of partying around here. But I really have to go now. I'll call you later if there's news."

"Now, Dana, don't forget to tell him—"

As a tall figure who must be Eversole slid out of the dust-caked SUV, Dana started faking static sounds. "Can't . . . hear you, Mom. I think the battery's . . . cutting out on me."

"Oh, for heaven's sake. Eight years of higher education and you can't even remember to recharge a simple—"

Dana switched off the phone, then killed the Beamer's engine and climbed into the blazing heat.

A gold-and-black dog followed the sheriff out of the Suburban. A lean and rangy shepherd mix, he eyed Dana suspiciously, as if he'd guessed how many animals she'd stuck with needles over the past years. Or how many intact males she had neutered.

When she took a good look at Rimrock County's freshly minted sheriff, he looked almost as leery.

"Dr. Vanover?" he asked, and stuck out a big hand.

Nodding, she took it, though Eversole wore nearly as much grime as the SUV. Except for his intense blue eyes and the sweat trails melting cleaner rivulets on his face, he might have been a figure chiseled out of sandstone.

Nicely chiseled, she thought, with the body of an athlete and strong features shaded by the brim of a sweat-stained Western hat.

"It's Dana," she managed before the café door across the street creaked open and Abe Hooks leaned out, wielding his spatula like a gavel. Dana's stomach clenched when he looked past her as if she were invisible. Hooks met the sheriff's gaze before nodding once and then disappearing back into what was clearly the real nerve center of this county.

The sheriff stared another moment at the Broken Spur before he let go of Dana's hand and cleared his throat. "As of this afternoon the search is over. Afraid I don't know where else to look."

"Have you asked the locals where to—"

"I *am* a local. Born and bred here."

If he meant that literally, Dana felt sorry for his mother. "Sorry," she said. "I understood that the last sheriff died, that you had recently been recruited."

He gave her an appraising look, one that lingered a bit too long for comfort. "Been checking up on me?"

She nodded. "The *Pecos Enterprise* is online. I read about it on the Web, tried to find out as much as possible about what I was getting into before I headed out here."

He hesitated before answering. "My uncle . . . he was the sheriff killed in the house fire that burned what used to be my grandfather's homestead."

"I'm sorry."

"So am I. But the paper had some of its facts wrong. I didn't get recruited. Before the Guard called up my unit I was a cop in Dallas, and by the time I got back stateside I was more than ready to head home."

"You were overseas?" she asked. It made sense to her: his rigid posture and directness, his terse way of speaking on the phone. All bespoke a military background.

But something had shifted in him with her question. Tension stiffened his limbs, and the light dimmed in those blue eyes.

"I was proud to serve," he said quietly.

She wondered about that but answered honestly: "You should be." Though she had a whole flock of reservations about the current conflict. None of them, however, dampened the respect her late father, who had served as a surgeon in Vietnam, had instilled in her for those who fought and sometimes died to fulfill what they saw as their duty.

But even if Eversole had served in hell, Dana couldn't imagine anyone willingly returning to Devil's Claw, Texas. Strong homing instinct, she decided—or the Dallas PD didn't want him back.

"Well, I'm home now," he said, "though I'm pretty sure I've wasted most of my first week on the job hunting a woman who took a notion to move on. That happens around here, especially among the squatters. And your sister has a history."

"She wouldn't leave her car."

"Could be she abandoned it. It'd cost more to fix than it's worth."

Dana cast a guilty look at her little blue convertible, a "pick-me-up" gift from her mother after the one-two punch of the surgery and breakup. Angie, on the other hand, had been driving an ancient Buick with a couple of hundred thousand miles and almost no paint on it. Anything better and she'd simply trade it for a high-grade hit of whatever she could find, or turn it into quick cash to donate to some crazy cause or a friend with a sob story.

"Maybe she left the car, but I've already told you she'd never go without that loom, especially with a nearly finished tapestry on it. I called the gallery owner she deals with, and he told me she has a buyer waiting. Angie stands to collect close to two grand on delivery."

He shook his head. "Drugs and alcohol can reshuffle a person's priorities. Your sister has both weaknesses, from the looks of her arrest record. Probably plenty more charges I haven't found, too, since she's skipped through a lot of jurisdictions."

"I *know* she's still around here." Dana stared up at the sheriff over her sunglasses' dark rims. "We can't quit looking. And you won't. You're just hot and tired and frustrated right now. And annoyed that I'm here to bother you in person."

"I wouldn't say annoyed"—beneath the grime there was the suggestion of a smile as his gaze skimmed over her—"exactly. But the rest is on the money. And I mean what I say. Always."

Aggravation tightened her mouth. One thing she was sure of: he was stiff-necked. Proud, too. But if he thought that she would give up, he was also clueless.

"You can't," she insisted. "What can I do to help you? I could go through her house."

"It's only a one-room adobe, and my deputy and I have both been over it twice already."

"Please, I'd like to see it."

Beneath his hat's brim, the sheriff squinted. "Damned blast furnace out here. Might want to finish this conversation inside. Not that it's going to change my answer."

"What's the real reason you want to drop this? Because some fry cook gave you the evil eye?"

Looking grimmer than ever, he slammed shut the SUV's door. "You'd better not let Judge Hooks hear you call him that."

A buzzing started in Dana's ears as a sense of unreality descended. With so few people, roles overlapped here, creating crosscurrents she could never hope to understand. The thought left her disoriented, as if she'd been dropped off in a country where she didn't know the customs and couldn't speak the language.

The sheriff took a step or two toward the courthouse, then turned to peer over his shoulder. "You'd better hurry. Estelle'll be turnin' off the air-conditioning in another twenty minutes. County budget cutbacks.

"I've got a little fridge behind my desk," he added, sweetening the deal. "Cold jug of water in it, maybe even a Coke or two."

Despite the hat, the dirt, and the creases, his blue eyes smiled as he said it. Maybe he guessed that the suggestion had her suddenly parched mouth begging for a sip of icy sweetness.

"I'll come in," said Dana. "I think I could learn to appreciate shade in a whole new way here."

Not that summer in Houston, with its stifling humidity, was any picnic, but even this late in the afternoon the desert sun seemed hell-bent on sucking every drop of moisture from her cells. For all her differences with Angie, it was that sun that most scared Dana. What if, instead of shacking up with some new lover, Angie was wandering somewhere in the featureless, flat scrubland, disoriented by the heat and sunburned lobster red?

*If she's out in that, she's as good as dead.* Dana closed her eyes as the horizon tilted. *And more than likely so is Nikki.*

The dog barked at the same moment the sheriff caught her arm. "Inside," he urged. "Gotta get you cooled down. Then we'll talk."

He held open the front door for her. The dog slipped through first, his short nails clicking on a marble floor dulled and scratched by years of sandy footsteps. The dark-paneled walls looked worn, too, and yellow splotches marked the ceiling tiles in places and accounted for the musty-stale smell, at least in part. A bucket of sand, bristling with cigar butts, offered further explanation. Dana figured they probably kept a spittoon tucked inside the men's room. Or maybe even in the ladies'.

"They had this place done up real nice back when the oil revenues were better," Eversole said as his boot heels struck a deeper note. He pulled off his hat, revealing short, light brown hair darkened in the places sweat had dampened it. "Been a while, though. Back when my granddad was the sheriff."

She heard the defensiveness in his voice, a warning that he wouldn't tolerate her looking down on the courthouse, town, and county he'd reclaimed as his own. It didn't much surprise her. She'd seen his mouth tighten when he'd caught sight of the Beamer. Besides that, the Anne Klein shorts and Talbots top she wore with her flat sandals were simple, classic—and as out of place as scuba gear in Rimrock County.

"So you've come back to the family business?" She preferred small talk over her mother's methods of persuasion.

He shrugged and opened a smoked-glass door labeled SHERIFF. "Pay's steadier than ranching, but I plan to keep a hand in that, too. Or will until the damned salad lovers take over the world."

She smiled. "That would be me. Vegetarian for five years. Since I toured a slaughterhouse in vet school."

He shook his head and snorted.

"Vegetarian veterinarian who sees fuzzy little pups and kitties instead of dosing heifers." His eyes glinted with amusement. "This is gonna be the greatest thing for local gossip since that pack of flying-saucer hunters took a wrong turn on the way to Roswell in the eighties. But not even those weirdoes would dare to stick their noses up at Abe Hooks's burgers."

She laughed and stepped inside the office, where a plump woman was rifling through the top drawer of the only desk.

"Help you find something, Estelle?"

As the woman looked up, Dana's focus remained stuck on the flypaper of that iron gray hairdo. Half pompadour, half beehive, with a neat little bun in back, it went well with the fifties checked dress and made Dana think of Aunt Bea from the reruns of that old *Mayberry* show.

With a start Dana recognized the small brown eyes and the nose, which clued her in that she had just met the she-male version of this woman at the Broken Spur. The one with the Clark Kent glasses, the gray hair, and what had turned out to be one foul mouth. There was no question that the two must be related, but talk about flip sides of the same coin.

"We're out of paper clips again, Jay. How on earth do people expect a tax office to run without a decent supply budget— Oh." Her expression closed as she noticed Dana. "You must be that other Vanover girl that Jay said would be coming."

"Dana Vanover." Smiling, she offered her hand, ridiculously eager to win over one person in this county. Especially someone clever enough to manage that feat of hairstyle engineering without a salon for miles around. Dana's own strategically messy blond hair had long since fallen limp around her shoulders.

Estelle didn't take her hand. "*Miss* Vanover?"

"Actually, it's Doctor, but Dana's fine," she said.

"Around here, Dr. Vanover, we're not so fast and loose with first-name privileges. I'm Mrs. Hooks, the county tax collector."

"And the judge's wife?"

"I am."

All hope of an ally fizzled. For all Dana knew, Abe Hooks had already phoned the woman since their run-in. Or perhaps in a town this small, gossip traveled by osmosis.

"Do you . . . do you have a sister?" Dana asked, grasping at one last straw.

The woman nodded stiffly and excused herself, but not

before giving Eversole a look as pointed as her husband's. As she closed the door behind her, Dana noticed that her right foot dragged.

"Sore subject." Eversole tossed his hat onto the desktop, where a small mushroom cloud of dust rose. "They may've shared a womb once, but Estelle and Dorothy haven't spoken for a lot of years."

The two were *twins*? Stranger and stranger . . . "Seems like that could get pretty inconvenient in a town this small."

"You'd be surprised at how much feuding we pack in per capita. Same old grudges I remember from when I was a kid." With that, Eversole gestured toward a straight-backed chair, then went to a peeling, square refrigerator wedged between two four-drawer file cabinets behind his desk. He pulled out a Coke for Dana before filling an aluminum pie pan with water and setting it on the floor beside the dog.

"There you go, Max," the sheriff said. As the animal lapped and splashed, his stub tail wagging, Eversole filled a huge plastic cup with more water from the gallon jug.

Because she liked a man who tended his animal before himself, Dana didn't ask him where Abe Hooks kept his puppet's strings. Instead she thanked him for the soda and savored each sweetly carbonated swallow while she watched the way his throat worked as he drained his cup. When he went for a second, her gaze lingered on the fit of his Levi's as he bent over.

Not half-bad for a marionette. He definitely had the whole cowboy thing working for him. She ought to take pictures for Lynette, since her partner—who had worked with equines until a fractious filly kicked her hard enough to shatter her knee—followed the pro rodeo riders' circuit with a devotion most often reserved for cult religions. Dana had always preferred a little more polish in her men, though considering Alex and his damned text message, she had decided that Ben and Jerry were male company enough for the foreseeable future.

Eversole sat in the wooden roller chair behind a beat-up desk. She lowered herself into the chair he'd indicated to her and took another sip of blessed cola. "The gallery owners who handled Angie's weavings haven't heard from her in months. The friends and former lovers I was able to track down haven't either. She hasn't contacted our mom to ask for money, and with her car out of commission, I would have expected that for sure. Angie's never liked to be tied down."

Eversole nodded, then pulled a bandanna from the pocket of his jeans, wet it with more water, and wiped some of the dirt from his face before he spoke. "I've made some more calls since we last talked, to law enforcement in surrounding counties and over in New Mexico. She hasn't been arrested in any of them, and no unidentified . . . uh . . . remains match her description."

"Which means she's still here," Dana insisted.

"Search hasn't turned up one sign, not even the plane."

"It's a big desert," she said. "And with all the shadows from those rills and washes I saw on the way here—"

"They're arroyos. They drain rainwater off the foothills. Funnel flash floods, too, on occasion."

Dana's heart sank. "Should we search downstream, then? Have there been any hard rains since she vanished?"

"No, and there is no *we* in this search, not out on the desert. It'd kill you fast this time of year—kill anybody who doesn't know what times of day to look and what to stay away from."

Though it rankled, she suspected he was right. Her nature experience mostly consisted of jogs along carefully manicured park trails. "I understand, but what if I offered to bring in an investigator and a couple more planes, with private pilots? My family will gladly pay for—"

The blue eyes narrowed. "While you've been sitting back in Houston dreaming up ways to throw around your money, my deputy, a few volunteers, and I have thoroughly searched all around the place where she was living. And I'm telling you we haven't found a single thing to indicate—"

"Why don't you just say it?" Dana asked him. "You want me gone from here, the same as Angie. You'd just as soon forget about my sister and that little girl in Houston."

When his jaw clenched, attraction stirred inside her, as annoying as it was disconcerting. But Dana knew relief, too, that she still had the capacity to feel it, though both the man and the timing were nonstarters.

"I want your sister found as much as you do." His eyes held a quiet sincerity that looked real.

But so did the mirages that shimmered in the afternoon heat. Thinking of what the Clark Kent woman had said as she was leaving the café, Dana decided it was time to let him know that she might be a long way from Houston, but she was even farther from being a gullible mouth-breather.

"Really?" She leaned toward him to ask. "Even if Angie was about to stop this county's latest salt-dome scheme?"

# *Chapter Three*

*Throughout history, salt has meant many things to many people. Some cultures considered it wealth, while others believed it an essential component of religious and magical ceremonies. People worshiped it, fought for it, died for it. And in some civilizations it became a weapon, best remembered in ancient Rome's legendary destruction of Carthage by the salting of its fields.*

*So with such a rich and varied history, why shouldn't the same salt that's deprived this community of so much for so long end up being its salvation?*

—Miriam Piper-Gold,
Spokeswoman for Haz-Vestment,
from the transcripts of community meeting 1A,
Devil's Claw, Texas

Jay had dreaded this moment, had braced himself for the explosion the way he'd once braced himself for incoming mortar fire. Yet in spite of her narrowed green eyes and angry tone, he realized that Dana Vanover—Dr. Vanover, he mentally corrected—had yet to connect the last dots of the ugly picture that had cost him so much sleep of late.

She still had not allowed herself to understand that while she'd been looking for her sister, he'd been searching for a corpse—and praying like hell his suspicion would prove false. Inconvenient as it would be if Angie Vanover—or Angelina Morningstar, as she had called herself here—turned up dead, he had made a thorough search. Far too thorough to please his new constituents, many of whom had been showing up most evenings to help with the restoration of Uncle R.C.'s charred home. Over the past few nights their collective disapproval had taken on the bitterness of ash.

"Don't know if I'd call the waste-disposal plan a 'scheme,'" he said cautiously. "I've looked over the specs, read up on the science. Haz-Vestment, Inc.'s got no record of complaints. No accidents, no leaks, and a history of positive community involvement. And Lord knows this county's about due for a little taste of progress."

Jay could have said more but didn't. He needed to find out what Dana Vanover knew already and who had been her source. For sure it hadn't been any of those who had complained he was squandering county resources on a trouble-making drifter. All week they'd been reminding him of how his deputy, Wallace Hooks, had found "Angelina" passed out in the middle of the road outside of town. The theory was, she'd gotten plastered because no one would sign that fool petition she'd been shoving under every nose in the county. Jay found it easy to imagine she'd moved on after that humiliation and rejection—if someone hadn't taken a notion to kill her.

"Waste disposal? What kind?"

"Low-level radiation. From what I hear it's mostly medical waste. About as safe as you can get."

Dana was shaking her head. "Angie wouldn't have been won over by any corporate propaganda. About sixteen, seventeen years back, she was wrapped up in some environmental protest group, picked up a few arrests for being part of human chains across the entrances of public buildings and busy intersections, mostly nuisance stuff."

"Nuisance stuff," he echoed flatly, chilled to the bone by the memory of a lone Iraqi woman whose idea of protest involved strapping explosives beneath her traditional black abaya and begging American soldiers to help the horribly burned child she held in her arms.

And just that quickly, Jay was back there, breathing the bitter smoke stench of that other desert, his stomach cramping as Angie Vanover's kohled eyes glared out at him from behind a thick, dark veil. *Run*, he tried to shout at his men, but the word caught in his throat, and the woman was reaching for the detonator, and—

"Are you listening?" Dana's gaze had zeroed in on him. A hunting cat's eyes, with a patient stillness masking predatory instinct.

*Careful there.* His muscles tensing, Jay sucked in a breath to clear his head, reminded himself he was back in the Texas desert and that he had seen Angie Vanover only in mug shots and outdated family photos of an unsmiling girl with long, ash-blond hair.

"Sorry," he said. "Little too much sun today, and anyway, it surprised me to hear that your sister was mixed up with radicals." Slowly and deliberately he drank from a plastic cup as damp with condensation as he was with sweat.

From outside he heard a car door slam, followed by the rumbling rev of an engine. Estelle leaving, he guessed, though she'd neglected to turn off the building's air-conditioning.

"It was mostly in the Northwest," Dana said, "and they weren't radicals, just a bunch of college dropouts trying to be heard. I managed to track down one of her old friends from those days. Trent said Angie called a few months back, trying to drum up interest in a lawsuit. He told her he'd left his rabble-rousing days behind him. Sells insurance now in Portland. But Angie barely listened, she was so wound up about some plan she had for getting word out to the media to cover demonstrations."

A new chill shook him. Protestors here, and reporters from the outside. What the hell would he do if that happened? If they started digging into his recent history—including the reasons his own police force had declined to welcome him back?

He shifted in his seat before shrugging. "Rimrock County might be small in terms of population, but we're big enough to handle a little difference of opinion."

Dana looked skeptical. "What are you, the president of the chamber of commerce, too?"

He tried for a smile. "If we ever get one, I'll be sure to put my hat in the ring for the position."

She didn't smile back. "I'm not leaving without her."

"Then you could be here a long stretch." Her stubbornness reminded him of the few women who made their homes in Rimrock County, the kind who hunkered down, teeth gritted, and toughed out this tough land. But that was where the similarity ended. Everything else about Dana Vanover, from the silk and linen she wore, to the high-dollar convertible she drove, to the shoulder-length, salon-highlighted hairstyle, bespoke the kind of privilege those born to it took for granted. That sense of entitlement didn't sit too well with people around here, and, fair or not, they especially didn't appreciate it in a woman.

The building's AC shuddered to a stop, and in the silence that followed Jay caught the *tap-slide, tap-slide* of Estelle's retreating footsteps. Must not have been her car he'd heard before. This close to dinnertime it was more likely a couple of oilfield workers or a rancher heading to the café than someone coming in to see him. At least, he hoped that was the case, for with the thought of food his stomach rumbled loudly.

Dana's expression eased a little. "Am I keeping you from dinner?"

"Missed lunch earlier," he said. "Went out to have a look around the Apache Mesa pour-off."

"What's that?"

"It's one of those spots where rain runs down from the mountains, about a forty-minute drive down some pretty bumpy dirt roads."

"You mean there's another kind here?"

He ignored the comment and the smile that went with it. He might have to deal with the woman for now, but he didn't have to—and didn't want to—like her. Didn't want to notice the way she was put together, either, or that pretty face.

"Whenever there's a storm up in the higher elevations," he said, "the water ends up drizzling off the flat top of the mesa. When I was a kid we used to drive out and splash around in the little freshwater pool that forms down at the bottom from time to time."

"You thought my sister might've gone there?"

He shrugged. "People do, and it was a place to look, somewhere I haven't been all over ten times. So I took a shot."

It had been a wasted trip. The rocky bowl at the pour-off had been bone dry, and the cave punched into the mesa just above it held no sign of life but ten thousand restless dreamers—Mexican free-tailed bats that rose like smoke each summer night to scour the skies for insects. Jay had clambered atop a van-sized rock and shone his flashlight back into the darkness, then sighed in relief at the realization that he wouldn't have to crawl inside. The thick layer of guano appeared undisturbed; there was no sign that anyone had wormed his or her way into the cave's dark recesses. No sign that anybody had shoved a body back there either.

"Thank you," Dana told him as she rose from her chair. "For giving up your lunch to go there. And for looking for my sister all this week. I'd offer to buy you some dinner for your trouble, but I'm afraid I've already gotten crosswise with the cook."

Enticing as her smile was, he couldn't let it get to him. "That's all right. I'm too filthy, anyway. And besides that, my trouble's not for sale. It's already bought and paid for by the people of this county. If your sister was still one of 'em, I'd have already found her by this time."

Dana cut a swath through the heat, her strides long and swift, her mind seething with frustration. Still, the image of Jay Eversole stayed with her, an image that sparked and crackled along her nerve endings. She had to get clear of this one-horse hell pit—and that meant finding Angie and hauling her straight back to Houston to have her marrow tested. Dana had brought her own car, despite the long drive, in case simple persuasion wasn't enough to convince her sister to cooperate. She had headaches enough without allowing one of Angie's fits to get them both escorted off a plane—and Dana refused to take no for an answer.

But the Angie situation wasn't the only thing under Dana's skin. As much as she hated to admit it, Eversole's body had reminded hers that she was still female, whatever the surgeons had removed.

*Idiot,* she told herself. *Leave the Marlboro men to Lynette.* Jay Eversole was just another roadblock between her and what she needed. He was simply humoring her, going through the motions of looking for her sister so she wouldn't pull some family strings to drag in the Texas Rangers. Wouldn't look good for the big, bad, new sheriff if outsiders barged in and elbowed him aside.

She opened her car door and slid inside, only to wince as the leather seat seared her thighs. Jamming the key in the ignition, she started up the engine and turned the air-conditioning somewhere between arctic and subzero. . . .

And felt a rough brush scrape past her left ankle. Adrenaline pulled its ripcord, jerking her attention downward. But before her eyes could make sense of the slide of scales, raw instinct kicked in at the rattling.

At the sound her muscles exploded into reflex, flinging the door open and sending her bursting from the car—or, rather, falling.

She hit the hard-baked dirt with both knees and felt flesh tear with the bruising impact. Yet it wasn't pain but horror that had her shrieking as she scrabbled several yards away.

*Rattlesnake.* In her car. A damned big one, from what she'd seen. And chances were it hadn't gotten inside on its own.

# *Chapter Four*

Dana had stopped screaming by the time Jay was halfway down the sidewalk, but a glimpse of blood across her legs kept him running, his pulse pounding in his ears.

"Snakesnakesnake," she blurted the moment she saw him.

"Where?" he asked, scanning the area. Out of the corner of his eye he spotted Hooks and a couple of regulars boiling out the front door of the Broken Spur. Mamie Lockett, who lived next door to the café, poked her gray head through her front window to stare, too.

Dana climbed to her feet and put more distance between herself and the open car door. Pointing toward it, she shouted, "A *humongous* freaking snake. In my car, across the floorboard."

In spite of the heat her teeth chattered, and her eyes were wide. Yet she was already bolstering herself against the terror, gathering whatever reserves of courage she could muster.

Though he still refused to like her, he appreciated that. Hysteria solved nothing—and inconvenienced the hell out of those working to set matters right.

"Somebody put it in there." Her whole body was shaking, her flesh crawling with revulsion. Her gaze locked onto his face. "What kind of nutcase puts a rattlesnake in someone's car?"

"You sure it was a real snake?" This place spooked some of those more used to human commerce. The quiet he needed to stay sane worked at city nerves. Though Dana Vanover had struck him as anything but flighty, she wouldn't be the first to mistake a purse strap or a set of jumper cables for a hissing viper.

"Are you crazy?" she demanded. "If you don't believe me, why don't you stick your head in there and see for yourself?"

"Don't need to," he said as he looked down past her knees. "You've already convinced me."

Or the wounds had. A pair of them, some four inches above the outside point of her left ankle. A few drops of blood marked the spots one fang had scratched and another had sunk into. Already the flesh around the wound looked puffy. As if that weren't proof enough, he heard the telltale buzz of rattling from the direction of the car.

She followed his gaze downward, then yelped as she saw the bites.

"Oh, God. I didn't even feel it. Now I do, though, plenty." After a pause she added, "Guess he didn't like being shut up in the heat."

As if to confirm it, an arrow-shaped head poked out of the door, and a tan-and-brown snake as thick as her forearm lowered itself to the ground. As she had claimed, a damned big snake—a Western diamondback. The dog leaped toward it, snarling, but Jay beat him to the punch, drawing his sidearm and shooting the serpent through its head. As the body twitched he put the sole of his boot across the rattler's neck and pulled the tail end from the vehicle. A lot more snake spilled out than he'd expected, five—no—five and a half feet of well-fed viper, which terminated in a set of rattles bordered by telltale black-and-white stripes.

Dana stared at it, her fair face flushing and her skin gleaming with perspiration. "Holy . . ."

When her knees wobbled he holstered his Colt Commander and scooped her up before she fell. She made a nice armful, all long legs and slender curves.

But she wasn't too far gone to protest. "Put me down. I don't need—"

"Keep real still. I'm getting you inside, where it's cooler. Then I'm calling an air ambulance." He remembered the deputy, Wallace, pointing out the number of the El Paso–based service posted on a corkboard in the office. Glancing up, he told their audience, "She's been bitten—going to need a medevac."

"Bring her on in here." Abe waved to indicate the Broken Spur, and his two customers, the Navarro brothers, rushed over to lend a hand.

Since the café was closer—and probably cooler—than the courthouse, Jay didn't argue.

"Let me take her legs." Bill, the older of the brothers, slid a grease-stained hand beneath Dana's thigh—or tried to.

When Jay caught the look in his eye, he stepped neatly out of range. "I've got her, thanks."

Eagerness turned to a scowl, reminding Jay of Bill's reputation for dealing with frustration with his fists. He and his more easygoing brother, Carl, considered themselves ranchers but earned most of their income in the oil patch. Both could always be counted on to help their neighbors, but neither could be trusted to resist the temptation to feel up a good-looking woman if the chance arose.

It didn't very often, since the county's female population

came in only two varieties: spoken for and old. Rumor had it that the Navarro brothers, both in their early forties, had grown so desperate that Bill was e-mailing foreign ladies eager to come to the U.S. Carl scoffed at the idea, but the area's other ranchers joked that in the last few years their livestock acted skittish when he showed up on a property alone.

With both Navarros and the dog, Max, bringing up the rear, Jay carried Dana into the café. Abe had pushed aside one of the three wooden tables.

"I'll need a chair," said Dana. "We'll want to keep the bite below heart level."

Since that meshed with what Jay knew, he bent to set her down on the chair Bill Navarro pulled out. Before he could straighten, Mrs. Lockett burst inside, too. Bird thin, she flapped around them, twisting an embroidered hankie in her liver-spotted hands.

"Oh, dear," she kept exclaiming, her faded yellow housedress aswirl around her stick legs. "You'd better cut a big X and suck out all that poison. My boy Nestor liked to've died when he got snakebit, and that rattler wasn't half the size of that Goliath you got out there."

After pulling off his apron, Abe wiped his hands on it and tossed it onto the chipped Formica countertop. "Get you anything, Dr. Vanover? Water? Soda?"

Dana slid a sharp look his way. "So you're okay with my being here?"

Hooks flushed beneath his mop of white hair. "I told him to bring you on in, didn't I? And I'm sorry about earlier. Shouldn'ta been hard on you for the way your sister acted."

"Water would be fine, thanks," she said stiffly before bending down to grasp her leg above the bite.

Max wagged his stub tail and attempted to lick her face as her fingers dug into the flesh of her calf muscle. Trying to squeeze back the pain, Jay figured. But as much as it must hurt, she didn't whimper and her eyes remained dry.

He found himself praying that the bite was dry, too, that

the rattler hadn't cut loose with its venom. In around half the cases he'd seen growing up here, it worked out that way. But just in case it didn't this time, he'd best get his ass across the street and make that call.

Before he reached the door, Mamie went to search the grill area behind the counter. "What we really need's a big knife."

"Nobody's cutting me." Dana's gaze swept the room, touching on each of them in turn. "That old nonsense about sucking out the venom does more harm than good."

Carl Navarro scrubbed a calloused hand over three days' growth of beard, probably to hide his disappointment at not being allowed a chance to put his ugly mouth to that sleek leg.

"Are you sure?" his older brother asked. "Our daddy always said to—"

"There'll be no cutting on Dr. Vanover," Jay said firmly. "Could you keep an eye on her, Abe, while I go call up that chopper?"

Abe cracked open a bottle of water from the icebox and handed it to Dana. Though he'd complained tirelessly about the cost of a search plane to look for her sister, Hooks nodded and said, "You can count on it," before asking Dana what else he could get her.

As Jay strode outside, both Navarros followed.

"Got any plans for that big boy out there, Sheriff?" Bill asked him.

Jay hesitated. "Not particularly. Why?"

Catching on, his brother flashed a crooked grin. "Rattlesnake chili, that's why. Come on, Bill, and let's go skin 'im."

As Jay broke into a jog, he glanced down at the dog beside him. "You know something, Toto, buddy? I've got a feeling we're not in Baghdad anymore."

"How're you doing?" Judge Hooks asked her for what seemed like the thousandth time as they waited for the sheriff to return. "You sure you don't want to lie down? I can push over this here table and spread a clean cloth for you."

To Dana, his tone sounded as insincere as his apology.

"That sounds like a wonderful idea," the old woman chirped. "I'll run next door to get a pillow."

"I'm fine right here in this chair." Dana would rather have a root canal than admit her leg was throbbing and her heart was racing. Especially since she was more than half convinced that Hooks and his two snake charmers had been the ones who had left the rattler in her car, unless he'd put Clark Kent Woman up to it. Of course the bastard was being magnanimous now that he had figured a quick way to drive her out of Rimrock County. Idiot probably imagined he was getting rid of her for good.

"I'll be right back with that pillow," the gray-haired woman sang as she hurried out, leaving Dana on her own with Abe Hooks and the greasy, burned stink of years' worth of burgers.

"*I'll* be right back, too," Dana promised, looking square into the small man's eyes. "I promise you I'll find my sister, Judge Hooks. This isn't going to stop me."

"Of course it won't."

The patronizing runt had the nerve to pat her hand. If her leg didn't hurt so badly, she swore she'd give him a swift kick.

"I mean it. This bite—it's not bad at all," she said, though already her mouth tasted of metal and her skin felt clammy-cool. Staying on top of her panic left her feeling strung out, reckless. And mad as all hell. "A vial or two of antivenin and I'll show up again—with help. Or maybe I'll just call in some reporters, let them get a whiff of how you people are trying to obstruct me. Let them put a camera on that dying girl, too, and interview her parents. Then you'll have more media in Devil's Claw than you know what to do with. And you can't run 'em all off with the local wildlife."

The county judge's face darkened, making his blue eyes appear brighter. "You have a lot of nerve, *Doctor*, sitting in my place and leveling an accusation like that. I don't know and I don't care what kind of pull you and your people have in Houston. You're in *my* county now, and it's about time you understood what that means."

"All I want is Angie," Dana repeated. "Once I find her, neither one of us will ever trouble you again."

"As appealing as that sounds"—Hooks's voice softened to a serpent's whisper—"how can you be so sure your sister's still alive?"

# *Chapter Five*

*Monday, June 25, 6:48 A.M.*
*67 Degrees Fahrenheit*
*Forecast High: 104 Degrees*

"It's bad enough I had to waste half my evening last night listenin' to Weevil Jenkins carry on about that missin' ATV of his. Now you want me to follow you in that little car of hers so I can drive you all the way back from El Paso. Three and a half hours each way." Across the table of the Broken Spur, where Abe had plunked down a breakfast of eggs and sausage links, Deputy Wallace Hooks's face took on the sour look that Jay was coming to know well. The easy translation was that Wallace would do things a hell of a lot differently if he'd been given a shot at being sheriff.

He probably would have had that chance had it not been for Dennis Riggins, who insisted the Hooks family already had too much power, and that twenty-nine-year-old Wallace lacked the "seasoning" to take on the position. Dennis had swayed the other county commissioners into seeing things his way, leaving Abe Hooks outvoted, and breathing new life into the Riggins-Hooks feud that had been a Rimrock County staple for generations. Wallace in particular was put out, since the sole deputy's position may have been created with him in mind, but it demanded long hours in exchange for near-starvation wages.

"Think about it this way," Jay said. "If we take Dr.

Vanover's car to her, express a little professional concern, and update her on the investigation while she's recovering, she'll more than likely head straight back to Houston as soon as she's healed up."

Abe looked up from the grill, where he was cooking his own breakfast, since no other customers had arrived. "Man's got a point, Wallace. We don't need her back here, stirring up more trouble. If we're to get this project under way . . ."

Wallace shut him up with a look of pure resentment. Beneath the thick, dark bangs, the son's hazel eyes were as striking as his cleft chin and even features. Though his father had struggled to steer him toward some practical endeavor, Wallace had defied him, running off and hitching his way to New York City after high school. Everybody in the county—except the Rigginses, Jay guessed—had been rooting for the kid to make good on the promise of his handsome face. But instead of shooting straight to stardom on the TV soaps or maybe Broadway, as he'd hoped, Wallace couldn't act his way into commercials; and the jockey's build he'd inherited from his father hadn't helped things. After six or seven years of knocking around the country working various dead-end jobs, he'd come back home to lick his wounds and take the deputy's position created for him. But if Abe had been counting on gratitude to keep Wallace in line, he'd been deluded. Though Jay had been back in Devil's Claw only a short time, he had quickly picked up on the friction between father and son.

Wallace used his fork to spear a chunk of scrambled egg swimming in hot sauce and then spoke around the mouthful. "To hell with all this door-to-door ass kissing. She and her nut-job sister, neither one had any business out here. And now we're supposed to hand-deliver that fancy car of hers and act like we're all concerned that she got snakebit?"

"I *am* concerned," Jay said as a vision of Dana Vanover's terrified face overtook him. He could feel her still, trembling as those tight curves filled his arms. That brief contact had figured prominently in his dreams since. His subconscious didn't give a damn that she was so far out of his league, he couldn't reach her with an Apache helicopter. "The way I see it, putting a big rattler in that car was nothing short of attempted murder. And doing a thing like that right in front of my office shows a fundamental disrespect for this county's law enforcement, disrespect for *me*."

He glanced toward Abe, who had sworn he hadn't seen or heard a thing in the minutes before Dana Vanover started screaming. Though Jay had questioned both Navarros, Mrs. Lockett, the always charming postmistress, Dorothy Hobarth—who had cursed him for his trouble—and the few other potential witnesses, each one had told a similar story. Suspiciously similar, to Jay's way of thinking, but it was possible that his late-night reading—the Haz-Vestment community meeting transcripts he'd liberated from Estelle's locked cabinet—could have left him feeling paranoid. Or maybe the memory of Baghdad, with its indecipherable mix of enemies and allies, had him looking for conspiracies at every turn.

Abe turned, swearing, to his grill, and scraped it as burning bacon smoked the tiny café. Rising from the table, Jay walked to the door and propped it open with a brick used for that purpose. A couple of hours from now the heat would come back with a vengeance, but Jay stayed by the door, enjoying fresher air while he still could.

"Who's to say it wasn't an accident?" asked Wallace. "What if she left her door ajar and the thing just crawled in looking for some shade?"

Jay shook his head in disbelief. "Parked car in the afternoon gets up to, what? A hundred thirty, hundred forty maybe. You don't honestly think that old snake lived long enough to get as big as he was without having enough sense not to wriggle up inside a furnace."

Wallace gusted out a pent-up breath, the surliness melting from his expression and leaving behind an earnestness that caught Jay by surprise.

"Maybe it's the idea of something like that happening *here* that I can't handle. Hell, Sheriff, we know the people around here—every one of 'em—and they aren't killers. These are the folks who're rebuilding your uncle's house so you can get out of that RV, the people who put in those wheelchair ramps for old man Parker and took up a collection to hire a home health-care aide from Pecos after Mrs. Lockett broke her hip last summer. This is Devil's Claw, not back where you worked in Dallas," Wallace said. "People don't kill people out here. Scare 'em, maybe, but that's all."

"If that snake had unloaded all his venom, she'd have been as dead as if a bullet did it." Or the explosion of a suicide vest at one of Baghdad's checkpoints. The thunder of it boomed through his memory, along with the hot splatter of crimson rain and the hail of fleshy chunks.

Heart pounding, he nearly dropped to the floor before he realized where he was. As Jay wiped sweat from his face with a folded bandanna from his pocket, Wallace rose and carried their plates to the counter.

As the deputy turned away, Jay caught Abe looking in the younger Hooks's direction and caught, too, something in the glance that passed between them. Was it more evidence of the father-son struggle he'd seen earlier, or were the two united in their contempt for the new sheriff the county commissioners had foisted upon them? Had he flinched or made some sound that gave his too-real memories away?

Yet as frightening as that thought was, another possibility raised the hairs on the back of Jay's neck. The prospect that both Abe and Wallace had fallen for Haz-Vestment's promises of a Devil's Claw transformed into some kind of oasis of prosperity. And that because of their belief, both father and son regretted Dana Vanover's survival.

"It's okay, Mom— *Hey.*" Moving the phone away from her mouth, Dana tried to catch the attention of the thickly built Hispanic woman making off with her lunch tray. "I wasn't finished with that."

But the food service worker had already escaped the private room, so Dana sighed and returned her attention to her long-distance conversation. "Sorry for the interruption, and I do appreciate the offer. It's just that there's no need for you to fly out. The swelling's way down, and I'm getting around fine with crutches. In fact, I'm doing so well the hospital's giving me the boot tomorrow."

"I would have made arrangements sooner if you'd called me. I would have been there for you, Dana."

Dana bit her tongue to keep from asking, *Who the hell are you and what have you done with Isabel Huffington?* Since Dana, long ago cast in the role of the good—or at least the functional—daughter, was normally the last person her mother worried over, it boggled the mind to hear her sounding so . . . maternal.

Maybe, Dana thought, she should have allowed the hospital staff to call when she'd been flown in. Instead she had delayed, telling herself she was better off waiting until she felt well enough to make the call herself. For one thing, she had a dread of Isabel swooping in to order around the doctors and nurses—a behavior Dana had long ago concluded was her version of a touch-free hug. Now that the crisis was past, Dana admitted to herself that she'd feared even more that her mother *wouldn't* care that she'd been hurt, that instead of showing up she would simply harangue Dana on the phone to get back to Devil's Claw—for her darling Nikki's sake.

*I am total scum, the poster child for sibling rivalry run horribly amok.* Her face burning, Dana gave herself a mental kick.

"They're making you leave the hospital already?" Isabel asked. "Don't those people know you were at death's door?"

She really did sound worried.

"No. Because I wasn't. Really, it was an extremely light

dose of venom. I was lucky." Dana glanced at her lower left leg, which had gone down to less than twice the size of her right. Though she had treated more than a few snakebites in canine patients, her stomach clenched at the thought of the lurid bruising beneath her bandages.

"You're flying back to Houston, of course. I'm sending you an open ticket. I'll hire a driver to see to your car."

"Why would you do that? Angie's still somewhere in Rimrock County. She *has* to be." Dana took the snake incident as proof that she had come too close to finding her sister for someone's comfort.

"I want her to be found, too. But those awful people tried to *kill* you." Her mother sounded both furious and frightened.

"I'm sure they didn't mean for me to die." Dana was far from certain of it, really, but the knee-jerk denial seemed like a fitting penance for her childish jealousy. "They just wanted me to go home without messing up their chances for that project they're so gung-ho about getting. They must think she'll come back and start rabble-rousing again if I find her and get her cleaned up."

*Either that or they know what's happened to her and don't want me to find out.*

"I won't have this, Dana. I won't lose you, too."

Dana's stomach tightened, and her limbs went cold as the implication sank in. "Angie might still be alive."

"Of course she is. She has to be." Her mother's voice cracked on the last word, betraying a concern she wouldn't—or couldn't—voice.

Dana hesitated a moment before admitting, "I'm really worried, Mom. Worried that the reason someone put that snake in my car is because he doesn't want me finding out he's done something to Angie."

*Killed her,* her subconscious whispered. *Why can't you just say it?*

"I'm not coming home, Mom. Not until I have her with me."

"But your leg is—"

"I'll be fine. The doctor's sure of it. I've already been walking on—"

"Dana, no. Whether Jerome approves or not, I'm sending out someone to help you—you remember Regina Lawler, don't you? She's good at getting to the bottom of things, and she's volunteered to—"

"Of all the reporters on the planet, *not* Regina. No, Mom." A longtime friend of her mother's, the forty-something Regina Lawler had been a popular Houston news anchor—until, in an unscripted, on-air meltdown, she'd called the news director a "perfidious prick" for demoting her to weekends in favor of some "bleached-blond bimbette out of Tulsa, Oklahoma." Summarily canned—and blackballed from the major markets—Regina was desperate for a story that would put her back on top.

The last time Dana had seen her, about two months ago, the woman had still been chain-smoking and profanely ranting—in spite of eight weeks of anger-management classes and all of Isabel's attempts to distract her from her favorite topic. The very idea of being stuck with the reporter in Devil's Claw was enough to make Dana break out in a cold sweat.

"I wanted to keep this in the family," said her mother, "but if the media's our only chance of finding Angie . . ."

Dana jumped at the sound of a firm rap at the room's door. "Hang on a minute. Someone's here."

Though she wasn't expecting anyone, she put a hand over the phone's mouthpiece. "Come in."

Jay Eversole stepped inside, his hat in hand and his expression serious. Far cleaner than he had been when she'd last seen him, the man looked like a Wild West fantasy in his tan-over-brown uniform, the silver star catching the light from the room's window. Lynette would faint dead away, thought Dana.

She twitched the sheet to cover her injured leg and then

held up an index finger to signal him to wait. Uncovering the phone, she said, "Promise me you won't do anything until we talk again. The doctor's here to see me now. I'll call you back this afternoon."

As she clicked off the phone, Eversole smiled. "Doctor, huh? That's quite a promotion."

She shrugged. "If I'd told my mother it was you, she would have demanded I pass over the phone so she could give you an earful."

"What makes you think she hasn't? Several times, including last night, after you got around to telling her about that snakebite."

Dana winced, imagining the conversation. "Sorry."

"Don't be. Upset mamas come with the territory. And your mother has every right to be unhappy, with one daughter hurt and the other missing."

Before she could say more, a tap at the door preceded another interruption, an elderly man in wire-rimmed glasses and a volunteer's vest who was mostly hidden behind an enormous spray of mixed flowers. He set the vase on the bed tray.

"Holy cow. Who died?" Dana asked.

The man laughed, his mostly bald pate turning pink. "Only my lower back from hauling that behemoth up here."

He plucked out the card and passed it to her before wishing her a good day and a quick recovery.

"Thanks," she said, as he waved and left them. Shaking her head at the arrangement, she added, "My mother really has no concept of proportion. . . . Weird."

She blinked at the tiny card, confused, then looked up. "It's signed, 'Bill Navarro.'"

Jay grinned. "It's a lonely life out there ranching with his brother."

"But I don't know who he is. . . . Oh, yeah," she said, remembering a somewhat shaggy man, fortyish, with eyes creased by the sun and a thin layer of grime she'd come to associate with the men of Rimrock County. And a cowboy hat, of course. "He was one of those guys skinning the snake behind the café."

She made a face before adding, "He gave me his card before the helicopter showed up."

Jay snorted. "I have to hand it to him. Man sees an opportunity, he seizes on it."

"Like a pit bull, apparently." Dana rubbed her nose, which itched from all the pollen.

"That's Bill in a nutshell. Pit bull. Might want to keep that in mind when you talk to him."

"Maybe just a note, then."

The sheriff nodded in approval.

She sniffled, thinking she'd better have a nurse give the bouquet to a patient in need of cheering up, or she'd be sneezing her head off before day's end.

"So what brings you here?" she asked. If he had had more questions, he could have called her as he had the past two days. Unless he had some news he didn't want to share over the phone. "Is it something about Angie? Ha-have you found her?"

He shook his head. "I'm sorry, but there's still no sign of your sister. I wanted to see for myself how you are, and I brought your car for you."

Walking to her bedside, he passed her the keys, attached to a fob made from a photo of her corgis. The glimpse of Ben and Jerry made her homesick. Probably the two were having a ball playing with Lynette's Australian cattle dog at her place, but she could really use some wagging tails and canine kisses at the moment.

"My car?" Bringing it seemed far beyond the call of duty.

"I thought maybe you'd need it here, whenever you're up to driving. Besides that, I've always wanted to see what one of those little numbers could do if you redlined it."

"You . . . you drove it here so you could race it?"

He pointed at her, smiling. "Gotcha. I promise you I shifted through those gears like an old lady. Mostly."

She couldn't help smiling back. Marlboro Man was making a convert of her in the cowboy department. Pretty soon she'd be drooling over the rodeo-guy pictures Lynette kept by her desk at the clinic.

"So, how's the leg, Doc?" he asked.

"It's *Dana*, please. And it's better, thanks. They're springing me tomorrow."

"I'm glad. You had us pretty worried."

She wondered whom he meant by "us." Certainly not Judge Hooks. The only thing that worried that glorified fry cook was the thought of her returning. Had he sent the sheriff on a mission to keep her far away? The thought tossed a bucket of cold water over her new big-hat-and-boots fixation.

"I appreciate your bringing me the car," she said, "but you know, I'll still have to go back to Devil's Claw to take care of Angie's things."

"My deputy and I'll see to 'em," he said. "We can have them boxed and shipped, though it might take me a week or two to arrange to have that loom trucked. We'll want to make sure it's not damaged in the move."

She looked hard into Eversole's blue eyes. "Such a friendly, helpful bunch."

"We're just—"

"Trying to make sure I have no reason to return to Rimrock County?"

She had expected an argument, but he said nothing; nor did he look away. His expression grave, he only stood there as the silence between them took on weight.

Dana couldn't stand it any longer. "I'm right, aren't I?"

He frowned. "I haven't found out who put the snake in your car. No one saw anything. Or so they're saying."

"I see."

"I don't mean to stop investigating. And I haven't given up on finding your sister, either. But I'd feel better if you stayed away till I get to the bottom of all this."

"Or until Nikki Harrison dies and I lose interest."

His expression darkened. "That's the second time you've made that accusation. You were wrong before. You're wrong now. I don't want you hurt again, that's all. Or maybe killed this time."

Dana picked up her water cup from the rolling bedside table and sipped from the bent straw. But she couldn't swallow back the question that still nagged her. "Like Angie, do you mean? You believe . . . You think she's dead, don't you?"

He hesitated before answering. "I don't know that."

"You suspect it."

"I think it's a possibility. One that would explain a few things." He pulled the room's single chair by the bedside.

She rearranged the sheets for better coverage. "Why? Why would anyone kill Angie? I know she was making noise about getting together some protest, but . . ."

"But what?"

Dana grimaced. "This isn't easy to say about my own sister, but it's true. She's binged on drugs her whole adult life, and God knows she's an alcoholic. Sure, she got worked up about this and that from time to time, but she was bound to lose her focus, fall off the wagon. Then she'd forget about the salt-dome project."

"Maybe she convinced the wrong folks she was serious, that she could be a problem. That project, it's pretty important to the people around Rimrock." He hesitated, brushing dust from his hat.

She waited him out, sensing there was something more on his mind.

"Haz-Vestment's held a series of meetings to gain community support," he said. "I've been reading through the transcripts and . . ."

"And what?"

He shook his head. "I'd already heard that their spokeswoman's a real piece of work. Flashy dresser, lots of jewelry, real compelling way about her. Shook the right hands, kissed the right asses, made a lot of slick-sounding promises."

Dana nodded, recognizing the type. "Sounds like half the veterinary pharmaceutical reps I've met. Only she came to sell a company, not a product."

"Oh, yeah. She was selling, all right. Selling dreams of a Devil's Claw with fresh, clean-running water, of workers moving in and spending money in local businesses. Young females among them."

"Water, workers, and women. Sounds like the Devil's Claw trifecta."

Jay smiled wryly. "According to the transcripts there weren't many dissenters."

"Other than Angie . . ."

He nodded in confirmation. "And she was shouted down every time she started asking questions."

"Asking questions?" Dana echoed, imagining her sister on the warpath. "Or screaming accusations?"

"My deputy told me she *was* carrying on about the rape of the earth or . . . No, that wasn't it. She talked about the Salt Woman being defiled."

"The Salt Woman?" Dana found herself thinking of the digital photos Jay had e-mailed to her before she'd made the drive to Devil's Claw, when he'd asked her if she could identify her sister's things. One in particular came to mind—of the tapestry on the abandoned loom, with its tightly woven field of starlit desert backing the resplendent figure of an impossibly beautiful old woman, her white hair whirling around her naked body, her thin legs stepping forward, her dark, determined eyes locked on an unfinished horizon. The detail was incredible, by far the best work of Angie's she had seen. "Is there some significance?"

Eversole shrugged. "Not that I've ever heard of. And

from the way Wallace talked about it, I got the idea it didn't mean anything to him either."

Dana thought of her sister's long-standing interest in mythology and wondered if there might be some connection. She'd do an Internet search on this Salt Woman once she regained access to the laptop locked in her trunk. Probably a waste of time, she thought, just one more of her sister's drunken outbursts.

With a sigh she changed the subject. "Before, when you were talking about those transcripts, I got the idea something bothered you about them. Was it the way that spokeswoman honed in on exactly what people in your county wanted?"

Again he hesitated before answering. "No, I'd have expected Miriam Piper-Gold—that's the woman's name—to make promises. And like I told you, I looked into Haz-Vestment's reputation, found they've made a name for themselves with good corporate citizenship."

"So what was it, then?"

He frowned off into space, his gaze shifting to the open blinds and the clear blue sky beyond them. "It was the warnings. Piper-Gold was pretty subtle, but she referred several times to the nervousness of her investors, how they'd been bitten twice when communities that seemed ready to welcome them ended up balking after considerable money had been spent. There was apparently some lawsuit by out-of-town interests. Environmentalists reacting on emotion and not facts, as she put it. The L-word came up a few times, too."

"L-word?"

He smiled. "Liberal. That's not something you call your worst enemy in Rimrock County."

"Why does that not surprise me?"

"Because you salad-munchin' eco nuts are all so intuitive."

A laugh slipped free before she asked him, "So she was

hinting, I presume, that Haz-Vestment wasn't interested in gracing a community of misguided hippies with its facility?"

"Exactly."

Dana's smile faded as the gravity of Eversole's concern sank in. "And my sister was the one 'misguided hippie' in the county."

As her eyes burned, she held off tears by telling herself the scenario he was suggesting wasn't so much different from the one she had imagined when she'd first heard about the salt-dome project. At the time Dana had figured that Angie's potential interference was the reason no one was too eager to find her sister. Though the specter of Angie's death had since crept into Dana's thinking, the suspicion had seemed almost as unreal as the thought of someone putting a live snake in her car. Until Jay Eversole admitted he shared her fear, Dana had been able to hold on to the idea that this was simply another false alarm, one of the countless rehearsals for grief that Angie had put her family through over the years.

"I promise you"—his blue gaze never wavered—"I'm going to find out what happened. And if there's any way—any possibility whatsoever—that your sister's alive somewhere in Rimrock County, I will personally escort her back to Houston so she can get her marrow tested. You can count on that, Dana."

Since he'd be working in a county where nepotism was a way of life, where infighting was the only organized sport, and the name Vanover appeared to be a curse word, she would have to be an idiot to buy what he'd just said. Maybe she was, or maybe hearing him call her by her first name had kick-started dormant hormones, because she did believe him.

But then, she had believed in Alex Hilliard, too, right until the moment his damned text message lit up her cell phone's screen.

# *Chapter Six*

*I think I saw her last night, her white hair gleaming in the starlight as she strode across the flats. The Salt Woman, wandering the desert, looking for a home among those worthy of her gift.*

*More likely she was just another hallucination, a parting gift from the DTs—as if the puking and the shaking haven't been enough. But I can tell you this much: before I saw her I was hell-bent on jumping in the beater and hauling ass to Pecos for a bottle. Afterward the craving lifted, and I stood staring in the direction of the salt domes as the rarest peace rained down from the night sky.*

—Entry four, March 2
Angie's sobriety journal

*Saturday, June 30, 6:36 P.M.*
*101 Degrees Fahrenheit*

The vehicle's progress could be seen for miles as it churned up dust that stood out against the stark blue like a signal fire's smoke plume. The Hunter lowered the binoculars and wiped sweat off the eyepieces with a shirtsleeve.

Foolish woman had come back to the desert. Not only to the desert, but to the perfect isolation of the dilapidated ranch house out near Lost Lake. She should have gone back to her fancy family to reclaim her fancy life. Should have taken the fluke that had saved her and run with it like a jackrabbit.

She'd been given a sporting chance the first time. An opportunity to learn from her mistakes and mend her ways.

But the Hunter did not believe in second chances, not with so very much at stake. Besides that, natural selection was less forgiving in Rimrock County than most places, and if there was one thing to be respected, it was the ancient order of this most ancient land.

"Out here it's survival of the fittest," came the parched whisper, a rasping hiss barely tempered by a swig from the canteen. "And you've already proven, by returning, that the fittest isn't you."

Jay had just stopped by his office when the phone on his desk started ringing. With a sigh he reached for the receiver, though he'd been on his way home from another long day spent rechecking quadrants where others had supposedly looked for Angie Vanover. As much as Jay wanted to believe in both his deputy and his volunteers, he wasn't taking any chances, especially after this morning's phone conversation with Special Agent Tomlin from the FBI. Just thinking of it tempted him to pin his star to the corkboard and skip town before the proverbial shit hit the fan.

"Dennis Riggins," the caller identified himself so loudly Jay moved the receiver six inches from his ear. Though he couldn't be much older than his early fifties, the county commissioner was just about deaf. Too proud to wear a hearing aid, he compensated by speaking at top volume.

"What's on your mind?" Jay bellowed back into the phone. Anything less and Dennis would simply shout back demands that he quit mumbling.

"Saw somethin' you might want to check out today. I was passin' by the old Webb place. . . ." Named for the original rancher who had abandoned it decades earlier, the adobe had attracted any number of squatters over the years—including, most recently, the artist calling herself Angelina Morningstar. "I spotted this big, new-lookin' Expedition parked there. Drove close enough to see it was a rental, but—"

"Did you see any people?" Jay asked, at the same time praying, *Please let it be Angie and whatever boyfriend she's been off with.* His mind conjured an image of himself driving her right up to the doorstep of Dana Vanover's place, which, in his mind, was an immense, white-columned mansion. She'd come out on her crutches, then throw her arms around his neck and kiss him before tearfully reuniting with her wayward sister.

Pleasant as it was to imagine himself as Dana's—or anybody's—hero, it didn't hold a candle to the dreams that had left him hard and hurting every night since meeting her.

"Didn't spot a soul," said Dennis. "You think that Vanover woman could be back with them protestors—or maybe some reporter?"

Dennis's nervousness came through as loud and clear as his words. A rancher who derived most of his income from oil royalties off his land, he had put a lot of his personal money into Haz-Vestment as a show of faith in its plans. Jay felt sick to think of telling him the FBI's suspicions. He'd been asked to keep the information to himself, since the principals had not yet been arrested. And, of course, the suspects remained innocent until proven guilty.

*Bullshit. You know damned well that salt-dome project isn't happening—and that Devil's Claw has seen the last of Miriam Piper-Gold and her slick cronies. Pied Piper-Gold is what they ought to call that woman.*

He said, "If it is Angie over there, you don't have to worry. I promised I'd haul her troublemaking ass straight back to Houston, and I meant it. But what were you doing over by the Webb place?"

The abandoned ranch, near the dry salt flat called Lost Lake, was at least an hour away.

"Well, I . . ." Dennis started. "I was headin' over to see if anybody's been out to the salt domes. Equipment was supposed to start arrivin' last week, but the gate across the access road's still locked."

Jay's conscience gave him a swift kick. He owed the family friend who had helped get him this job when he'd been running out of options. He'd confessed to Dennis about the bridge in Baghdad and how it haunted him, even admitted to the psychiatric evaluation that he'd undergone before his relocation.

*"Far as I can see, you're a goddamned hero, not a liability."* A Vietnam vet himself, Dennis had been adamant—as well as loud enough that Jay had wished for earplugs. *"Besides that, you're R.C.'s nephew, and that's good enough for me."*

As far as Jay knew, Dennis had kept the knowledge of his recent history to himself, bragging of the "decorated veteran" part to others. To his way of thinking, the lives Jay had saved in an earlier incident, while stationed in Fallujah, absolved him of the possibility of guilt.

"I got a call this morning, Dennis," Jay said, "from the FBI, about Haz-Vestment."

*"What?"*

Jay realized he had unconsciously lowered his voice. For good reason, too. Estelle Hooks was working late this evening, and she was known to alleviate the boredom of tax-statement preparation by eavesdropping on his conversations.

"I'll talk to you later," Jay promised. "You still coming by the house tonight?"

More than anyone else, Dennis had thrown himself into the job of remodeling the late sheriff's fire-damaged adobe house. Both Abe and Wallace Hooks insisted that, being a Riggins, Dennis came for the free beer Jay provided, but Jay suspected it was the man's way of dealing with the death of an old friend, since he and Uncle R.C. had long been buddies. Drinking buddies, anyway, since the only thing Jay could remember the two doing together was sitting out on Uncle R.C.'s back steps and throwing back some cool ones at the end of a long day. While Jay, who had come to live with his bachelor relation at the age of twelve, attempted to do homework, Dennis—his hearing already fading—would boom out schemes to solve the county's problems, most of which involved running the Hooks clan out of town. Uncle R.C. would smile and puff one of his cigars, pausing every so often to speak of things he might have done if he had left the county, or to wave away a cloud of smelly smoke.

Jay smiled to recall it, though he'd been damned unhappy in those days after a single-car wreck killed his mother, and his father left abruptly to work on an offshore oil rig. As his father's calls and visits dwindled down to nothing, Jay had given Uncle R.C. nine kinds of hell, something that now shamed him as much as his failure to come back for so much as a visit after escaping Devil's Claw. Though his uncle had been the one to recommend that he "hit the ground runnin' and never look back," Jay regretted that he'd missed the chance to tell the man he was sorry for his behavior, or to thank R.C. for holding his rebellion in check with a firm but fair hand. God knew it was more than his old man— who had died five years back—had cared to do.

"I'll be there," Dennis told him. "But I wanted to let you know I called Haz-Vestment's office, and the fella there assured me work's gonna start on schedule."

*I'll just bet he did,* Jay thought miserably—and hoped the special agent nailed the conniving bastards to the wall.

After excusing himself for a quick cleanup in the men's room, Jay headed for the Webb place to find out who was there. Best-case scenario would be Angie: by herself and in one piece, though mad as hell that he had padlocked the house's doors to secure her belongings. But there were other possibilities as well, visitors who would make short work of his security measure, the drug dealers and coyotes who occasionally used such isolated places as safe houses while smuggling dope or illegals out of Mexico.

Still, he hadn't bothered calling Wallace, and he wouldn't unless he saw something suspicious. With only the two of them in the department, backup was a luxury reserved for bigger things than long shots. He'd have to settle for the company of Max, who rode shotgun as the rough road jolted man and dog alike.

In the rearview mirror, a choking plume of dust rose in the

SUV's wake. As he looked past the plastic hula dancer on the dashboard—a last vestige of his uncle's aimless talk of retiring to Tahiti—Jay's view was even less inviting. Tortilla-flat and hard-baked by a brutal sun, the Lost Lake area looked about as likely to support life as the surface of Mars. Jay tried to imagine what had prompted some misguided soul—Jonas Webb, according to local lore—to attempt to ranch along the salt flat's edge decades earlier. Had to have been a freakishly wet season, one of those rare events that briefly veiled the desert's harshness in soft green grasses. A joke played by the land to lure the unwitting into its grasp.

But all too soon the lush grass would have withered, leaving only the thorny seedpods of the devil's claw to catch the hooves of starving stock and the dungarees of the defeated. Had Webb cursed this place when he'd abandoned the adobe shelter he had built of earth and sweat and hope? Had he wept to leave the crosses that still stood sentry over the pair of nameless graves whose mounds still scarred the stony soil? More than once during his search for the missing woman, Jay had paused beside those two mounds, which someone had decorated with colored stones and desiccated petals, even a few iridescent feathers and a single, tiny skull bleached white save for the long orange incisors. Maybe a ground squirrel's, he figured, and most likely Angie's work. He wondered if the company of the dead had disturbed her or given comfort.

Ahead he spotted the one-room dwelling she had claimed, an adobe with splotched, cracked walls painted gold by the late sunlight. Still some fifty yards distant, the house hunkered low and mean, a brick-shaped blot against the blue smudge of the distant foothills. Though a succession of squatters had attempted to improve it over the years, the covered front porch had collapsed on one end, and shutters dangled beside glassless windows. The peeling wooden screen door hung askew, as if in testimony to the pointlessness of his attempts to secure the place.

Angie's ancient Buick crouched beside the building, decaying just as quickly. Since Jay had last stopped by, a third dry-rotted tire had gone flat, giving the rusty brown sedan a drunken tilt. But his attention focused on the unfamiliar Ford that Dennis had reported.

As Jay shifted the Suburban into park behind the vehicle, the hula dancer wriggled plastic hips. Staring past her, Max plunked his paws against the dashboard and raised his hackles with a growl.

"What's the matter, boy?" Jay asked. In the two weeks since he'd found the dog, hungry and abandoned at a roadside rest stop, Max had shown no signs of aggression other than his ill-advised lunge toward the snake. But clearly something was troubling him now, something Jay could neither see nor hear.

Something that stirred the uneasiness he had been carrying inside him these past four months.

His gun hand quaked as wraithlike figures took form in the shimmer of heat that rose from every solid surface.

"*Ali Baba, Ali Baba!*" Baghdad's children cried out, using the generic term for bad guys as they gestured toward the house.

Jay looked in the direction their skinny fingers pointed, only to spot a sniper squatting with an AK-47 on the rooftop, his robe as black as his turban. A second terrorist peered out from the doorway, a Molotov cocktail in his hand.

With a strangled shout Jay ducked low, his heart pounding and his eyes stinging with sweat. Distracted from whatever had captured his attention outside, Max gave himself over to this new game, his tail wagging and his tongue licking at his master's face.

"Shit." Jay fended off the kisses and blinked hard, struggling to regain the when and where of his position. Once it came to him, he peered over the dash and forced himself to focus.

The house, though homely, was certainly West Texan, a crumbling adobe in a familiar land. The only Ali Baba had sprung from his damned imagination.

Screwing his eyes shut, Jay sat before the chill gale of the AC vents and cursed himself. He could have applied for work anywhere in the country, someplace with soft, green mountains or towering pine forests. The seaside might have been nice, or somewhere with a lake. Instead he'd dragged his sorry ass back to the one place whose sprawling expanses and limitless horizons kept him tied to that *other* desert, the desert that had swallowed up his foolish promises to bring all his men home safely.

When he looked again, he saw a woman in the shadows of the porch's standing section. For a bare instant terror clothed her in a dark abaya, but Jay willed himself to still-ness until the illusion bled away.

In its wake stood not Angie, as he'd hoped, but Dana Vanover, dressed in rumpled khaki shorts and a somewhat grimy pale green T-shirt. She held a broom in one hand, and her blond bangs had fallen limply across her eyes.

Had she heard him, seen him spook at nothing? Maybe not, for she smiled and raised a bottle of water toward him in a casual greeting, not in the least alarmed.

Thank God for that, at least . . . but still, she shouldn't be here.

Frowning, Jay shut off his engine and climbed out into what felt like a solid wall of heat. Max burst past him, his whole body wagging in his rush to greet her, though he was usually cautious around those he didn't know well. His cau-tion made a lot of sense, considering that Jay had found pockmarks on the dog's side where some mean bastard had used the stray for target practice with a pellet gun.

"Hey, there, boy." Dana shifted her bottle and reached down to rub the dog's ears. "How're you doing, Max boy?"

Jay stood a moment, troubled by the way pleasure punched

through his irritation. So she had a pretty smile and the kind of body that did a clingy little T-shirt proud. He had no business being glad to see her—and no sense for thinking of the things they'd done in those damned dreams that did an end run around his self-control each night. Her presence only complicated an already tense situation. Once the news about Haz-Vestment got out, there were going to be some seriously unhappy folks in Rimrock County. Folks who might not think so clearly in their rush to assign blame.

"You found this place," he said as he moved nearer. "And you're walking on that leg."

"I can certainly see why they hired you as sheriff. You're an observant fellow, aren't you?"

"That's not the half of it. I noticed that it's hot, too, you've been cleaning, and you showed up in a different vehicle."

He nodded toward the far side of the house, in the direction of a gas generator's hum. "With some serious supplies. Which means you plan on staying awhile and not just picking up your sister's belongings and scooting home, like anybody with a lick of sense would."

Grin stretching, she said, "God, you *are* good. I had to rent the SUV in Pecos. The convertible was too small, and I thought I'd need the higher clearance to get back here."

"So who gave you directions?" He was surprised he hadn't heard about it.

"It was, uh, Bill Navarro—you remember, flower guy, snake charmer." She wrinkled her nose as she said it. "I still had his card, so I called to ask him—and of course to say thanks for the arrangement."

Jay resisted the temptation to fill her in about the rumors regarding Russian brides and Bill's history of fighting, not to mention the stories of a painkiller addiction in his past after he had injured his back in some mishap with a steer. For one thing, Bill was always on his best behavior with women. For another, Dana had too much class to string the man along.

"So how'd you get in, anyway?" Jay asked. "Did you pry off my padlocks?"

"That wood's so far gone, all I had to do was pull a little and it crumbled. And it's not as if anybody couldn't crawl in through those windows. But listen, I've got some more water inside. Want some while we talk?"

He shook his head, since he'd just finished a bottle. Even so, he squeezed past her into the leaning porch's shade, eager to avoid the searing sun.

Dana excused herself and ducked inside. In under a minute she returned with a small plastic tub of water, which she put down for Max to drink. After giving him a pat, she said, "Nice dog. A little skinny . . ."

"We're working on that," Jay said. "I found him only a couple of weeks back. Or he found me—jumped inside my RV when I got out at a rest stop. I thought I'd take him to a shelter, but . . ." He shrugged his shoulders. "He makes for decent company."

"A stray, huh?" she asked before giving him a more professional appraisal. To the dog she said, "Looks like you've had a rough go of it, poor guy. But I don't see anything a little TLC won't cure."

Afterward she sat on one end of a rough-hewn bench as Jay took the side opposite. It was still damned hot here, but she'd run an extension cord to an oscillating fan she'd set up, and its dry breeze offered at least the suggestion of comfort.

The blond tips of her hair stirred as she looked straight at him. "I told you I'd be back, just like I told you I was staying till I find her. I'm starting off by going over this house inch by inch."

He shook his head. "This is no place for you. All the sweeping in the world won't fix that, and neither will that generator."

Her lips pursed before she answered. "My sister managed with a lot less, and she lived here for, what, five months?"

He hesitated before saying, "Your sister might have *died*

here, Dana. And I can't concentrate on finding her if I have to keep an eye on you, too."

"I didn't ask for a babysitter, Sheriff." Her voice roughened as she added, "The only thing I want is Angie—one way or another."

He leaned forward to watch a scorpion crawl out from a crack in the adobe, lured by the shade into coming out of hiding before nightfall. Rushing forward, the creature seized a centipede with its tiny claws. He could have stepped on both but didn't bother. Both predator and prey would have enough stinging relatives close by that their annihilation wouldn't make a difference. And besides, humans were the interlopers here.

"I said I'll find her if she's anywhere around," Jay told her. "And I'll do it a lot faster than you will, hobbling around on that bum leg."

He gestured toward the bandaged ankle. It looked somewhat swollen, though not as much as he'd expected.

For a long while Dana said nothing, looking off into the distance as he watched the scorpion thrust its stinger into its victim. The centipede writhed desperately, but soon its movements slowed, and the little hunter dragged it back inside its lair.

"I never meant to care about her," Dana said at last, her voice as soft as Dennis Riggins's had been loud. "Angie's daughter, I mean. I didn't want to get involved."

"Makes a lot of sense," Jay told her. "Life hands out enough heartache as it is. Taking on somebody else's portion—that's a tough call."

"She seems like a sweet kid, but I can't say I really know her. Not after just meeting her the one time."

"So why do all of this, then?" He waved a hand, his gesture sweeping from the run-down old house to the rental. "Why make it your problem?"

She shrugged, looking like a child herself, tired and defeated. "Her parents . . . they're so desperate. You can tell

Nikki's their whole world. And my mother—she's taking it so hard, too. It's almost as if she's losing my sister all over. The two of them have been estranged for years now."

A chill overtook him, despite the ovenlike heat. "Makes me glad I don't have kids of my own," he said. "I'm not sure how I'd stand that."

He shook his head and rubbed one of Max's ears while his mind dredged up the grief of Baghdad, the mothers wailing for dead children. He thought, too, of weeping children, the sons and daughters of his men, who'd learned their fathers wouldn't come home.

Dana was quiet for several moments before speaking. "As much as I feel for the Harrisons, I'm not sure that's why I came either. I think part of it's avoidance. I have some things I need to deal with that I'd just as soon put off."

"Trouble with a man?" he guessed.

She smiled wryly. "If you could call the jerk that."

He smiled back, wondering if maybe on the rebound she could be persuaded . . . While his better nature called him a slimy opportunist—and far worse—the part of him that hadn't had a woman in what seemed like forever got down on its knees and prayed.

"Sorry, but I don't see you as the kind who hides out from her problems," he said. "Not the way you've been ridin' my case. If some guy's giving you garbage, I figure you'd take him on directly—or run his ass out of town."

"I would've," she admitted, "but he was already making a sprint for it when I finally figured things out."

"So he's a damned chickenshit, not just a fool."

She seemed to consider this, then nodded. "I won't argue over the coward part."

He looked into her face. "Trust me, if he's giving a woman like you grief, 'fool' definitely applies. And then some."

She tried for a smile, but it didn't quite take. "Thanks, but all that's in the past now. I've wasted more than enough time already."

"That's good to hear," he ventured, his heart pounding out a warning that he was about to make a monumental fool of himself. *Oh, what the hell?* "That you're through with him, I mean."

She turned her face from his view, but not in time to hide the single tear that broke loose. "Everything's so screwed up. My personal life, my practice, this business with my sister. This is going to sound stupid, but I thought that if I could fix this one thing for the Harrisons, maybe then the rest would start to make sense. And maybe saving the daughter she gave up would give Angie some purpose, something else besides her own problems to think about."

He couldn't help himself. He leaned close enough to pull her into his arms. He meant it as a simple, human gesture, but it had been so long since he'd reached out to offer anybody comfort, he felt as awkward as a boy.

She stiffened and then stood, as if to escape him.

Rising, too, he cursed his clumsiness. He'd crossed a line, a line he'd had no trouble maintaining as a cop in Dallas or a soldier in Iraq. But he'd never met a Dana Vanover in either of those places.

"I'm sorry," he blurted.

When she merely blinked at him, he wished he could shrink down small enough to follow the scorpion into its crevice.

Shaking his head, he went on, "Wish you'd forget I did that. It's got to be the heat."

"Well, it's for sure not the humidity. But don't apologize," she said quickly. "To tell you the truth, it's a relief."

He stared a question at her.

She nodded. "I, uh, I don't want you to take this wrong, but I was sort of hoping that would happen."

The breath he'd been holding gusted free. "There's a way to take that *wrong?*"

"Yes, because it's . . . it's such a bad idea."

Jay didn't say anything, but any number of *bad* ideas had

flared up—among other things. Instead of speaking, he leaned forward and gave her the gentlest, most restrained kiss he could manage, partly to keep her from looking down.

The diversion worked out even better than he'd hoped. From the moment their lips touched he let go of his awkwardness like a child releasing a balloon. And for just that moment he was again the man he had been before that night in Baghdad: confident with women, sure of his ability to lead and do his job. The National Guard staff sergeant the younger men looked up to. A man who knew his duty and never shrank from imaginary shadows.

Jay Eversole wanted that man back, wanted so badly to be him that he rolled with the emotion, pouring every bit of it into a mouth that feasted on Dana's acquiescence, into hands that skimmed the curve of her waist and held her when she seemed to weaken.

Seconds stretched to minutes that magnified the heat. Dana's surrender flared into an urgent murmur as her short nails dug into his back, pulling him tight to her. When her breasts spread against his chest, he thought he'd lose it right there. Unable to control himself, he reached up to find and cup her as his mouth tasted the sweat-salt column of her neck.

She was moaning now, something he'd forgotten how much he liked in a woman. But finally he registered her words.

"No. Don't." And she was pushing, pushing back his shoulders, a realization that doused him like a freezing shower.

Jerking back abruptly, he stood staring at her, breathing as hard as if he'd just finished his morning PT. And wondering if that strange expression in her green eyes was terror, if in his eagerness to reclaim the man he'd once been, he had damned near forced himself on an unwilling woman.

# *Chapter Seven*

A *wise woman puts a grain of sugar into everything she says to
a man, and takes a grain of salt with everything he says to her.*
                                                    —Helen Rowland

Dana's shudder had nothing to do with fear and everything
to do with the realization that Jay Eversole wanted her here
and now.

He saw her as desirable. He saw her as a woman, regardless of the way Alex had felt about her since her surgery.

And she wanted him as well. She'd grown hot and damp
at his touch. But that didn't mean acting on desire was a
good idea.

"I can't do this," she said, then cleared her throat, embarrassed by the huskiness in her voice. "I'm sorry if I . . . if you
thought I . . . I never should have . . ."

Defeated by the tangle of words inside her, she sighed and
wished she were the sort of woman who could let him take
her healing body for a test drive. Or that she had ever been
the type for a casual affair.

Jay picked up his hat, which their embrace had knocked
free. As he brushed the dirt from it he asked, "You all
right?"

She shook her head, her resolve nearly undone by his
concern. "I'm an idiot."

He winced. "Not exactly the reaction I was hoping for.
I'll grant you I'm a little out of practice, but still—"

"It wasn't anything you did."

With a pained look he asked, "This isn't going to be one
of those, 'It's not you, it's me' talks, is it? I might've been out
of circulation for a while, but I'm pretty sure I remember
that one."

She smiled. "How about, 'It's not you *or* me, it's Angie'? Would that make you feel better?"

"Not at all. But I suppose you're right." He gave her a look of such intensity her mouth went chalk dry. "Because if I get started on you, Dana, I'm not going to want to come up for air, much less bother with an investigation. And I told you I'd find your sister."

At the carnal promise in his voice, Dana's brain misfired, wiping out the knowledge that she was standing on the half-collapsed porch of a grimy old adobe in the middle of a godforsaken desert. For a moment she couldn't even remember her own name.

"Dana?" He frowned at her. "You all right?"

*Dana.* That was it. She nodded, wondering if the heat had melted her common sense. But another glance at Jay's expression assured her that he and not the temperature was the culprit.

"This isn't a good time for me. I'm worried sick about my sister and her little girl." The words tumbled out too quickly, but she couldn't seem to slow down. "And the jerk who left me cut out three weeks before our wedding. I still have about three hundred stupid notes to write, and everyone's embarrassed for me, and . . ."

She felt her control slipping out from under her, felt the first bubble of panic break the surface. She wouldn't do this, wouldn't let fear and isolation and Alex's rejection start her babbling.

Shaking his head, he said, "You don't have to—"

She couldn't seem to stop. "And I'm still recovering from surgery, and—"

"You don't have to make excuses, Dana."

"Sorry." Her face flamed. "Sorry I unloaded on you. You didn't ask for the life story."

He shrugged. "Sounds like you've been through a lot. Sometimes that kind of stuff swells up inside until you just bust open with it."

When his blue eyes took on a faraway look, she wondered what sadness he was seeing. She remembered that he had recently come back from a war zone, that he must have witnessed suffering on a far grander scale than the ordinary dramas that loomed so large in her life.

His reverie vanished in a blink, and he refocused his attention on her. "You shouldn't be out here. It's dirty, hot—the snakebite's bad enough, but if you're getting over some kind of operation—"

"It's no big deal," she told him, just as if it weren't. She swallowed hard, steeling herself by imagining how appalled her mother would be to see her on the edge of tears with this near stranger, her mother, who had leaned toward her, arms outstretched, only to pull back at the last instant.

*"Well, at least you have your career,"* she'd said. *"And you could always rescue another little dog or something."* Though Isabel had immediately afterward surprised her with the convertible, the memory didn't stand out as any kind of hall-of-fame highlight from the annals of empathy.

Back under control, Dana said, "You're a good guy to worry about me. And if I weren't in such a bad place in my life, I'd be—"

"Anywhere but six hundred miles from home, in the armpit of West Texas," he finished for her.

She smiled at him. "True."

"Maybe I'd better go now. It's about time to meet my crew," he said.

"Your crew?"

He nodded and explained how, in the absence of emergency services, Rimrock County residents helped one another get back on their feet whenever disaster struck. The fire that had taken his uncle's life had badly damaged the interior of the ranch house he'd left to his nephew, so his neighbors had been helping to restore it. "They started on it as soon as I agreed to take the job. Didn't even wait for me to get here."

"That's amazing," she said. "No insurance, no contractors, just mutual assistance. Sounds almost like the Amish, with their barn raisings."

He grinned. "I can guarantee the Amish never have to make so many beer runs. But we're getting there. I'll be moving in a couple of weeks from now, after we install the cabinets and clean up the debris. And not a moment too soon. I'm more than ready to get out of that old motor home I've been using."

He pulled a small pad of paper and a pen from his shirt pocket and started jotting. "Place isn't all that far from here. Only about twenty minutes."

She saw him sketching out a map.

"There's one of those big, wrought-iron gates with a Texas Lone Star on it across the driveway," he explained. "Visitors have to get out to unchain it, but I never keep it locked. Long drive back to the house. You have to follow it up a little rise and to the right to reach the house.

"If anyone bothers you out here, you call me," he said. "Doesn't matter what time. You still have your satellite phone and my numbers?"

Dana nodded.

"But if you can't get hold of me for any reason, or you're feeling nervous, you come right on over. Nobody's going to think less of you, not after what you've been through lately."

"Thanks," she said. "I guess I'll see you around."

Rather than leaving, he lingered until she thought—and began to hope—that he might try to kiss her again.

Instead he said, "Why don't I leave Max here with you? I'd feel better if you had him. I doubt he'd bite anybody, but his bark's pretty convincing. And like I told you, he's good company."

She meant to turn him down, but animals had been the one consistent comfort in her life. Though she'd stubbornly resisted Regina Lawler's persistent offers to join her, Dana felt queasy at the thought of spending the night completely on her own here, with no locks on the doors and no neighbor for miles around.

"That would be great," she said, "but the food I brought won't do for him."

"He's already had his dinner, so he'll be all right until tomorrow morning. I'll drop off some feed for him on my way to work."

She looked down at Max. "So how about it, boy? You want to bed down with me?"

When the docked tail wagged in answer, Jay headed toward his Suburban. But under his breath Dana heard him mutter, "That makes two of us, buddy."

It had cooled down to the eighties by ten-thirty, when Dennis stormed out to his pickup and threw open the door. Jay had waited to tell him until Bill Navarro, Henry Schlitz, and Weevil Jenkins all left. Even though the FBI special agent had asked him to keep news of the investigation quiet, Jay had felt obligated to share what he knew, in part because he needed some sage advice about how to handle folks once word of the situation went public.

"I don't give a good goddamn what you tell the others," Dennis hollered before climbing into the cab of his dark green Chevy. "I've gotta let Suzanne know. I need to talk to 'er right now."

Jay rushed to catch up—at six-feet-six, Dennis outpaced him with his long strides—and grabbed the handle of the door before it shut. "It's not for sure, Dennis. And even if it is true, the FBI is closing in on them. Maybe they'll recover at least part of the money—"

Dennis glowered through the thicket of his unruly red-gray beard. "Don't give me that bullshit, Jay. When's the last time anybody ever caught con artists with their loot? I'm calling back that lyin' piece of shit I talked to about the equipment, and I'm tellin' him to expect a visit shortly."

His right arm slipped behind the seat where, like nearly all of Rimrock's citizens, Dennis kept at least one hunting rifle.

Alarm pulsed through Jay's system. "Don't be stupid, Dennis. Keep your hands where I can see 'em."

"You're not the one who needs to worry. It's those bastards in Albuquerque who'd better—"

"You can't call them, can't do anything but hold tight for the moment. You want them to rabbit out of the country so the FBI can't find them? The agent told me they're just waiting to move in until they get a bead on the location of Miriam Piper-Gold and her husband. They have the rest of them under tight surveillance."

"I'd rather dispense some good, old-fashioned West Texas justice than take my chances on the ACLU or one of them liberal outfits gettin' their sorry asses off the hook."

"That's not happening, and besides"—Jay struggled to dredge up a smile—"it would be an all-day job to hunt up a tree around here tall enough for hanging anybody. Come on, Dennis; let's go back inside and talk awhile longer. I don't want you tearing off and getting hurt out there, and I sure as hell don't want you giving Suzanne another heart scare by running in there bellowing about how y'all are ruined."

Something hardened in Dennis's expression, a reminder that he didn't like to talk about his wife's health. "You just don't want her callin' Estelle and lettin' that loose-lipped Hooks bunch in on this mess."

Jay nodded. "That *is* a consideration."

Despite the animosity between the Riggins family and the Hooks clan, Suzanne and Estelle had been close friends before their marriages and somehow managed to remain so. Once Estelle heard about Haz-Vestment she'd tell Abe, and the disaster would be common knowledge within hours. Which meant that anyone with a phone could tip off the criminals before they were arrested.

"I'll tell Suzanne to keep it quiet," Dennis growled.

"Something this big tends to slip out. Which means the

word will spread. Dennis, I took a big chance telling you, and I only did it because I appreciate the way you've—"

Within the thicket of beard, Dennis's mouth turned down. "Next time don't do me any goddamned favors. Now let go, before I end up pinchin' off your fingers in this door."

"Careful, Dennis," Jay warned.

The pickup spun its wheels before rocketing out of the driveway so quickly that Jay heard small stones ping off the RV's metal side. One popped off his hat, denting its straw brim.

"Wonderful," he told the full moon, which had risen while they'd been talking in the kitchen. Clear and bright, it shone down like a spotlight on his stupidity.

He'd been an idiot to spill his guts to Dennis. Of course the man would be upset; of course he'd tell his wife. And she would spread the so-called secret to another, who would no doubt spread it even further, with God-alone-could-guess what consequences.

And it wasn't the only thing he'd done that made Jay wonder if his superiors in the Dallas PD had been right about him. *"The department can't take the chance"*—his memory twisted the captain's voice, drenching the measured words in malice—*"that you're ill-equipped to interact with members of the public. The incident at the movie theater suggests that more treatment is the best course. When the department's psychologist assures us there's been progress, perhaps then . . ."*

Jay swore and slammed his fist against the RV's side, but the damned thing was so rusted, his hand punched partway through the metal. Pulling free he felt the moisture first, then saw a rivulet trickling from a cut near his wrist.

In the full moon's light the blood dripped as black as crude oil, black as the stained space between the man he'd been as a cop in Dallas and the wreck who'd slunk back to the salt-scrub desert he should have long since left behind.

# *Chapter Eight*

*Back before I switched my major from cultural anthropology to tequila (with a minor in hashish), I got really into the mythos of the native people of what's now the western U.S. From Kokopelli to Coyote to the Kachinas, I listened to visiting story-tellers and read up until I dreamed their legends in fluorescent colors (which might have been the hallucinogens talking, now that I think back on it). But the stories that spoke loudest to me focused on the sacred feminine, powerful chicks like White Buffalo Calf Maiden, Corn Woman, and, of course, the Salt Woman. My veins might not carry a single drop of native blood (biologically, at least, I'm a child of the oppressor), but these are the figures that show up when my fingers touch the loom's shuttle.*

*Maybe that's why it wasn't Mother Mary or even the Wiccan goddess who guided me to my place of healing, but that white-haired desert wanderer who moved westward through my night-time dreamscape, until I followed her steps past the domes that form her rounded breasts to the sparkling, salt-white cavern of her empty womb.*

—Entry seven, March 13
Angie's sobriety journal

With the full moon shining through the window and her eyes watering with exhaustion, Dana decided it was high time to collapse on the cot she'd picked up in the camping aisle of the Pecos Wal-Mart. After dragging it a safe distance from the grungy old mattress her sister had been using, she sank back against her pillow. But as she reached to shut off the battery-operated lantern, she spotted a slitlike hole partly hidden behind a leg of Angie's big, freestanding loom.

"I'll check it out tomorrow," she told the dog, who had stretched out across the newly swept floor near her feet. She was far too tired to get down on her hands and knees tonight.

But the thought of that hole—which probably meant nothing—kept her from sleeping, even more than the aching of her healing leg and her regrets about what had happened—and what hadn't—with the sheriff. Besides that, whenever she was still for too long, she saw images of a little girl with Angie's brown eyes shrinking down to nothing amid a tangle of IV tubes.

The silence proved equally unnerving. Dana had shut down the generator to save gas, since the temperature was cooling. But she missed its friendly hum and the oscillating fan's buzz, thin reassurance that she still lived in the twenty-first century.

After tossing and turning for an eternity beneath a light throw—a tricky business on the narrow cot—she finally sat straight upright and huffed out, "Screw it."

She slipped into her sandals and pushed back the heavy loom. Then she squatted down to peer into the opening, setting the lantern close beside her.

The hole was so small—a three-inch slit, only a half inch or so across at its widest—Dana couldn't see much, except for a dried curl of torn paper. Maybe a rat's nest, she thought. Pack rats were common in this area, and they were known for incorporating human possessions into their nests.

In this part of the country they were also known to carry the fleas that transmitted bubonic plague. Dana decided that anyone unlucky enough to be bitten by a diamondback in her own car had no business tempting fate with the Black Death. So she tied a T-shirt over her lower face, pulled on a pair of latex gloves from her first-aid kit, and hoped like hell she wasn't risking killer cooties to pull out shreds of decades-old newspaper.

But the scrap she prized free was marked with blue ink and not newsprint. As she held it closer to the light, Dana could make out only isolated words and fragments, but her nerve endings buzzed with recognition. The messy script was clearly Angie's.

Dana looked over to where the dog was watching and said, "There has to be more."

Desperately she chipped at the hole's edges with a Swiss army knife, another addition to what was sure to be a record credit-card bill. Soon a few more inches of adobe crumbled. With the stump of his tail wagging, Max pawed at the debris.

"No, boy," she said as she pushed the dog out of the way. "Go lie down, will you?"

To her surprise the shepherd mix trotted over to the old mattress and then jumped on it. After turning in three tight circles, he lowered himself with a groan of satisfaction.

"Go ahead and sleep there if you want to," Dana told him, "but don't blame me if you end up with bedbugs."

She poked her blade into the hole's depths, trusting that her banging had scared off any occupants. A fat black spider scuttled up the handle and onto her gloved hand. With a shriek, she shook it off. Landing on its back, the widow flashed a bright red hourglass before Dana reflexively crushed it with a sandal.

"I've had enough venom for one week, thanks." She shuddered before forcing herself back to her explorations.

Beneath the hole's edge there was a metallic clink, followed by a rustle that had Dana reaching down with two fingers and pulling out not more scraps, as she'd expected, but a thin sheaf of notebook pages that had been folded and refolded, as if someone had wanted to quickly fit them in the slotlike hole.

So what had jingled? Holding her breath, she reached in with her gloved hand and prayed the black widow had no revenge-minded relations. Once she snagged something she withdrew, pulling out a small key that hung suspended from a loop of dark blue yarn. A glance at the unfinished tapestry confirmed that the color was the same as Angie had used to form the star field's background. Since she hadn't come across a lock, Dana dropped both key and "necklace" into a pocket of her shorts.

Moving away from both the hole and loom, she set the lantern on the only other furnishing, a tilted and paint-spattered table. Standing beside it she smoothed the papers and noticed that only the outermost pages near the back appeared to have been gnawed by rodents.

Near the center of the relatively clean front page, Dana once more recognized her sister's script. In her usual bold and messy slash strokes, she had scrawled, *Angie's Sobriety Journal, Devil's Claw, Texas*, and dated it January of that year.

But as Dana turned the page, she started at a crunching sound from outside—a footstep on the gravel? Max leaped off the mattress and bounded toward the window, his deep, aggressive woofs echoing. Terror slamming through her, Dana bumped the table.

Its skewed leg gave way, which sent the lantern sliding to the hard floor with a splintering sound. She was plunged into velvet darkness, a void so black she had to bite her tongue to keep from screaming.

She crouched instinctively, her heart pummeling her chest wall. *Just an animal of some kind. It has to be an animal.* When the blazing eye of the sun closed, nocturnal desert creatures went about their business. She tried to picture furry rodents, the scrappy little wild pigs called javelinas, comically waddling armadillos. Tried to pretend the heavy tread hadn't sounded human.

"Quiet, Max," she ordered, so desperate to think it was a harmless animal that she was half-annoyed the dog had scared her.

*Unless it isn't harmless.* While Max went on barking, her stomach spasmed at the thought of what else could be out there.

Or perhaps *who* else.

Within an hour of her first arrival in Rimrock County

someone had nearly gotten her killed. She'd been furious, defiant—enough that she'd told Abe Hooks she was coming back to find her sister.

What if he had told whoever had put the snake in her car? Or what if he had been the one who'd done it in the first place? Could the guilty party have been watching for a sign of her return?

More agitated than ever, Max tried to scramble out the empty window. Dana sprang to her feet and grabbed his collar to keep him from getting hurt.

"No, boy. Please. Settle down." Lingering near the opening, she scanned the salt flat . . .

. . . and spotted an unmistakably human silhouette standing perhaps twenty yards distant. The person held something long and slender, a shape that could have been a walking stick—except it glinted in the moonlight like the barrel of a gun.

With a strangled cry she dropped to the hard floor and fumbled in the darkness. She felt for her purse, which held her phone and SUV keys, her tickets out of hell.

*Sunday, July 1, 12:04 A.M.*
*78 Degrees Fahrenheit*

Though he'd gone to bed nearly an hour earlier, Jay's brain was still running on nervous energy when his phone broke the silence. He caught it on the second ring.

"Eversole," he said as he clicked on the bedside light.

"I'm coming over."

The fear in Dana's voice sent worry hurtling through him, had him reaching for a shirt. "What's wrong?"

In the background he heard frantic barking.

"I have to get out of here. Come on, Max." There was a double chirp, as if she'd deactivated her vehicle's alarm. "Hurry."

"What's going on?" His pulse thundered in his ears. How could he have left her out there? "Is someone at the house?"

She didn't answer right away, but he recognized the sounds of movement, of the SUV's door closing. The dog fell quiet, so Jay could make out the jingling of keys and the chiming of the seat belt reminder.

"Dana, answer me right now." He tasted bile as a new thought shook him. "Is someone with you?"

As he shoved his feet into his boots, he heard her engine starting.

"No, I'm all right," she said. "He's gone."

"Who's gone?" he asked, but she was talking over him.

"Max and I are heading your way. I, uh, I forgot to grab the directions you left me, but I think I remember. Follow this road to the left. Is that it?"

"Yeah, for six miles. Then you'll catch the rural ranch road that Y's off to the right and follow it for another ten-point-six miles. Now tell me, what's this all about?"

"I saw somebody outside. Couldn't see who it was, but I'm sure it was human."

"Shit." He should have brought her here with him, should have kept her safe. "How close?"

"I think he was right outside—I heard a footstep, but when Max barked he ran to the salt flat. He was armed, I'm pretty sure. Rifle, shotgun—one of those with a long barrel. It was hard to get a good look. Max was going crazy, and when I looked back, the guy was gone."

Jay grabbed his keys. "I need you to check your rearview. Do you see anyone behind you?"

After a short pause she said, "I don't see anything at all. But the moon's behind a cloud now, and it's dark as death."

He knew the desert blackness shook those used to man-made lights. That terror was as instinctive as the fear of isolation. Could the combination have led her to imagine she'd seen something she hadn't? Could it have been the same animal that had stirred up Max?

He'd be damned if he took that chance, even though she'd made it more than clear that she was only interested in him as the sheriff. Not the man who chose to live in exile, nor the would-be lover who was sure to complicate her life. If he had any sense, he would quit hoping she might change her mind.

"I'm heading your way, Dana. When you see headlights, flash yours. Then I'll flash twice to signal for you to pull over."

"All right." She sounded shaky, breathless with the exhaustion that followed hard on adrenaline's heels.

"Stay on the line," he told her as he headed out to his Suburban. "But don't panic if I lose you. My phone isn't that reliable, especially in your area."

Unlike Dana Vanover, Rimrock County couldn't afford expensive satellite phone service. And she didn't have a radio, which was what he and Wallace used to keep in contact.

"I'll watch for you," she said. An easy promise, since there was almost no chance of meeting another vehicle at this hour.

Almost no chance of meeting anyone except the stranger with his weapon, as he came in pursuit.

# *Chapter Nine*

Hey, sis,

The birth mother's sister has been calling a lot lately, asking after Nikki. Asking after John and me, too. It's funny the way she acted all stiff and distant the day she came to visit. Guarded, like she didn't want to get involved. But it turns out she's the one who's gone out looking. The one who refuses to give up.

I even heard that she was bitten by a rattlesnake. But when I asked, she changed the subject. What she really wants to talk about, she can't bring herself to ask me. But then, only God could answer that one, and I'm afraid I'm not on speaking terms with Him these days.

So the next time you bow your head, maybe you should ask Him for us. How long do we have left to find a donor? How late is really too late—for my daughter, for my marriage? And while you're at it, O, almighty Father, how could You do this to a child I prayed for so hard? How could You do something like this to any child at all?

—E-mail message from Laurie Harrison

As his Suburban slewed around a long curve, Jay fought off the panic pounding at his temples. He should have met her by now. Where the hell was she?

The roads out here were shit. Rutted, dusty, unlit. Probably they'd slowed her down more than he'd figured, since she would be far more used to driving freeways.

The moon, at least, had emerged from its veil of clouds. Emerged to light the carcass of an armored vehicle with dark streamers of smoke rising . . .

*Goddammit, no.* He blinked hard, willed the nightmare image back into the shadows. Scanned the empty stretch of road that took its place.

"Come on, Dana," he murmured as he tried the phone

again. But the signal was no stronger than when he'd dropped out of range ten minutes earlier.

Might as well forget that and try Wallace on the radio for backup. He grabbed the handset, only to replace it as he finally spotted headlights. When they flashed he gave a whoop and thanked the same God who had let him down in Baghdad.

Signaling back, he pulled over, then bailed out of his vehicle. With the gravel still crunching underneath her Ford's tires, he pulled open the SUV's door.

"You all right?"

She killed the engine, then nodded as she slid down from the seat. Max jumped down behind her, looking no worse for the unholy racket he'd been making.

When Dana threw herself into his arms, Jay stroked her back to soothe her shaking. And hoped she wouldn't think him weak if she felt his own.

"It wasn't my imagination. I really saw somebody out there," she said. "Scared the snot out of me."

"You're safe now." He breathed the words into her hair, gave her another squeeze of reassurance. Then he let her go before he reacted in a way that would make her doubt his motives. "You never saw anything else on the road?"

She shook her head. "Somehow the emptiness made it that much worse, the idea that headlights might come up on me at any second. It's really creepy out here after dark."

"I've been told it's not exactly a garden spot by daylight either." He smiled at her and was relieved to see some of the tension melt out of her posture.

"You okay to follow me back?" he asked. "To my place, that is. If you're not feeling up to driving I can bring you back here in the morning."

"I'll follow," she said. "I've already caused you enough trouble."

"Not you, but someone sure as hell has. And starting at

first light I mean to find out exactly who's behind this." Jay could already imagine Wallace's grumbling about city women and their overactive imaginations, but that was too damned bad. They were going to scour the area where she had seen the armed man—and then he meant to rattle some cages by questioning whatever possible suspects came to mind.

Fifteen minutes later the two had pulled into the long driveway and were climbing out of their vehicles beside the old RV next to his uncle's house.

"I'd invite you inside the house, but it's still a mess with the construction. So why don't you come on in the Beast here."

He gestured toward the hulk at his right.

"What happened to your hand?" she asked.

He glanced down at the bandage, embarrassed to think of his earlier fit of temper. "Oh, uh, I cut it earlier, working on the cabinets."

Something in his voice must have clued her in that he was lying, because she looked at him oddly. But instead of saying anything she mounted the concrete-block steps and pulled at the RV's door.

"It's locked," she said when it didn't open.

"Pull harder," he suggested, and the nearly frozen hinges squealed a protest as they opened.

The space inside was dated, but thanks to military habits he kept it spotless, with his possessions all stowed neatly. He'd picked up the nearly thirty-year-old relic outside of San Antonio for a song. After loading his few things, he had babied it through a journey fraught with two breakdowns and a flat. Jay was pretty sure the Beast had made its last road trip, but it served his purposes for the time being—and more important, his jury-rigged AC system worked well.

"There's something I wanted to show you." Dana slipped a hand inside her purse and pulled out some folded papers. "I found this tucked down inside a slot in the adobe, back behind the loom. It's some kind of diary my sister was keeping."

"You've read it?"

"I was about to when Max here went ballistic." When she said his name, the black-and-gold dog looked up at her and wagged his tail until she murmured, "That's a good boy, Max. Good dog."

Soon they were seated on either side of the RV's kitchen table with the papers spread between them while the coffeemaker made indelicate sounds atop the nearby counter. Max had slunk off to bed down in his favorite spot, the driver's seat, where he curled in a ball and closed his eyes.

"Can't read it upside down," Jay said as the rich aroma percolated through the small space. "Scoot over, will you?"

She complied, and he moved around to sit next to her. Their thighs touched in the tight booth. The contact dragged his attention downward, where the hem of her shorts had ridden up to bare her leg.

*Don't look,* he ordered himself, and concentrated on the first of Angie's entries. Dana winced at the reference to a certain "clueless little sister."

"Guess she'll be glad to hear how my so-called 'perfect life' has turned out," Dana grumbled before flipping to the next page, but Jay glimpsed the raw pain in her expression.

The entries that followed appeared sporadic, though it was difficult to tell for sure, since so many were undated. The handwriting, never neat, became so shaky in some places that neither Jay nor Dana could make sense of what was written. But often the problem lay not in the writing but the writer, as Angie vacillated between anger and despondence, vulgarity and surprisingly poetic prose. At times she graphically described alcohol withdrawal—pulling no punches about its physical effects. In other cases she lapsed into what appeared to be delusion as she spoke of almost otherworldly visitations and what might be either a lover or a simple flight of fancy.

Jay glanced beside him to see tears rolling down Dana's

cheek. Putting a hand on top of hers, he prevented her from turning the next page. "That's enough for now."

Already it was past one-thirty, and despite the empty coffee mugs before them, each of them had paused to rub at tired eyes.

"She was so sick," said Dana, "and to suffer like that all alone, without anyone to help her . . ."

After squeezing Dana's hand, Jay said, "She knew you'd be here in a minute if she asked you. That counts for a lot, Dana."

She chewed her lower lip, then said, "Angie resented everything about me."

"And at times you've probably resented everything about her. I've never had a sibling, but I've been around enough to know that's how it usually works."

"I love my sister, Jay. But sometimes I do hate her. For all the things she's put my mother through. For giving away that beautiful little girl when I'd give anything to . . ." Dana shook her head, either unwilling or unable to finish the thought. After clearing her throat, she added, "For the way I've always had to be so strong to make up for her weakness."

"What if I told you"—he picked a lock of blond hair off her cheek, then ran it, sleek and silky, through his fingers— "you don't have to be the tough one?"

He feathered a caress along her jawline, then lifted her mouth close to his.

"What if I asked you to hand it over? If I told you I would take it off your shoulders"—he kissed all around her parted lips—"just for this one night?"

She looked into his eyes, her green gaze searching, worry etching furrows across her forehead. But a moment later a smile smoothed the lines away. Reaching to cup the back of his head, she whispered, "Tonight I'd tell you yes, Jay. *Yes.* Please. Now, before I overthink—"

He silenced her with a kiss, half-afraid she would pull back as she had earlier, run to her SUV, and drive all night to Houston. Half-afraid that she *should*, that his hunger for her would erupt into something fast and selfish instead of the careful loving she needed and deserved.

But instead of running Dana kissed him back, as sweet and hot as melted honey. With a flick of his tongue her mouth opened to his, and her body pressed so close he could feel the pounding of her heart.

He didn't move on for a long time, instead reacquainting himself with the forgotten pleasure of a kiss, allowing the warmth and moisture of their mouths to simmer, heating every square inch of his body. Allowing himself the luxury of languid exploration, in spite of the painful hardness that threatened to overwhelm his senses.

*Make it last*, he urged himself, pausing for a deep breath before he ran a palm along her side to trace the gentle flare between her waist and hip. Breaking contact with her mouth, he feasted on a second curve between her neck and shoulder and smiled when she caught her breath. A murmur rose from her throat, a rumbling, feminine purr that made him want to sweep the papers from the table and spread her out on top.

*Make it last*, he thought again, so he fought back the impulse, instead taking her by the hand and drawing her to her feet. She followed, unresisting, standing on her toes to nip his neck. Afterward she soothed the hurt with the most sensual of kisses as her fingers squeezed one of his nipples.

Pleasure arcing through him, he peeled off her T-shirt, running his hands along her back and kneading her buttocks, pulling her body to rub against his length. Not exactly subtle, but by this time his senses were too aroused for him to care.

He reached around, unhooking her bra with a single deft move, then kissed his way down to circle a small, pink areola with his tongue. When he sucked in a plump and perfect breast she gasped, and he gave himself over to drinking in her pleasure, dividing his attention left and right.

His fingers made brief forays, dipping beneath her waistband, grazing her bare thigh. Dropping to his knees, he swirled his mouth in a teasing circle all around her navel.

"Jay," she whimpered. "Jay, I . . ."

Her knees wobbled as he unsnapped her shorts, and again she gasped at the sound of her zipper losing its purchase tooth by tooth. He rose to strip off his own clothing, and soon they stood together naked, kissing, touching with abandon.

This felt so different from the wild dreams he had been having. So much deeper and more powerful, with her taste filling his mouth and her scent inflaming him. He wanted to devour her, to feel the whole of her, to take her in all of the ways he had imagined in such vivid detail.

So he swept her into his arms and carried her to the bed. Before he laid her down, he looked into her eyes and asked, "Is this what you want, Dana?"

She hesitated, and in that moment he saw how badly her trust in men had been shaken. In that moment he thought he had to be the biggest damned fool in West Texas to offer her the chance to back out now. But after blowing out a long breath, she nodded as she repeated in a silken whisper, "For tonight."

Even so, he sensed an edge of fear in her, so he forced himself to take his time, his mouth once more lingering at each breast, his fingers teasing before testing. Bowing between her thighs, he explored her damp folds and tasted the heaven of her center, and as her writhing turned to a shuddering cry, the words *Make it last* morphed into *Make it count.* . . .

After sheathing himself in a condom he moved over her, and their gazes locked before she slanted her hot mouth against his, then flexed her hips to take the solid length of his hard thrust.

Though Jay had returned to his country four months earlier and had recently marked two weeks back in Rimrock County, Dana's body felt like his true homecoming. In her he forgot about the desiccated desert, forgot the way that death could slip up from its sands with stealthy menace. . . .

Forgot all else but the lush heat of the woman rocking like the ocean just beneath him.

# Chapter Ten

*The cure for anything is salt water: sweat, tears, or the sea.*
> —Isak Dinesen

Dana woke from a deep and healing sleep as dawn's first rays bathed the bed in coppery light. Smiling lazily, she sighed at the warm weight of Jay's arm draped over her hip, at the solidity of his body spooning hers from behind.

Tempting to roll toward him, to rouse him again with kisses. Or to duck her head beneath the sheets and give him a proper wake-up call.

But the thought of the last few pages of her sister's journal lying unread on the table reminded her that this was no vacation. She could accept that she'd been human, allowing fear and loneliness—and raw attraction—to land her in Jay's bed. But she couldn't indulge herself by enjoying endless encores of last night's incredible performance.

Even as she thought it, Dana knew Jay hadn't been *performing*. He wasn't some lothario intent on showing off his technique or scoring a conquest. What had arced between them had felt more honest and elemental than even the best sex, forging a deeper connection that she refused to name—to even think about for fear of opening herself to any more pain.

She closed her eyes, forcing herself to refocus; she had come here to find her sister, not shack up with some small-town sheriff. *Angie. Angie. Angie.* The one-two beat turned to ticking, a countdown clock's race toward a tiny coffin. . . .

When Nikki's face flashed through her consciousness, Dana wriggled free of Jay's embrace. With shaking hands she unearthed a comb and travel toothbrush from the depths of her purse and then used the bathroom's cramped shower stall.

The water felt hard and tasted briny—better than nothing, but she didn't linger. Because she'd left Angie's place in such a panic, she had to dress in the same shorts and T-shirt she'd changed into before collapsing on the cot last night, but she could make do until she headed back to the adobe.

Her stomach fluttered at the memory of Max lunging toward the window, of the silhouetted figure lurking on the moonlit salt plain. If the dog hadn't warned her, would the gunman have come right up to the house? Would he have balanced the barrel of his weapon on the window ledge and shot her in her sleep?

She leaned over the counter as a wave of dizziness broke over her. Forcing her gaze higher, she stared into her hazy reflection in the still-steamy mirror.

"I'm not letting this stop me," she told her double as a stubborn impulse reared up, one that made her want to dig in her heels, drive to Pecos, and buy herself the biggest, loudest rifle she could find. Or an elephant gun, maybe.

Except she'd never fired a weapon, probably wouldn't if she could. Since she couldn't even bring herself to eat shellfish—which had all the self-awareness of animated snot—it was ridiculous to think she'd turn into Dirty Harriet overnight.

Not only ridiculous but dangerously delusional. No way could she outgun or outfight this skulking shadow. Her only hope was to outthink him if she could.

Emerging from the bathroom, she smelled fresh coffee brewing. The outside door had been propped open, letting in the cool breath of the morning, and both Jay and Max were missing.

She stuck her head outside and spotted the Suburban. So they couldn't have gone far, maybe to the house for something. After swiping half a mug of coffee from the still-dripping machine, she sat back down at the table—and saw that someone had flipped to the last legible page of Angie's journal.

Had Jay read further while she'd been in the shower? As she scanned the paper, her gaze snagged on two words amidst the scribbles, a name that made her gut tighten in response.

*Sheriff Eversole*, it said in Angie's angry slash strokes.

His uncle's bedroom had been one of the first spots the volunteer restorers tackled before Jay's arrival. He had been relieved beyond measure to find the walls torn down to the studs and the furnishings and rugs all hauled off. Though no one had come right out and said it, he knew his neighbors didn't want him facing the room where his uncle R.C. had burned to death, where the fire appeared to have ignited.

As stunned as Jay had been to lose the one unshakable fixture of his childhood, in retrospect he might have seen it coming. During his years living here, he'd often spotted a red-orange cigar tip glowing in the darkness. Most times Uncle R.C. would be reclining in an old chair that permanently reeked of burning tobacco. *"Thinking the day through and the people,"* as R.C. had always put it, adding only once, *"and maybe wondering a little over how things could've been."* But every now and again Jay would catch Rimrock County's sheriff smoking in his bed with the lights off.

If Jay had visited after his discharge, as he should have, would he have thought to warn his uncle of the danger? Or would he have remained as fixated on his own wounds as he had been as a kid?

Grimacing, he squatted to survey the bare wood flooring, his gaze searching out the uneven slats Angie had mentioned in her journal.

*Old R.C.'s stashed Haz-Vestment's money somewhere. He thinks I've just been screwing him out of gratitude for bringing me those groceries—like I'm so hard up I'd put out for canned tuna, wheat crackers, and a few goddamned rolls of toilet paper.*

*I'd probably do him for tequila, or maybe even beer (my
mouth's watering to think of it, though I've been dry for
three whole months now!) but Eversole's never offered that
much. Only his lectures and his johnson—tight-assed old
man . . .*

At around that point Angie's handwriting disintegrated
into a rat-chewed patchwork. A few recognizable words remained, including *bedroom*, *floorboards*, and the one that
seared Jay's gut like a hot coal: *bribes.*

He damned well didn't buy it, refused to believe that his
uncle, a lifelong bachelor with a reputation as straight-
edged as a ruler, would get mixed up in anything of the kind.

Still, Jay needed to look for himself, to put his mind at
ease. The trouble was, the flooring had been sanded and re-
finished. Carl Navarro had mentioned that a few boards had
to be replaced, and Jay picked them out by their slightly
darker color. But there was no discernible unevenness, and
certainly no one had mentioned finding hidden money during the repairs. There had been a few smiles over the few
well-thumbed *Penthouse* magazines they'd unearthed, but
nothing more notable than the same naked women most of
the county's bachelors knew by heart.

Max turned toward the doorway, his short nails clicking
on the wood floor as he pranced in excitement.

"I-I figured I'd find the two of you . . . here." Dana's words
came out off-kilter, and she ignored the dog to lock eyes
with Jay instead. "Considering what I read at your table."

As he looked up at the gorgeous blonde fresh out of his
bed, regret hit him. He'd expected tenderness, maybe a little nervous joking this morning, or, if he didn't go and say
the wrong thing, the chance to lay her on that kitchen
table and have a fantasy for breakfast. But Angie's journal
had taken up that spot, and he saw in Dana's face that she
had swallowed the whole damned pack of lies.

"Caught my eye while I was making coffee," he said.

Dana thrust one of the two mugs she carried toward him, its contents black as his mood. "At first, when I read 'Eversole,' I thought she was talking about you."

"Me? Angie was long gone before I ever got here. And besides that—"

"Yes, I know now. When I read further I could see she meant your uncle. Your uncle who was taking bribes, who was using my sister—"

"That's bullshit." The surface of Jay's coffee trembled, even after he stood. "My uncle mostly raised me. Taught me to work cattle. Taught me to handle life—at least when I would listen."

He'd been the one to push, too, for Jay to take a stab at making himself a life outside of Rimrock County—handing Jay a bus ticket to Dallas and three hundred dollars right after his high school graduation, saying, "*It's not a lot, but it's sure a hell of a lot more of a chance than I was given. So don't blow it.*"

Jay had felt lost—and scared shitless—but he'd never doubted the good intentions of the man who'd given him the boot. "He was the most honest man I knew, a man who always stepped up to do what needed doing. He took care of my grandfather when he was dying. Took me in when no one else would. In all the time I knew him, I never saw him take a cent he hadn't earned. And I sure as hell can't imagine him taking advantage of a woman in your sister's situa—"

"I'll admit, it's obvious Angie had her own agenda. But I can't help wondering how your uncle felt about *that*."

What the hell was she implying? Jay sipped the bitter brew to give himself a moment.

"She was delusional," he told her, trying to keep it a professional rather than a personal judgment. "When alcoholics dry out they can get pretty paranoid. This one old

man in Dallas kept calling nine-one-one to report bats flying out of his TV set. He insisted they were working under
the orders of Jay Leno. Some of the stuff your sister wrote
made just about as much sense."

Dana shook her head. "The thing is, the part about your
uncle seemed lucid. Not like that nonsense about the Salt
Woman she was going on about."

"So you're saying you believe it? The accusations of your
drug-addled, drunken sister against a man I know damned
well would never—"

She threw up a hand, anger sparking in her green eyes.
"Whoa, there, cowboy. Angie has her problems, but pur-
poseful dishonesty's never been one of them. If anything it's
the opposite. It's her penchant for blurting out the brutal
truth that's gotten her into trouble in the past. Besides, who
would she be lying to in the pages of a journal she kept hidden? Herself?"

He thought about it as he swallowed another mouthful before conceding, "You've got a point there, and I'm sorry. I was
out of line to talk that way about your sister. It's just that—"

"If you'd ever met her," Dana told him, "you'd understand
there's a whole lot more to Angie than chemical dependen-
cy and a history of hell-raising. She's smart, Jay, and she's
talented, and for all the trouble she's caused me, I still miss
her—every bit as much as I'm sure you miss your uncle."

He nodded stiffly, wishing again that he had been a better
nephew.

"But I'm still wondering," she said, "if he ever figured out
my sister was looking for that cash."

"If there was even money—which I'm not saying I
believe—what if Angie found it? Maybe she stole it and ran
off to Aruba or wherever, and that's why no one's heard
from her."

Dana blew across the surface of her coffee, and the sight
of her pursed lips filled Jay with sharp regret.

"Angie wouldn't leave her loom behind," she said.

"She could buy a hell of a lot of looms with that money, if it was as much as she implied. Drugs, too, and whatever she was drinking."

"But *that* loom meant something to her. It was her one constant, the only thing I knew she'd never hock. She told me that some old *curandero* put some kind of mojo on it, cast a spell so it could never turn against her. She believed in all that stuff. She loved it. Besides, Angie doesn't give a rat's rump about money. The trust fund I told you about earlier, the one that pays us each a monthly stipend—she's due to get the balance before the year is up. And it's . . . it's substantial money by most people's standards, a couple of million plus. Maybe more by now, I don't know. I haven't really kept up with my statements."

Jay had known Dana's family had money, but not that she and Angie were both rich in their own right. He'd slept with a *millionaire*. An *heiress*. But instead of cheering him, the thought felt wrong. After all, who was he but some screwed-up Dallas PD reject, a man who'd fouled up in the army so badly he'd gotten his men killed, then couldn't even handle—

"Whenever she's gotten into trouble, my mother's always bailed her out," Dana went on, "and so have I, on occasion."

Jay sucked in a deep breath, tried to focus his mind on her point.

"So *if* this money's real, and *if* your sister wouldn't steal it for her own sake"—he heard the skepticism in his own voice; saw Dana glower at it. Clearly sex on the RV's table had moved beyond the realm of possibility—"what the hell are you saying about my uncle?"

"I'm saying that a lot of men would kill to keep that kind of money. Especially a guy who's crossed the line to get it in the first place."

"So first you're accusing him of being dirty, and now you're calling him a killer." Jay's anger hammered flat each word. "Guess it's a good thing you weren't available to do his eulogy. Too busy back in Houston, living rich, while your sister scraped by like some kind of two-bit crack whore—"

"Stop. Right there. Right now." She pointed at him, making it an order.

"And who's to say your sister's way of getting to that money wasn't to set fire to her so-called 'lover' in his bed?"

"But Angie'd never hurt a—"

"That 'never' slices both ways, Dana. If you expect me to consider your theory about a sheriff well-known for his honesty, you can at least open yourself to the chance that your sister's not the victim in all this."

Dana stared at him. "Last night. Last night I thought you were someone different."

"If you thought I was someone different from a lawman, then I'm sorry. I . . . I can't let my relationship with my uncle affect my investigation. Any more than I can let what happened between us . . ."

When she nodded he let the rest go.

"So what's next?" she asked to end the unwieldy silence. "Do you want me to help you pry up this wood flooring?"

Jay felt a muscle twitch beside his mouth. Though he still meant to do it himself, her suggestion grated.

"That'll have to wait," he told her. "Right now it's more important to get a look around the Webb place, see if your evening visitor left anything behind. Wallace's meeting me out there at seven, so I need to grab some breakfast and get moving. I've got a couple extra honey-oat muffins if you want 'em. Mrs. Lockett bakes 'em, and they're pretty good."

"Okay, and then I'll follow you out to the adobe."

He hesitated before saying, "I don't think so, Dana."

"Look—if it's about this . . . disagreement, we're both adults. We should be able to put aside our differences and do what needs to be—"

"It's not that. I just think it would be better if you stay here, out of sight."

"If I'm not with you, how will you and Wallace know where to look? Max's the only other witness, and he's not much of a talker."

"Just give me a description of the area and let me take care of it. It'll be a lot of walking on that bad leg, and the terrain around there's dangerous. You could meet up with tarantulas or scorpions, maybe another snake. Or you might get heatstroke. Stay here and keep Max company—I'm leaving him at home today."

Yesterday morning at the courthouse the normally well-behaved dog had knocked over a trash can, torn up the contents, and left a steaming tribute outside of Estelle's office. Estelle had raised such a hue and cry that, after cleaning up the evidence, Jay figured he had better keep *canis non grata* out of sight for a few days.

"You don't want me around," she guessed. "Or are you really worried your deputy will see us and put two and two together about what happened here last night?" A light flush stole over her, but she didn't look away.

He reached out on an impulse, meaning to caress the curve of her cheek, but she turned her head to avoid the contact.

"I'm not ashamed," he told her, a truth he tainted by adding, "and I'm not sorry, either."

"Then prove it," she challenged. "We'll ride there together."

As the Suburban parted the Red Sea of desert stillness, a deeper silence welled between its occupants.

Dana wished she'd taken her own vehicle. At least then she wouldn't be trapped in this pocket of awkwardness, unwilling to speak of what had happened last night and unable to pretend that it meant nothing to her.

She wished that she could take it back, that she'd insisted upon sleeping on the floor last night—or even driving back to Pecos to rent a hotel room. Because she couldn't stop worrying whether she had pushed him too far, and wondering whether Angie's accusations would put an end to their relationship.

*What relationship?* As a light breeze snaked ribbons of dust across the road before them, Dana gave herself a mental kick, then recalled a detail she'd let slip.

*The key.* Digging into her shorts pocket, she said, "I forgot to show you what I found with the journal."

She pulled it free, letting it dangle on its deep blue necklace. When he glanced over, she explained, "The yarn's from Angie's tapestry, but I don't know what the key's for. It's not to her car, and I didn't see another lock around there."

"Except the one you pried off the door," he reminded her.

"But this can't be to your lock," she said. "It was left inside the wall."

He looked over again before staring past the gyrations of the idiotically smiling hula girl toward the rutted dirt road. A small desert cottontail looked up from where it had been nibbling the sparse grasses at the margin, then raised its tail like a white flag as it zigzagged toward the shelter of scraggly tarbush. Silhouetted against the morning sky, a dark-winged hunter changed course but was too far off to pose a threat.

"Looks to me like a key to the same kind of padlock," he said. "But I can't think of where I've seen another. . . ."

She waited for him to continue before quickly losing patience. "What?"

He shook his head. "It's just a hunch, but we're going to make a little detour."

Though he didn't explain further, Dana's heart picked up speed when he radioed his deputy to tell him he was making a stop to check the salt-dome access road.

"Do you remember that part in Angie's journal about the Salt Woman and her womb?" she asked excitedly when Jay replaced the radio's handset. "There's really a cavern, isn't there? A salt cavern somewhere past the 'round breasts' of the domes? West of them, maybe?"

"I never heard of any cavern," he said. "But this land is known for keeping secrets, so I wouldn't rule it out."

As they turned onto an even rougher dirt road, Dana caught a flash at the corner of her eye. Glancing behind them, she was distracted by the sight of the hawk tucking in its wings and dropping well beyond the dust of the Suburban's passage.

When it rose again its flight was burdened by the weight of the young rabbit dangling limp beneath its claws.

To the uninitiated, the Chihuahuan Desert's basins appeared as flat and unbroken as the surface of a windless sea. But the Hunter had learned its creosote-lined ridges and its deeply carved arroyos. He knew the hidden places prowled by coyotes and bobcats, and even an occasional mountain lion ranging down out of the foothills.

He knew because during the past two months he had become one with the predators that stalked these arid lands. Not out of choice, but because *she* had driven him to it—his wicked Angelina.

While he chewed the strip of raw flesh from his last kill, his memory marked out the best spots to linger in the shade to wait out the murderous afternoon sun. As well as the places where a good pair of field glasses could reward a watcher with a glimmer from a windshield miles distant.

As the breeze shifted, it streamed across the cavern's gaping mouth behind him, dragging a mournful echo from the depths below.

Untroubled by its lament, he raised his binoculars to follow the movement of the new sheriff's Suburban across a rural ranch road some twenty miles away. He watched for a long time as the SUV drew nearer, but still he couldn't discern whether it was carrying one occupant or two.

Swearing under his breath, he willed the image to come clearer. Willed Jay Eversole to be alone.

Because that would mean that he'd left Dana Vanover at his place. That she would be unarmed and alone while the lawman wasted hours searching the area around the abandoned Webb ranch.

But instead of continuing in the direction of the dry lake, Eversole slowed and took the turnoff that would lead him to the salt domes, the very access road the Hunter had used the night before.

He crossed a stony wash and trudged up a rocky outcrop to a spot that overlooked the locked gate. Squatting low so as to remain unnoticed, he watched from that vantage point as the sheriff climbed out of his vehicle.

Moments later, he was joined by a second figure, smaller, with a flutter of wheat-gold hair. He recognized the woman. The same woman the Hunter would have taken down last night, if he had had surprise on his side.

The pair approached the gate and apparently unlocked it, for the sheriff pushed it open with a creaking sound that carried on the wind.

The Hunter didn't wait around to track their progress further. Instead he trotted off to get his rifle and find the perfect cover, the perfect spot from which to make his kill.

# Chapter Eleven

*He comes to me by night, on the heels of the Salt Woman's visitations.*

*As hard and hurried as he ever was, he is a selfish lover, often rough,*
*skirting the edges of raw violence.*

*He's pissed off I have come again.*
*Even more pissed when I come first.*
*Because, as unevolved as it seems,*
*his animal rutting turns me on at some elemental level.*
*No matter how I protest and wish it wasn't so.*

*Has the goddess sent him as a warning,*
*Or a way to pass this endless night of my withdrawal?*
                                              —Entry nine, March (illegible)
                                              Angie's sobriety journal

As Jay used binoculars to survey the hillside rising from the end of the access road, Dana shaded her vision and looked, too, until the windblown sand forced her to turn away. As she wiped her watering eyes, she listened intently but registered nothing but silence.

"Where *are* you, Angie?" she asked through gritted teeth.

Jay gave her a bare nod of understanding before returning his attention to the land.

Lifeless, lonely, and far too vast to search on foot, it rose gently, shielding what she imagined as a limitless expanse. If the cavern wasn't somewhere in sight, the two of them could search for weeks—for *years*—and never find it.

Despair billowing inside her, Dana turned back toward the Suburban, then cocked her head at a faint sound. It was only a dry hiss: coarse grains blown over rocks and rattling through desiccated creosote as brown and barren as the sun-bleached soil.

"Where are all the cactus?" she asked, realizing this area was missing the friendly forms that desert travelers expected. Organ-pipe, saguaro, barrel cactus with their bright flowers. Even a stand of prickly pear would be a welcome patch of green amid the scraggly scrub.

"Too dry and too salty for most of 'em," Jay said before glancing down around their feet. After walking a few paces to the left, he pointed out a pile of small, fissured gray rocks. "Here's your cactus."

She moved closer and bent forward, then lifted her fluttering hair away to look. "That's the best you can do? A dead one?"

"Oh, it's alive, just waiting for a rain to perk it up and help it put out big, pink blossoms. They call this one living rock. There's a resurrection plant, too—and if you're not careful you'll pick up some hitchhikers: seedpods from the devil's claw and half a dozen thorny relatives. Life's tough as all hell out here. Yet it hangs on against all odds."

His words fanned the embers of a hope that somehow so had Angie. But before Dana could say as much, another sound intruded on the quiet. The hollow tone reminded her of childhood, when she and her sister would drive their mother crazy blowing across the glass tops of old-fashioned soda bottles. Only this note droned far deeper, as if the vessel held not eight ounces but untold thousands.

"Hear that?" she asked, half convinced she was dredging up the note from memory.

But Jay's stance told her he was listening, too, his head turned toward the hill's right side.

"Sounds like the wind's blowing across an opening or between some rocks," he said. "But let's not read too much into it even if we do find something. There are lots of little caves around here, and most of 'em . . ."

But Dana was already scrambling uphill like a mountain goat, heading toward a spot that she had at first taken for a band of shadow. The harder she looked, the more she imagined it was a hole of some sort, perhaps the same cavern Angie had mentioned in her journal.

"Slow down," Jay called from behind her. "You'll break an ankle in those sandals."

But Dana couldn't slow down, not with the low tone growing deeper and more ominous with each step. It drew her like a siren's song, her skin prickling with the conviction that this was the place where her sister, like the living rock, lay waiting for a signal to spring forth and flourish. This was the battleground where Nikki's life would be won.

Dana ignored the throbbing of her healing leg, the burning of the dry air in her lungs. Jay's footsteps closed in, his boots sending pebbles clattering downhill.

Blood thrumming with exertion, she approached a mouthlike opening. Larger than it had looked from below, perhaps twelve feet wide and four and a half feet high at the tallest, it seemed to frown at her as she drew level with it. As they watched, a pair of cave swallows swooped out past a dangling spider, their beaks snapping at a host of tiny insects.

"Stop." Jay forced the issue, grasping her arm. The shadowed void returned his word an instant later, but was too black to offer up its secrets.

"Let go of me." She panted and cupped a hand around her mouth. *"Angie. Angie!"*

The shouted word reverberated in the emptiness around them, echoing not only from the cave but from the rocky slope itself. No other sound came back to them; even the wind had fallen silent.

"She has to be around here," Dana insisted.

"She *was*." He pointed downward, where Dana would have stepped.

Dried petals lay at their feet, along with feathers weighted down by pebbles in a pattern far too regular to be explained by random chance, a subtle mosaic that underscored the mouth from one corner to the other. At the center of it sat a skull, clearly canine. And probably coyote, considering the scabrous patch of clinging hairs.

Though the sun shone warm at her back, a sick chill rippled along her sides. "I've seen . . . I've seen this somewhere before."

He nodded. "Near the adobe. There are a couple of old graves, and I'm pretty sure your sister marked them this way. Looks like something somebody like Angie—I mean an artist—would've done."

As Dana stared, it came to her: "That same pattern's in her star field, the one she was weaving in the tapestry. This is *Angie's* place, my sister's. *This* is where she went."

She pulled away from him, or tried to, but Jay's grip tightened.

"Those petals have been here a long time, but someone's come since your sister." He gestured toward the ground beneath the opening's tallest point. "See that? It's disturbed there—and that looks like a footprint."

Dana didn't care about that, not now, with her instincts shouting that Angie was nearby. "I'll need that flashlight," she said, nodding toward the leather holster he'd attached to his belt next to his weapon before they'd left the SUV. "I have to know if she's still in there."

She noted the grim set of his jaw, the sweat gleaming at his temple. In his eyes she saw what he was thinking, what she was trying so hard not to let herself understand.

"If she's inside," he started, "she can't possibly be living. It's been two months since she vanished, Dana. Two months without water, food . . ."

She held his gaze and resisted the urge to blink back

moisture. "I ran away from what I had to face in Houston. I'm not running from this, too."

Yet she did a moment later, when the first gunshots rang out.

# *Chapter Twelve*

*Police responded Saturday to an incident at the AMC 16 at the Valley View Center, where witnesses claim a patron assaulted a man of Arabic descent as he carried a snack tray into a movie theater. The victim was transported to a minor emergency center with a head laceration but declined to press charges. The alleged assailant, recently separated from military service overseas, was escorted to Dallas VA Medical Center, where he agreed to undergo voluntary psychiatric evaluation.*

—Police blotter item,
*Dallas Morning News*

Behind and between them, rock exploded with a crack that instantly took Jay back to a Baghdad hotspot his unit had been defending.

"What was tha—" Dana started before a second report echoed from everywhere at once.

Jay was already reaching for her when she leaped out of range, instinct and adrenaline pushing her to bolt. Which would take her out into the open, straight into harm's way.

He'd seen it before in his men, so he was ready, propelling himself after her, hooking his left arm around her waist and dragging her to the closest cover—the black maw of the cave.

He bent low to hurry them inside, pulling her past a row of rocks that jutted upward like a crone's teeth. Dana lost a sandal, but he couldn't stop to grab it.

"Quiet," he barked before she had the chance to cry out. He hauled her farther back, picking his way by feel amid the stony rubble.

He didn't dare turn on his flashlight, couldn't give the sniper any greater advantage than he had already. Leaving her behind him, Jay growled, "Don't move; don't speak," and belly-crawled behind a large rock to peer outside.

The pistol in his hand felt all wrong. What he needed was his AK-47 and enough battle rattle to encase his head and body like a beetle's. He felt naked out here with the hajji firing on their position, with the terrorists who'd streamed in like a swarm of stinging ants on a fresh carcass—

*That's not right,* Jay realized. He wasn't in *that* desert, wasn't even someplace it was okay to call them hajjis, much less tackle a man wearing a turban as he walked into a matinee.

Horror body-slammed him, the same shame that had hit after he'd realized the man wasn't some bomb-strapped radical but an adjunct professor from a local college who'd been taking popcorn to his twelve-year-old son.

"What . . . what's happening?" Dana whispered from the spot where she crouched, breathing hard.

He glanced back at her, looking for confirmation that the shots he'd heard had been real. That she wasn't cowering because she'd been dragged in here by an insane man.

"Can you see him? Is he coming?" Her expression was barely visible, but she was clearly tense. Yet he saw trust in her eyes, enough to reassure him that he hadn't just assaulted her over a mirage.

"Can't see anyone," he said. "Did *you*, before I pulled you in here?"

His words reverberated in what sounded like a good-size space. Bigger than any of the wormhole caves he'd seen around here. Maybe they'd found Angie's cavern, after all, or at least its antechamber.

"No, I just . . . I heard the shots, and I remembered the man with the gun last night. After that all I could think of was running back to the Suburban, where I left my purse and phone. If you hadn't pulled me in here . . ."

So what he'd heard *had* been real. Jay would have been relieved—except a live sniper wasn't a reality worth celebrating.

"You might've made it," he said. "It's tough to hit a running target. But we're better off here, behind cover—except the bastard can keep us pinned down for a while. At least till Wallace comes looking for us."

"Will he?"

Jay nodded. "If I don't check in within the next hour he'll start to wonder. We don't carry handheld radios—they don't work around here well enough to bother, and it's a dead zone for my cell phone, too. But when I don't answer my truck radio, he'll worry something's happened and drive out here."

Wallace might not be his number-one fan, but he knew as well as Jay did that they had to watch each other's backs. In a place this desolate, every mother's son—and daughter—respected the necessity of mutual assistance. Especially in the hot months, when the "inconvenience" of a dead battery or flat tire could prove fatal.

Jay tried to think of some way to warn his deputy. If the shooter lingered, he could easily take Wallace by surprise.

"But what if he climbs up here first—the man who fired at us?" Dana asked him. "What if he—"

"He'll have to leave cover to get to a spot where he can sight us. For a decent angle he'll have to come in close, too. And if he does that, I'll drop him." *Just another enemy target,* he thought. *Not an old friend or a neighbor.* He couldn't afford to hesitate, couldn't afford to let the shooter squeeze off another round.

"Chances are he won't risk it," Jay added. "After all, he's already blown his best chance, when he had both time and surprise on his side. That tells me he's nervous, just like he got nervous last night when Max started barking. If he ran then, he'll run now. More than likely."

"More than likely," Dana echoed with prayerlike fervor.

They remained in place a long time, but no matter how hard Jay stared he saw no movement except that caused by the renewed stirring of the wind, heard no sound but its haunted voice whispering across the cave's face.

"I can't take this anymore," said Dana. "It . . . it stinks in here. Like death. G-give me the flashlight."

He had smelled it, too, and had been hoping that she hadn't: a pungent background odor mingled with the moldy, barnyard reek of guano. "No, Dana."

"He's gone by now; he has to be. But I'll point the beam away from the opening in case he's watching."

"There're other things to think of, too. Bats have been here. They'll be deeper than the swallows' nests, but they could be close enough, covering the ceiling. You disturb them and they'll swarm out, maybe by the thousands. And it only takes one with rabies. Besides that, snakes hole up where there's shade, and—"

"Ugh—does this place have any *non*disgusting fauna?" she asked sharply. Without waiting for an answer she said, "I'll keep my voice down and my beam low. So come on, Jay. Let me look."

Still he hesitated, until she said, "I've been to vet school. I've done necropsies on dead dogs. I've put down sick and injured animals while their owners stood there bawling. I'll handle this the same way. Because I have to."

*Even if it's Angie?* He couldn't ask her that, though, couldn't give voice to the suspicion. Because he'd smelled the odor that hovered in this cave before, a peculiar strain that had him thinking, *Human.*

"It's not my sister," she said nonetheless. "Do you really think Angie would've stopped on her way to her own death to decorate the tomb?"

When he'd patrolled the streets of Dallas, Jay had been first responder to a lot of strange stuff. Suicides, in particular, had a tendency to ritualize their own deaths, maybe in some last-ditch quest for meaning. Considering what he'd read of her journal, "Angelina Morningstar" would have been the type.

Again he scanned the slope below them. This time he spotted movement, but it was only the agitated darting of the swallows and a trio of scaled quails pecking among the scraggly brown weeds. He could have cited the pretty little birds as examples of the land's "nondisgusting" creatures, but he didn't have the heart.

Instead he passed the flashlight back toward Dana. When she grasped its end, he did not immediately let go.

"First you have to promise me," he told her, "you won't move from where you're sitting. No matter what you see, you stay put. There could be holes and passages and side chambers, and I'm *not* running after you again. You hear that?"

There could also be a crime scene, one that needed to be preserved.

"I hear you," she said grudgingly. "And I promise I'll stay right here."

With a nod, he let go of the light, and then looked back out on the desert. Though he was nearly convinced they were alone here, he'd seen men and women die when they took things for granted.

A split second later Dana's gasp turned him around. A circle of light skimmed along the guano-stained floor and rocky walls that glittered white with sparkling crystals.

"This has to be it," she said, her voice bouncing off of salted walls.

The space was smaller than he'd imagined, smaller than his RV. But as her beam shifted, he saw a darker spot off to the right, a second opening that led downward, deeper inside the hill.

It might have been his imagination, but the smell of death seemed to come from that direction. From the blackness of that hole.

"I'll bet an animal wandered in here." Thin and eerily childlike, Dana's voice floated in the darkness. "It got confused and lost, and when Angie found its body later she built the tribute outside. Because this spot was sacred to her."

Turning from the cave's mouth, Jay holstered his pistol and then crept over rock to reach her. He laid a hand on her bare leg where she crouched.

"Let me take the flashlight," he said softly. "Let me have a look."

Nodding, she relinquished it and waited, her tension a more palpable presence than the unseen sea of living fur above. After taking one last glance back toward daylight, he stood up awkwardly and made his way toward the cavern's throat.

The smell strengthened with his progress, a stench he had smelled far too often overseas. Though he hoped—prayed—he was wrong and that he would discover a mule deer or a bobcat, the closer he came to the opening the more convinced he was he'd find a human, a body already partly mummified within the chamber's arid confines.

He reached the nearly round portal and, using one hand, braced himself within its rock frame. Then, leaning in, he shone the flashlight downward—down into a grotto whose sole inhabitant lay curled and naked as a fetus on its floor.

# *Chapter Thirteen*

*The Navajo call her Usheenasun, salt spirit.*
*The Zuni know her as the Salt Mother.*
*But to the Cochiti and so many others, she is simply Salt Woman.*

*To the people Salt Woman's flesh is sacred.*
*They use it to preserve food, to give simple stews their savor.*
*Often it's important in religious ceremonies.*

*When gathering her flesh, they are instructed to move*
*with quiet dignity, keeping her realm pure.*
*But often, in the stories, she is disrespected*
*by those who should revere her.*
*Refused food and lodging, polluted,*
*her gifts squandered without thought.*

*So she leaves the people she loves.*
*She turns her back and walks deep into the desert.*

*Can I do any less?*

—Final entry (undated)
Angie's sobriety journal

Dana stared straight through the grimy windshield without registering the rocky slope before her.

Once they'd heard the slam of a truck door, Jay had ventured outside the cavern and then called down the hill to Wallace. Afterward he'd taken Dana down to sit inside the Suburban with its engine idling while she waited out Those Things That Must Be Done.

He hadn't let her see the body, though he had promised that he would once it was recovered. First, though, would come the photographs, the measurements, the collection of whatever trace evidence remained.

Jay had used his radio to contact someone, perhaps Estelle Hooks, at the courthouse. He had asked the woman's husband, the county judge, to collect and bring out the supplies they would need. Dana couldn't recall what he had wanted, other than a stretcher and a body bag, and perhaps a camera.

She was horrified to realize that other men would see the corpse the way Jay had described it: curve-spined, withered, and entirely unclothed. The thought of Angie so heart-breakingly helpless and exposed in death seized Dana with a desire to protect her sister's dignity—to race back and *demand* that they turn away their prying gazes.

Yet she sat shivering in the AC vents' arctic blast. When Abe Hooks pulled up and climbed out of his old pickup, he glanced curiously in her direction, but she couldn't meet his eyes. Couldn't do a damned thing except stare numbly while her brain spun desperately through possible explanations for the presence of a blond female corpse inside the remote cavern Angie's journal had described.

Even so, when her satellite phone rang perhaps fifteen minutes later, Dana answered without thinking.

"Hello." The word was listless and mechanical, more a reflex than a greeting.

"I just called to say I'm so, so sorry."

Dana jerked to awareness at her mother's words. How could she know? Who on earth would have told her before the body was officially identified?

"Sorry?" she asked cautiously.

"Yes, about that stupid Regina—who is no longer any friend of mine. Jerome says I should have my head examined for crying on her shoulder, that the only reason she listened in the first place was to come up with some angle to turn to her own advantage. Now it seems he was right, and you know how I hate *that.*"

"Regina called and pestered me in El Paso. I told her not to come," Dana said flatly, while inside she screamed and wept and wondered, *What the hell does any of it matter now?*

"That's just it. Regina said that when it comes to the news, she doesn't need *anyone's* permission."

"Regina Lawler's not the news. She's just some flipped-out has-been." Dana knew it was a harsh assessment, but she had no energy for tact now, not while she was bleeding inside and helpless to tell her mother what was happening at that very moment beneath the desert's blank face.

As she thought about the withered corpse there, hot tears hazed her vision.

"She's on her way," said Isabel. "That's what I called to warn you about. She's found a freelance cameraman, and they're coming out to get the story. That's all this is—a *story* to her. My daughter, my granddaughter—everything you're doing. She's already shown up at the hospital and gotten footage of Nikki's birthday party from the doorway. She turned seven the other day, and there was cake and ice cream with her parents and the nurses. They didn't want the extra visitors, but Nikki got so excited when she saw the microphone and TV camera, they didn't have it in their hearts to tell her no."

*Say something. Just say it,* Dana thought. *Don't let her sit there thinking that anything we do or don't do will make one damned bit of difference. Not for Angie, not for Nikki, not for any of us in the end.*

Because she couldn't force out those words, Dana settled for a stammered, "For-forget about Regina. I-I'll handle her when she gets here."

"Is something wrong?" Isabel asked. "You sound terrible. Is your nose clogged? I knew you'd catch something in that horrible place. Did you remember your antihistamines?"

"I'm fine. It's just . . . let me call you later."

"What's going on? Dana? Is there anything you need?"

*A mother who could stand to hug me. A mother who was willing to accept Angie as she was.* But her anger was only a thin shroud draped over a monolith of sadness.

"Just to say I love you," Dana managed. *And I'll be home sooner than I thought.*

Once the call was over she shut off the Suburban and stuck Jay's keys in her pockets. Rubbing her arms for warmth, she stepped out into the already oppressive heat and started up the hill.

*How far have you gone this time, Angie?*

The answer came back to Dana on a moan of wind across the cavern's mouth: *Far enough to finally break your heart . . .*

"She's lighter than I would've thought," said Wallace Hooks as he and the sheriff carefully maneuvered the stiffened figure inside the body bag.

The deputy was mouth-breathing and trying not to look down. Jay suspected he'd appear green when they stepped out into the daylight. No surprise there. The odor, while not as harrowing as wet-rotted putrefaction, was plenty strong in the enclosed space. And besides that, Wallace had already told him this was only his second corpse, after the charred remains of the sheriff with whom he had worked for more than three years.

Wallace's father, who held the flashlight where he stood at the portal, looked unhappy but resigned to the morbid tasks at hand. He had clearly left his grill in a hurry, for his thick white hair stood up in clumps, probably from where he'd hurriedly pulled off his apron. "That's what happens when they dry out. Henry Schlitz and I went out with the last sheriff, when a couple of illegals got found by Weevil Jenkins's stock tank. Guess they didn't make it to the water soon enough, 'cause they were light like this, too. Or I should say what was left was. After the coyotes."

"Gently," Jay instructed Wallace. "We'll need the body intact for the medical examination, and she's . . . fragile."

"This is going to cost the county a damned fortune," Abe complained.

Both Jay and Wallace looked up sharply, though Jay knew Abe was right, since Rimrock County was far too small to have its own ME and so contracted with the county of El Paso.

"Listen, I'm sorry the girl's gone and killed herself," the older Hooks grumbled. "I'm just being practical, that's all."

"We don't know it's a suicide," Jay reminded him. "There hasn't been a formal—"

"I know you worked in the big city, but around here we rely on the sense the Lord God gave us. That gun under the body, tangled in the fingers of her right hand. Face shot half off—you don't have to be a goddamned coroner to figure out she blew that booze-soaked brain of hers all over this cavern. Left all of us her goddamned mess to deal with, that rich family of hers to explain to—"

"A forty-five-caliber handgun's not typically a woman's weapon," Jay said as he shone his own flashlight around the walls. "Besides that, I don't see any dark stains. No blood spatter either, like I'd expect if it was done here."

Looking down he added, "Just some pooling on the floor, where the body fluids leaked out before evaporating."

"Right back." Wallace pushed past his father. Before he made it clear of the cave, both men heard him retching.

Moving forward, Abe bent down to help Jay with the body. "Let's get a move on with this. I could use some fresh air myself."

"I could stand the help," Jay said, "but I need you to let me deal with Dr. Vanover."

Abe shrugged. "Suits me fine. Only when you do, be careful. Don't want her thinking there's more to this than there is."

Jay hammered him with a hard look. "Somebody already gave her that impression when they shot at us this morning."

The smaller man grunted with what sounded like surprise. "Shot at you? Here?"

"Yeah—like he knew what we were going to find."

Abe cursed. "The goddamned *idiot*. I expect he figured he would make things better, shutting her up before she could call in her environmeddlers or what have you. But to shoot at that woman's sister, too—and with you here for a witness."

"What idiot? Abe, do you have some idea who might've done this?"

Another shrug. A hesitation. And then: "Dennis Riggins, who else? I heard he has near everything he owned tied up in Haz-Vestment. If that deal doesn't go through, he's sunk."

Jay stared, unable to comprehend that Abe Hooks would take the two men's family feud to this level, that he would accuse Dennis, a man the Eversoles had considered a good friend for decades. Jay wanted to tell the old judge where he could shove his theory—except he couldn't quite dismiss it out of hand. Not considering Dennis's reaction to last night's news about the Haz-Vestment investigation.

As furious as Dennis had been, Jay could almost picture the huge man stalking over to Angie's adobe, intent on scaring Dana out of town. Or maybe Angie herself, since he suspected that she'd come back to stir up trouble. Maybe somehow he blamed her for the FBI's investigation— thought she'd put them up to looking where they had no business.

But never in a million years could Jay picture Dennis firing in his direction. No matter how upset the man had been about his failed investment, he couldn't possibly—

"I know what you're thinking," Abe said. "You're thinking this is all about that mad-on my family's had with the Riggins bunch since I was just a kid. And you're thinking how your uncle R.C.'s buddy wouldn't have it in him to kill someone. But you don't really know that bastard. Nobody knows him the way I do. If you had any idea what he's done . . ."

Jay wanted to demand an explanation, but he heard the low murmur of voices outside, voices he assumed to be Wallace's and Dana's. He should have figured she wouldn't wait too long, alone, with nothing left to do but brood. He wished he'd thought to ask Estelle to come, too, to sit with her. The county clerk might not have been friendly when Dana had first arrived in Devil's Claw, but now that the worst had come to pass, Jay knew Estelle would call her friend Suzanne Riggins, and the two of them would righteously downshift into full-fledged comfort-the-bereaved mode, armed with an array of casseroles and sweet Rice Krispies Treats.

"Excuse me a minute, Abe," Jay said. Maybe he could talk Dana into going back to the Suburban—or at least make sure Wallace didn't set her off with some remark about her sister.

But Wallace proved to be Estelle's son. When Jay stepped outside he saw his deputy take Dana's hand and tell her how sorry he was for her loss.

She nodded stiffly before noticing Jay's presence and abruptly withdrawing to move toward him. "I can't wait any longer—can't talk to my mother on the phone as if nothing's happened. I need to see the body, Jay. I have to know for certain."

Wallace's sharp glance banked from Dana to Jay and back again, and the deputy's expression soured. Clearly he had connected the dots between her use of Jay's first name and their arrival here together. Since Jay had already told him she had fled the adobe late last night, Wallace would have to suspect where she had stayed until morning.

"You look like you're feeling better," Jay told him, "so why don't you go back inside and help your father with that stretcher while I speak to Dr. Vanover?"

Wallace pressed his lips together, and frown lines furrowed his expression. But after a moment's hesitation he did as he was asked.

"Dana," Jay said as he pulled her into his arms and

squeezed her, "I know you think you want to see her, but it's not a good idea. Trust me. You don't want to remember her this way."

"I know it will be hard. I know the . . . the body's been there quite a while. But she needs to be identified. What difference does it make whether I do it here or in whatever morgue you end up sending her to? Do you think a cold steel slab in some strange city's going to make things any easier?"

"I think . . ." His heart ached as he said it. "I think this will have to be one of those IDs done by dental records. Or maybe DNA. The face . . . a lot of the face is missing. And quite a bit of skin, too."

He felt Dana's muscles tense against him, felt the warmth of her tears soaking the light fabric of his duty shirt.

"Do you mean . . . Was it animals?"

"Not that killed her." Though perhaps something had gnawed later to tear flesh from both the abdomen and upper legs. "The medical examiner will tell us more, but you need to know we found a gun beneath the body, in the victim's right hand. There's a possibility the damage to the face was self-inflicted, but we won't be certain until the—"

Shaking her head, she pulled away to stare up into his face. "Are you sure it was the right hand?"

He thought about it, nodded. "I'm certain. And I documented it with photos. Why?"

"Because my sister is left-handed, Jay. She didn't shoot herself."

"I'll be sure to note that, Dana. But right now it's just one piece in the puzzle. I don't want you jumping to some conclusion that'll only cause your family even more pain in the long run."

Moisture glimmered in her green eyes, tears that welled up from a soul-deep wound. "More pain than what, Sheriff? Than knowing that my sister's dead—or that the people running Rimrock County will be overjoyed to hear it?"

*   *   *

As the passing hours slowly dragged the day toward darkness, Dana felt her heart pulled toward an even blacker chasm. Jay had wanted her taken somewhere more comfortable, but she'd refused to leave, thinking that at any moment she would get out of his Suburban and insist on seeing Angie's body. Instead she struggled to find her way past his warning that she wouldn't want to remember Angie as she was now. But as the minutes ticked down, Dana couldn't force herself to move, and finally the van left for El Paso with its somber cargo.

Sometime later Jay opened the driver's-side door and climbed inside, the last to leave the scene.

"How are you holding up?" he asked her, and reached over to pull off her sunglasses and brush a stray lock from her eyes.

His kindness cracked the shell of her inertia, and she sagged into his arms and exhaled. "I know you're not glad she's gone. I'm sorry if I lumped you in with Abe Hooks and those others. I'm sorry—you've been nothing but kind to me from the start."

He stroked her back. "No apologies needed. It's been a rough day for you—a lot of rough days strung together. If snapping at me could make it any easier, I'd volunteer for a hell of a lot more than you dished out."

She dredged up what she hoped would pass for a smile. "I can't stop thinking about Angie, about the way she was when she was younger. She wasn't always . . . troubled. Not until the summer she turned sixteen."

"Did something happen that year?"

"We lost Dad that June. It was awful." Even now, so many years later, her eyes stung at the memory. "He was so young, only forty-three. A cardiologist who liked to set a good example for his patients. He didn't smoke or drink. He ran at least five days a week, no matter what the weather. It was misting rain the day a lady cutting through our subdivision hit him with her minivan. His head slammed down on the concrete—it was very quick."

"I'm sorry. That must've been tough on you."

She nodded. "Brutal. I was thirteen at the time, and I thought my daddy was—how's that song go?—ten feet tall and bulletproof. And my mother—she was devastated. Dad was the only person she ever really opened up around. Afterward she withdrew from Angie and me almost completely. And that's when Angie started getting into trouble. I think at first all she really wanted was some attention. When that didn't work she seemed hell-bent on punishing Mom for not caring.

"I tried everything I could to save what family I had left," Dana went on. "I told Angie she was wrong about Mom. She did care—*does* care. She just doesn't show it the same way most mothers do. She can't— Oh, God, I don't know how to tell her. I should have called already, but how can . . . ?"

His calloused hand cupped her chin, while his thumb caressed the line of her jaw. "Don't beat yourself up about it. Let me make the phone call. That's part of my job."

Though she felt like a coward for grasping at his offer, she dug her phone out of her purse and gave it to him, then turned her face away to press her forehead to the window glass. "Just hold down the number one. I've got her programmed on the speed dial."

Outside she watched the dimming sky and picked out the first few bright stars. *I wish I may, I wish I might, disappear for this one night,* she thought as the knowledge of her failure and its consequences pounded at her temples.

"Mrs. Huffington?" Jay asked, using that grave calm that so often presaged bad news in lawmen's voices.

Dana closed her eyes and pinched her lower lip between her teeth.

"We've recovered human remains from a location in the desert," Jay said. "We have no way of knowing how long they might have been there or whether the body has any connection with your daughter's disappearance. But if we want to rule that possibility out, we'll need you to gather a few items and get them to us as soon as possible. We're looking for dental records—even old ones—names, dates, and locations of medical procedures you're aware of."

Dana remembered Angie's appendectomy in Santa Fe, the fractured wrist she'd suffered while living near Phoenix, and several rounds of residential rehab—all cut short when she'd prematurely checked herself out and taken off for parts unknown. Though her sister had refused for years to see their mother, she had never hesitated to list Isabel under the "responsible party" section of her admittance papers. In spite of her husband's disapproval, Isabel had paid each bill without complaint. . . .

Except, Dana realized, her mother had never gotten any statements related to Angie's prenatal care or labor and delivery. Angie might have turned to a charity that helped unwed mothers or to the adoptive family themselves, if she'd had any involvement in choosing who would raise her child. Dana was seized with an impulse to ask Laurie Harrison about it, though she had no idea why the question felt so critically important.

"Yes," Jay said into the phone, "Dana's here with me. She's a little shaken, but she's strong. Would you like to speak to her now?"

After a slight delay to listen, he added, "I'm sure she'll understand you need a little time first. I'll contact you as soon as I can with details about where your courier can bring those records."

He ended the call a moment later and laid a hand on Dana's shoulder. "Your mother's a strong woman, too. She's going to get through this. She wanted to compose herself before she spoke to you."

Dana nodded, understanding her mother's need to regain some semblance of control. "Thank you. Thank you for being so . . . You handled that far better than I could have."

"Unfortunately, I have experience."

Despite the lump thickening her throat, she changed the subject. "So what's next? Do you have to go to your office?"

"I do, but first we're stopping back by my place. I'm making us some dinner, and we're going to get you packed."

"I told you, I'm not hungry, and what do you mean, packed?"

"You've been through a shock. Your body doesn't know what it needs. You wouldn't eat the sandwich Estelle brought earlier, and I see you've only had one bottle of water the whole day. You need decent food, drink, and sleep tonight—in Pecos. I'll drive you there myself if you're not up to it."

"But why? Can't I stay with you again?"

He shook his head. "As much as I'd like that, Dana, we can't do it. I need to keep my head clear and my mind focused, without risking any bias. Even if I felt sure you would be safe in Devil's Claw, there's no fit place for you to lodge."

"I don't want to sit in some hotel room an hour away waiting for the phone to ring."

"And I don't want to have to worry about you every minute while I'm doing my job."

"So take me with you."

He shook his head, his expression regretful but unyielding. "No, Dana. This isn't Nancy Drew. It's an investigation into a suspicious death, one that could turn out to be a murder. Do you know what a defense attorney could do with the fact that the sheriff was sleeping with the victim's sister while looking into this? Not to mention what the FBI would make of it."

"The FBI? Why would they be involved?"

"I can't give you any details, except to say they'll be looking into this because of a related investigation."

She stared a hole into him. "You can't do this now, Jay. You can't cut me off like this, treat me like I'm just anybody, as if last night we didn't—"

"Last night meant a lot to me." He met her gaze directly. "But I can't let it mean more than justice for the woman we found."

She turned away to stare back out the window, where a few more stars had joined the evening offering. She understood what he was saying, even respected his professionalism. But that didn't stop the hurt—and the feeling of rejection—from welling up like blood out of a fresh wound.

"Fine," she said. "Just take me back to your place to pick up my rental. Then I'll gather up my sister's things and—"

"Your sister's belongings have to stay for now. I've already sent Wallace to secure the adobe, and I'll be taking her journal into evidence as well."

"I want that journal, Jay. It's mine and my family's. I'm the one who found it, and we both know it could end up in custody pretty much forever if I let you take it."

"I'll make you a copy, all right? It's the best that I can offer."

When he touched her shoulder she shrugged off the contact. So without another word he put the Suburban into drive.

As Dana glanced back one last time toward the lonely hillside, the bright streak of a meteor caught her attention. But almost before she recognized what she was seeing, it faded out against the blackness of the summer sky.

The Hunter should have ended it last night, while he had her all alone. Should have taken out the damned dog and overpowered her quickly, before she'd had the chance to call for help.

Instead he'd backed off, overwhelmed by the dog's noise—the barking that would carry for miles in the silence. Worried that, with such a warning, Dana Vanover would produce a weapon; that cornered, she might try to fight him hand to hand.

If the desert had taught him anything, it was that even the most formidable predator had to choose his opportunities, to minimize the risk of an injury that might slow him. And if the desert hadn't convinced the Hunter, Angelina had certainly driven home the point by demonstrating that even the weakest prey could inflict one hell of a lot of damage when struggling for its life. He'd been afraid to take the chance that her sister might as well.

But fear was just another word for weakness, a weakness that must be faced and conquered if he meant to survive.

# *Chapter Fourteen*

*I met a traveller from an antique land*
*Who said: "Two vast and trunkless legs of stone*
*Stand in the desert. Near them, on the sand,*
*Half sunk, a shattered visage lies . . .*

—Percy Bysshe Shelley,
from "Ozymandias"

*Tuesday, July 3, 4:37 P.M.*
*99 Degrees Fahrenheit*

Jay glowered at his ringing office phone and swore. Within hours of the first reporter—a fox-faced, forty-something brunette out of Houston—breaking the story of Dana Vanover's "heroic quest" to find her missing sister and save a dying child, other members of the press had clogged his phone lines in an effort to get his take on the search. And when word got out about the partially mummified female recovered from the salt cavern they'd gone absolutely ape shit, racing one another to get here first and sniff out even juicier details.

But ignoring the call was not an option, so he picked up and said, "Sheriff's office."

"Jay? Is that you?"

"Dana." He wanted to say more—wanted to pull her into a hard hug and stroke her sleek blond hair while he kissed away her grief. But the chances of that were right up there with the likelihood of snow in the day's forecast. For one thing, Dana was staying in Pecos.

It hurt to remember her driving away last night, taking little more than her purse and the photocopy of her sister's journal. He'd kept a second copy for himself before leaving the original in FBI hands, for whatever good they'd get out of it. He had called Dana later to make sure she'd gotten safely to the motel, but she'd seemed both guarded and distracted. Understandable, considering the circumstances.

Still, he hated the distance between them, as well as the chasm that had opened with their discovery in the cavern.

"Are you all right?" he asked her. "The reporters haven't found you, have they?"

"It's not that. It's . . . Did you see the news this morning—that FBI press conference?"

"Yeah." He grimaced. "Estelle dragged me over to her office. She keeps a TV over there to catch her soaps."

It pissed him off that the damned feds couldn't have given him a heads-up, though he had spoken personally with the pair of special agents who'd arrived just after dawn to stake their claim on his investigation. Tomlin had been a little on the officious side, but he and Petit had been polite enough—clearly well trained to minimize friction with the locals. Yet neither one had warned him that their boss, the special agent in charge of the FBI's Albuquerque field office, was about to publicly announce the arrest of two individuals involved in a scheme that bilked investors out of millions.

"Haz-Vestment was the outfit that got Angie so upset, right?" Dana asked. "The same people she was threatening to shut down."

"I see where you're heading with this"—as would any reporter worth his daily java—"and believe me, it's an angle that'll be fully investi—"

But Dana went on as if she hadn't heard him. "What if those people killed her? That Roman Goldsmith and his wife? They still haven't been caught, have they?"

"The FBI's made finding them a top priority." Not that they'd seen fit to confide in him, but along with the rest of the country, Jay had heard the announcement that Roman Goldsmith and his wife, whose most recently reported alias was Miriam Piper-Gold, remained at large. A substantial reward was offered for information leading to their arrest, and a poolside photo was flashed on screen of a leather-skinned, tanned fifty-something male wearing a man-thong below a slight paunch and a set of polar-white capped choppers. At his side was a much younger redhead looking hotter than the record high in a lime-green string bikini. Reporters had already caught onto the fact that Piper-Gold's last known appearance was in Rimrock County, where a hazardous-waste-storage scheme was under way, and they were breaking their necks in the race to put together the connection to the body presumed to be that of the missing heiress.

"Listen, Dana," he warned, "maybe you should think about going back to Houston. It's only a matter of time before the media figures out your sister was the only real opposition to the salt-dome project—and then you'll get no peace." Already three network news vans had collected outside of the courthouse, and he'd had to tape a sign reading, ABSOLUTELY NO PRESS—THIS MEANS YOU! beneath the word SHERIFF on the smoked glass of his door, or he'd spend the whole of his day telling the idiots, "No comment." He hoped to God the round of thunderstorms the weather people were predicting washed the streets clean of the pests and all their interruptions.

"You want me to go?" she asked, though they both knew she was gone already. The brief respite they'd shared was finished, never to be repeated.

"Hell, no," he said honestly, for there was nothing he'd rather have than the privilege of one more chance, one more night to get to know her better. "But the last thing you need is to be stranded an hour away in Pecos, bein' pecked to death by vultures."

"I can handle a few reporters," she said. "What I can't handle is the idea of my sister's killer or killers running around loose while she's—"

"The FBI's on this case. I'm on this case, and Wallace,

too. With that reward and the nationwide publicity, we're going to find them, Dana. It's okay for you to trust us."

She was silent for so long that he wondered if something had gone wrong with the connection. "Are you still there? Dana?"

From across the miles he heard tapping.

"Sorry," she said. "There's someone at the door. Probably the maid. I forgot to put out the 'Do Not Disturb' sign."

"Check the peephole," he warned, unable to get the attempts on her life out of his mind. Though the incidents had occurred here in Rimrock County, Pecos was only an hour away. "You've got the chain on, don't you?"

There was another pause, followed by the muffled sound of voices, as if she'd covered up the phone with her hand. Anxiety bored holes in him. "Dana. *Dana?*"

"Just housekeeping," she reported. "I sent her away. Listen, Sheriff, just because we've been . . . been together, I'm not your responsibility. But Angie is, and she's still mine, too. And that's an obligation I mean to see through."

A few minutes later he was still pondering their conversation—and stewing over the fact that she had called him *Sheriff* instead of using his name—when a sharp rap at the door made him jump. Probably some jackass reporter who hadn't bothered to read his sign. Though he hadn't peered out through his window lately, he suspected they were coming close to outnumbering the residents of Devil's Claw.

He dreaded the moment when one showed up to confront him with his own recent history. More than likely, *he'd* be history once that happened and the leeches slimed him in the cesspool of insinuation. Rimrock County voters might be a fiercely independent lot, but they'd be looking for someone to hang for this debacle. Why not a long-absent prodigal who'd hidden psychiatric trouble in his past?

But when the door flew open it was Estelle Hooks, her

face flushed rosy pink and an iron-gray escapee from her up-swept hair bouncing girlishly about her shoulder. "You have to see this. Hurry, Sheriff. My boy's on the television."

Jay's stomach plunged into his boot heels. Of all the harebrained . . . What the hell was Wallace doing yapping to reporters?

He followed Estelle back into her office, where the set usually devoted to *Days of Our Lives* instead showed Wallace Hooks on CNN. He looked happier than Jay had ever seen him, with his thumbs hooked in his gun belt and his broad-brimmed hat cocked rodeo-stud style. Clearly the deputy was making the most of his moment in the spotlight. But before Jay could catch much more than the word *body*, Estelle drowned out his voice.

"Doesn't he look *tall* on TV?" she asked as she pressed her hands together. "Why, Wallace looks as tall as anybody."

Instead of risking life and limb to shush her, Jay simply turned up the set's volume. If he was going to put Mr. Media's ass in a sling, he needed proper ammunition.

"It was like half a mummy, dry and shriveled, with salt crystals sticking to the skin," said Wallace, above a graphic that incorrectly identified him as the Rimrock County sheriff. "Long blond hair too, though it was comin' out in big clumps."

"Jesus," Jay fumed. What if Dana was watching the live broadcast? What if her mother or the adoptive parents of Angie's daughter saw it? When he had called her, Isabel Huffington had immediately seized on the sliver of hope that the remains belonged to some stranger. But if she heard Wallace's description . . .

As the reporter, a serious young man wearing an early Dan Rather–style safari shirt with a panama fedora, began wrapping up the segment, Wallace—his face lighting—burst out, "It was kinda like that lady she was carrying on about at the town meeting. That Salt Maiden we was supposedly raping with our project."

The reporter looked momentarily annoyed at the unexpected interruption, but, recovering quickly, he asked, "What do you mean, the Salt Maiden?"

*The Salt* Woman, *you moron*, Jay thought. Bad enough Wallace had to spill his guts; he could at least be accurate. And grammatically correct, while he was at it.

Wallace nodded vigorously. "Some Indian thing, I guess. Maybe some kind of a spirit. Ms. Vanover started yelling during the Haz-Vestment meeting that using the salt domes to store hazardous wastes was *defiling* the Salt Maiden. And now she ends up getting turned t'one herself."

"And he's so well-spoken, too," Estelle gushed as the reporter regained enough control to wrap up the segment. "I wouldn't be a bit surprised if those casting people from *Law & Order* call the woman who used to be his agent."

Too bad he couldn't act, because once Jay got finished with him, Wallace was going to *need* a new job—perhaps something set up through the Witness Protection Program, to keep his former boss from hunting him down to wring his neck. "Wallace has no business insinuating that we have an ID on that body. Until the ME makes the call, we can't—"

"She's a Jew, that agent," Estelle went on, "but perfectly nice. I talked to her once when she called for Wallace not long after he left New York City. She wanted him to read for a part on one of the soap operas. She was so disappointed I didn't have a number for poor Wallace at the time. He was chasing around the country somewhere—looking for community theater work, I think. If he'd come straight home like he should have—or at least told me how to reach him—that could have been his big break, don't you think?"

"I'll give him a big break," Jay growled, though his gaze was glued to the screen again, which had erupted with a news flash.

In the heart of Baghdad another suicide bomber had blown up twenty in a marketplace. Jay leaned in close to scan the littered street and the grieving faces of Iraqis. At the sound of gunfire somewhere offscreen he saw a soldier spin, his blue eyes ablaze with terror. The soldier looked exactly like PFC Mike Daugherty, who had been killed on his watch. And the smell . . . the smoke and burning flesh were—

"Sheriff . . . Sheriff—Jay." The alarm in Estelle's voice finally reached him where he crouched behind her metal desk. When he blinked in her direction she shook her head at him. "My goodness. Maybe you should go home and lie down with a cool washcloth for a while."

What he really wanted was to crawl into a hole and die. "I'm sorry," he said, rising. He wanted to say more, to explain away his actions somehow, but anything he could think of would sound ridiculous, even worse than cowering and shaking like a frightened child.

The sympathy in Estelle's eyes somehow made it harder. "War's a terrible thing, isn't it? My father was in Normandy during the Second World War. Mercy, how that man suffered with his nightmares—disrupted the whole house with his shouting. He wanted to move us to a bigger city, somewhere there'd be more opportunity for my brothers and me. But any little thing could set him off—a car backfiring or a big crowd—"

"I can't talk about this," Jay said miserably, avoiding her gaze. "It's just . . . it's hard to watch the news, that's all."

As traumatic as he found the war coverage, the rest was equally disturbing. On nearly every channel, nearly all the time, Americans went in for entertainment as usual: chittering along with laugh tracks from old sitcoms, hawking gaudy jewelry, stalking vacuous celebrities like rare game, and advertising fat-soaked fast foods while, half a world away, children starved and bled as bombs blew apart their schools and parents. He'd put a foot through his TV set the week after he had come home, and he hadn't yet bothered to replace it.

But he had dared to hope that he could, had dared to believe that he was getting better.

Estelle shook her head and told him, "I understand, dear. He couldn't talk about it, either. But don't worry. I won't tell a soul about this."

Since secrets were the highest form of currency in this town, he wasn't sure how long her promise would hold. Yet Jay thanked her nonetheless before excusing himself to find her camera-hungry son—who was about to have another sort of worry altogether.

An El Paso meteorologist led the evening newscast with a warning that the moisture streaming across Mexico, where a Pacific tropical storm had landed, could spark not only thunderstorms but possible flash flooding. According to "Doppler Dave," over three inches of rain were possible in some locations, and clips were played of last summer's devastating mudslides.

Accustomed to coastal Houston's legendary "toad stranglers," Dana decided it was another example of TV hype gone wild. As was the story that followed on the latest developments in tiny Devil's Claw.

"If I ever get my hands on you, Regina Lawler," said Dana as she paced the narrow confines of her hotel room, "I'm going to suture your mouth shut."

Oblivious to the threat, the reporter whose narrow face filled the TV screen went on speaking to the camera.

"I've been a close friend of Mrs. Smith-Vanover Huffington for years." Regina had plastered on her stoic look, with crocodile tears gleaming in her brown eyes. "It breaks my heart to see her family coping with this tragedy."

"If you're so damned concerned," Dana demanded of the TV, "why the hell aren't you in Houston with my mother, you ungrateful, bottom-feeding troll?"

Instead the woman had been appearing on every newscast that would have her—and generating enough media interest that Dana's mother had hired security to keep reporters off her property. Dana, too, had started having problems after two reporters unearthed her cell phone number. Another somehow learned where she was staying and showed up at the door to her room. Though Dana had quickly gotten rid of them, she had the terrible feeling she had been too quick to dismiss Jay's worry for her on that count. She pictured many more on their way—as endless and voracious as a column of army ants intent on stripping every scrap of flesh from her bones. Unwilling to barricade herself in this room, she had already decided to pile into her newly reclaimed convertible and retreat to Houston, where she could monitor the investigation as well as she could from here.

The screen shifted to a montage of Rimrock County footage, starting with the courthouse and ending with the hillside where the body had been found. All the while Regina went on talking, exploiting her relationship with Dana's family for all that she was worth. She spoke of Angie's troubled history, from protest arrests to rehab, and—just to sweeten the pot—threw in a bit about Dana having recently been "abandoned at the altar."

The report concluded with an image of Nikki Harrison wearing a birthday hat and a look of pale exhaustion as her gloved and masked adoptive parents tried to interest her in cake. As the camera zoomed in on the child's face, someone asked her what her wish was.

"To sleep in my own bed." Wistful and translucent, a smile lit her brown eyes. "With my kitty, Goldie, and no more needles."

"For this little girl"—on the voice-over, Regina Lawler's words trembled with emotion—"this birthday wish, and all her wishes for the future, may hinge on one mystery: the identity of the body now known as the Salt Maiden."

"That does it." Dana angrily switched off the television and gathered the few belongings she had purchased for her stay. She'd be damned if she would hide out while that woman—the same basket case her mother had steadfastly supported through the worst months of her life—continued to make her family's life into some made-for-the-masses melodrama.

Grabbing her purse and keys as well, Dana slammed out of the room and headed for her car. Though the additional distance would prevent her from making Houston by morning, as she'd planned, she was heading out to Devil's Claw to have a few off-camera—and undoubtedly off-color—words with the reporter.

As she rolled into the tiny town past midnight, Dana began to realize how badly unsettled the stress of the past few weeks had left her. What had she thought to accomplish, arriving here so late at night? Except for the dimly lit windows of a few houses and the lights of the two news vans parked near the courthouse, the place was black and silent as the deepest cavern. And the last thing she wanted to do was rouse the scavengers, then create a scene for them to film.

With thunder murmuring its disapproval, she turned the car around and cursed the angry impulse that had brought her back here. After checking her fuel gauge and seeing she could make it back to Pecos, she braced herself for yet another long drive.

But how could she leave Devil's Claw, perhaps for the last time, without a word to Jay? She glanced at the dark courthouse, though she knew he must have gone home hours earlier. Probably he was sleeping. Had he moved into the house Angie had mentioned in her journal? Or was he still in the RV, lying in the same bed where they had made love only days before?

*It's history—just a one-night wonder.* But the more Dana told herself not to think about it, the more overwhelmed she grew with memories of the only real emotional connection she had had since leaving home.

Since long *before* she'd left home, if she let herself admit it. Even before he'd checked out physically, Alex had long since left the building. She hadn't allowed herself to see it, but her charming golden boy, a man who had almost effort-lessly racked up achievement after achievement in his thirty-two years, had withdrawn from her the moment their planned "for better" lurched toward "worse."

"*I was sure we'd have the perfect life . . . the perfect family,*" he'd told her once her hysterectomy was over. Though they should have been celebrating, or at least relieved, to learn that the mass in her uterus had turned out not to be malig-nant, the very idea of her imperfection left him as per-plexed and hurt as a child who had been slapped.

As a glimmer on the horizon presaged a growl of thunder, Dana thought she shouldn't have been all that surprised that he had left her. He was a man who'd traded in his new Mercedes after a parking-lot mishap had creased a fender. Though the dealership's body shop had made it look like new, he had told her the *idea* of the accident had ruined the car for him. When a longtime friend came out of the closet, Alex had backed away, saying the whole thing made him feel "too weird." If he had seen her family's story on TV in New York, he was probably out congratulating himself for escaping an entanglement with such defectives. And Dana would bet the whole of her inheritance that his celebration would include a shiny new blonde on his arm.

*Spoiled ass,* she thought—the polar opposite of Jay Ever-sole, a man tempered by both family tragedy and war. A man who understood firsthand that real life could get messy but hadn't allowed that knowledge to turn him cruel or bitter.

*So go and see him while you still can.* At the very least she could thank him for his help, make sure he had her contact information, and then get back on the road.

And at best? She smiled to herself as she took the turnoff that would take her to Jay Eversole's place. At best she might end up delaying her drive home until morning and pushing her troubles to the back burner for one more night.

She didn't allow herself to imagine anything more than a

brief respite. Didn't—couldn't—think about the yawning loneliness that awaited her back home, despite the presence of her friends, her dogs, her work, and a mother who would need—but couldn't offer—her support as they both waited for the other shoe to drop.

From the purse beside her, her phone began to ring. Pulling over on the dark road, she started digging. By the time she found the phone it had clicked over to voice mail, but the number on the screen identified the caller as her mother.

Had there been some news? Had Angie's body been officially identified, perhaps even released so they could plan the funeral? Dread rose like bile, though in Dana's heart she had known this news was coming. Impatiently she waited for the voice mail to come through.

Before she could retrieve it, the phone rang again. UN-KNOWN CALLER, the display said, and Dana nearly let this one, too, go to voice mail, figuring it was another loathsome pitch from a reporter.

But after the second ring she answered, eager to dispose of the irritation and clear the line as quickly as she could.

"If you're looking for a story," she said without preamble, "you can damned well look somewhere else."

Instead of the polished plea she had expected, she heard only parched-sounding laughter through static that crackled in time to another flash of distant lightning. "Dana—same as always."

Dana froze, eyes flaring and both hands tightening reflexively as her stomach dropped down through the floorboard. She knew that laugh—she would swear it. But before she found her own voice, the caller started speaking.

"How far would you go," rasped Angie, "to give a girl a lift?"

Not long after Jay had finished taking out his frustrations on the bedroom floor of the house—where he'd found no trace of hidden money—Special Agent Emil Tomlin called him on his cell phone at the RV. "We have an ID on the body, and it isn't what you think."

Jay glanced down at the copy of the sobriety journal, which he'd been studying at the table after kicking off his boots. "It's not Angie Vanover?"

On the floor at his feet Max rolled over, clearly hoping his master's distraction would net him a belly rub.

"No, sir," said Tomlin. "The woman is Delilah Lawrence-Goldsmith—better known in your county as Miriam Piper-Gold."

"The scam artist from Haz-Vestment?" The image of the woman in her green bikini flashed through his mind, juxtaposed beside the withered, browned flesh of a corpse with half its face blown off. "I understood she was a redhead."

"In her business," Emil told him, "hair color changes often. We found several sets of colored contacts and different-styled eyeglasses, too, at her house, which has been empty for a couple of months, at least. No sign of the husband, either—though now we're more interested than ever in his whereabouts."

Jay's mind immediately sketched out two scenarios. Whether victim or killer, Goldsmith definitely needed to be found.

"So how'd this ID come about?" he asked Tomlin. A fair question in view of the condition of the corpse.

"When the partial on the dentals didn't match Vanover, we started thinking, and then got a rush on DNA to confirm it."

Jay was impressed. Because of the backlog of requests, DNA matches normally took months. Tomlin must have pull.

"So this means that Angie Vanover's still missing." As Max pawed at his ankle, Jay's thoughts leaped to Dana. Would she be relieved or disappointed to have the possibility of closure snatched away?

"What this means," Tomlin confided, "is that Angie

Vanover is also very much a person of interest in this case."

"You're thinking she's a suspect?" Considering Angie's background and her reaction to Haz-Vestment's proposal, it made sense, though the lack of violence in her history and the journal entries he'd read made Jay skeptical.

"I'm thinking that the FBI is going to move mountains to find Ms. Vanover—whether she's dead or alive."

# *Chapter Fifteen*

*In the desert*
*I saw a creature, naked, bestial,*
*Who, squatting upon the ground,*
*Held his heart in his hands,*
*And ate of it.*
*I said, "Is it good, friend?"*
*"It is bitter—bitter," he answered;*
*"But I like it*
*"Because it is bitter,*
*"And because it is my heart."*

—Stephen Crane,
"The Black Riders and Other Lines"

The Hunter was watching the reporters when he spotted her. Watching them and swearing, all but spitting in his fury.

*She* had led them here, where they would dig and prod like the scavengers they were. Where they would destroy the future finally coming his way—a future he had risked everything to secure.

His hatred focused on the blonde behind the car's wheel, despising her for drawing them but hating her far more on account of what her sister and the desert had made him.

For two months the bitch had eluded him, though he knew damned well she was nearby: laughing, mocking, and always a step beyond his grasp . . . with every penny of his money hidden in some secret cache. And all the while he was living like an animal, driven so far from the person he remembered that he barely recognized himself.

He longed to catch her in his rifle's scope. Longed to take her down like the diseased bitch that she was.

But since that wouldn't lead him to his money, he would move in on her sister. Only this time he didn't mean to kill her.

For he'd thought of a better use for Dana Vanover. A use that would bring her sister out of hiding and deliver both his money and his vengeance.

When Dana saw the headlights pull onto the road behind her, she first thought of Jay and then suspected that some reporter must have recognized her and decided to give chase. But as the tiny town fell away, the driver dropped back into the distance. Smiling nervously, she said, "At last, someone whose life doesn't revolve around mine."

But it was impossible to relax. With her mind racing and her convertible rocking, jolting, and sometimes bouncing on the rutted dirt road, she had to focus every bit of her attention on getting to the rendezvous in one piece.

Barely audible over the car's rattle, her phone once more rang from where it had slid onto the floor mat. Unable to reach it—and unwilling to delay even a moment—Dana ignored the noise.

If she'd thought Devil's Claw was dark, this stretch of road was far blacker. Dead ahead, the upper half of the rising moon disappeared into a cloudbank that blotted out the stars. Hemmed in by obsidian, her headlights reached into the void, illuminating nothing but a creosote-lined dirt road and a handful of fluttering white moths. She hunched forward, straining to watch for the mile marker her sister had described.

Her sister. Angie. Alive and waiting for her.

As a bruised glow pulsed through the low clouds, the tiny hairs on Dana's arms stood at attention. A sick chill snaked through her before suspicion sank in its fangs.

*What if I only heard what I wanted?* Pressed by grief and desperation, had her mind sifted sounds from random static, then shaped them into the voice she remembered?

On TV she'd heard a withered old black man once who

had claimed his dead wife spoke to him through the static on his radio. He was pitiful, with childlike belief shining from his clouded eyes—a terrible contrast to the puffed-up condescension of the program's narrator. Though Dana had been quick to switch the channel, she still remembered the jab of embarrassment she'd felt on the poor old man's behalf.

At the thought that she could be as unhinged by her own grief, her foot slipped from the accelerator. After braking slowly, she leaned over to retrieve the phone where it had fallen and whispered, "Dear God, please let her be there. Please let this be real. . . ."

Dana scrolled back through the last calls and blinked away the threat of tears so she could read the tiny screen. On the list, sandwiched between a pair of missed calls from her mother, she spotted an unidentified number. She didn't recognize it, save for the 432 area code that encompassed a broad swath of West Texas, including Rimrock County.

With the first fat raindrops popping against her windshield, she pushed the button to connect. As much as she hated to delay her journey, she had to reassure herself she wasn't hurtling into the desert darkness to meet with a delusion. Breath held, she listened to a few clicks, followed by the sound of ringing.

"Damn it, pick up," Dana ordered at the sixth ring. By the twentieth she hung up before trying once again. But it was no use; no one answered. She tried to call Jay, too, but heard only a recorded message asking her to try again later because of some problem with the circuits.

Which left her with only one choice, as far as she could see.

Max growled at a thunderous rumble while the RV shuddered with the gusting wind. As a few drops of rain pinged off the skin of rusted metal, Jay flipped the last page of

Angie's journal, disappointed that rereading it had yielded no further secrets.

"Come on, dog." He stood, stretching, and spoke through a yawn. "You'd better go out one more time before bed."

And one more time before the clouds burst. Desert thunderstorms might be infrequent, but they more than made up for their rarity in fierceness. On those occasions when the tropical moisture of a Pacific storm collided with the arid heat, the resulting lightning struck fear into the stoutest hearts, and rain ran off of earth baked too hard to absorb it. The summer Jay turned fifteen, his uncle had shown him the rotting carcasses of half a dozen head of cattle drowned when such a storm caught them grazing in the grassy bottom of a narrow-walled arroyo. With the water long gone, the bodies lay bloated, baking in the sun as buzzing flies swarmed in the shimmering stench.

Jay opened the door for him, but Max only tucked his tail between his legs and whined, clearly unnerved by the thunder.

"Last chance, you big sissy," Jay offered, but the dog slunk off and hid beneath the table. "Suit yourself, then."

Before Jay could close the door, something fluttered through the rectangle of light that spilled out through the opening. He turned, following the motion, but the object had already vanished in the darkness.

Then another something flew past, and, as he watched, yet a third thin shape twisted through.

"What the hell?" he asked as he pulled a flashlight from a kitchen drawer. Hurrying back, he leaned out the open doorway and shone the strong beam outward.

"Son of a bitch," he burst out, eyes wide as his light scanned a flock of green bills tumbling on the wind. There was no telling how much money had been snagged among dry grasses or caught on the barbed spikes of a yucca. Most, however—at least a score of loose notes—simply blew past to skim along the desert floor, save for one caught on the open door—a hundred-dollar bill that he peeled off and shoved into a pocket.

Racing outside, he resisted the temptation to chase after them, instead turning his light in the opposite direction of the strange migration. If only he could find the source, maybe he could stop whatever cash remained from following its companions.

With the wind whistling around him, he trotted upstream of the flow as fast as his bare feet would allow him, pausing to curse as a lechuguilla's leafy daggers scraped his ankle and a sharp stone bruised his heel. Unwilling to waste time getting his boots, he rounded the corner of his uncle's house . . .

. . . and found the shrinking pile lying in a shallow dug-out hole, perhaps two feet across and not even half as deep. To save what he could of the contents, Jay tore off his shirt, then threw it over the bills as lightning streaked across the sky and thunder shook the air.

That quickly the spattering became a torrent. Raindrops stung his bare skin, exploding in a kamikaze assault against the land. Jay knelt, raking loose clods of sandy dirt over the fresh excavation. Gritty mud gloved his hands when at last he crowded beneath the eaves in an attempt to save his hide.

But the overhang was too narrow to offer him much shelter, so he decided to make a run for cover, back to the RV to call for help. With a violent tattoo pounding the ranch house roof above him, he glanced at the nearest window to get a bead on his position.

And sucked in a startled breath as inside his uncle's bedroom, the red glow of a cigar butt caught his eye.

Hunched over the steering wheel, Dana struggled to see through the driving rain. She'd had no choice except to slow down to avoid mistaking a gap in the scrub for the single-lane road.

Yet as the miles spun away behind her, her speed gradually crept higher while she recalled the voice she'd taken as her sister's.

*"If you take the right branch, where it splits off past Lost Lake, you'll come up on an old mile marker, painted white."* The line had crackled loudly then, so that something could have been missed. Once the sound cleared, the last words followed. *"I'll be waiting near there, off the road where you can't see me. But I'll be watching for you, so pull over and I'll come out."*

*"Where are you calling from?"* Dana had asked. She remembered the wild leap of her heart, the murmur of her tires on the hard-packed surface, the very texture of the silence as the line went dead.

She remembered in such detail that she told herself that it had to have been more than her imagination. That it had to have been Angie, leading her into the night.

*"How far would you go . . . ?"* the echo asked her—just as a shuddering flash strobe-lit a human figure that stepped into her path. Head ducked against the silvery nails of rain, it raised an arm as if blinded by the glare of her approaching headlights.

Dana took in the sight the instant before her right foot all but slammed through the car's floorboard and her arms twisted the wheel to avoid impact.

The convertible fishtailed, its front brakes biting into the dirt road a critical half second before the rear tires grabbed hold. Thrown against her seat belt harness, Dana felt herself losing control, felt that at any moment she'd lose contact with the desert and flip onto the convertible's roll bar.

But instead the car came to a stop with a bone-jarring lurch that threatened to fling her stomach worlds away. More concerned with whether she had struck the pedestrian, Dana twisted her head around but could see nothing but rain slanting across the empty field.

Unfastening her seat belt, she threw open the car door and leaped into the downpour.

"Angie," she cried as she stepped out into the darkness. "Angie—"

"Dana," came the answer an instant before cold, wet arms grabbed her from behind.

# Chapter Sixteen

Patient Name: Nikki Harrison
Patient Number: 9360277513
Date of Admission: 6/07/2007

Texas Children's Hospital, Houston Medical Center

Nursing Entry
Date: 7/03/2007
Time: 1600

Patient reports feeling cold, warm to touch. Rigors severe, shivering throughout PM. IV site warm to touch, red with darker line spreading proximally from right hand to elbow. Informed Dr. Ybarra @ 1542. Lethargic, difficult to initiate eye contact. Mottled skin. Mother unable to engage with favorite stuffed toy.

0400 tympanic temp. 103.7° F at 1538. Continue alternating acetaminophen with ibuprofen every two hours. IV antibiotics to continue every four hours as ordered. Use cooling blanket. Continue to do lab work as ordered every 12 hours and change IV to left arm. Reassess 2X per hour and report further temp. increase or change in mental status to Dr. Ybarra ASAP.

Jay burst into the house's back door and clicked on the mudroom's light switch. Nothing happened, and when he followed his flashlight's beam into the kitchen, only darkness greeted him instead of the glowing time display on the newly installed microwave.

Power outage from the lightning, he decided. Which made the red light he'd seen even more alarming. Since he'd left his weapon in the RV, Jay picked a stubby section of two-by-four from the pile of discarded construction remnants. Steeling himself to the task, he dripped a slow path

down the hall. Each time he reached an open doorway—
first the bathroom, then two bedrooms—he paused to listen
but heard nothing except the storm's assault. When he
sniffed he smelled only new paint and sawdust, along with
the vaguest suggestion of charred wood.

Neither the murmur of his uncle's voice nor the odor of
cigar smoke lingered. Just that ghostly red glow that had
buried him in memory.

Jay took a deep breath before approaching the final closed
door at the hall's end. As he reached the master bedroom,
he wondered if the shock of his discovery and the wild
night had prompted yet another hallucination. Had the
bomblike thunder launched another flashback? Had the
wind's howl reminded him of Baghdad's cries of anguish?

Or could he have been fooled by more mundane emotions? As he'd torn up the flooring earlier, Jay's thoughts had
been full of the uncle who had died here. The man who'd
burned to death inside this very house. Probably as a result
of his late-night smoking habit.

But even if his memory had tricked him, the gritty filth
covering Jay's hands was very real. As had been the hole
he'd tried to cover and the money he'd seen blowing.
Which meant that someone must have dug it up. Someone
who had come while he'd been inside the RV reading.

Had the storm interrupted the culprit? Or had something, maybe even some*one*, else? In either case, it only
made sense that someone would be nearby, watching as he
waited for the coast to clear.

Or as *she* waited, perhaps, for it came to Jay that Angie
Vanover had written of that money and that, since she
wasn't the so-called "Salt Maiden," she might have come
back to claim it.

After taking a deep breath to steady himself, Jay told
himself this might be his chance to return the missing
woman to her family after all. Flinging the door open, he or-

dered, "Drop to the floor and spread 'em. *Now*—before I shoot."

Dana screamed and fought to jerk free, her instincts revolting against what felt like death's embrace. For the flesh felt cool as glass against her warm skin, and the moan that issued from the lips at her ear sounded inhuman.

"No," it said. "Don't fight me. Please, Da—"

But Dana broke loose, whirling toward the voice and staring, seeing in another flash of lightning.

And crying out as recognition was followed by a wave of anguish. "Angie, my God . . ."

For this *was* her sister, or what was left of her. Drenched and shivering, with her long, sun-bleached hair hanging in thick cords about blade-thin shoulders browned like parchment. Nearly naked—the rain had plastered only a few rags to her body—Angie was emaciated, in by far the worst shape Dana had ever seen her. What in heaven's name had happened to her these past months?

"So cold," rasped Angie as she hoisted a soaked and battered backpack onto her shoulder. "And so fucking glad to see you."

Dana gave her a quick hug before saying, "In the car."

She half led, half pulled her sister to the passenger-side door. Once she opened it she placed a hand on top of Angie's pale head to protect her as she ducked inside.

"I set it free." As Angie threw her head back, her thin laughter skirted the edge of hysteria. "I took that bastard's money, and I gave it to the desert so I could finally go on home. A sacrifice to salt, a tribute to the gods of . . ."

From the corner of her eye Dana caught the flash of what looked like a truck's headlights and was flooded by a wave of pure relief. Until her sister, staring in the same direction, cried out, "Hurry. If he catches us we're as good as dead."

With the shooting on the hillside still fresh in her mem-

ory, Dana didn't have to be told twice. After racing around
the vehicle's back bumper, she slid into the driver's seat and
shifted into gear. In the rearview mirror she saw the twin
lights approaching, their movement too swift and purpose-
ful to be explained by anything but malice.

She hit the gas, and the passenger door clapped shut with
the BMW's forward motion. Dana glanced over, wondering
why Angie had left it open. But Angie had slumped forward
with her eyes closed, looking far more like an ancient crone
than a thirty-four-year-old heiress from a privileged family
in Houston.

"Wake up," Dana shouted as she shifted swiftly through
the gears. "I have to know what's happening."

Angie jerked and groaned, then flopped bonelessly as
they bounced over the road's rutted surface.

"Dammit, Angie, open your eyes. Or buckle up, at least,
before you break something." Dana wished she had a free
hand to help her—or to buckle herself in—but she needed
both of hers to keep the car on the road.

Angie roused enough to grumble something as she pulled
her seat belt across her waist. She was shuddering so vio-
lently it took a number of attempts before the buckle finally
clicked home.

The truck closed in, now only a few car lengths behind
them. It swung slightly to the left, as if the driver meant to
pass them—or intended to bump her rear wheels and send
the convertible flying off the road. Smashing her foot down
on the gas, Dana was rewarded by a burst of power from the
engine, and at last their smaller vehicle began to pull away.

The road ahead looked like a dark river, with the water
pouring off it. In spots the flow split into confusing tributar-
ies, any one of which could trick her into driving off the
graded track.

"He must've followed you," slurred Angie. "H-he must
have watched and—"

"Who? Who is it, Angie?"

"It's— Dana, look out for the road!"

Dana manhandled the convertible around a curve, but managed to make the turn without sliding off onto the shoulder. Forced to slow, the bulkier vehicle behind them lost more ground. Gripping the wheel tightly, Dana mumbled desperate prayers, and the speedometer crept upward.

"We're doing it. We're going to outrun him." If they really did, Dana swore she'd build a shrine to the genius of German engineering.

With her sticklike arm braced against the dashboard, Angie turned to look behind them. But before Dana could ask a question, the road dipped downward and the hood splashed down into a torrent that pushed the front end sideways and spun them downstream with its flow.

Shrieking, Dana fought to steer the car back onto the gravel. But no matter how she turned the wheel, it made no difference—they were floating. Water was pouring in beneath the door and spilling through the engine's firewall.

"Oh, shit." Angie was looking frantically from side to side. "How deep is—"

The tires bumped, then caught, leaving them perhaps ten feet from where they'd started. But the engine had drowned, and nothing Dana did could revive it.

Peering over her shoulder she saw the truck's relentless advance, knew in an instant that the higher-clearance, heavier vehicle would have no difficulty negotiating the water that had crippled them.

*Damn German engineering, anyhow.*

"Get out, get out," she ordered. And, taking her own advice, she snatched up her phone and flung open the door. More water poured inside, raising the floorboard tide so that it lapped well past her ankles.

Hoping the darkness would hide them, she fumbled to shut off the headlights before climbing out into knee-deep water.

Angie called after her, "Door won't open—stuck against something. Dana, help me."

Instead of going around the car Dana leaned far inside, unhooked her sister's belt, and grabbed her under the arms. Propelled by a burst of pure adrenaline Dana dragged her, ignoring the screaming muscles in her lower back.

Angie got her legs under her and scrambled out the driver's side, her movements loose and jerky. With Dana's help she lurched to her feet, her elbow knocking into her sister's hand and sending the satellite phone splashing beneath the water.

"No," Dana cried as she groped for it. But at that moment headlights flashed across them, and she knew their time was up.

Abandoning the search, she hooked her arm through Angie's and blindly towed her into the driving rain.

# GET UP TO 4 FREE BOOKS!

You can have the best romance delivered to your door for less than what you'd pay in a bookstore or online. Sign up for one of our book clubs today, and we'll send you **FREE\* BOOKS** just for trying it out...**with no obligation to buy, ever!**

## HISTORICAL ROMANCE BOOK CLUB

Travel from the Scottish Highlands to the American West, the decadent ballrooms of Regency England to Viking ships. Your shipments will include authors such as CONNIE MASON, CASSIE EDWARDS, LYNSAY SANDS, LEIGH GREENWOOD, and many, many more.

## LOVE SPELL BOOK CLUB

Bring a little magic into your life with the romances of Love Spell—fun contemporaries, paranormals, time-travels, futuristics, and more. Your shipments will include authors such as KATIE MACALISTER, SUSAN GRANT, NINA BANGS, SANDRA HILL, and more.

As a book club member you also receive the following special benefits:

- **30% OFF all orders through our website & telecenter!**
  (Plus, you still get 1 book FREE for every 5 books you buy!)
- **Exclusive access to** special discounts!
- **Convenient** home delivery **and 10 days to return any books you don't want to keep.**

**There is no minimum number of books to buy,** and you may cancel membership at any time. See back to sign up!

\*Please include $2.00 for shipping and handling.

# YES! ☐

Sign me up for the **Historical Romance Book Club** and send my TWO FREE BOOKS! If I choose to stay in the club, I will pay only $8.50* each month, a savings of $5.48!

# YES! ☐

Sign me up for the **Love Spell Book Club** and send my TWO FREE BOOKS! If I choose to stay in the club, I will pay only $8.50* each month, a savings of $5.48!

**NAME:** _____

**ADDRESS:** _____

_____

**TELEPHONE:** _____

**E-MAIL:** _____

☐ **I WANT TO PAY BY CREDIT CARD.**

☐ VISA          ☐ MasterCard.          ☐ DISCOVER

**ACCOUNT #:** _____

**EXPIRATION DATE:** _____

**SIGNATURE:** _____

Send this card along with $2.00 shipping & handling for each club you wish to join, to:

**Romance Book Clubs
1 Mechanic Street
Norwalk, CT 06850-3431**

Or fax (must include credit card information!) to: 610.995.9274.
You can also sign up online at www.dorchesterpub.com.

*Plus $2.00 for shipping. Offer open to residents of the U.S. and Canada only.
Canadian residents please call 1.800.481.9191 for pricing information.

If under 18, a parent or guardian must sign. Terms, prices and conditions subject to change. Subscription subject to acceptance. Dorchester Publishing reserves the right to reject any order or cancel any subscription.

JOIN NOW!

# *Chapter Seventeen*

*Today was my best day in months, years maybe.*

*As dawn painted the eastern sky, I walked out into what most people would consider an ugly stretch of wasteland. But bathed in that sweet light, I called it beautiful. Life stirred in the morning coolness. Jackrabbits out to nibble. Red-tailed hawks out to hunt.*

*Then something stirred in me, too. A need that came on so strong and sudden, it pushed aside all other cravings.*

*I raced back to my loom and started working, weaving the living images in my head into the cloth. Consumed with the rhythm of my movements, I thought of nothing. Not food or tequila or the sparkling dust I snorted to set the world on fire. Not the way I'd screwed my life up, or the people left in my wake.*

*A damned good day, all things considered. So I think I'll stick around awhile more.*

—Undated entry (loose page)
Angie's sobriety journal


Wednesday, July 4, 12:32 A.M.
72 Degrees Fahrenheit


Jay might have laughed at himself, embarrassed at his misinterpretation of the red battery-backup indicator light of the room's newly installed smoke alarm. Laughter would have been a relief, if he could have managed. But as he stepped among the litter of loose floorboards, something thin and brittle crunched.

With thunder stuttering outside, he lifted his bare foot and shone down his light, which reflected off white shards that looked like bone.

He picked up the largest portion and recognized the hollowed orbit of a missing eye. A chill unrelated to his wet clothes gripped him as he took in what had been a tiny skull, perhaps a pack rat's. A more thorough search revealed a familiar scattering of petals and small pebbles. His flesh crawled as he thought of the displays near both the salt cavern and the Webb adobe. Those had been far better organized, but the essential ingredients remained the same.

And none of it, he was certain, had been here earlier.

"Angie?" he called, heart pounding, as he re-searched the small house room by room. But all he found were a few remaining mementos of the man who'd lived and died here.

A man who must have been lured off course by the siren call of Miriam Piper-Gold and her illicit cash, as Angie's journal claimed. Nothing else explained the money buried just outside his bedroom window. Still, the idea of R.C. Eversole accepting bribes went against everything Jay had always taken for a fact about him, everything that had inspired Jay to pursue his own career in law enforcement despite the trouble he had caused the old man and the way he'd been unceremoniously sent out on his own. Jay could have simply apologized for the outbursts and the fighting, could have come right out and told his uncle that he loved him and appreciated all he'd done. But by then the two of them had forgotten how to speak of such things—or anything of consequence. Easier to simply *prove* how he felt, just as R.C. had proven his love by giving a lost boy the security and structure he most needed.

And by setting an example that told Jay what he must now do. Whatever his feelings about his uncle's unexpected failings, they didn't absolve Jay of his responsibility. Miriam Piper-Gold's murder was an FBI case, so he'd have to let the special agents know what he had found here. Even though it meant blackening the family name.

As Jay checked the window latches and secured the house, questions clamored for attention. Why would Piper-

Gold see fit to bribe a county sheriff? And why would R.C. hide the cash where he had? Unless he hadn't. Maybe Angie had buried it there after stealing it from the hiding place beneath the bedroom floor. He'd been in on enough drug busts to know that large amounts of money could be bulky. Perhaps she'd only had the time or energy to conceal it somewhere close by.

But if she had, why would she come back now, two months after the man's death—and her own disappearance—to leave her macabre display in the bedroom and expose the money? Had she meant to take it before the fierceness of the storm scared her off? Could that mean, as Steve Petit clearly thought, that Angie was somehow involved in Piper-Gold's death? And what of his own uncle's?

This time, when he left, Jay locked both the doors. Though thunder snarled at his progress, he reached the RV with no more than a fresh dousing. He stripped out of his wet clothing and dried off, then wrapped a towel around his waist and went to find the telephone.

But he needn't have bothered. His cell phone screen told him ALL CIRCUITS BUSY, and his portable phone was dead, since its base had no power. The radio was no help, either, for it, too, ran on electricity.

He decided to try the one inside the Suburban. If he couldn't raise Wallace, Jay would drive back into town and use the office phones to make his call. He didn't like the idea of leaving, since Angie—or whoever the digger was— could still be somewhere on the property. But it would be the height of stupidity to go looking in perfect darkness, all alone.

Just as it would be criminal to leave the remaining money lying in that hole unguarded. Which meant, Jay thought, he'd have to gather what he could before going anywhere— and pray that no one was waiting in the darkness for the chance to shoot him in the back.

He dressed in a fresh uniform and strapped on his weapon

before making an impromptu rain poncho from a black garbage bag out of the kitchen.

Edging out from beneath the table, Max eyed him suspiciously as Jay poked his head through the newly made hole.

"What are you looking at?" Jay asked the shepherd as he grabbed a second bag for the money. "It might not stop any bullets, but at least it'll keep me from getting soaked again."

*Maybe*, he thought as he grabbed his flashlight and headed out the door.

"Not—not that way." Angie resisted, gasping to catch her breath. "O-over here."

Dana couldn't see a thing, except in those fractured glimpses lit by lightning. But that seemed to be enough for Angie, for she moved resolutely in the direction she had chosen, even though she staggered and fell twice.

Dana wrapped an arm around her sister's waist, and together the two of them scrambled up a slope.

Behind them the truck's door slammed as someone got out, and the sound of shouting followed. The words were lost amid the storm sounds and their scraping, halting progress, but there was no mistaking the fury in that voice—or was Dana just imagining murderous intent?

In her haste to get away she stumbled into some thorny horror that snagged her soaked shirt and flesh alike.

"I'm caught," she cried as Angie tried to tug her forward.

The wind snatched away her words, betraying her, she realized, as light caught her attention, a beam searching too near the spot where they stood. Panicking, she jerked loose, barely feeling the tearing bite of needles.

"Hurry," she had time to say—before the shooting started.

Crack followed crack, sharper than the thunder. Dana wasn't sure how many shots, wasn't sure of anything but the terror prompting her to pull her sister forward, higher up the slope.

Angie went down heavily, her breathing so loud and labored that Dana was sure their pursuer must hear.

"Get up," she whispered urgently.

"Go away," Angie sobbed. "Just run. While you still can. There's . . . there's an ATV. Outside the building. When it quits raining, you . . . you can ride for help."

"A building?" Shelter was exactly what they needed. Gritting her teeth, Dana took her sister's backpack and then hauled her to her feet and started moving. Despite Angie's gauntness, her weight felt like an anchor. But after a few steps she must have caught her breath, for she began to move on her own once again.

The shooting had stopped, leaving Dana to wonder if their attacker had given up or simply paused to reload. Yet she didn't dare slow down, despite her stinging cuts, her straining lungs and throbbing muscles. Terror pushed her past her limits, the fear that any second might bring the bullet that would put an end to everything.

*Not now that I've found her,* Dana prayed as she tightened her hold around her sister. *Not now, please, God.*

As if in answer to her prayer, only thunder punctuated their progress for the next few minutes, and it seemed to be farther away with every rumble. The rain, too, was slackening, or spending its fury on points beyond their struggle.

They must have crested the incline, for Dana felt the pull of gravity hastening her steps downhill. She dared to think that it was helping them to safety, moving them beyond their pursuer's line of fire. Maybe even past the worst that this night had to offer. But as momentum sped her progress, Dana lost her balance and plunged forward with a shriek.

She came down hard on hands and knees, while beside her Angie fell with an explosion of air forced from her lungs.

"Sorry. I'm so sorry," Dana told her. "But we can't stay here. Let me help you up."

Groaning, Angie snapped, "Don't touch me."

The sharpness of her voice prompted a backlash of fury. With tears burning in her eyes, Dana wanted to snarl back, to lash out at the sister who had not only disrupted her life, but now endangered it. But fighting each other wouldn't save them. At this point only escape to shelter would accomplish that.

"Where's this building? Where'd you call me from?" she asked. "If you tell me the way I'll get us both there. I can do it, Angie. *We* can do it, both of us together."

As lightning lit the world in strobelike flashes, Dana saw her sister curled into a ball on her side.

"I can't. I can't get up again," Angie murmured.

"Then I'll lift you, damn it." Dana felt for her sister's shoulder—and drew back at Angie's scream of pain.

"No. I said, don't touch me."

"What?" asked Dana, even as the warmth of the spot she'd touched registered. "Are you . . . are you bleeding?"

"Just leave it alone."

"Is it your shoulder, Angie?" Dana's heart pounded wildly.

"It . . . hurts so much."

"He shot you, didn't he? Back there. When you fell."

"I . . . I don't know. I guess. . . ." Angie's confusion downshifted into anguish. "Damn him. After all this time—the bastard caught me with a wild shot."

Dana prayed that she was wrong, that somehow they were both mistaken or that the wound was minor. But without light there was no telling. "We have to stop the bleeding, but there's nothing here—not even a scrap of dry cloth for a bandage."

"Just let . . . let me rest awhile." Exhaustion hollowed out the words. "Then we'll go 'n find the . . ."

"Angie? *Angie?*" When her sister didn't answer or respond to her shaking, Dana felt the shoulder until she found the round opening, near the topmost portion of the upper arm. No exit wound that she could find. Dana applied direct pressure to the wound, hoping to stanch the bleeding until someone—

*Don't kid yourself. Help isn't coming. And if we stay out in the elements, exposure's going to kill her—maybe kill us both.*

With no better option, Dana grabbed her sister and struggled to pull her to her feet. But it was like trying to hoist a sack of rocks over her head.

"Damn it," Dana cried, tears streaming down her face to mingle with rainwater. "I'm *not* letting you die here. You hear that, you s-self-centered, sc-screwed-up little . . . *Help me.*"

Angie roused a little, as least enough to stand hunched once Dana hauled her upright.

"Wh-what the hell is wrong with you?" Rage—or weakness—shook Angie's words. "Why the hell aren't you back in Houston with Mr. Wonderful and your animals? Are you some kind of freaking masochist or what?"

"Probably," said Dana. "Remind me to sue your ass off for my therapy bills as soon as we get out of this."

That drew a sound that might have been laughter out of Angie. "Maybe . . . maybe there's hope for you yet."

"We have to move now. And you're going to have to do your part."

"Dana . . . I can't. I just—"

As Dana felt Angie start to sink again, she said the only thing she could think of that might jolt her sister into trying. "You had damned well better. For your daughter's sake, if not ours."

"F-for my . . . I don't have a—"

"You have a daughter, Nikki. And she needs you strong and well if she's to have a chance to live."

# *Chapter Eighteen*

*They cannot scare me with their empty spaces*
*Between stars—on stars where no human race is.*
*I have it in me so much nearer home*
*To scare myself with my own desert places.*

—Robert Frost,
"Desert Places"

Despite the cutting-edge black outerwear, Jay was plenty wet by the time he slid past the sole remaining news van to park beside the courthouse. Using a key on a large, old-fashioned brass ring, he opened the door and slipped inside, hoping to remain unnoticed. But either the news crew was sleeping or had accurately predicted yet another no-comment, for no one came to bother him as he stripped off one bag and plunked the second—full of sodden currency—on top of his desk.

After pulling out the special agents' numbers, he called and woke Petit, a younger agent who had grown up only an hour outside of Rimrock County. Though he hadn't played the hometown-boy card too hard, he'd seemed friendlier than the veteran, Tomlin, who had turned out to be even more stiff-necked than he'd seemed at first. After a brief preamble to apologize about the hour, Jay explained the situation as thoroughly as possible.

"Disturbin' the scene," said Petit. "That was strictly necessary, was it?"

Jay hesitated, catching the disdainful note in the special agent's words. Jay guessed he'd been with the feds long enough that this was the kind of amateur-hour fuckup he'd expect from such a small-town yokel. But since Petit didn't come right out and say so, Jay let it slide and laid out the reasons for his choice.

That got a grunt of acknowledgment, followed by a request that he not handle the evidence, meaning the money, until both agents showed up. "Just so there aren't any misunderstandin's later," Petit added.

Allowing that comment to slide was not an option.

"Let's not beat around the bush," Jay said. "I'm not planning on stuffing a bundle down my pants. If I had stealing in mind, I never would've called you. Unless you think I'm such a hick, I'm too damned stupid to cover up my theft."

There was a pause before Petit said, "They call me Cowboy in the bureau." The sourness of his voice indicated he was less than pleased with the handle. "On account of the way I talk and how some smart-ass Houston cop spread it around that I used to ride the bulls in high school. So I could tell you a thing or two about what these federal boys think of rural Texas lawmen. And how I'd hear about it if you did anything that might be *misconstrued*."

"Got it," Jay replied, glad that he'd remembered to take the stray hundred-dollar bill out of his pocket and put it in the bag.

"Besides that," Petit said, reverting to what Jay took to be the bureau's latest don't-rile-the-natives manifesto, "we need to be certain that any remaining forensic evidence survives intact."

Jay knew damned well that any possible forensics had already been hopelessly contaminated, but he decided, at least for now, to ignore the insult.

"We'll be there in two hours, tops," Petit told him.

"I'll be here waiting," Jay said.

Once the call ended he looked at the bag that sat dripping on his desktop. Sandy soil clung to the black plastic, but it was the bag's interior that had him curious. Some of the currency he'd blindly thrown in had been loose, but far more of it was bundled. How many packets had he gathered?

It would take only a peek to note the bills' denomination, to see if all of them were hundreds like the one he'd picked off of his door. And a half minute's more work to count the number of intact bundles among the unbound notes. Then he could take a stab at answering the questions chewing his insides. How much money did it take to turn an honest lawman dirty? How much had proved irresistible to Uncle R.C.? And what could the bachelor sheriff have wanted with it in the first place?

Jay touched the plastic with a mud-spattered hand. Yet he hesitated, doubt seeping through his curiosity. Had it been enough to have cost the man his life? The medical examiner had had no reason to look beyond the obvious burns and smoke inhalation as R.C. Eversole's cause of death. If he went back and re-examined the body, would he find blunt trauma to the head, a stab wound, even a bullet he'd missed during his first examination? Or had Uncle R.C. been drugged before his house was set on fire?

Jay swore, knowing he had already ruined any chance of answers, since he'd respected his uncle's wish to have his body cremated. Not even the ashes remained, since Dennis had scattered them on the desert as requested.

The phone rang, interrupting Jay's remorse.

He picked up the receiver, but before he got his name out a woman started screaming, crying out his name.

"Help us. You have to help us. Please—we're out at some . . . I guess it's a bunkhouse for oil-field workers, but no one's here now. The door . . . the door says 'Red Wolf Wildcatters,' and it's . . . I don't know where—"

"Dana?" He jolted out of his seat, his nerves buzzing like a wasps' nest. She was supposed to be staying in Pecos, so how could she have gotten all the way out past Arroyo Hueso, here in Rimrock County?

"Jay—please. My sister's been shot. You have to come. You have to come right now." Her words burst out in a torrent, followed by another gush so fast he didn't catch it.

"Calm down. Take a deep breath and repeat that, only slow it down a little." His heart was pounding so hard, he struggled to take his own advice. *You can't help her if you can't think. Can't help anybody if you put your gut—or heart—in charge of your brain.*

"Please. Call the helicopter, the medevac people. She's . . . she can't die." Still, Dana was all but screaming, far from the self-possessed woman he had come to know, the woman who had so quickly regained control after her own injury.

"I'll call," he said, though he was far from sure that anyone would be flying in this weather, in the darkness. "And I'm on my way—twenty, twenty-five minutes, tops. Meanwhile, you're going to have to do what you can on your own. It might've been with animals, but you've been trained to handle medical emergencies. So settle down right now and focus. Hear me?"

At the sharpness of his tone she sucked in a startled breath. When she spoke next she sounded calmer. "Okay, okay. I found a first-aid kit here . . . but her injury is way beyond that. What if she's already lost too much blood?"

"I'll be there quick as I can, Dana. Just hang tight. You can do this."

He heard her draw a deep breath, heard her fighting off a sob. "Jay—"

Static crackled loudly.

"Dana? Dana, are you still there?" he asked.

But the line had gone dead, leaving him to pray the interruption was the storm's doing, not a man's.

Dana held on to the sound of Jay's voice like a drowning woman clutching at a lifeline. *Settle down right now and focus,* he had told her, and she used those words to float above the chaos roaring in her ears.

The rain had resumed, as hard as ever, just after she'd half dragged, half carried Angie inside a small building marked with KEEP OUT signs. As the storm pounded out a rattling rhythm on the metal roof, Dana lowered her now-incoherent sister to the dry floor near the door and went in search of light. The switches were all dead, but she had found a

rechargeable flashlight hanging on the wall. A quick scan of
the small space showed a Spartan bathroom, a minifridge
beside a sink, and half a dozen bunks tucked against the
corrugated-metal walls. One of the beds contained a stack
of folded blankets. Since she didn't have the strength to
drag Angie another inch, much less lift her onto a mattress,
Dana settled for using the blankets to cover up her sister
where she lay. Afterward she also came across a first-aid kit
and an old black wall phone, which—miracle of miracles—
had worked long enough for her to call Jay.

Long enough to gather a measure of his strength and let
it flow into her aching limbs to steady her. After rubbing life
into her arms, she knelt and set the flashlight on the ground
so that it pointed at her sister.

The light cast deep shadows on a hunger-ravaged face.
Though it was impossible to judge her color, Angie's breath
seemed quick and shallow and her eyes remained closed
tight, even after Dana called her name repeatedly and shook
her.

"Please wake up." She felt panic scrabbling at her, eager
for a toehold.

Stifling a sob, Dana forced herself to make a thorough examination. Still, she could find no wound other than the
quarter-size hole in the upper humerus, which meant the
bullet was lodged somewhere in the shoulder joint or possibly deeper. There was no way to measure blood loss; the rain
could have washed away a few teaspoons or a few pints, but
the blood she saw now seeped instead of gushed. Even so
she found a blanket wadded up a corner and wedged it carefully to conserve every drop of life she could.

Dana rummaged through the meager contents of the
first-aid kit and put aside the antibiotic ointment, since the
wound would have to be thoroughly cleaned at the hospital.
Instead she pulled out gauze and tape and opened one of
several wrapped sanitary napkins included in the box to

provide a sterile dressing. After patting the area as dry as she could, she jury-rigged a proper pressure bandage.

She dumped out Angie's sodden backpack to see if there was anything inside that might prove helpful. Digging through the meager contents, Dana found only a pocketknife, a disposable lighter, a half-empty water bottle, and a key only a little smaller than one for a car's ignition.

It must be to the ATV her sister had mentioned. Though Dana hadn't seen it in the darkness, she saw no point in looking for it now. Little more than a three- or four-wheeled motorcycle, it couldn't carry an unconscious woman, and even if she could figure out how to drive it, the ride would leave them both exposed to the storm's fury.

She pushed aside the backpack and the items it held and rubbed life back into her own arms, which trembled with exhaustion. She felt chilled, too, with her wet clothes clinging to her skin. To fortify herself against the pain of her scratches and bruises, she dry-swallowed a couple of aspirins from the kit. But she was powerless to head off the fatigue that swamped her, the nearly overwhelming urge to close her eyes for just a moment. . . .

*Focus*, her brain prompted her, but the mostly dark room started spinning, stars sparkling at its edges, and the snare-drum rattle of the rain turned to a hiss. *Have to stay alert, awake for Angie. Have to . . . but right now I'd trade my practice for a strong, black cup of coffee, for anything to keep me warm and moving.*

Her sister moaned, her head turning to one side.

Dana blinked and straightened. "Angie? Can you look at me? Can you squeeze my hand?"

The cold fingers didn't tighten, but Angie's eyes moved behind their deeply shadowed lids.

"Help's coming," Dana promised. "A helicopter with a paramedic on board. And the sheriff's coming, too, soon."

Agitated, Angie tossed her head from side to side.

"Who was in that truck?" Dana asked her. "Who was it that shot you?"

But as her moaning ceased, Angie Vanover went as still as she was silent.

Jay found them lying on the bare floor, their damp bodies wrapped haphazardly in blankets. Dana was curled around her sister with her arm draped over the frail form as if to offer her protection against further violence.

His breath froze in his lungs, and his heart stumbled. A vision of the Baghdad checkpoint's carnage spun through his mind. Too late—he'd been too late *again*, and this time he had no idea how he could survive it.

Then his flashlight's beam caught the gentle rise and fall of Dana's chest.

"Oh, God. *Dana*. Dana, wake up," he said as he knelt beside the pair. Unprofessional as it might be, he leaned his head down to hers and hugged her to him in sheer relief.

He kissed her temple before whispering, "I'm here now, so you're safe. It's going to be all right."

When Dana looked up at him, Jay realized she had neither been sleeping nor unconscious. Dirt and scratches marred her tearstained face, but they could not hide the misery there.

"It's going to be all right," he repeated.

But before he could say more, she sobbed, "It's never going to be all right. Not now, not ever again."

Alarm catapulting through his system, Jay checked on Angie. But even before he found her first pulse point, he understood that Dana spoke the truth.

# Chapter Nineteen

*Full many a flower is born to blush unseen,*
*And waste its sweetness on the desert air.*

—Thomas Gray,
"Elegy Written in a Country Churchyard"

"If I was the sheriff, we for damn sure wouldn't be out here sweatin' our balls off, playin' Stepin Fetchit for some feeb," Wallace growled as he and Jay plucked twenties from the thorny stalks of a sticklike ocotillo.

The federal agent stood in the scant shade beneath the house's eaves, offering assistance in the form of supervision. Though he'd abandoned his suit jacket, loosened his collar, and pulled off his tie, Emil Tomlin was no match for the noon heat. The skies had cleared to brilliant azure, but last night's rain had left the air stiflingly humid by desert standards.

Since he'd been up the whole night, Jay wasn't thrilled about this detail either. And he sure as hell was in no kind of mood for any more lip from his own deputy.

"You *aren't* the sheriff, Wallace, and you damned well never will be if you don't quit your constant bitching and your sucking up for cameras."

Though the deputy's hat shaded eyes hidden by sunglasses, there was no mistaking Hooks's glare. "I told you I was sorry about that interview. I explained how that guy sort of tricked me into—"

"Save it." Jay rubbed sweat from his face with a forearm and pointed to a grouping of low, spiny plants. "There's more money stuck on those shin daggers. Go and grab those, will you?"

Wallace did it grudgingly, but that didn't stop him from bitching about how his work gloves were already in tatters.

Jay wished him a lacerated tongue, too, while he was at it. He didn't have time for his chickenshit petulance and second-guessing. He simply wanted to get this done and escape from Special Agent Tomlin's endless questions, which were feeling less collegial and more like an interrogation all the time. Both Tomlin and his partner, Petit, who was currently transporting the recovered money to a secure location, had had problems with Jay leaving the bag locked in one of the empty upstairs jail cells after Dana's frantic call last night. He supposed he could have called in Wallace to look after it, but how could he have delayed with lives at risk?

Though neither of the agents could answer that question when he'd posed it, they seemed to disapprove of it—along with every one of Jay's decisions. Or maybe it was his relationship to the former sheriff that had them suspicious, considering the evidence.

Jay would have gladly dealt with the special agents' scorn if his actions could have saved Angie Vanover or eased her sister's grief. The thought of Dana, battered, wet, and weeping last night, made his gut clench and his eyes burn, and he wished that he could get away to see how she was doing.

Wallace glanced back toward the agent and abruptly broke out laughing. Jay turned to see what could have possibly amused the deputy in his foul mood.

The tall, graying fed had drawn his gun on something and was backing away from it as it crawled past. Jay couldn't help joining in Wallace's laughter at the man's reaction to what must be a male tarantula, driven from his home by water and looking for some love. He and Wallace had already spotted several of the hairy-legged suitors, including one as big as his hand.

It was always the males who went out searching, and he'd heard that between the spiders' predators and their exertion, they didn't live long after they got laid. The females, on the other hand, might last through twenty years and almost as many lovers, as long as they stayed in the place where they belonged.

It made him think of getting Dana back to her safe, clean home in Houston before the same desert that had broken her heart found some way to stop it, too.

Dusk cloaked the small bedroom where Dana awakened. Or maybe it was dawn; she was as unsure of the time of day as of her location. Where on earth *was* this?

When she sat up to rub her eyes, their gritty soreness surprised her. Blinking did nothing but reveal another mystery: the flowered nightgown she was wearing. Edged in lace, it looked nothing like the worn sleep T-shirts she usually favored. Looked more, in fact, like something from Gramma Gifts "R" Us.

She couldn't remember dressing in it, couldn't remember anything after . . .

A cry caught in her throat, and an electric impulse quivered through her muscles. No, that couldn't be. It had to be a nightmare; that was all.

As she rolled onto her side she pulled her knees toward her breasts. Pain lanced through her muscles, a tearing soreness that made her clamp down on another cry. Had she been hurt somehow? Was that it? Maybe an accident of some kind . . . Some incident with her car teased the frayed edge of a memory.

Frowning, she studied the dim shapes of the furnishings around her: the old-fashioned dresser-and-mirror set, the nightstand, the small chair, and the looming presence that turned out to be an armoire in the corner. She twisted the brass key of an electric hurricane lamp. With a click it bathed the room in quiet yellow light. From the rag rug to the crown-of-thorns Jesus picture to the faded, moss green walls, the room remained utterly unfamiliar—and about as far from a hospital as she could imagine.

Outside the closed door a floorboard creaked beneath a heavy footstep. Moments later a soft tap followed.

A premonition prickled in her stomach, a sense that whoever came would solve the mystery of where she was and how she'd come to be here, and that the answer to those questions would be far more difficult to bear than curiosity.

By the time the door cracked open, she was trembling.

"Dana? Mrs. Lockett thought she'd heard you stirring, and I saw the light under the door." Jay's voice floated over her, quiet and reassuring. "Are you awake?"

She turned toward him, her eyes full of tears that she still could not explain.

"Hey, now. Dana, I'm so sorry." He sat on the bed beside her and let her fit herself into his embrace.

As he rubbed her back and rocked her, knowledge seeped in slowly. The nightmare hadn't been a mere dream; her sister had drawn her last breath in her arms.

Tensing, Dana pulled away. "I have to tell my mother. I have to tell her about Angie."

"It's all right," he assured her. "I've already taken care of it. Your father's with her—"

"My stepfather," she corrected without thinking.

"That's right, your stepfather. He's taking care of her. I told them, too, that you refused medical treatment, but you were in no shape to go anywhere. Mrs. Lockett said you're welcome to stay at her house for as long as you need to."

"Mrs. . . . Mrs. Lockett?"

"Mamie Lockett. Remember the elderly lady from the café the day that you were bitten by the snake?"

Dana shuddered at the memory of a skinny, gray-haired woman fluttering around the kitchen, searching for the biggest knife she could find. "The one who wanted to carve up my leg?"

"She meant well, I'm sure of it. Mrs. Lockett doesn't have a mean bone in her body. Bakes the best cookies in West Texas, too. Would you like me to bring you a couple?

Or how about one of those muffins to hold you over until dinner?"

Dana shook her aching head, her stomach rebelling at the thought.

He pulled her even closer. "You're going to have to eat and drink. You've slept straight through the whole day."

"I didn't remember anything when I woke up. Couldn't imagine how I'd gotten here or why I was dressed in this." She pinched at tiny flowers her sister would have laughed at. She could almost hear a younger Angie teasing, *"The nursing home staff called this morning. They want the nightie back, but they'll let you hold on to the adult diapers."*

"You were pretty out of it," Jay said. "I probably should've dragged you to the hospital in Pecos, no matter how much of a fit you pitched. But Mrs. Hooks and Mrs. Lockett volunteered to clean you up and put you to bed, and it seemed like the best thing at the moment—"

"Mrs. Hooks did? *Judge* Hooks's wife?" Dana's face went hot as she remembered snippets of the two women helping her dress. "But I thought Fry Cook and the missus hated me."

"Estelle's got her notions of what's proper, that's all, but that includes treating someone who's been through a bad time with Christian kindness."

Dana thought about the way Jay's neighbors pitched in during times of trouble. But she was an outsider, with a sister who'd caused trouble and whose death would only bring more unwelcome publicity. Dana's throat tightened, and she felt the salty sting of tears at the corners of her eyes.

"I tried to hold on to her. Tried everything I could think of to keep her from slipping—"

"You did all the right things, Dana. It wasn't your fault—"

"That I let her die, or that I led him to her?" She struggled free of his arms, the words painful as acid on her tongue. "Because that had to be what happened. He must have followed me from Devil's Claw when I went out to meet her."

"Even if that's true, you meant to save your sister. You were doing everything you could to—"

"Tell that to the Harrisons," she said bitterly. "Tell that to my mother."

He looked at her a long time, his blue eyes wells of sadness. "I know what you're doing, taking everything on yourself. I did it, too, after Baghdad. The other guys, my superiors, they all kept explaining that it was the suicide bomber's act that killed my men, and I'd shake my head and say, 'Yes, sir, I understand that.' But I damned well should have realized she was reaching for the detonator a split second sooner. Should have shouted out a warning so they could've stopped her."

Dana wanted to tell him that was war and this was different, that in war, death was expected. Not like Angie's, not like being hunted and helpless in the stormy desert in the dead of night. But the pain in his expression was so present and the fatigue shadowing his eyes so deep that Dana crushed the lit fuse of that impulse. "I'm sorry, Jay. It must have been horrible."

He nodded an acknowledgment. "More than I can tell you. But I didn't say it for your sympathy. I only wanted you to know that what you're doing, it's like swallowing a fistful of razor blades. They'll cut you all to pieces on the inside. Pieces that will bleed where no one sees. If you have to be pissed, be pissed, Dana. Mad as all hell at the son of a bitch who killed her. At me, for not finding her soon enough. Even at Angie, if you have to. But don't swallow all this down. You're too . . . I can't stand the idea of your hurting yourself any worse than this bastard's already hurt you."

She squeezed her eyes shut. Praying that maybe when she opened them, she'd wake up in her hotel room in Pecos. Or better yet, at home in Houston the day before she'd learned of Nikki Harrison's existence. Angie would be somewhere, on the lam as usual, always in the back of Dana's mind but no better or worse than ever. And Dana would spend her day off writing notes, returning gifts, and mailing that jerk Alex a present of her own: a beautifully wrapped, beribboned box of dog shit for his birthday.

But when she counted to ten and looked again, all she saw was Jay, gazing back at her.

*Time to face this*, she thought, for what other option was there? Sadness overpowered her, cloying as the scent of lilies at a funeral.

"We never even got a chance to talk," she said.

"Not at all?"

"Not about anything that mattered—except . . . except I said that Nikki needed her. I told her she had to keep trying for her daughter's sake." Dana sank into his arms again. "And now she'll never even get the chance to meet her."

"It's a hard thing. I understand that," he said as he enfolded her. "Still, I have to ask you: have you remembered any more? Anything about the shooter or his vehicle?"

Bits of last night came at her, assembling themselves into a warped jigsaw with several pieces missing. "Angie didn't tell me who. I asked, but by then she'd . . ." Dana bit her lip as another fragment of memory snapped into place. "There was something about an ATV, I think."

"We found it—out of gas. It had been reported missing a couple of weeks ago. We're guessing that your sister 'borrowed' it to get around in the desert."

"But other than that I don't remember anything."

Jay didn't try to hurry her. He simply pulled her into his arms and held her, the steady beating of his heart and the rhythm of his slow breaths a guide that she could follow. He pressed a tender kiss against her crown, and before she could stop herself she tipped back her head to meet his lips. Warm and lingering, the kiss settled over her like an unexpected benediction. But the bittersweetness of it tilted into shock as hunger slipped in uninvited. She needed to lose herself in the wet heat of hard kisses, the ripple of muscle beneath tanned skin, the ancient rhythm called up when he had moved inside her. She wanted desperately to bridge the gap between raw grief and the place where the pounding of their two hearts would hammer her emotions flat.

She withdrew from him once more, shame throbbing through her. She had no right to visit that place, not with Angie lying cold and friendless, shrouded on a slab.

"Dana." Jay's voice was weighted by exhaustion and a longing that made her own name sound foreign to her. But with a shake of his head he dismissed whatever he'd been about to say.

Unable to meet his gaze, she forced herself back to the only subject that should matter. "I never really saw the shooter, but I'm pretty sure he drove a pickup. Could've been an SUV, but my impression was a truck."

Within the space of a few heartbeats he struggled back to sheriff mode. "Do you know what make or model the truck was? Did you catch a glimpse of the paint color?"

She shook her head. "Something on the darker side. I'm not certain, though. And as for what kind, I have absolutely no idea. Even if there'd been light, I've never paid a lot of attention to truck styles. Wouldn't know a Ford from a Chevy from a . . . well, I don't know. Who else makes a pickup?"

"Was it older? Newer?"

"I'm so sorry. I want to remember it, *want* to think of something that will help you catch him. But aside from the lightning it was pitch-black out there, so dark he must have fired toward the sound of my voice. He couldn't even see what he was shooting. If I'd only kept quiet when the thorns caught—"

"I *will* get this person, Dana. I swear it to you."

In his eyes she saw him beg her to forget that he had also promised he'd find Angie. His fingers glided through her hair and caressed the side of her neck. She wanted to believe him. God only knew she needed to believe in *something*.

"Can you tell me," she asked, "where my sister's . . . where's her body?"

"El Paso ME's office. The FBI's put a rush on the post-mortem."

Dana tried not to think about the Y incision. Closed her eyes but couldn't keep back the image of gloved hands lifting out the mass of dripping entrails. She wanted to ask if he could stop it, to beg them not to put Angie through that final assault. But to do that she'd have to hold the horror in her head long enough to form a cogent argument, and she couldn't bear it. Probably *shouldn't*, since Angie's body might offer up the evidence she could no longer share in words.

"That's enough for now," Jay said as he pulled away. "Why don't you rest a few more minutes, and I'll bring you some food and . . . Do you drink milk?"

When she didn't answer he offered a brief smile. "What if I told you it came from free-range dairy cows with all-organic diets, weekly massages, and plush retirement packages?"

Against her will, she smiled back, and almost imperceptibly the anguish knotted hard inside her eased. "I'd call you a liar," she managed, "but I'd drink it."

"Okay." He kissed her forehead, teasing the knot a little looser.

When he pulled away she tumbled headlong into his gaze. "I'll be right back," he told her.

As the door closed she stared after him, her teeth pinching her lower lip until it hurt. What she felt for him was gratitude, a knee-jerk response to the kindness any decent person might feel obliged to offer.

*It can't possibly be love.*

She was smart enough to understand that she was caught up in a perfect storm of conditions guaranteed to obliterate good judgment. Grieving for her sister, on the rebound from a breakup, and recovering from the loss of her fertility, she had no business even thinking of Jay Eversole as anything but a momentary oasis in this hell.

And no business whatsoever imagining that a man still raw from his own traumas would have any better sense than she did. If she'd glimpsed love in his gaze, it was simply an illusion, a mirage so cunning he couldn't tell it from reality.

It was up to her, then, to remember the distinction. And up to her to ramrod some sort of justice for her sister, if she could only find the strength.

When the knock at her back door came, Mrs. Lockett was ladling vegetable soup into a bowl while Jay threw together a cheese sandwich made with two thick slabs of the home-made jalapeño beer bread famous throughout the county. Without waiting for an answer Estelle Hooks came in, her heels making their familiar *click-drag* on the tile.

"Turn on the TV," she blurted. "Hurry."

"If your son's giving interviews again . . ." Jay growled, wondering how Wallace could have already forgotten the first-rate ass-chewing he'd gotten the last time. Certainly he'd acted resentful enough to let Jay know his words had made an impact.

"It's not Wallace. It's you," Estelle said.

Mamie Lockett scuttled out of the kitchen to turn on the set in her parlor, her movements so swift and unexpected that her orange tabby tomcat jumped off the couch and ran be-hind it, yowling. With a fleet of knickknacks weighing down the doilies, the room looked like something from the forties, but the television's reception was a credit to the satellite dish on her roof.

"What channel?" she asked as she squinted down at the remote. Her reading glasses, as usual, were perched atop her head.

Estelle snatched away the clicker while Jay protested, "But I didn't talk to anybody."

The station Estelle punched in was running a terrifically annoying commercial for some headache medication.

Jay wished he had some, then frowned and said, "We must have missed the story. What was it—"

She shook her head and shushed them. "It's about to come on, they said. Right before they went to the commercials that pretty little reporter lady promised some exciting new information on the sheriff connected with the Rimrock County Salt Maiden case. Or do you think she could've meant my Wallace? After all, it's not the first time he's been mistaken for a sheriff. And even Suzanne Riggins had to admit he looked authoritative."

Unfazed by her pride, Jay stared at the television. Fear smoldered in his belly while his hands went icy cold.

Mamie patted his arm. "I'll bet they're going to point out that you're a real American hero, that's what you are."

He nearly choked on disbelief. "A *hero?*"

"*All* our boys in uniform are heroes." Her gaze drifted to the faded photo on her sideboard of a boyish-looking man wearing sailor's whites and a cocky grin beneath his tilted hat. Her late husband, Jay remembered, had been a navy squid in World War II. Lost a leg on some Pacific island hellhole after his Japanese captors let it go gangrenous. People had spoken reverently of him for decades, how his actions had saved dozens, how after coming home with every reason in the world to feel angry and defeated, he had never been known to step out his front door without a smile.

In spite of the medals he had been awarded, it made Jay sick that Mamie Lockett would compare him to a real hero like her husband. That the circumstances of his discharge would bring him anything like honor.

Yet unearned praise turned out to be the last thing he needed to sweat over. Instead he watched his worst fear play out in slow motion. Noted the sparkle in the anchor's eye as she heightened the suspense by cobbling a recap out of sound bites. Brave little girl struggling for her life in Houston. Heroic search for the missing birth mother. Mummified body in the salt tomb with its links to a well-organized scheme to bilk retirees across the country out of millions. And finally the tragic murder of Angie Vanover herself, under the watch of a sheriff whose "fitness to hold office has been called into question."

And then she came right out and told them—told the whole world what had happened in that theater. How a respected professor bringing snacks to his boy had been set upon in an unprovoked attack that smacked of ethnic hatred. How the man sustained a cut requiring seven stitches to the side of his head, from where he'd fallen hard against the armrest of a stadium-style seat.

The shot switched to a large and frizzy-haired young woman sausage-stuffed into a hot-pink tube top. *Izzy Jablonski, Terrified Movie Patron*, read the graphic beneath her Lycra-flattened breasts. Her head dipped toward the proffered microphone, her wide mouth opening as if she meant to eat it.

"The man was a *maniac*," she raved, waving her hands and bugging out her bulgy blue eyes for effect. "Totally deranged. I had to go to *counseling* for the trauma, like they tell you to on *Dr. Phil*. And I was shaking so hard there was no way I could work over at Hair by Harriet's on Valley View Lane, where ho-hum hair's made history. That's three whole days of pay lost, plus tip money, but after what I saw . . ."

She shook her head, her eyes now all but bursting from their orbits.

*You'd last about three seconds on the ground in Baghdad,* Jay wanted to tell her as a dark tangle of broken corpses overlaid her pale face, and soul-rending ululations drowned out the whipped-up histrionics. With an effort he tore away the past that filmed over the present.

"It's just *terrifying*." Good old Izzy was on a roll now, tearing visibly. "Imagine anyone giving a man like that a badge and, worse yet, allowing him to carry around a loaded *weapon*. What on earth were those people out there *thinking*? I won't sleep nights worrying about this. I might have to go on *disability* for my stress! And who's going to pay for *that*?"

"I'm not listening to one more second of this bullshit." Turning from the screen, Jay felt the women's stares as he stalked back toward the kitchen. "I'm taking Dana her dinner, but I'll do my best not to be a damned maniac about it."

He didn't wait for a reply before snatching the tray off the counter. But that didn't save him from hearing them whispering in the parlor, Estelle confiding how she'd seen him drop into a crouch behind her desk.

He nearly bumped into Dana in the hallway, which was lit only by a tiny night-light at knee level. She was emerging from the bathroom, and she smelled of Ivory soap and spearmint. He hesitated, worried that she might have overheard the TV. That she'd believe she had made love to some kind of psycho.

"It was . . . it was so kind of Mrs. Lockett to leave me the toothbrush and the comb and everything. I need to thank her for it, to thank her for everything she's done."

Relief rippled through his tensed limbs. She didn't know, not yet.

Her gaze dropped to the tray in his hands. "And this is nice, too, but I still don't think I can—"

"That's the trick," he said. "Don't think. Do you want to eat it in the bedroom?"

"I'm not . . . I'm not ready to face anyone. Anyone else, I mean." Without meeting his gaze she slipped back into the room.

He followed her and closed the door behind them, giving in to the absurd fear that Estelle's story would scuttle in on spider's legs to whisper the ugly truth in Dana's ear. *Tell her first*, his conscience urged him. *Before she hears the Izzy Jablonski version from someone else.*

She propped the pillows against the headboard, then sat

down and pulled the sheet over her thighs. In the lamplight she looked a little better for her cleanup, but her face was pale, and she had a raw-looking scrape beneath her right eye.

With a sigh she told him, "I could sleep forever. And you look tired, too."

He pulled a delicate cane-bottomed chair next to the bed, and then thought better of putting his weight on it. As he set the tray down on the nightstand, he said, "I caught a few Zs this afternoon, but there's been lots to do."

*Say it.* But the warmth in her expression made it harder. It could be a long, dry stretch before anybody looked at him that way again. The kind of women he craved tended to be skittish around nationally known nut jobs. Especially those given to unprovoked attacks.

"Soup or sandwich first?" he asked.

She reached for the milk instead and took a polite sip, apparently thinking to appease him. She moved to put it down again, but seemed to change her mind before draining three-quarters of the glass.

"I didn't realize I was so thirsty." At her stomach's growl she glanced down. "Hungry, too, apparently."

"Your body has its own agenda, no matter what's going on in your head." His pulse quickened and his muscles tensed. *It won't get any easier, so just go ahead and do it.* "It was like that for me in the hospital."

She touched the side of the soup bowl, then took the sandwich plate instead. "You were in the hospital? Were you hurt when your men . . . Were you injured in the Middle East?"

"Not physically." It was all he could do to meet her gaze directly.

"Post-traumatic stress?"

He swallowed painfully, hating this, hating himself. And then he forced himself to nod.

"That's perfectly understandable," she said. "Anyone who saw what you did, who saw people killed, would naturally be shaken. Even animals, after something scares them badly—"

"There was . . . there was an incident when I came home. A mistake I made. In a crowded theater. First movie I saw stateside—or tried to see." It had damned sure been the last one, too.

She picked a few green chunks of jalapeño from the beer bread and laid them on the plate's rim like a garnish. "Tell me," she invited, no judgment in her voice.

He grimaced. "With everything you've been through, maybe now's not the time. You've got plenty on your mind without me—"

"Could be I'll feel better hearing about somebody else's trouble for a change." She nibbled a corner of the sandwich half and chewed it woodenly. Moisture seeped from one eye, and she reached up to wipe it.

"Don't do that." He shook out her white cloth napkin. "You get jalapeño oil in that eye, you'll really have something to cry over."

She went very still while he carefully blotted the leaking tear. Once he had finished she scooted over. "Sit down, will you, please? My neck's stiff, and it hurts to look up."

He sat on the edge of the bed. If Estelle and Mamie saw, there'd be talk around town. But considering the newscast, that toothless bit of gossip would have to take a number.

"I wouldn't have brought it up now," he said. "Except . . . this thing that happened . . . they've put it on the news. Made it sound like I'm some kind of menace—and maybe that's what I am."

"Then tell me what really happened," she said. "Because I've already seen how twisted up these stories get once they pass through the vulture's bowels. Believe me, a certain reporter who's been spreading vile dirt about my family is about to have a day of reckoning. She's my mother's friend, or so we all thought. She wasn't the same witch trashing you? Regina Lawler?"

Jay shook his head. "I don't think so."

Then he told her the true story. How carefully he'd chosen the movie in the first place: a mindless comedy a cop buddy had suggested might help him remember how to laugh. How a preview trailer for another flick had put him all wrong with its billowing explosions that conjured up the smoke and smells and screams of that night at the checkpoint. How when he'd seen a tall man in a turban, silhouetted over pyrotechnics, he had leaped on instinct, his shoulder slamming the man's sternum and bringing him down hard.

How his "terrorist" had shamed Jay with his understanding, despite the blood and stitches and his own son's horror. Or maybe the professor had been scared to raise a fuss, fearful of calling any more attention to his heritage in a post-9/11 world.

"But the worst part was the screaming—and how everybody looked at me when my friend said I was just back from the Middle East. They'd started out scared, confused about what happened. Then I saw it turn to pity, heard some people start to argue that we shouldn't even be there. That I was no better than any of the psycho baby-killers back from Vietnam."

"Oh, Jay. I'm so sorry." Dana put down the sandwich. "I don't care how people feel about the war. There's no excuse for that behavior. You made a commitment and stood by it, a commitment to your country."

"Sure, they had an excuse for talking that way. I *was* crazy, Dana—acting like a first-class nutcase."

"It was an *accident*."

"What I did was dangerous, and it could've been a lot worse if my buddy hadn't been there to restrain me. That's why I checked into the VA to get myself evaluated."

"But they helped you? Right? I mean, I haven't seen any signs—"

"I did a few of the group sessions—counseling, I guess

you'd call it. But it was hard being around a lot of people stateside. Their priorities . . . I didn't get them. And the noise. The cell phones and the TVs and the Starbucks and the strip malls and the music and—"

"So that's why you came out here," she guessed, "to escape America—or as much of it as you could."

He nodded, shrugged a shoulder. "That and the fact that the Dallas PD wouldn't have me back. Not without extensive treatment. Maybe not even after that."

"It would've been a good idea, Jay, to work things through in counseling. Hiding from the problem—"

"You think I want to live off the government on some kind of psychiatric disability?" he burst out. "That even if I could work again with something like that on my record, I'd beg and plead and jump through hoops to get help from the system? Who'd ever let me carry a gun, knowing something could set me off again? I was broken up about my uncle's death, but I was also damned lucky to have an offer from the one place where the name Eversole's worth something, where they wouldn't look too closely at my references or background. Because not everybody's got a rich family to help them. Not everybody's got a safety net when things don't pan out like they should."

Dana stiffened. "I'm well aware of that, Jay. But I'm not about to apologize for mine. For one thing, as you might have noticed, it hasn't exactly bought me a special dispensation against all things unpleasant."

The chill in her voice lingered, freezing the narrow space between them.

"You didn't deserve that. See? It's just one more way of lashing out at others. And one more reason you should stay away from me. Because I'm screwed up, Dana."

She smiled without a trace of humor. "Maybe *that's* the big attraction. Because anybody else would take one look at my life and start running. Even before the thing with Angie, my fiancé already decided I was a bad bet."

Relieved at the change of subject, he said, "I thought we'd pretty well established the man's an idiot with no taste."

"But possibly good survival instincts."

He faltered through a smile. "Well, you'd have to have suicidal instincts to take a chance on me. For one thing, now that that story's out, my days as sheriff here are probably numbered. And even if I stay, this is no place for any woman. No place for anyone but scorpions and rattlers and a very few lost souls."

"Everybody gets lost, Jay. We all wander through one desert or another in our lifetime. There's still time for you to get whatever help you need to put yourself back on track and return to Dallas, or go anywhere you like."

"Cops handle things. They don't go cry on some shrink's shoulder or snivel around some lame-ass sharing circle and pass the tissue box. And they sure as hell don't respect any cop who does."

She made a face. "Oh, so it's a macho issue. I see. Then you'll forgive me if I don't make time to listen to it anymore."

"You don't have to listen. Just eat."

When she only stared, he added, "Unless you want me to feed you. Or call the old-lady brigade in here to do it."

Her look reflected his mood: sullen, bordering on mean. But she picked up the soup bowl nonetheless and started spooning.

"I've got some other things to see to," he said. "I'll check in with you in the morning. Meanwhile, I want you to get some rest and lie low. As far as I'm concerned, you're still in danger as long as you're here and there's a killer out there, God knows where."

# *Chapter Twenty*

Dear sis,

Those prayers you promised must have helped, because it seems we've dodged a bullet. Nikki's fever's finally down, and she's eating a little this morning, even smiling.

For how long, no one can guess. With the birth mother dead, we're almost out of other options. If she'd only listed the father on the original certificate, there might have been some chance. But now? Now we're using the publicity (or the "public evisceration," as John is calling it) to go out on the news and ask perfect strangers to be typed for the National Marrow Donor Registry. I know it would take a miracle to find a match in time, but aren't we due a big break about now?

—E-mail message from Laurie Harrison

*Thursday, July 5, 10:49 P.M.*
*82 Degrees Fahrenheit*

The house lay in dark silence when Dana awakened, saturated with too much sleep, too many aches, and far too many memories that cut like shards of broken glass.

Though she'd met with the FBI special agents earlier, cried with her mother in a wrenching phone call later, and finally arranged a flight home for tomorrow evening, Dana had retreated to Mrs. Lockett's guest room several times and fallen down the mine shaft of exhausted, dreamless sleep. Her recovering body craved rest, but her mind needed the escape more, for every time she woke it was to tears.

Tonight she held them at bay, her mind drifting through the misty layers of Special Agent Tomlin's endless questions.

A tall man whose gray eyes matched his short hair, he had rolled through the obligatory sympathetic statement quickly before peppering her with a fresh round of questions about last night, the weeks leading up to last night, and so many details about her sister's history that Dana felt as if her brain had been turned inside out. Each time she started to tire or lose patience, his partner, Petit, an athletic-looking blond man with a slightly chipped front tooth and a homegrown West Texas accent, interrupted the barrage by offering her water or holding up a palm to slow Tomlin down and suggesting, "How 'bout we give Dr. Vanover a minute to catch her breath?"

Which only went to prove that federal agents, too, resorted to the classic good-cop/bad-cop method, not only with prime suspects but with cranky witnesses as well. During one of these breaks she had told the two men, "I've been answering your questions long enough. Now I need some answers to mine."

She tried not to take it personally when the agents denied her every query about gathering both her belongings and her sister's and having them sent home. The clothing and supplies Dana had left in the adobe were now considered evidence, along with her flooded convertible. Angie's loom and the tapestry on it were evidence as well, and her clothing, art supplies, few mementos, and abandoned clunker all must be thoroughly examined. Neither man would venture to predict when they might be released. Most frustrating—and something Dana couldn't help taking personally—was the matter of her sister's body.

"What about the funeral?" she'd asked. "Surely you can't expect us to go on waiting, wondering. How can we move on with our lives without knowing when this might be over?"

"I realize it's not ideal." Petit leaned forward in his seat to touch her hand. "But most people in your situation opt to hold a memorial service to provide some sense of closure. Then, when the time comes, they hold a private burial for the immediate family."

The younger agent was an attractive man who seemed genuinely committed to the apprehension of her sister's killer, yet Dana had jerked her hand away from him without understanding why.

But later, in the wakeful darkness, she knew that his show of concern—though more professional than personal—had touched off thoughts of the man who wasn't there. The man she wanted desperately to talk to.

"This investigation is now in federal hands," Special Agent Tomlin said when she had asked about Jay. "You won't have to bother dealing with these locals anymore."

She hadn't liked the way he'd said, "these locals," hadn't liked it, either, when Jay had simply dropped her purse and the clothing from her car at the house while she slept. His note said, *Even the feds ought to know better than to come between a lady and her handbag, and I figured you could use those clothes you picked up, too.* There had been no mention of how he'd charmed these items out of the inflexible Tomlin, or if Jay had found a way to hijack them somehow.

When he didn't stop by later, she worried each time he crossed her mind. Was his career in jeopardy because of the publicity about the theater incident near Dallas? Or did he fear that rumors of their personal involvement would add fuel to the debate about his fitness?

*"Well, Dana, why don't you just ask him?"* Angie challenged.

Dana turned to see her sister sitting in the delicate chair beside her. Her waist-length, sun-bleached hair gave off light enough to illuminate her thin face. Hollow-cheeked but strangely radiant, she looked as clean as thin, blue moonlight and far younger than she had the night before.

"You're alive." Relief cascaded through Dana, beginning in her center, radiating through her pores. With joy bubbling inside her, Dana used her arms to push herself upright, launching herself toward an embrace—

The movement, and the pain of sore limbs, woke her to a room as still and black and silent as that salty tomb beneath the desert floor.

"No . . ." she moaned. "No, Angie. Please don't do this."
But Angie wasn't there to either argue or explain.

*Friday, July 6, 8:17 A.M.*
*76 Degrees Fahrenheit*
*Forecast High: 103 Degrees*

"I wonder where the sheriff's been." Dana kept her voice as
carefully casual as she could and her eyes cast down toward
the cinnamon-raisin toast she was eating.

"Poor young Jay's been running himself ragged, that's all.
You needn't worry about him," Mrs. Lockett told her. Between them sat a carb lover's fantasy: fresh-baked breads,
sweet yellow butter, and strawberry preserves.

As far as Dana had been able to establish, the old woman
spent nearly all her waking hours filling the counters of her
kitchen with cooling racks of muffins, cakes, and breads,
biscuits, pies, and honey-nut rolls. She repeatedly mentioned her need to feed her hungry children—children pictured in the faded photos she kept all around the house.
Apparently she had lapses, forgetting that her sons and
daughter were decades grown and gone. But she happily fed
her friends and neighbors who stopped by to bring her gifts
of sugar, flour—all her groceries—and whatever cash she
would accept.

Dana thought it wasn't a half-bad arrangement, but she
was happy she had finally arranged a flight home. If she didn't
get out of this house soon she'd be sure to gain ten pounds on
the warm and yeasty smells alone. The thought came out of
habit, though she'd probably lost that much weight over the
past two months from stress.

The old woman swiped a crumb from her lip with a bony
finger. "Don't you fret. Our Jay will overcome this nonsense."

"Do you mean the—"

"I mean all of it. Those lies about his uncle taking
bribes—as if a good man like R.C. would ever do any such

thing—and that foolishness on the TV about something that happened right after Jay came home from the war." The creases of her forehead folded into hard pleats. "Bunch of soft outsiders telling us who we should and shouldn't have for a sheriff. As if country folk aren't smart enough to know a crazy man when we see one. We've got a lot of experience dealin' with that sort of thinking. And a lot of practice diggin' in our heels when some slick city people waltz in and tell us what we should do."

Dana took a deep breath, let it expand inside her. She, too, had taken the locals for a backward bunch when she had first arrived, with their petty feuds, their prickly natures, and the deprivations imposed by this harsh land. Only unlike most outsiders—and utterly against her will—she'd stuck around long enough to learn that there was more to them than that. Including a streak of stubborn independence that ran so deep it resonated to the core of a cinnamon-sweet woman in her mid-eighties.

"So the sheriff won't lose his job?" Dana ventured, then repeated herself when Mrs. Lockett looked confused.

"I'm not saying he won't have a tough fight on his hands. Since he was appointed to fill a vacated term of office, the county commissioners can fire him, if that's what they decide. I figure Judge Hooks will try to use this news as an excuse to give his badge to Wallace. Estelle'll lobby hard, too, even though she has a soft spot for Jay on account of what happened to his mother."

"His mother?" Dana had wondered how his uncle had come to raise him.

The old woman's gaze warmed, and the past drifted across her eyes like thin clouds. "Such a shame, all that was. That Gayla was the prettiest little thing—I taught her in my Sunday-school class when she was just a tiny bit of fluff. As she started getting older the boys buzzed all about her like bees on a blossom. Why, even my Nestor took a shine to her, but he was always the bookish type, my boy. He could never—now, don't you go repeatin' this, or I'll deny it—hold a candle to those handsome Eversole brothers or big Dennis Riggins."

"So what happened to her?" Dana prompted.

"Why, she ran off with Lewis Eversole, she surely did. Didn't come back till they were married and she was in the family way. But Devil's Claw never suited Gayla—or Lewis either, for that matter. Restless types, those two, always chasing after some opportunity in another town, then bouncing back home when it didn't pan out. But still, she always was a sweet thing. And always kept herself lookin' pretty as a picture. Why, she was heading back from the beauty parlor over to Pecos when it happened—wanted to look nice for Christmas, cold as it was that year. But she spun out on an icy patch and flipped that cute little convertible she always loved to tool around in."

"That's terrible," said Dana.

Mrs. Lockett's eyes filmed, and she reached under her bra strap and pulled out a lace-edged handkerchief, thin with age. Dabbing her eyes, she said, "Killed her instantly, it did—and that precious boy of hers was only twelve. His daddy was so broken up, he could hardly stand to look at poor Jay after. That's when Lewis finally got himself a job that took him out of Devil's Claw for good."

"Poor Jay . . ." Dana, too, had lost a parent young, but she couldn't imagine how she would have survived had her mother turned her back on her in her grief. Except . . . wasn't that exactly what Isabel had done by withdrawing as she had from both her daughters?

"Don't you worry about our Jay," Mrs. Lockett told her. "That boy's a genuine Eversole, like R.C. And everyone in these parts knows that Eversoles make the best sheriffs."

"Everyone except the Hookses," Dana said.

"That's only because blood is thicker—and Wallace is always carryin' on about how he needs a fatter salary so he can move out of the family house."

"The deputy still lives at home?"

Mrs. Lockett bobbed her head in answer. "Has since he's moved back here, and the way I hear it, it's not a situation that's to anybody's liking."

"So Hooks will try to fire Jay to get his own house in order."

"That's part of it, but I'd say far as Abe's concerned, it's more about getting one up on Dennis Riggins—he's another of the county commissioners. Abe'd just as soon dip him in barbecue sauce and leave him in the foothills for a lion. But since he can't, he'll try to thwart him 'cause Dennis was the one that swung the vote for Jay's hiring over Wallace."

"Hmm . . ." Dana wished she had a scorecard.

"R.C. was Dennis's good friend, you see, ever since the two of 'em were knee-high," said Mrs. Lockett. "He took it awful hard after the fire. And Rigginses and Hookses have been oil and water ever since I can recall—something about a land deal that went sour between their folks. Or maybe it was their granddaddies."

No wonder these people hated outside interference. Anyone raised elsewhere would need years of study to avoid stepping in the middle of alliances and enmities that were apparently passed down through the generations.

"But then," Mrs. Lockett continued, "my youngest boy, Nestor, always said that there was more spite between those two families than in a sack of scalded bobcats. And worse 'n ever these past fifteen years or so—ever since that one term Dennis got himself elected county judge and Abe accused him of buying votes."

"It was nice of your son to offer to drive me to the airport this afternoon," Dana said to change the subject.

Mrs. Lockett's thin hand fluttered in dismissal. "I'm afraid Nestor got tied up in that business of his over in Kermit. So my nephew Bill Navarro's going to take you. You remember Billy, don't you, from the Broken Spur?"

Dana nodded, trying not to wince at the memory of the huge bouquet back in El Paso and how disappointed he had sounded when she'd asked directions to Jay Eversole's place after thanking him for the flowers. This could turn awkward if she wasn't careful.

"That's a lot of trouble to put him to," she said uneasily. "A lot of hours on the road to run me into New Mexico. Why don't I just hire a driver out of—"

"Nonsense," Mrs. Lockett said. "By West Texas standards, the drive to Carlsbad's nothing. Three hours round-trip at the most. Quicker than that, the way Bill drives."

Dana's stomach quivered. After her wild ride two nights before, the idea of speeding along these desert roads unnerved her. Along with the thought of speeding along *any* road with some lovesick cattleman. If the insurance company ended up totaling her Beamer, she decided she'd buy something slow, low-flash, with lots and lots of air bags. Maybe a higher-clearance vehicle, one that wouldn't be swept off course by a piddling, knee-deep flood. If she had driven something like that, something safe and practical, maybe she wouldn't be aching in a dozen places. And maybe her sister would be living, the two of them laughing during the long drive back to Houston, Angie asking anxiously, *"So, does Nikki look like me?"*

"Dana? Dana, dear, I asked if you'd like more tea."

Dana blinked to hide the misting of her eyes. "I'm sorry. I'm afraid my mind's been wandering. And I'd better not have more tea or I'll be squatting behind every bush from here to Carlsbad. I have enough troubles without getting a bunch of spines in my keister."

She shivered at a premonition of Bill Navarro volunteering to pull them out. And kiss the hurt to make it better, while he was at it.

Mrs. Lockett smiled, showing yellowed dentures. "If you're still thinking of Sheriff Eversole, why don't you go and see him?"

"I *do* need to ask him a few questions about the investigation. And thank him for bringing me my purse and clothes."

Kindness settled over the old woman's expression. "Call it what you like, dear."

Dana's face heated, and her gaze drifted toward the closed shades of the front window, which looked out onto the court-house, as well as the spot where Jay habitually parked his county SUV. Before sitting down to breakfast she had twice peered out, but had seen only Wallace's blue pickup. Mrs. Lockett must have noticed—or heard something in her voice.

"He probably won't be in till later," she said, "but you can take my car to his place if you'd like. I imagine it would do you some good to get out on your own a spell."

Dana looked at her, surprised—not so much that Mrs. Lockett had picked up on her concern for Jay, but at the offer of the ancient relic gathering dust behind the house. "It . . . The car still runs?" she asked, and then heated as she realized how snobbish her question must have sounded. "I-I'm sorry. Of course, it must. Or you wouldn't have offered."

Mrs. Lockett laughed. "Say what you want about my Ed-sel. Like you and me, she's built to last."

Except for the high-clearance part, the cream-colored Edsel turned out to be everything Dana wanted: low-flash, slow, and put together like a Sherman tank. Even so, she kept nervously checking her mirrors on the way to Jay's place, looking for the big grille of the shooter's truck.

*He was only after Angie,* she told herself. *And before that, he wanted to keep us away from the other woman he'd killed, the Salt Maiden.* An image of Angie's sun-bleached hair merged with a memory of the weaving on the loom. *He's not after me, not really. . . .*

But Dana couldn't stop thinking of her night in the adobe, when he'd crept so close with what might have been a rifle. Had he mistaken her for Angie that night? Or had his rage spilled over onto her?

One thing was for certain: Jay would have a fit about her driving out here all alone. It was the sole reason she hadn't called to let him know that she was coming. If she had, he might have driven into town to see her, but she needed time alone before she saw him to collect her thoughts.

*Don't make it complicated. Just tell him good-bye.* But that was her head talking, not the part of her behind the wheel.

The good-girl portion, the one that made top grades and sensible decisions, hadn't made much headway by the time she pulled into his driveway. She was relieved to see Jay's SUV there and pleased when Max raced over and wagged his little stub tail feverishly.

"Hey, Maxie," she said as she climbed out of the car to greet him. "Down, boy."

The dog broke off his attempts to slurp her face and dropped into a down position, though his whole body wriggled in frustrated enthusiasm.

"Somebody's been working with you," she said as she bent to scratch the silky fuzz behind his ears. Feeding him well, too, from the way he was beginning to fill out.

"That somebody would be me," Jay said, from behind her. "Too bad you're not as amenable to following directions. I thought you'd keep a low profile. Isn't that what we agreed on?"

She turned her head to see him dressed in khaki shorts and a faded Grateful Dead T-shirt. That took her by surprise, since she'd figured him for country all the way.

She leavened her shrug with a smile. "I'm not the obedient type. So sue me."

He answered with a wry grin. "Maybe I just will. Rumor has it that you're loaded."

She snorted. "You'd better hurry, before my next credit-card statement shows up. You wouldn't believe the cost of a last-minute, one-way flight from Carlsbad to Houston. And then there's the fact that I'm not working."

"That could make two of us soon."

"So I've heard. I'm sorry, Jay. Sorry about everything, including the way our last talk ended."

Their gazes locked, and she saw in his a reflection of her struggle, her ambivalence about leaving the only good thing to come out of her trip here. Because as unlikely as it was, the connection between them felt real. As real as anything she'd ever known.

He tossed aside the hammer he'd been holding, dropped the bag of nails into the dirt. When she took a step forward he met her, clasping her against him and pulling her into a blazing kiss. Her every nerve ending fired at the contact, and the tears trickling from the corners of her sore eyes signaled joy instead of pain. As his tongue slipped into her mouth, stroking and exploring, a white light seared away the cold, black shadow of her grief.

His hand skimmed along her side before sliding between them to stroke her breast.

He thumbed the nipple, and she pulled her mouth away to whisper, "Yes, Jay. Yes, this, please—before I have to go."

As his hardness sprang against her, Dana thrilled to the thought that she had caused it, that she meant to set off a lot more than hydraulics. Without a word he scooped her into his arms and carried her to the RV, his only pause to struggle with its stubborn door.

Breathing hard, he said, "This doesn't make a lot of sense. Not for you and not for me—and if those federal agents see us, I'm in even deeper shit than—"

"Just open the damned door and shut up," Dana told him, "unless you want them to spot me doing you right here."

Inside they didn't make it to the bed. Instead he cleared the breakfast things from the table with a sweep of his arm that sent a coffee mug, a small plate, and a stack of papers flying. Something shattered, but she didn't see what, didn't care as he pushed up her T-shirt and made short work of her bra's front closure, his mouth sucking in her nipple and sending more bliss streaking southward.

She nearly screamed with the pleasure of it as tiny detonations quivered low and deep, building to the first real shudder as he stripped her of her shorts and panties, then laid her out like a dessert and started kissing at two tiny, reddish scars on either side of her lower abdomen.

And then he shifted, kissing his way around her navel and flicking his tongue around its dimple.

"You aren't going to . . ." she began, some primly proper corner balking as his lips tickled the inside of her thigh. "People have to eat here."

He looked up, his eyes laughing, and said, "Damned straight. People do."

He delved lower, sinking to his knees for access, stroking the center of her until a storm of mindless pleasure crackled all around her. Her neck arched back until she saw nothing, heard nothing but the rasping of her breath, the building of her moans, then the thrumming of her blood like thunder in her ears. When two of his fingers tested her depths she exploded, her cry so loud that from some distant recess she heard Max bark outside.

When the waves at last subsided and she could see again, Jay was fumbling with his own clothes, searching through a pocket, looking. Cursing softly.

Smiling, she told him, "You don't need a condom. The surgery I mentioned . . . those scars . . . I'll never get pregnant, and I'm not sick."

"There's been no one else but you," he said, "not since the army gave me a clean bill on that count."

"Why don't you come up here," she invited, patting the table as she rose from it, "and let me give you a very personal examination?"

They tangled in another deep kiss that tasted of her own excitement. When her mouth dropped to his neck and her fingers tweaked his nipples, she smiled at his sharp intake of air.

"If you . . ." he said as she trailed kisses lower. "I won't last if you don't stop that."

She pushed him backward, smiling. "I've been told you should lie back and think of England."

"It's not working," he said as she kissed along his length.

She feathered touches, eliciting a low moan that made her smile at the thought of her own power, a power that remained to her despite the surgery. "Then try the queen. That ought to do."

Apparently it did, for he not only survived what came next, he rallied well enough to flip her over afterward and take her from behind.

She moved in time to his thrusts, her own excitement building as he reached around to touch her, setting her ablaze. As he cried her name and spilled the river of himself inside her, the table cracked and canted and they had to scramble off to keep from sliding to the floor.

"That was some kind of good-bye," she said as she leaned her head against his chest, nuzzling the coarse hairs. "But I am sorry about your table."

He kissed her, then smiled down like sunlight. "Maybe someday we'll take ourselves a trip to England. Seems like I should stop by and thank the queen."

Sometime later, as he sat with Dana nestled in his arms, Jay felt the shift of her emotions in the warmth of tears against his skin.

"If you're going to do this every time we make love," he said as he kissed her temple, "you're going to give me some kind of complex. You know, on top of the ones I have already."

As she wiped at her green eyes she tried to laugh, but her expression trembled before collapsing into misery. "I-I'm sorry, Jay. It just seems wrong. Being with you this way. Laughing as if nothing's happened. And then there's the part where I stepped outside myself this morning, coming here and throwing myself at you like some sort of a—"

He stopped her with a lingering kiss. When he felt her

tension melt into it, he cupped her face and stared at her, intent on memorizing each beautiful detail.

"There's nothing in the world wrong in this, with us," he said. "It's only simple, human comfort at a time we both can use it. And I expect we're both behind on our quota of laughter these past few months. God only knows we're due a share."

"But this afternoon I'm leaving," she said. "I have to go home to my mother. To my clinic."

"To your life," he finished for her. "I wish it could be different, but we both know it's the right thing. Me and you together—it's something to fill a need, that's all. It could never work out long-term. I think we both know that."

It hurt to say those words, hurt to know that they were true. Because impossible as it was, he wanted her at his side—not in a place like Rimrock County, but in a community with all the advantages and comforts she deserved. The trouble was, though, back in her city she had friends and family and her own expectations about the kind of man she would accept. None of which had anything to do with some shell-shocked reject who might easily end up out of work and on the street.

"I know it, but I want . . ." She squeezed him tight around the middle. "I need . . ."

She sighed and let him go. "I need to grow up, that's what. This is crazy, thinking there's some way for us . . . Even if it weren't for the logistics, Jay . . . I'm as barren as this desert, and twice as prickly."

"Prickly?" he asked. "You? Maybe by Houston standards, but you can't hold a candle to the average Rimrock County resident. Or its vegetation."

He started dressing as she did the same. Once they had finished he added, "And the desert isn't barren, Dana. Come out here a minute. Let me show you."

He took her outside, where the air was heating, then

moved to the ladder at the back of the RV. "Climb it," he said. "I'll be right behind you."

Dana looked distrustfully at the ladder. "Oh, come on, Jay, it's got to be ninety already, and I'm sore and—"

"It'll be worth it, I promise. And I've tested and retested this ladder. It's secure as it can be. Come on, Dana, just for a minute."

She shrugged and muttered, "In the spirit of humoring you . . ." before making her slow way up the ladder toward the top, with Max barking in frustrated longing from below.

"Hands to yourself," she groused when he tried to boost her bottom.

"I just thought, with all that groaning you were doing—"

"That it would be a great excuse to cop a feel?"

"Hadn't thought of that angle," he lied, grinning, before he joined her on the top deck. "Careful of that rusty spot."

"So what," she started, "was so important to show me up . . . here . . ."

Her words trailed off as she looked out at the vastness of the desert all around them: a vista unbroken, save for the earth-colored adobe ranch house and outbuildings, by any other sign of human habitation.

"It's . . . it's so *green*." Her words were hushed with reverence. "And I see flowers—right there."

He followed the line of her slim arm to where she pointed out a mass of bright purple blooms decorating a stand of cholla cactus. "And over there? What's that?"

He spotted the pale yellow-green patches clothing rocks that had been dull gray days before. "That's lichen. And over there, those little white blossoms—tangled fishhooks. And enough grass to keep the cattle chewing quite a while."

In the distance he saw several cow-and-calf pairs doing just that, and he felt the first stirring of eagerness to be out there among them working, a job that Dennis Riggins had been tending in his stead since Uncle R.C. had died. Den-

nis was keeping his uncle's horses, too, a pair of sturdy geld-
ings sometimes used for desert searches.

"But how can this be?" asked Dana. "Just two days ago
this was all . . . empty."

"Dormant," he said, "that's all. Just waiting for the rain.
Never barren, Dana, any more than you."

As if to hide her face, she turned. "Thank you so much
for showing me, Jay. There really is a beauty here if you
know where and when to look."

He inhaled the dry air's clarity, gazed out across the salt
flat to the foothills that looked for all the world like shapes
cut out of purple construction paper. . . .

Where he formed a silhouetted target within a distant rifle's scope.

# Chapter Twenty-one

*A belief developed in the Middle Ages that the ingestion of the preserved flesh of the Egyptian mummy could cure all manner of infirmity and illness. This practice, which persisted well into the nineteenth century, accounted for the looting of innumerable desert tombs in order to support the grisly trade.*

*When mummies were no longer readily available, the dried, ground flesh of executed felons or diseased poor ensured that profits could continue to flow uninterrupted.*

—From *Medical Oddities Through the Ages*,
Professor Elizabeth Farnum, Ph.D

An explosion of scarlet, flecked with shards of skull and splatters of gray matter. A burst of will communicated in the trajectory of a single, deadly missile.

A pulse of lethal power, *his* power, that would fall like a killing bolt from the clear blue.

The Hunter hardened with the thought of it, with the justness and the rightness. With an answer to the frustration and raw hatred that cut like broken glass inside him. With the avalanche of pain and destruction he would hurl down at the bitch's sister ... if he but squeezed a little harder on the trigger of his gun.

Sweat poured off him, more in response to the weight of his decision than to the day's heat. As he stared through the rifle's scope, the salt sting forced him to pull away, to blink.

And to consider the sacrifices he had made to get that money. And the sheer stupidity of killing the one woman he could have forced to lead him to it.

If he had only run the sisters to ground that storm-slashed night as he had planned, had only held his gun to Dana Vanover's head and started flaying strips of her flesh with his skinning knife. Then Angelina surely would have told him the location, would have wept and begged him to let her take him to it.

But instead he had allowed his hunting instincts and his rage to call the shots—that and his terror that Angelina would escape beyond his reach. If he had been smart enough to think beyond that, he would have aimed high to pin the pair down until he could get to them.

But his intentions hardly mattered, since he had been unable to track them in the darkness. Worse yet, he'd later learned that he had killed her—accidentally shot dead the one person in the world who could have led him to the cash.

Fury and frustration crashed around the Hunter, deep red waves as thick and salty as congealing blood. After all the sacrifice, all the deprivation, to lose his prize through such stupidity . . .

Sometimes he heard the woman he had murdered laughing from the grave. For she'd unearthed his due, leaving it for Sheriff Jay Eversole to find.

And that bastard had turned it over to the goddamned FBI. . . .

The Hunter's index finger spasmed, and he barely controlled the urge to squeeze off a killing shot. Or better yet a pair of them, to take out both of those who had helped to ruin everything for him.

But this time he pushed back the predator, which allowed his human remnant to think through the likely consequences—the law officers that would swarm like angry hornets, stopping at nothing to seek him out.

Through his scope he saw that Eversole was moving, climbing down from the RV after Dana Vanover. Even from this distance he saw their casual touches, the body language that hinted they were either lovers or soon would be.

At the realization the Hunter's finger moved to stroke the rifle's barrel and then caress the well-worn handle of his favorite skinning knife. His breathing intensified as his thoughts turned to the smooth strips of pale flesh he had peeled from the pale body, to the sweet-salty iron taste that he had held for hours between his teeth and gum.

As a youth he had been taught to honor the valor and the cunning of his prey by taking such a tribute, and he still recalled the first steaming sliver of buck's heart pressed bloody to his lips. When he had gagged at that initiation, his father's friends had mockingly asked if he was certain that he wished to be a real man, had had themselves a good laugh at his expense.

Never guessing that much later the lesson would sink in.

Never guessing the bitterness of his regret that he had lost the chance to taste of Angelina, who had been by far the worthiest prey that he had ever taken. Brilliant and resourceful, strong enough to elude him on his own turf for months, in spite of her condition.

Was it possible Angelina's sister was all she had been and more? For twice she had escaped his bullets. Her sister, who was charming the county sheriff, just as Angelina had before her.

A smile pulled at dry lips until the lower split and oozed out bloody droplets. Because the thought of Dana Vanover gave the Hunter an idea . . .

One that had him smiling as he stroked both the knife's shaft and his own.

Dana's gaze lingered on the pickup's rearview mirror as the tiny clutch of buildings disappeared over the horizon. One hand fiddled with the truck's air-conditioning vent in an attempt to direct some cool air toward her face. What breeze she felt was hot and gritty, dry as the afternoon outside.

"Sorry, Dana, but this old girl's AC takes a few miles to get crankin'." Bill Navarro patted the dashboard, then pulled a bandanna from his pocket and brushed at sun-faded plastic as if he'd noticed the thin film of dust there.

Dana sneezed twice, which had him stammering more

apologies as he tucked the blue cloth in the front pocket of a freshly pressed shirt.

"Please don't do that," she said. "Say you're sorry, I mean. I really do appreciate your taking half your day to drive me."

A smile warmed a deeply tanned, broad face that smelled of drugstore aftershave. A decent-looking face, since he'd taken time to clean up. "The pleasure's all mine."

She nodded before turning in her seat to look out the rear window, desperate for a last glimpse of the place—of all the godforsaken places in the country—her older sister had chosen to call home. Here it was less green than Jay's ranch, but nevertheless, patches of bright color caught her eye.

Jay's voice flowed from her memory, cool and unexpected as a wellspring in the rocky soil. *"Never barren, Dana, any more than you."*

She wished he was here now, that he could have put aside his duties to drive her to the airport. Even though she knew it would only make it more difficult to leave him.

"If you're worryin' about that nutcase coming after us," Bill told her, "you don't have to."

He hunkered low and reached beneath the seat between his feet, then drew out the largest pistol she had ever seen.

Her eyes widened at the sight of it, as well as at the memory of Angie bleeding, dying, a bullet in her shoulder.

"I feel much safer," Dana said too quickly. "Now could you please put that away?"

When he blinked at her blankly, she added, "My . . . my sister. That's how she . . ."

His tanned face reddening, Bill shoved the gun back out of sight, his movement so abrupt that she lifted her feet for fear he might squeeze off a shot. He looked disappointed at her reaction, maybe even angry, but he didn't push her.

As the trip wore on she felt guilty for playing the grief card, using it as an excuse to draw into herself for the remainder of their journey. Clearly Bill had harbored hopes of a little conversation. But even for the sake of manners she couldn't manage such a thing.

Not with her heart aching for both the hope and the man she was leaving behind in Rimrock County.

Later that same afternoon in his office, Jay talked to Special Agent Steve Petit. With the officious Tomlin busy elsewhere, Petit loosened up a little more as he talked about his years in the town of Monahans, where his father still raised cattle, a living he supplemented by hot-shotting oil-field equipment from site to site in his old pickup.

Jay listened, waiting for the other shoe to drop, but Petit never said a word about the news reports regarding the theater incident. Probably the agent already knew far more than the reporters. The bureau could have his medical records opened in a heartbeat, or those of any present or past member of the military.

More than likely both Petit's reticence and his trip down memory lane were tactics meant to ease the local yokel into talking about his uncle's possible corruption. Still, Jay found himself confessing his suspicions that R.C.'s death might be related to both the Piper-Gold and Vanover killings. As he pulled a couple of sodas from his office fridge, he suggested, "Maybe we could brainstorm together. God knows I want to get to the bottom of this as much as you do."

Petit immediately agreed.

"No idea's too wild," the special agent said, setting the ground rules for the exercise. "So no calling bullshit on me, saying this old buddy or that neighbor would never do such a thing."

Jay felt a muscle tic in his jaw, but he nodded all the same. However difficult this might be, it would keep him from being shunted aside, then bulldozed by the widening FBI investigation. And it beat the hell out of staring at the clock and wondering if Dana had yet reached the Carlsbad airport, whether she had boarded the plane that would take her out of his life once and for all. He wondered, too, about Bill Navarro, in a truck alone with her for an hour and a half. Would the rough-hewn and short-tempered rancher have it in him to play the gentleman so long? Jay worried that he should have insisted upon taking her himself, in spite of his appointment with Petit and Dana's insistence that she could handle Bill.

"We've gotta consider the possibility"—Petit's voice pulled Jay's thoughts back on track—"that R.C. Eversole was murdered by Piper-Gold and her husband. Maybe the money wasn't so much a bribe as blackmail. He could've figured out their angle, but eventually he squeezed a little too hard."

Since that didn't sit well with him, Jay threw in, "Or maybe they killed him after he *wouldn't* take their cash."

Petit looked doubtful, which was natural, considering the money buried outside of R.C.'s bedroom window. But he obeyed his own rule, which prompted Jay to mention his earlier suspicion that Angie Vanover had killed his uncle before her own eventual murder.

Petit nodded. "Could've been her way of shutting down the project, if she believed Eversole was bought off. She could've murdered the woman you found in the cavern, too, maybe at the same time. But if Vanover killed one or both, who'd be left to look for her?"

"Roman Goldsmith," Jay guessed. "Maybe after *he* killed his wife, he figured out she really hadn't known the location of the money."

"That's a possibility, especially considering that we've linked Goldsmith to an unsolved murder in Miami, where he was running a real estate scam back in the nineties."

"Seems off, though, somehow, doesn't it, to have a city type traipsing out to a salt cavern in the Rimrock County desert?"

"Not necessarily, since Haz-Vestment did a survey of the area around the domes to make their scam look legitimate. Goldsmith could have known about that cavern. . . . Or maybe your uncle had a local partner who wanted to avenge his death. And find the missing money, if Angie was the one who hid it."

"Considering the skull and petals I found in the bedroom, that part seems to fit."

Both men lapsed into silence as they thought for several minutes.

Petit spoke next. "Or what if somebody else found out about the money? Someone local with a pressing need for it."

Jay recalled Dennis Riggins's reaction to the news of Haz-Vestment's investigation. Remembered, too, Abe Hooks saying, "*You don't really know that bastard. Nobody knows him the way I do.*"

"Have you taken a good look around here? Just about everybody living in these parts scratches out a pretty thin living," Jay said instead, thinking it was bad enough speculating about his uncle, but at least R.C. Eversole was not around to hear it. Dennis, on the other hand, would die a thousand deaths if agents came to question him. Better that Jay should talk to him, though Dennis might try to kick his ass for daring.

Petit grinned, revealing the chipped front tooth. "If people in Devil's Claw're anything like folks where I'm from, the whole damned bunch of 'em would just as soon starve as admit it."

A beep interrupted, alerting Jay a moment before the fax machine hummed and spit out the first of several pages.

"Let me check this, see if it's anything important." Jay put down his Dr Pepper and stood from where he had been sitting on the corner of his desk. After walking to the low ledge of the counter, he said, "It's from the El Paso ME's office. A summary of their preliminary findings."

"Already?" Petit rose from the straight-backed chair where he'd been taking notes. Reaching for the papers, he said, "That was mighty speedy, even with an FBI rush on it."

Jay turned from his proprietary grab. "Not so fast. This isn't Angie Vanover's autopsy. It's Miriam Piper-Gold's—and that's my name on the cover sheet."

Petit looked disgusted. "Listen, Sheriff, you know as well as I do her death falls in our territory."

"The name's Eversole, not Sheriff. And since I found this body and rode herd on this examination, let's just say we look at the report together."

Petit regarded him coolly for a minute, and in his gaze Jay saw the battle raging between West Texas good old boy and the bureau's more-professional-than-thou way of thinking. Shrugging, the agent opted for the path of least resistance.

"All right," he said. "I don't see any reason why we can't have it your way."

Jay pulled his desk chair around the corner and laid the papers out where they could both see. He frowned as he read.

"So they're ruling it a homicide."

"Just the way you figured," Petit responded, giving him his due.

"But I didn't figure this." Jay reread a few lines to make sure he hadn't misunderstood them. "They're calling the facial injuries postmortem, especially in light of the damage to the fingers."

"What damage?" Petit asked. "I don't remember your saying anything about that."

Jay shook his head. "Because I missed it, even though I was the one who bagged her hands."

He tried to recall the fingertips, but he'd been mostly concentrating on the nails, which might hold evidence beneath them. These and the general condition of the mummified body had prevented him from focusing on one macabre detail: the fleshy pads, it seemed, had been pared away.

"Somebody didn't want her ID'd, destroying the face, damaging the dentals, carving off those fingerprints," said Petit.

Jay tapped another paragraph on the report. "I do remember seeing *these* cuts. Thought maybe an animal had been going at the internal organs. But the edges did seem pretty regular, now that I think on it."

According to the medical examiner, strips of flesh appeared to have been flayed from the victim's inner thighs and belly region. The cause of death, while remaining inconclusive, likely involved "circulatory collapse due to exsanguination."

"So she bled out," Petit concluded. "After being cut, possibly tortured, with something very sharp. A hunting knife? A scalpel?"

Jay nodded. "Someone wanted her to tell 'em the location of that money, I'm thinking."

So far, forty-seven grand and change had been recovered. Some of the original total might have been spent already, while more had doubtless blown across the desert. Jay figured many of his neighbors would take an interest in dry-country hiking once the news got out.

"Either that," said Petit, "or somebody meant to punish her for something. She surely didn't die a quiet death. Nor the kind of death a female perpetrator would be statistically likely to inflict."

Jay reread another line, trying to extract every shade of meaning from the clinical details. Seeing nothing more of interest, he said, "Full report'll come in after they've had a chance to run the tox screen."

Petit frowned before picking up the pages. "Too bad they can't get more specific with the time of death. Would've helped a lot to know when she'd been killed. I guess because of the body's desiccation, they weren't able to use the usual insect evidence."

Jay nodded, his mind perversely drifting to a distant history lesson on Western frontier life. "I guess the old-timers had one thing right," he said. "Looks like salt's not a half-bad preservative after all."

*Saturday, July 7, 1:02 P.M.*
*95 Degrees Fahrenheit*

When Dennis Riggins's wife opened the door to their ranch house, Jay couldn't believe this was the same woman he remembered. In the time he'd been away, Suzanne's once-dark hair had gone completely white, and her full, pink face had paled, falling on dark, crepey circles beneath once-vibrant gray eyes. Jay had expected change over the course of the sixteen years since he had seen her, and he had heard she'd had a mild heart attack last winter. But she looked terrible, as if she'd received the shock of her life, such as her husband telling her they'd lost everything to the con artists who called themselves Haz-Vestment.

"Why, Jay Eversole." She smiled in recognition and stepped back to wave him inside the Mexican-tiled foyer. Her voice might be thinner than he remembered—as was her tall frame—but her West Texan accent remained the same. And so did the personality that sparkled just beneath the surface. "Come on in. It's so good to see you all grown up, and I have to say you've filled out real fine."

His face grew warm at the compliment.

"Thanks, Suzanne." She'd never taken kindly to being called "Mrs. Riggins." "You're a sight for sore eyes, too."

She waved off his reflexive statement, the look in her eyes telling him that she knew bullshit when she heard it. But instead of chastising him, she said, "Sorry I'm not dressed for company. . . . Would've slapped on my boots 'n ball gown if Dennis had given me any kind of warning."

Though it was early afternoon, she wore a green-and-white-striped cotton bathrobe.

"That was my fault, not your husband's. I'm sorry I didn't call first." Jay would have, but he wasn't sure his uncle's old friend would have stuck around the house if he had had fair warning. "But next time I'll be sure to do that. Wouldn't want to miss a chance of seein' a pretty lady all dressed up."

She laughed at their foolishness and led him toward the sound of a TV playing at high volume in a den that hadn't changed at all. As worn and comfortable as the rest of the house, the room was decorated with cross-stitched patterns in antique frames, a Victorian washstand with a flowered basin and a matching pitcher, and Dennis's moth-eaten old trophies, the mounted heads of a pair of mule deer bucks whose racks were lightly laced with cobwebs.

Dennis's huge form was ensconced in an oversize recliner as he watched baseball on ESPN.

"Who's playing?" Jay called to him, all but shouting to be heard over the TV.

Dennis looked at him morosely, his frown nearly hidden by the bushy red-gray beard. Shrugging, he answered, "Who the hell cares?" before using the remote to mute the sound.

Suzanne shot her husband a worried look before glancing back at Jay. "I was heading for the tub when I heard you knocking. If you'll excuse me, I'll leave the two of you to talk. There's Cokes and lemonade out in the fridge, so make yourself at home, Jay."

"Thanks," he said, and waited for her to leave before sitting in the smaller of the two chairs, which was covered in the same faded plaid fabric as the "his" version. The rocker-recliner creaked beneath his weight. "How's she taking the news about Haz-Vestment?"

Dennis turned to make sure his wife was out of earshot before meeting Jay's gaze and dropping his voice to a loud whisper. "Haven't told her yet how bad it is. For us personally, I mean. I know I oughta, but . . . Suzie's got more'n enough to worry over right now."

"What's going on?" Jay dreaded the answer, but the change in Suzanne's appearance was too drastic to ignore.

The pain flashing through Dennis's blue eyes was unmistakable, though his features hardened almost instantly. "You didn't come here to talk about her."

"But I care about her, Dennis." Jay nearly told the older man he was worried about him, too, but Rimrock County was the kind of place where a man helped another man sink postholes, castrate calves, or shore up a sagging feed shed. Expressions of sentiment between males were considered useless, if not positively suspect.

"A prayer wouldn't go amiss," Dennis admitted as he looked away. "And that's all I've got to say on the subject. So tell me, what the hell brings you here? And it had god-damned well better not be to question me like some damned suspect."

*Well, hell,* thought Jay. He stood and took a step in the direction of the kitchen.

"Think I'll go for that Coke," he said. "Can I get you anything?"

Might as well be civil while he still could. Because Jay sensed this conversation was about to go downhill fast.

# Chapter Twenty-two

Dear sis,

The birth mother's sister, Dana, arranged to meet me yesterday while John stayed with Nikki at the hospital. (More problems with the new IV site, so they're putting in a central line this morning.)

Dana looked so sad, I told her how sorry I was for her family's loss—as if it weren't our family's loss, too. I told her how much I would have liked to thank her sister for the gift she shared with us. But it must have been too hard for Dana to hear, because she changed the subject to the purpose of her visit, the documents she wanted John and me to gather from Nikki's adoption file.

I can't imagine what good she thinks they'll do her. I explained that the father was listed as "unknown," that the hospital in Odessa wouldn't give out any further information. Our attorney says there's nothing more for them to give, but maybe the Vanovers have their own resources.

Better light another candle. Better say another prayer. Because the next infection Nikki gets could be her last one. And I swear to you, if my baby dies, I'm going to die with her. Because a heart can't keep beating through that kind of pain, can it? At some point it has to scream, "ENOUGH!"

—E-mail message from Laurie Harrison

*Thursday, July 12, 9:33 A.M.*
*82 Degrees Fahrenheit*

As they sat at her mother's backyard patio set, Dana wondered how to break the news that she was leaving Houston first thing tomorrow morning. She swallowed fresh-squeezed orange juice to moisten her dry throat, but before she could come up with the right words, Isabel put down her fork and started talking.

"Your sister called me that night to get your number." Dana's mother's eyes reddened, a startling contrast to irises that matched the lush green of the landscaping around her pool. "That's why I tried to reach you, to let you know about it."

After the time she had spent surrounded by the desert's subtler palette, Dana found the sight of so much verdure overwhelming, almost painful. The blaze of hibiscus blossoms seemed extravagant, the bougainvillea blooms too gaudy—even the pool's turquoise made her wince and turn away, her cheese omelet forgotten.

"That's what I figured," Dana said, still wrung out from the previous night. Her mother and Jerome's circle had attended a restrained but elegant memorial service. Of Dana's friends, Lynette and their two vet techs had come from the clinic, along with a few others who had seen the announcement in the paper. But not a soul showed who had known Angie personally, though Dana had heard from her sister's art agent and a couple of friends she had met in rehab, each of whom promised to remember her in their own way.

Including one Dana had called back three times in the past three days, between her visits with John and Laurie Harrison.

"Once I told Angie you were out there, the only thing she wanted was to call you." Isabel sipped the ginger-peach iced tea she drank in place of coffee on warm mornings. Like her daughter's, her own breakfast lay abandoned after a few bites. "She didn't even tell me good-bye."

"She was in bad shape, Mom, and desperate to get out of there. If she had known it would be the last time, I'm sure she would have—"

"You don't have to do that. To make excuses for your sister. You know as well as I do why she was the way she was. . . . I was never the sort of mother Angie needed."

Moisture glittered in her eyes. "And probably not much better when it came to you."

Dana said gently, "You did the best you could. And like I told you, Angie planned to come home. She wouldn't have said that if she didn't love you."

Dana had repeated the same thing perhaps a dozen times over the past few days. This time, like all the others, Isabel didn't look as though she believed a word of it. Avoiding Dana's gaze, she fussed with the wrinkled linen of her sundress and turned her attention to a hummingbird's worship of a garish blossom.

Finished with their squirrel patrol, Ben and Jerry trotted over and sat near Dana's feet. The corgis' thick red-blond tails fanned in unison as they stared a reminder that the two unfinished breakfasts need not go to waste.

Ignoring the dogs' telepathic messages, Dana thought of asking her mother about the rumors she had heard years earlier, the talk that hinted of sexual abuse while Isabel was still a child. Maybe if she sought help, things could be different in the future. Or would the suggestion merely make Isabel wonder if she could have saved Angie with such an effort?

Too dangerous to try now, Dana decided, especially since she wouldn't be around to watch her mother. Though Jerome had taken the week off, it wouldn't be fair to leave him with the fallout of yet another emotional upheaval—especially since he'd undoubtedly disagree with the idea of dredging up the painful past. Like most men, he believed in living in the present and burying whatever memories might prove too messy.

Like Jay Eversole, who would prefer to avoid any reminder of the traumas that had left him with his own psychic wounds. Apparently Dana was one more aspect of the past to put behind him, since he hadn't called or e-mailed since she had returned home. He *had* sent both flowers to the service and a handwritten letter of condolence, though the latter had been stiffly formal and addressed to the whole family, without a single hint of the intimacies the two of them had shared.

But as much as that note rankled, it was another that had convinced Dana of the need to head back to the desert. A tersely worded, unsigned message with the postmark DEV-IL'S CLAW. Thanks to the anonymous typed letter, she was one aspect of Jay's past that he was going to have to deal with—whether he wanted to or not.

Jay tipped his hat to the postmistress as he unlocked the mailbox that had once belonged to Uncle R.C. "Good mornin'. How're you?"

Behind her mannish horn-rimmed glasses, Dorothy Hobarth merely glared by way of greeting. In spite of regulations banning smoking in the tiny federal building, a lit cigarette dangled from her downturned lips, an inch of glowing ash drooping from its business end.

*So who pissed in your cornflakes?* Jay wanted to ask her. But he didn't, since in the unlikely event that he was still here for November's election, he'd need every vote he could muster if he hoped to keep his job. Including the vote of one of Devil's Claw's most famously eccentric characters.

Predictably, Judge Hooks had been gunning for his removal, and Dennis Riggins was arguing that the new sheriff was doing "a damned fine job keepin' the peace," despite the upheaval that had broken out after he took office. But Jay half expected Dennis to withdraw his support any minute, so angry had he been over their visit a few days earlier.

For all his bluster, maybe Dennis considered Jay's decision to question him the hallmark of a professional who wouldn't allow his personal feelings to interfere with duty. Or more likely Dennis simply didn't want Abe Hooks to "win" by running off his choice.

Jay frowned at the empty metal box. "What happened to my uncle's mail?"

He hadn't checked it in days, so he'd expected the usual barrage of farm and ranch catalogs, flyers from various businesses in Pecos, perhaps a statement from one of the utilities. Not even the dead got a pass on either junk mail or their bills.

"That FBI man, Tomlin, showed up with a court order." Beneath the slicked-back gray hair, the grooves in Dorothy's forehead deepened, making her look like a thinner version of her twin. "Snooped in several boxes. Yours included, though they only emptied the old sheriff's."

"They looked in mine, too?"

Dorothy nodded. "I don't like this one damned bit. Ever since that Vanover girl—Angelina, I mean—set foot in this town, it's been nothin' but one outsider after another messin' in our business. Them reporters're bad enough, traipsin' through here with their questions, hoggin' the whole counter over to the Broken Spur. But now we got the goddamned FBI, too. Wish they'd all just stayed where they belong."

"So you would rather the FBI had left us in the dark about Haz-Vestment?"

Tension crackled between them like power arcing from a downed line. But finally she answered, "We got our own way of dealing with thieves and liars here in Rimrock. I figured, growing up with old R.C., you'd have known that."

Devil's Claw's postmistress was as famous for her morosely ominous statements as her artistry with swear words, but even so, her statement prickled at the back of Jay's neck.

"Miz Hobarth, I believe we need to have a serious conversation." He didn't want anyone else interrupting. "But not here."

"If you think I'm settin' foot in that office of yours, you're as crazy as they're sayin'. Probably can't turn around in there without bumping your ass against an FBI bug."

Jay wondered for a moment if she could be right about the feds bugging his office, but decided it was more than likely her paranoia talking. "How about I swing by your place this afternoon, then, once you're off work?"

Dorothy lived in an old trailer home just beyond Dead Horse Run. After last week's storms, flash flooding washed out the track and stranded the postmistress there for two days. When enough neighbors tired of waiting for their mail, a detail was organized to regrade the dirt road for her.

Predictably, she hadn't thanked them with a batch of homemade cookies. Instead she'd asked what the hell had taken the goddamned bunch of them so long.

She considered before nodding. "All right, all right. But leave that mutt of yours at home. My girls would likely rip off his balls and feed 'em to him."

Jay wasn't sure who—or what—Dorothy's "girls" were, but he agreed and gave her an exact time, then warned her to be on the lookout for his SUV. Like nearly everyone in Rimrock County, she was known to keep loaded weapons, one of which had been accidentally discharged when her twin sister had dropped by unannounced. Though the incident had taken place more than two decades earlier, Estelle was still waiting for an apology for the blast that had nearly cost her her right foot.

Besides that, Jay decided it would be damned embarrassing to come back from a war zone only to get his head blown off by someone Wallace laughingly referred to (though never in his mother's presence) as "Uncle Dorothy."

After sorting through and discarding most of the junk mail from his own box, Jay returned to his office, where he found Wallace himself going through the largest side drawer of the desk. This was getting to be a habit for members of the Hooks family.

"Can I help you find something, Deputy?" Jay asked without preamble.

Wallace jerked to attention, his face reddening. "I, uh, I was looking for a file. Uh, my mom said it was missing—this transcript from the community meetings for Haz-Vestment.

The feebs were askin' her about it, and I . . . I thought I'd make sure you hadn't accidentally—"

"Lifted it out of her locked cabinet?" Jay watched how his deputy's color deepened at the question.

Jay went to his own file cabinet and pulled his key ring from his pocket. As he unlocked it he said, "I did borrow it a while back—forgot to tell her. Meant to remind her, too, to be more careful with her own keys. She left 'em sitting on her desk when she went home. . . ."

As Jay's fingers walked the top tabs of file after file, his words trailed off. Frowning, he rechecked before looking up at Wallace, who had closed the open desk drawer.

"It's gone," Jay told him. "The folder's not here."

"You sure that's where you left it?"

Jay nodded. He distinctly remembered the morning he had brought the transcripts back from his place. Estelle hadn't yet been in her office, so he'd unlocked his file cabinet and slipped the manila folder into the front with the intention of returning it to her once she arrived, along with an apology for borrowing it without a word. But at about that time Abe Hooks had burst in ranting that Dennis Riggins had overturned the Broken Spur's trash barrel—when any idiot could see the javelina hoofprints all around it. By the time he had talked the judge out of tossing his archrival in the hoosegow, Jay had forgotten all about the transcript.

"So are you sure *you* locked your file drawer?"

Though Wallace looked smug, Jay could hardly fault him, since he'd made the mistake of criticizing Estelle to her son's face. As Dennis was so fond of saying, *Never get between one Hooks and another.*

"Can't exactly recall it," Jay said, "but I try to make a habit of securing all my evi—"

"What?" Wallace asked when Jay stopped abruptly. Anxiety put a tremor in the deputy's words. "What're you thinkin'?"

"I was just wondering," Jay said, masking his nervousness. "You'd have a copy of those drawer keys, right?"

Wallace blinked at him. "So you think *I* took the file? Why the hell would I do that? I was at that meeting. I don't need any transcript to tell me what went on there. Besides, if I had it, why would I be rooting around your desk drawer looking for it for my mama?"

"That's a damned good question." Unless the file—which Wallace would have been given for the asking—wasn't what he'd been hunting after all. Jay thought of one piece of evidence his deputy had not seen, though they had discussed it in a general way the week before. Had he been looking for Jay's copy—left locked up back at the house—of Angie Vanover's journal? Or was there something else that Wallace hoped to find?

"You aren't looking to throw me in the grease with those federal agents, are you?" Jay asked. "Or maybe looking for something you can use to sway the other commissioners to your daddy's way of thinking?"

Wallace stiffened, his jaw locking and his hazel eyes turning fierce. "*Hell*, no, and screw you for even asking—"

"Come on, Wallace. It's no secret that you wanted this job. No secret that you'll have it if I get myself run off. From what I hear, you could use the money."

"I was completely loyal to R.C., loyal even though I knew damned well that he was . . ." Wallace looked away, cutting himself short as he did so.

"That he was *what*?" Jay demanded, moving into Wallace's space to stare him down. "What have you told the feds about my uncle?"

The deputy shrugged and spit out a sullen, "Nothin'."

"Saving it for the reporters, are you? Or did Tomlin and Petit ask you not to tell me?"

When Wallace's jaw clenched tighter, Jay decided to change tacks. Gesturing toward a chair, he said, "Look, I'm sorry I insulted you. It's been a rough few weeks."

His deputy said nothing, so Jay extended his right hand and looked into the younger man's face. "Apology accepted?"

Wallace shook his hand and warned, "Just don't do that again—accusin' me like I'm some kind of freakin' Riggins. I might've wanted this job, but I'd be a damned liar if I didn't admit I've been glad that all this Haz-Vestment/Vanover mess didn't hit the fan on my watch. Then I'd be the one under the feebs' watchful eye."

Jay wondered how much more Wallace knew but wasn't saying. He gestured toward the peeling box-shaped fridge. "Want a drink?"

"Not unless you got a six-pack stashed in there."

"No way am I keeping alcohol in this office. Not with everybody from my deputy to some damned transcript-napper to a couple of special agents pawin' through my stuff. But if you'll stop by the house later, I'll be sure to set you up right."

Wallace rolled his eyes. "Why? You got some woodwork that needs stainin'? Or is it heavy liftin' this time?"

"Nope. I'm all moved in and settled. That house is as finished as it's gonna get." Since Dana had left town he'd lost whatever enthusiasm he'd been able to muster for the project.

"So this invitation's purely social?" Wallace's brows rose suspiciously. "It has nothing to do with wanting to pick my brain about old R.C.?"

Jay didn't answer, unwilling to insult his deputy a second time.

"You don't need to bust open a bottle for me." Wallace sighed. "He—your uncle R.C.—uh, *entertained* that Piper-Gold bitch a couple times at his house. I figured she was screwin' him, and frankly it pissed me off."

Shrugging, he added, "She was one fine-lookin' woman—haven't seen a set like that since I left New York City. And I, uh, I gotta tell you, I'd hinted more than once I might be open to that sort of visit my own self. Hell, I never knew that she was *married*."

Jay looked at him, disgusted, though he was most disturbed by what Wallace had said about his uncle. Had the old man changed so much after Jay left, or had he always hidden a dark side? Dorothy Hobarth's words reverberated through his thoughts: "*We got our own way of dealing with thieves and liars here in Rimrock. I figured, growing up with old R.C., you'd have known that.*"

"Kinda insultin' that she didn't see as how a deputy could have all that much influence. Even if I am the county judge's son."

"The way you and your dad argue," Jay said, "maybe she didn't figure your good word would cut much ice with him."

"Could be. Or maybe she was into old men. Way I understand it, she turned out to be married to that leather-skinned geezer from the TV." Wallace shuddered. "He had to have twenty years on her at least."

Jay snorted. "Must've been that banana hammock he was wearing drew her to him."

"Only if he was packin' wads of cash down there," Wallace shot back with a grin.

"You said earlier you never saw Goldsmith here in Rimrock. Are you still sure on that count?"

"I'm sure. And if anybody else around here saw a fellow like that, for sure it would've got around."

Jay imagined that was so. He also figured a man like Goldsmith, who had a record of small- and big-time grifting that dated back for decades, would be smart enough to keep out of sight.

Was it possible that jealousy, and not financial motives, had been the catalyst that pushed the scam artist into violence? What if he had caught his wife in bed with Uncle R.C.? Jay imagined the scenario unfolding, pictured the con man shooting R.C., then setting fire to the bed to hide his crime. When Dennis had called to tell Jay what had happened to his uncle, he hadn't spoken of the condition of the body. And Jay, who'd already been coping with more images of violent death than he could handle, hadn't pushed for details.

But it was high time to put that squeamishness behind him, because whether or not he'd known his uncle's darker side, Jay still owed the man a debt. Far too great a debt to leave to the FBI the solution of what might well have been his murder.

A thin sliver of moon was rising when the Hunter saw her, her white hair swinging down past her slim waist. Her bare feet barely skimmed the crystals of the dry lake's surface as she made her way into the dusk-robed desert.

"Angelina?" he asked, though she was too far away to hear him. Though he could barely hear himself over the sudden thunder of his heartbeat.

But she turned nonetheless, showing him a smile so cold and feral it shook him to his soul. Lowering his binoculars, he strained his eyes and muttered, "You're dead. You're dead. I killed you. You can't be . . . Jesus . . ."

Something *was* there, something moving, though it was past the margins of the salt flat. Hands trembling, he once more lifted the field glasses—and laughed at what he saw.

A trio of pronghorn antelope looked up from their browsing, their delicate ears turned in his direction and their slender legs tensing as they watched him for signs of movement. They must have been drawn by the grasses that had sprouted after last week's rain, for they rarely traveled so deep into the desert.

But not so rarely as a woman who had passed beyond death's borders.

The Hunter breathed again and took this transformation as a sign, a sign that if he watched carefully, he would see an opportunity to reverse his losses. Perhaps his plans would lead him to the money Angelina must have hidden elsewhere before his shot took her down.

The authorities had recovered less than fifty thousand, according to his sources. A fraction of the total. A last sting on the ass, but nothing lethal.

Daunted by its bulk, she had to have been moving it in stages, probably beginning before the new sheriff's arrival, when she'd have had ample privacy. Though the storm had clearly interrupted her last attempt, he had to concentrate on finding where she'd hidden all the rest.

There was only one person in the world Angelina might have had the chance to tell about it, and he was watching carefully for that woman to come back within his reach. Once he had her, he would use his skinning knife to find out in short order whether her sister had told her the location of the stolen money.

One way or another, the Hunter was going to get his million from her—as well as his revenge.

# *Chapter Twenty-three*

*Before you trust a man, eat a peck of salt with him.*
—Proverb, anonymous

Jay's Suburban bobbed and wallowed as he followed the otherwise deserted road's power lines into a rutted driveway. He steered between a huge agave's ring of spear-tipped leaves and a hard-luck patch of creosote to park behind Dorothy Hobarth's vintage Jeep. Nearby a single-wide mobile home squatted beneath a freestanding gabled roof that someone had built to keep the trailer from cooking like a TV dinner in the sun. In spite of this, heat rose from every surface, making the air swim.

He gave the horn two short blasts to alert Dorothy to his arrival. After sucking in a breath of cooled air, Jay shut off his engine and climbed out into the heat. People who didn't live here assumed that, without humidity, the summers must be bearable. People who didn't live here should try spending an afternoon inside their ovens and then rethink that opinion.

As Jay approached the peeling brown front door, a few spent yellow flowers dropped exhausted from a sotol's spiky stalk and landed amid the narrow, sharp-toothed leaves below. The loss drew a hum of protest from the assembled blue-black bees, a sound nearly lost to the pulsing drone of the mobile home's swamp cooler and the barking swarm of ill-tempered little dogs inside. He heard small pops as they launched themselves against the inner door with fanatical fervor, their tiny toenails scrabbling against the metal.

Dorothy's "girls," he figured. Maybe she should have warned him about his own balls instead of Max's.

"Cut it out, girls. Settle down," Dorothy told them. But

the riot continued unabated until she finally shouted, "Sit. Hush. *Now*."

The barking stopped as if someone had yanked out the yappers' batteries, and the door opened. Dorothy gestured for him to come in, while beside her three nearly identical fat black-and-white rat terriers sat growling, their lips curled back to show vibrating teeth.

"Nice smiles," he commented as he stepped inside a living room paneled in dark wood. Blinded by the abrupt transition, he waited for his eyes to adjust to the dim light.

"They know how to use 'em, too," Dorothy assured him with what sounded like parental pride. "Now go lie down, girls."

The trio didn't budge but continued to monitor him closely. Probably looking for a sign of weakness.

"Sorry. They don't like men. Don't know where they get that."

Since he didn't want to spend the next week picking fibers from his work pants out of bite wounds, he resisted the temptation to supply the obvious answer.

"Want a beer? Or water?" Dorothy invited.

"Water'd be good, thanks."

After reminding the three dogs, "Stay. Hush," she went into the kitchen, which allowed Jay the opportunity to look around the place. The rust-colored carpeting was dated, but looked clean enough, as did the furnishings and the antique oval mirror that hung from the mounted head of a huge, well-antlered mule deer. A crocheted afghan lay, precisely folded, atop the back of a worn but decent green sofa. A matching chair sat beside a lamp table holding—of all things—a leather-bound edition of the collected works of William Shakespeare. A bookmark sat near the halfway point, and when he looked carefully he saw the wine-red cover was cracked with age and dehydration.

With Dorothy still rattling around in the kitchen, he picked up the heavy book and allowed it to fall open. To his surprise the pages were heavily marked in red ink, with underlines and handwritten exclamations.

The play was *Hamlet*, he saw, and the line most vigorously marked read, *Frailty, thy name is woman.*

*True!* someone, presumably Dorothy, had written, followed by the word, *Why?*

Embarrassed to have intruded on her privacy, he closed the book as she came in with his water. Her gaze lingered on his hand until he removed it from the cover.

"Shakespeare, huh?" he said. "Would've figured you more for private-eye stuff, or maybe Westerns."

She smiled, revealing a yellowed set of teeth. "Been readin' on that one since high school. It's got everythin' you need right there in one spot. Killin', sex stuff, people turnin' on each other. Just like the Good Book."

One of the terriers sprang forward, but she smacked it on the snout and snarled, "Down, Ophelia."

All three dogs dropped, and Jay took the distraction as an opportunity to shift from chitchat to the reason for his visit. As he cracked open the bottle's top, he said, "I want to know what you meant by that remark at the post office. The one about my uncle, and how certain things got handled here in Rimrock County."

She took a swallow from the longneck beer she'd brought for herself before dropping gracelessly into the chair. She didn't invite him, but he took the sofa, though the dogs' growls deepened with his daring.

"No mystery there, Sheriff," Dorothy said flatly. "Only that we freeze folks out when they don't behave. You know, like not speakin' to 'em when we see 'em. Or not helpin' out when they have trouble."

Jay frowned, knowing bullshit when he heard it. "Backing down's not like you. You're known for calling 'em the way you see 'em."

Her mouth tightened, and she put down the beer to clean her glasses on the tail of her federal-blue work shirt.

"You aren't scared of me, are you?" he asked. "Because you don't have to worry—"

She gave a little bark of laughter that had her terriers popping up and yapping. Once she silenced the unholy trio, she shook her head and told him, "I'm scared of no man. It's just . . . you've been away a long time. Probably picked up a few strange ideas."

"I tried to," he admitted before attempting to appease her. "But there's no place in the world like Devil's Claw. In the Dallas PD they've got heads of this, departments of that, and activists and lawyers squalling if you so much as color outside the lines."

"Damn lawyers," she droned. "First day one sets up shop here, I'm packing up my girls and heading into the backcountry."

Despite the growling delivery, terror glittered in her eyes, as dark and sharp as chips of onyx. Jay recognized it instantly, had seen it in the mirror of his apartment after he'd left the hospital.

Was he as irrational as this woman, as in danger of turning into another eccentric desert hermit? Dana's words filled his mind: *"You're far from a lost cause, Jay. There's still time for you to get whatever help you need to put yourself back on track. . . ."*

He cleared his throat, buying a moment to get his head back in the game. "What I'm saying, Dorothy, is that we both know Devil's Claw's run by a different set of rules than your ordinary town. Just the way you operate by a different set of rules than an ordinary woman."

Her lower lip dropped, and behind the horn-rimmed glasses something changed in her eyes in the split second before her gaze fixed onto the TV's blank screen.

He was on the verge of apologizing when she ran her fingers through her graying hair and muttered, "Too bad 'Stelle could never get that."

But Jay didn't want to step into the minefield of the twin sisters' years-long grudge. So once again he tried to steer her back on course. "How'd my uncle run things? I'll need to know to do my job, keep people out here happy the way he did."

She blinked hard, then downed another swig of beer. "He'd just run some of the lowlifes outta town when it was needful, that's all. You know, drug smugglers, men whose women turned up with one too many black eyes or busted lips, and thieves. Goddamn, but that man always hated the kind that feel entitled to whatever they can cart off."

"How'd he manage to get rid of 'em?"

She shrugged. "Him and a few others used to pay a visit, suggest the fella might be happier somewhere else. If he didn't take the hint, an old-fashioned ass-whippin' was in order. And if he squawked too much about that, well . . . Devil's Claw don't have no hydrants, if you get my meanin'."

"They *burned* them out? Set fire to their houses?" Unable to keep still, Jay stood and started pacing. When one of the terriers snarled and made for his leg, he ordered, "*Down*."

The dog wheeled and slunk out of the room, closely followed by the others.

"You've gone and hurt the Weird Sisters' feelings. They'll hold a grudge for sure now."

Jay didn't give a damn about that, not with long-forgotten memories from his teen years rising like the undead. Of an unlucky "fall" that had cost a drunken bully most of his teeth before he slunk out of town. Of a burning bungalow whose flames had lit the night sky, killing one of the two hippie squatters who had lived there. A tragic accident, everyone had called it, though no one had been too sorry to see the dead man's old lady pack their ancient van and go.

Jay's stomach knotted. The uncle he'd looked up to—and belatedly learned to love—had been no more than a whitewashed facade over a dark reality.

"My uncle R.C. *died* in a fire," he reminded Dorothy. "Didn't anyone ever wonder about that, considering? Who were these other men who helped him? After he was hired was Wallace in on it, too?"

She shook her head. "Lord, not that one. That sawed-off little peacock was always too busy starin' into mirrors and workin' on lines for high school plays to pay much attention when he was younger. And then he went off to make a fool of himself in *New York City*."

She pronounced the name with the same contempt hellfire-and-brimstone preachers reserved for sermons featuring Sodom and Gomorrah.

So who would Uncle R.C. have trusted? "Dennis? Or Henry Schlitz—or what about Abe?"

Dorothy's lips pursed, wrinkling around their outer margins. "I only told you what I did because the sheriff was kin to you. And you're the sheriff now, so you ought to know how we handle the likes of these outsiders."

"What about Angie Vanover? Was she 'handled' after making a big fuss at the Haz-Vestment meeting?"

Dorothy shrugged, but behind the glasses malice smoldered in her brown eyes.

"You were part of it," he guessed, thinking her participation would be one way of proving she was just "one of the boys." "You could tell me everything."

"No, I damn well couldn't," she said sharply. "Now it's time for you to leave."

He tried persuading her, only to be met with stony silence.

"We'll talk again later," he assured her before opening the door to leave.

As he started his Suburban, Jay got one last glimpse of the postmistress through the window. Or rather, of the middle finger she used to wave good-bye.

*Friday, July 13, 4:48 P.M.*
*102 Degrees Fahrenheit*

It wasn't lost on Dana that she rolled across the Rimrock County line on the afternoon of Friday the thirteenth. But given how bad her luck had been during her prior visits, she couldn't conceive that the desert had any worse fortune left to hurl in her direction.

She hoped this wasn't merely a failure of imagination on her part.

She had flown into Carlsbad, New Mexico, where she had picked up a rental SUV. Paranoid about being caught out on Rimrock County's rugged roads, she'd swallowed the premium and sprung for a four-wheel-drive model with GPS. She had also rented another satellite phone before leaving Houston, but had stopped short of picking up the elephant gun she'd been daydreaming about with alarming frequency.

But last night's dreams had leaned less toward violence and more toward sex, a sign that her subconscious had picked up on her proximity to Jay. Erotic as the scenes were—including the schmaltziest, where they'd made love as a wild surf crashed around them—each one had gradually twisted into wrongness. At four-twenty this morning she'd awakened trembling and weeping after seeing Angie rising from the depths to point an accusation their way. She shuddered, recalling how her sister's mummified hand dripped with seaweed and—worse yet—most of her face was a black and charred-edged hole.

*It's that letter working on me, that's all,* Dana told herself. Sent to her clinic address and not her home, it had raised goose bumps when she'd read the coffee-stained and crumpled sheet.

*Dear ~~Miss~~ Doc Vanover,*

*Too bad about that little girl. But your sister got what she had coming.*

*Shouldn't have come out here in the first place, stirring up trouble for the father.*

*Only thing that man wants is to forget that time, be left alone. After what he's been ~~threw~~ through, he deserves that much.*

*So a word to the wise. You and yours stay the FUCK clear into the future if you know what's good for you!!!*

The writer was no Hemingway, but the message came through loud and clear. As Dana spotted Devil's Claw on the horizon, her stomach tightened in a delayed reaction to the threat.

Up until this point she had managed to keep from focusing on the danger. Though she hadn't wanted to get either her mother's or the Harrisons' hopes up by giving them the details, she'd concentrated on the fact that the father of Angie's child was somewhere in or around Devil's Claw, and that if she could find him, there still might be a shot at salvaging something—namely Nikki—from this horror. A shot at salvaging something worthwhile from her sister's life.

After counting backward nine months from the child's birth date and cross-matching the dates against her mother's records, Dana had been excited to learn that Angie had been in rehab around that time at a facility in Las Cruces, New Mexico. With a place and time period to work with, Dana felt certain she could track down the man who had fathered Nikki, especially if she could talk Jay into helping.

She couldn't be certain he'd be willing, or that he wouldn't insist on taking the letter to the FBI team now handling the investigation into the Haz-Vestment murders. She might have gone to them herself, except that the last time they'd spoken—in a brief call before the arrival of the letter—Agent Tomlin had informed her that the bureau's investigation was limited in scope. He had neither the time nor the authority to expand it to include what he'd called a "snipe hunt" for the father of the child one of the two victims had given up years before.

Dana worried about keeping what could be relevant evidence to herself, and she felt guilty for lying to her mother, telling her she'd been asked to come back to be reinterviewed about the night of Angie's murder. To ease her conscience she instead focused on the excitement of making contact with a friend Angie had met around that time—a woman with vague memories of Angie "sneaking off" to meet some lover. But Rainbow, as she called herself, had no memory of the man involved—couldn't even say for certain whether he had been another patient or someone who worked at the facility. Since Rainbow had volunteered the fact that she'd been sweating out some "majorly warped" acid flashbacks at the time, Dana was surprised she recalled anything at all from those weeks.

She was also more than a little suspicious that the "memories" were manufactured, a conscious or unconscious attempt to please a grieving sister or simply gain attention. Yet Dana refused to let suspicion stop her, any more than she would allow fear to keep her from making up for the part she'd played in getting Angie killed.

She lifted her foot from the accelerator and coasted as something loped across the road before her. Though the shimmer of rising heat obscured the gray-brown form, its size and movement made her think coyote before it disappeared into the scrub.

Beside her the satellite phone began to ring. Dana considered ignoring it, since the only person with the number was her mother. Had she found out Dana had lied about her reason for leaving Houston? Or was it Jerome calling to say Isabel had taken a high dive off the deep end?

Guilt kicked in, so she answered before the voice mail could pick up. "Everything okay, Mom?"

"Dana . . ."

Fumbling the phone, Dana pulled off onto the road's margin. Rocks crunched beneath the tires, sending a tan snake whipping off toward safety. With an involuntary shudder—more at the voice than the serpent—she picked up the dropped phone and demanded, "How the hell did you manage to charm my mother, of all people, into giving you this number? Do you have any idea how much money she lost on dresses and deposits—not to mention how embarrassed she was to have her daughter dumped the way you—"

"I know, and I'm sorry." Alex sounded like a chastened schoolboy. "It's just . . . I was having cold feet, that's all. I was so confused and . . . Dana, I'm an idiot."

"At last, one thing we can agree on." An ugly desire rocketed to the surface, a need to wound him a fraction of the amount he had hurt her. "My new lover thinks so, too."

There was a long pause before he managed, "I guess I deserved that. But you don't have to make up stories to get me to realize how badly I've screwed things up. If I could do anything to take it back, Day, if I could do anything to fix this . . ."

Instead of relief to hear him groveling, she felt the insult mushrooming inside her. He didn't believe she'd found another lover. Didn't think it possible.

"So what brought you to this conclusion?" she asked coolly. "Figure out you didn't want little Alex clones after all?"

"I figured out I wanted *you*. I want to stand by you through this crisis."

She rolled her eyes and thought, *How freaking noble of him.*

"I . . . I heard about your sister," he added, "and I'm so, so sorry."

She was tempted to agree that yes, he was certainly that. But since her last bit of vitriol had backfired, Dana forced herself to take the high road and to acknowledge what this phone call must have cost the man in pride. "I appreciate that, Alex. And I understand it's natural, after a transition, to have second thoughts. But—"

"Don't say 'but,' Dana. Please don't close the door on what I'm saying. Please don't close the door on us."

She spotted first the dust cloud and then the dark blue pickup heading her way. But it barely registered, so caught up was she in the swirl of her emotions.

"You made me feel like garbage, Alex. Like some broken piece of trash. You humiliated me and then skipped town so you wouldn't have to face people looking at you like you were the biggest jerk in Houston—which, I might add, you were. You even stuck me with returning all the gifts with 'I'm sorry I'm such a pathetic loser' notes."

Notes she'd begun tackling a few days earlier, since putting it off hadn't solved the problem—or gotten rid of all the boxed gifts stacked in her condo's dining room.

"I'm the one who's a pathetic loser," he told her. "And if you give me one more chance, I swear I'll spend every day of my life making it up to you."

As the pickup closed the gap between them, a frisson of alarm skated up her spine. She squinted through her sunglasses, but she honestly couldn't tell if the truck's grille looked familiar. And the sun's glare across the windshield prevented her from seeing inside.

As it neared, the truck slowed.

"I have to go, Alex."

"Just tell me I've got some chance. If you want, I'll fly out there and help you. Your mom said you could use a man looking out for you in that place. I saw it on the news, Day. It's appalling, practically a third-world country—and after everything that's happened—"

"Sorry. No chance at all, but thanks for calling. Gotta run now." Every tiny hair stood on end as Dana switched off the phone and jammed her rental back in gear. What was she *doing*, sitting on the roadside, presenting a target for anyone with a good pair of field glasses—or a rifle scope?

But before she could mash down on the pedal, the pickup's driver's-side window glided downward, giving her a glimpse of a face she had been hoping to avoid.

Heart pummeling her chest wall, she rolled down her own window.

"You're back. Surprised to see that," Bill Navarro said. His sun-creased blue eyes were as flat as his voice.

"Umm, yes. I have a few last things to wrap up." Clearly

she'd offended him the last time they had spoken. She wondered if he still had that enormous pistol of his tucked beneath his front seat.

"Don't mean to intrude or anything, but I was on my way to pick up some supplies in Pecos when I saw this vehicle pulled over. Just wanted to make sure you hadn't overheated. Or broke a belt or something. Hot day like this one, person could expire walkin'. 'Specially a woman not used to the sun."

"My rental's fine, thanks." Dana tried to keep a quaver from her voice but only partially succeeded. "I just stopped to take a phone call."

The disturbing emptiness of his expression made the explanation seem important, to let him know she was connected, in case of an emergency. His gaze lingered on hers for several moments longer before he tipped his hat and nodded.

Both rolled up their windows, but Dana didn't breathe again until Bill continued on his way. Leaving her to wonder why he was heading off toward the New Mexico border instead of south toward Pecos, as he'd claimed.

# *Chapter Twenty-four*

DEVIL'S CLAW, July 13—Area rancher Bo "Weevil" Jenkins, 47, complained to Rimrock County Commissioners that the recently hired sheriff, embattled Jay Eversole, has failed to adequately investigate the deaths of three Angus heifer calves in separate range incidents occurring over the past two months.

"They all had the exact same damage," Jenkins reported. "Missing eyes and lips and parts that I won't mention in a lady's presence. And there was [were] grooves down their flanks, too, like they'd been carved up with a knife."

Sheriff Eversole, 34, dismissed Jenkins's claims that "some weird cult" was responsible and suggested that the damage to the one carcass he was called to examine was consistent with natural predation by the area's coyotes or possibly a mountain lion. After Eversole was called away to respond to another matter, a heated debate broke out regarding his possible "preoccupation" with matters related to the recent salt-dome project murders.

County Judge Abraham "Abe" Hooks, 62, said, "Regardless of any other issues, Rimrock County officials, including whoever holds the office of sheriff, must remain mindful of the welfare of the ranchers who have forged the area's past and will continue to shape its future."

—Front page item,
Pecos Enterprise

It was late afternoon when Jay took the accident report: Hereford bull versus TV news van on the ranch road leading toward the Lost Lake area. No human injuries, but the bull was down and bellowing, and according to a furious Henry Schlitz, the female field reporter was bawling her fool head off.

Just what Jay needed to cap a week already brimful of aggravations: a hysterical reporter and a rancher spitting mad about the loss of his valuable herd sire, which would almost undoubtedly end up as ground beef before the day was out.

After asking Wallace to stand by in the office and letting Estelle know where he was headed, Jay piled into the Suburban with Max, who was back on duty, and raced toward the scene, his hurry due in part to a desire to prevent Henry from making hamburger out of the news crew. Who—the way Jay's luck was running—would probably have a camera rolling with a live link, via satellite.

As he crossed the metal grating of a cattle guard, Jay automatically slowed down and scanned the area for loose stock, as every local had been brought up to do. Outsiders, unfortunately, rarely paid the warning signs much heed. It simply never occurred to most that there were rural areas where the grazing was so sparse that cattle were allowed to freely cross public roads for better forage. Predictably this resulted in periodic collisions, which killed not only cattle but the occasional driver.

Even more predictably, Rimrock County ranchers shed more tears about the former losses than the latter, which they considered a fitting punishment for the stupidity of those behind the wheel. But as Jay approached a trio of familiar pickups—evidently Henry had called in reinforcements—he saw no sign of either the news van or the injured bull, only miles of desert and a twinkling, pale expanse that bore witness to what had once been a salt lake.

No van, no beef, no accident, he realized. Only a different brand of trouble, one he ought to have seen coming.

He parked behind a truck he recognized as Abe Hooks's before striding toward the assembled men. Their arms were crossed and their expressions hard beneath the shadows of the hats' brims. Beside him Max growled softly as Jay recognized Carl Navarro standing at Abe's right, and Henry Schlitz, who took the left flank. Jay fought both the urge to grimace and the impulse to rest his right hand on his Colt's butt.

They appeared to be unarmed, though Jay didn't have to look to know that each truck's gun rack would hold at least one rifle. He tried to remember that these were the same men who had welcomed him back to Rimrock County, that each had worked his ass off rebuilding the burned house he now called home. In the past few weeks they'd drunk his beer and swapped old stories, commiserated over the "hard luck" of Haz-Vestment as if they were old friends.

But what had passed for camaraderie had abruptly ended after the report of Jay's past troubles had hit the news. Abe Hooks had been the most outspoken, openly suggesting that the county had mistakenly "acted on sentiment instead of good sense" in choosing R.C. Eversole's nephew to complete the dead man's term of office. So it didn't surprise Jay when the county judge stepped forward to signal his intention to speak for the group.

Rather than allowing Hooks to start or asking pointless questions about the so-called accident, Jay snatched the offensive. "You three had better have a damned good explanation. Otherwise don't think I won't charge you with filing a false report. You could get six months for that, along with a stiff fine."

The threat hung in the heated air. Though all three knew the odds of Jay's getting a conviction in this county ranged from long to laughable, they also knew he could throw their asses in jail and drag his heels with the proceedings, creating an ordeal as inconvenient as it would be embarrassing.

Abe raised his palms as if in supplication. "There's no need to get excited, Jay. We just wanted a private word, that's all."

"Well, you damned sure could've picked a cooler spot for it." But not one less likely to be witnessed.

"The last few weeks have been pretty rough." Carl

scrubbed his hand over whiskers silvered with an early frost of gray.

"Rough on everybody." Peering from behind his round-rimmed glasses, Henry Schlitz crossed thick arms over a barrel chest. "And 'specially on you, what with them federal agents runnin' you off your own case and that bullshit story playin' on the TV—like anybody gives a rat's ass that you pounded some towel-headed asshole."

Though Jay had heard worse slurs during his time overseas, he winced. The need to dehumanize the enemy was the common denominator in all conflicts—one that had damned sure left a bad taste in his mouth.

"That was a mistake," he said, "and not one that I'm proud of."

"The thing is," Abe Hooks said, "that's the kind of mistake that opens the county up to a chance of getting sued. If something happens, that is."

"Nothing else's going to happen," Jay said, as if Angie Vanover's dead body hadn't been making nightly appearances in his recent Baghdad nightmares. More disturbing still had been his dream of making love to Dana, only to find her flesh drying like a mummy's and peeling away with every touch, and her eyes staring, opaquely white, from her dead face. Though it had left him exhausted and irritable, he'd spent the better part of the past few nights pacing and downing strong black coffee, for fear that the images would return to haunt him if he lay down again.

"I know what's real and what isn't," he said, willing it to be so, "and what's appropriate."

"Do you?" Abe asked. "Because the way I see it, screwing a missing woman's sister *isn't*. And it looks even worse since Angelina's turned up dead."

Jay stared, wondering if Abe really did know about him and Dana. Or was he just guessing, bluffing in the hope that the new sheriff would simply admit the impropriety and leave town? Jay was pretty sure that Wallace had figured out where Dana had spent the night after she'd left the adobe. Had he bitched about it to the old man the way he'd bitched to Jay about R.C.'s supposed affair with Miriam Piper-Gold?

It seemed plausible—one more step in his deputy's campaign to snatch the top job—but Jay wasn't so certain. Because for all of Wallace's flaws, he had his own notions, like his mother, of the right and wrong of any situation. And if he was to be believed, those opinions had prevented him from reporting the last sheriff's affair with Miriam Piper-Gold.

"I do my job," Jay told them, "and I do it without prejudice. Whatever you think of anything that might or might not happen during my off time."

"What we were thinking"—Abe's voice was as icy as the sun was blistering—"is that you might be happier somewhere else."

The statement hit Jay with the precision of a laser-guided smart bomb. So these three were among those who had worked with his uncle to root out Rimrock's "undesirables." And now they had decided he was one of them.

"And if I refuse, what's next? The ass-whipping, or will you jump straight to the arson? Because I promise you, not even all three of you together want to meet me on a dark night. And I wouldn't recommend you get within ten miles of my place with gasoline and matches either. I'd hate to accidentally leave Estelle a widow, or your Mae-Anna, Henry." He zeroed in on Carl. "Just like I'd hate to get on the wrong side of Bill's temper. But I'd do it."

His words had an immediate effect. Henry turned pale behind his round-rimmed glasses, and Carl's normally placid demeanor fell away, revealing a barely controlled fury. Abe's upper lip curled back, reminding Jay of Dorothy Hobarth's "smiling" terriers. Clearly they understood that someone had been talking. One of their own, or maybe even one of those assembled.

"You might want to look for someplace else," Abe said,

"that's all. Of course, we didn't mean to threaten, if that's how you took it."

"That's a damned good thing," Jay told them as the dog trotted over to investigate a rustling near the base of a tarbush, "because even in the unlikely event that you got the drop on me, two dead Sheriff Eversoles would raise a lot of eyebrows. From the FBI to the Texas Rangers, this county—and your asses—would come under the kind of scrutiny that'd turn this past week into a pleasant memory from a bygone day. You get my meaning?"

Abe shrugged and flashed a creased version of his son's sullen look. "You're mistaken. But we heard you loud and clear."

Jay stood sweating in the heat as all three filed past his Suburban on the way to their respective pickups. As he turned to catch Max's collar and—with some difficulty—drag the dog from the spot where he was industriously digging, doors clunked shut and engines started. Jay looked up in time to see the gritty sand from each truck swirl up behind it, and watched until three dust devils danced on the horizon's heat waves like harbingers of hell.

So it should have come as no surprise, when he was driving home some ten minutes later, that his right front tire failed as he hit a bump.

The click of Dana's low-heeled sandals echoed off the marble of the Rimrock County courthouse. The sound conspired with the musty smell to resurrect the memory of the first day she had arrived here, exactly three weeks earlier. Only that day she'd had no idea of what she was walking into.

Anxiety pulsed inside her, for this time she knew that the venom found in so many of the desert's creatures extended to its human inhabitants as well. Or at least to some of them, she thought, recalling Mamie Lockett's kindness and the way Estelle Hooks had stepped up to help her after Angie's death. And Dana would never forget how Jay had touched her, the words he'd used to chip away at her self-loathing.

*But all that's over now*, she warned herself, unable to bear the thought of walking away from that beautiful mirage again. He had been right when he'd told her there could be no future for them. Just as she'd been right to say that it was time for her to grow up and take care of what she must.

And right now she was here to take care of her niece and not her own needs. Jay was a means to that end and nothing more. But before she could convince him to help her with her search, she had to find him. And she figured that Deputy Wallace Hooks, whose pickup sat beside the empty spot where Jay most often parked, would be the best person to tell her where his boss was.

She paused to read the ABSOLUTELY NO PRESS—THIS MEANS YOU sign taped to the door, and smiled to see that some frustrated reporter had scrawled, *Read Up on the First Amendment, Sheriff! This Means* You!

She tapped on the door before poking her head inside. Wallace, who was on the telephone, took his feet off of his boss's desk and gave her a wait-a-minute gesture, irritation spreading across his handsome features like a rash.

He might have been politely respectful after Angie's death, but Dana suspected that his manners formed no more than the thinnest veneer over his disdain for her sister's lifestyle choices. She recalled Jay telling her that Wallace had found Angie drunk once, not long before her disappearance. Though her journal had made no mention of a time she'd fallen off the wagon, Dana had seen such lapses in the past and knew that they weren't pretty. Her sister could have easily earned the deputy's contempt that day, and then some.

"I'll check it out as soon as I can," Wallace said into the telephone. "And I'll be sure to pass on your message to Eversole as soon as I hear from him."

The deputy cradled the old-fashioned black telephone's receiver, then came around the desk and gestured to a chair. "I hadn't heard anything about you coming back."

Instead of sitting she offered him her hand, and for the first time realized that at five-six she was a shade taller than he, in spite of his boot heels. His mouth gave an irritated twitch, as if he noticed, too, and didn't like it. What *was* it with men and their obsession with height?

"I thought I was finished here, too," she explained. "But something else has come up, and I'd like to discuss it with the sheriff. Do you know if he's out on a call somewhere? I tried him a little bit ago, but I wasn't able to reach him."

Even as she said it, a disturbing thought struck her, provoked in part by the sight of Wallace sitting at the sheriff's desk, comfortable enough to rest his feet there. Could Jay have been dismissed already? She recalled how adamant he'd been about refusing to accept help from the government in the form of either disability or treatment. What on earth would he do if he'd lost his job? And how would she figure out the identity of Nikki's father without his help?

"You know, I haven't been able to get hold of him either the last little while," Wallace told him. "Don't know where he's off to at the moment."

His gaze skated toward the window. Was he looking for a sign of Jay's SUV or avoiding her eyes to hide his own dishonesty?

After glancing back at her, he shrugged. "I'll try again in a few minutes. He must be driving through a dead spot. Plenty of those around here."

Her discomfort deepened, though she couldn't pinpoint why. "So he *is* on duty?" she pressed.

Once more Wallace shrugged. And once more he avoided her gaze. "Could be. Him and me, we're all there is here, when it comes to law enforcement. We don't punch a time clock. We just work whenever things need doing, any hour of the day or night. Lots of hours lately. But sometimes we have to squeeze in our own personal business, too. And the sheriff doesn't always check in with me about his visits to his women and the like."

So that was it, she realized. Wallace somehow knew that she and Jay had been together, and the deputy was jealous. No, that couldn't be it, for he'd never seemed the slightest bit interested in her as a woman. More likely he disapproved of the relationship for other reasons. Maybe he considered it a conflict of interest on Jay's part.

She could have assured Wallace she had no intention of falling into Jay's bed again—or onto his kitchen table, she thought regretfully. But she wasn't about to either confirm his suspicions or acknowledge his ridiculous attempt to make her jealous.

She leaned over the desk and picked up a message pad, then jotted, *Jay, I'm back in town. Please call me*, along with the number of her new satellite phone, once she had fished it from her purse. Glancing up at Wallace, she said, "I'd appreciate it if you'd see that he gets this message."

"Sure thing," he told her, but his eyes said the note would be confetti before she left the building.

"I need to run down some paperwork for the insurance," she said, though it aggravated her to have to whip up a lie to gain his cooperation. "They're insisting I get their stupid papers signed by both the sheriff and whichever FBI agent's in charge of the investigation."

Wallace's expression eased, making her wish she'd dreamed up this story sooner. Almost everyone, at some point, had to jump through insurance company hoops to settle a claim. And everyone, to a person, hated it.

"I'm kind of in a hurry," she added. "I need to get back to my practice as soon as possible."

"Well, the feebs—I mean, the special agents—have left town already. I'm pretty sure they're back in Albuquerque. Still workin' on our case, they tell me." Wallace surprised her with a cocky grin and added, "If we don't beat 'em to an answer."

"You think you'll find out who . . . who shot my sister?" she asked.

"Nothing would make me happier than to be the one to do that, Dr. Vanover," he said with what sounded like genuine conviction. "Nothing in this world."

As Dana left the office, she suspected Wallace's desire was based less on a need for justice than a desire to boost his own career. Clearly he had no love for the federal agents who had taken over the investigation, but she'd be willing to bet that the person he most hoped to outshine was Jay himself.

Wondering where to go from there, Dana made a pit stop in the ladies' room. On her way out, she came face-to-face with Rimrock County's tax collector.

"Why, isn't this a surprise?" Estelle Hooks asked, looking as pleased as, say, the average kidney-stone patient.

"Hello, Mrs. Hooks." Dana decided to trot out her lie sooner rather than later this time. "I'm afraid my insurance company's made me come back for some signatures—they're giving me a tough time about the damage to my car."

"After all you and your family have been through!" Estelle exclaimed. "Is there any way that I can help you?"

"Not unless you can tell me where Sheriff Eversole might be."

"He told me he was heading to an accident scene," Estelle said. "No one's hurt, but there's a bull down over on Ranch-to-Market Road One-seventy."

Dana squinted, thinking. "Is that the one I passed on the way to the adobe where my sister lived?"

Estelle nodded. "He said it was about a mile and a half west of that junction."

"Do you think it would be okay if I drove out there? I'd, ah, I'd like to get this business taken care of as soon as possible. So I can get back to my mother."

A slight nod attested to Estelle's approval. "I don't see why not. But maybe you should ask Wallace first if Jay is still there. He should have called in by now."

"Jay would tell him?"

"Oh, yes. He always lets my boy know where he's going and when he might be back, and Wallace does the same. Otherwise, if there was trouble, one of them could get stuck—and in this heat, that's no small matter."

"I see." Apprehension tightened Dana's stomach. So Wallace *had* been lying to her from the start. Was it only out of casual malice, or was there some darker reason that Jay was incommunicado? "I'll be sure to check in with him, then. Thank you, Mrs. Hooks."

A smile bloomed beneath the beehive hairdo. "I hope you won't mind if I call you Dana. And please, it's Estelle, dear."

# Chapter Twenty-five

*The strange thing is, he told me about this place back in rehab,*
*told me about its empty spaces and its defeated dwellings baking*
*in the desert sun.*
*He claimed he hated it, that he was never going back there.*
*Yet who should I run into within days of my arrival*
*but the man who now pretends he doesn't know me?*

*For old times' sake, I pretend right back,*
*even though it hurts like hell and has me wishing for a bottle or a*
*little magic dust.*
*For anything to take the edge off of the memories . . .*
*But I'm finished running.*
*Finished, so I breathe in a deep draft of desert*
*and turn back to my loom.*

—February 3 (loose page)
Angie's sobriety journal
(recovered following close of investigation near Red Wolf
Wildcatters bunkhouse)

"Looks like it's just you and me, dog," Jay told Max, who stood panting in the shade of the Suburban.

Still jittery from his struggle to slow his vehicle without rolling over, Jay glared down at his cell phone's tiny screen. Not a single bar, of course—though he'd had service earlier, at the location of the alleged accident. And Estelle and Wallace either didn't hear his radio or wouldn't answer.

If he stuck around this county, Jay vowed to convince the commissioners to fund the cost of a foolproof satellite communications system. His second order of business, he determined, would be finding someone other than a damned Hooks to watch his back. Or better yet, he'd throw in with

Dennis to run the whole bunch of them right out of Rimrock.

*If* Dennis was still speaking to him . . .

Jay pulled a gallon jug from the emergency stash he kept in the rear of the Suburban. The water was warm and tasted of plastic, but it would keep both him and Max going through the tire change.

One way or another, Jay would have ended up doing the work himself, but he'd feel better if he could have told someone his location. Though the sun rested on the horizon, the rock and soil cast off a day's worth of hellish heat, enough that Jay would bet his next cold beer that it remained close to one hundred in the shade.

Even a healthy man could die exerting himself in such conditions. He took another drink and looked to see what had happened to his tire. The roads were so rough around here, he expected to see a spot where a sharp stone had torn through the shoulder. He was surprised to find that neither rock nor rut had caused this flat.

Instead he spotted a slash across the sidewall. Though it would be impossible to prove, it looked to him as if someone had sliced through it with something sharp. A hunting knife, perhaps, and the idea nudged a memory. Something he'd discussed with the agent from Monahans, Steve Petit. What the hell had it been? Tough to remember at the moment, with both heat and fatigue pressing in on him. Hard to concentrate . . . He shook his head in an attempt to clear it.

As Jay twisted off each frozen lug nut and laid it in his upturned hat's crown, he cursed Hooks, Navarro, and Schlitz under his breath. Angry that he'd turned the tables on their attempt to intimidate him, one of them must have done the damage while Jay was busy with the dog. Probably they'd simply meant to cause him the aggravation of a tire change, but because the cutter had been in a hurry the tire hadn't immediately gone flat. Instead, after heating and bumping

along the dusty road, it had suddenly given up the ghost—
in a manner that could have gotten Jay killed if he'd been
driving any faster.

As he pulled off the ruined tire, a different sort of remains came to mind. Miriam Piper-Gold's, to be specific, or
whatever her real name was.

The medical examiner had made note of the strips of
flesh removed from the body's thighs and abdomen. *That*
was what Jay had been trying to remember—Petit's suggestion that the victim might have been tortured antemortem
by someone with a sharp knife.

And Jay recalled something else as well. The three young
heifers Weevil Jenkins thought had been slaughtered by
some weird cult, or maybe aliens. Though Jay hadn't been
around when the first two animals died, he remembered
hearing his uncle complain about Weevil's passion for con-
spiracy theories. Besides, the third carcass hadn't looked
particularly suspicious. Sometimes predators brought down
an animal and got scared off by something before they finished eating. Other times they killed when they were too
full to do more than nibble on the tenderest portions.

He'd assumed that was all it had been, but when he put it
into the larger context, Jay now wondered if the pattern
might be part of something more disturbing. Something
that involved one of the three men who had lured him to
the desert far from town before slashing his tires.

Dana's best-laid plans went awry when Mrs. Lockett flagged
her down on her way out of the courthouse.

"Come in and have some cheesecake," she'd invited. "I
made some for the children, but they haven't come in from
playing yet. I could have sworn . . . I think . . . I don't know."

The old woman turned around, the hem of her thin
housedress fluttering around her bony knees. Shielding her
eyes from the sun, she asked, "Where *are* those children off

to? Trudy-Lynn, Nestor, Sheldon! Come inside—it's getting dark."

She looked so bereft in her confusion, so vulnerable and hopeless, that Dana had gone in and had a slice of cheesecake with her. She'd intended to stay only long enough to set the old woman happily adrift among her memories, but when Dana caught sight of a huge—and undoubtedly painful—abscess on the orange tom's neck, she decided to do a makeshift procedure to alleviate the old cat's suffering.

"You know, if you'd have this boy neutered he wouldn't get into so many catfights," she suggested, "or leave the neighborhood knee-deep in kittens, either."

Mrs. Lockett tittered and waved off the suggestion. "But Eleanor's a girl cat. I named her after Mrs. Roosevelt."

"And a fine name it is, too," Dana told her, *except* this *Eleanor has testes.*

"Why, just this winter she had the cutest babies," Mrs. Lockett claimed. "The children had such fun playing with them."

The woman was too disoriented to be left alone, Dana decided, before she went to the old woman's telephone, where she kept a list of numbers posted.

By the time her son Nestor arrived and Dana was able to leave—along with the part-time preacher's thanks and a bag of fresh-baked muffins—the desert sky was strewn with stars, and her rental was the sole remaining vehicle outside the courthouse.

"Well, damn," she muttered, then decided that now that it was dark, Jay was likely to be home. She tried his number, only to get voice mail. Might as well stop by his place anyway and show him the letter she'd received before she headed to the hotel room she'd reserved in Pecos.

*If I need the room.*

No sooner had the thought slipped through than Dana slapped it down. She wasn't putting Jay's job at further risk;

nor was she climbing back aboard the emotional roller coaster—not for a few scant hours' pleasure.

She groaned, fighting the memory of his hands and mouth on her heated flesh. *No more hiding from reality,* she told herself. *It's time to face the facts and get on with your life.*

As she headed out of town, she concentrated on that thought. As if, with repetition, she could force it to sink in.

With each long scrape of blade against steel, the knife sang, a whirring note that rose to a bright *zing.*

A thrill of sheer excitement set the Hunter's pulse to racing as its music blended with the memory of the spatter of hot blood and the bawling of the half-grown heifers. For Angelina's sister had been lured by his letter like a doe drawn to a feeder on the first day of open season.

Or the first *night,* better yet. Because after the last failure he had made some preparations, one of which involved a very special addition to his arsenal: night-vision field glasses that would allow him to track her in the dark with the efficiency of a big lion. He expected to use them, but not quite yet.

Not when he could easily follow the taillights as they receded on a lonely road heading out of town. He wasn't certain where Dana Vanover thought she was going.

But he damned sure knew where she would end up before this night was through.

# Chapter Twenty-six

*One of the strangest plants of the desert, the night-blooming cereus is a member of the cactus family that resembles nothing more than a dead bush most of the year. It is rarely seen in the wild because of its inconspicuousness. But for one midsummer's night each year, its exquisitely scented flower opens as night falls, then closes forever with the first rays of the morning sun.*

— "Night-Blooming Cereus," entry by A.R. Royo, from www.DesertUSA.com

"I'll head out tonight—should be down your way first thing in the morning," Special Agent Steve Petit told Jay over the phone. "Meanwhile, I wouldn't advise you to go out on any calls alone."

Jay put his coffee down on the kitchen counter and rubbed his burning eyes. "Sure, Petit. I'll be puttin' *all* our vast reserves on babysitting duty."

"No need for sarcasm. It'd put me to a lot of trouble if I had to investigate your murder along with all the rest."

*All the rest*, Jay knew, included both his and the agent's presumption that R.C. Eversole, too, had met with foul play, later disguised by the fire that ravaged his home. With the forensic evidence—including the body—gone forever, their only chance to prove his murder would be to solve both the Vanover and the Piper-Gold killings. Once a suspect or suspects were in custody, there was always a chance of wringing out a confession, particularly if the investigators played one conspirator against the other.

"Hell knows, I wouldn't want to put the FBI to any *inconvenience*," Jay said. "But I don't imagine Hooks and his buddies will come after me. For one thing, they know I'll be watching for 'em. And they'll have to figure I'll pass their names on to you and Tomlin."

"Speaking of which, I'll get started on those background checks tonight," Petit promised. "See if the FBI computers turn up anything of interest on the three of them."

"While you're at it," Jay suggested as he stifled a yawn, "maybe you ought to take a look at Bill Navarro. He's supposed to have had some kind of a drug thing a few years back. And Wallace Hooks, too, just to see. Since he *is* Abe Hooks's son."

"Your deputy? His record's clean, as far as we've learned, other than the one marijuana-possession charge back in New York City about ten years ago."

Jay wasn't terribly surprised. As an aspiring actor just out of high school, Hooks had probably been trying to fit in with a faster-living crowd. Or the arrest had simply been a part of what he sardonically referred to as his "wild oats" years.

"There's nothing since then," Petit told him. "And nothing suspicious about his banking situation, either."

"You dug into Wallace's *accounts*?" Annoyance flared at the invasion of privacy.

"Well, yeah, we ran him earlier, when we checked on . . . We had to check out both the local—"

"There's no need to play coy," Jay said. "I've long since figured you've thoroughly investigated me. Can't say I'm thrilled about it, but I would've done the same in your shoes."

Petit hesitated before saying, "You should know that my partner, Agent Tomlin . . . he's not so sure you're fit for office. Not after the incident in Dallas, and what we read in the VA file on your . . . medical history."

Jay waited for his irritation to flash over before responding, "Then I guess it's a lucky thing for me he's not a county commissioner in these parts. So what about you? You think I'm a few fries short of a Happy Meal, too?"

"Hell, I think *anybody* who'd willingly live in that one-horse hellhole fits that description." The chip-toothed grin came through loud and clear, though Jay couldn't see it. "But I don't suppose you're any worse than most."

"Comin' from you, that means a whole lot . . . *Cowboy.*" Jay smiled as he tossed off Petit's hated nickname.

Petit lobbed back a good-natured but anatomically impossible suggestion before sobering. "Seriously, Eversole. If I didn't think you were okay, would I have faxed you copies of those extra journal pages we recovered inside the wall of that adobe? Especially with my partner suggestin' we keep you out of the loop."

"So why'd you do it, then?"

"Thought maybe all that crazy journal stuff would make more sense to you than us, since you've been digging into this mess longer. So did it?"

As Jay considered the two entries, something important hovered at the edge of his awareness. But when he tried to bring it into focus, his tired brain lost its grip.

"Let me get back to you on that," he said. "I need to take another look."

"Meanwhile," Petit told him, "you need to stay alive till I can get there. These people may be playing for a lot more than we thought. We've uncovered evidence that Miriam Piper-Gold took a hell of a lot more than fifty K with her to grease some wheels in Rimrock County."

"How much?"

"As far as we've determined, it could've been a million, maybe more."

When he'd served as a cop in Dallas, Jay had been in on million-dollar drug busts. Though his salary as a public servant was far humbler, he had grown used to seeing ads touting multimillion-dollar mansions and reading reports of million-dollar-plus contracts for everyone from CEOs to sports stars. After a while the number had begun to lose its magic.

But here in Rimrock County a million dollars was still considered an obscene amount of money. A wild dream that the average man could work his whole life without approaching.

Even a man as grounded as his uncle might have his head turned by such a figure. And a man like Abe Hooks, who had scrambled for decades to build a two-bit empire, might be willing to kill to secure a portion of that sum.

"Way we hear it," Petit said, "Roman Goldsmith was mad as hell when he discovered the amount. Wish we could get a line on that slick son of a bitch, but so far, nothing. I'm starting to think he's fled the country."

"If he isn't dead."

"Could be. But those kind of scum suckers are like roaches. No matter what else has gone down, we usually find 'em hiding under some rock. Eventually, anyway."

"So where do you go from here?"

"Believe it or not we've been talking to some people at *America's Most Wanted*. Walsh lives to go after assholes who fleece little old ladies out of their life savings. Besides, Goldsmith's starting to look good for his wife's death, and with the public's interest in the Salt Maiden mummy and the tie-in to an adorable cancer kid, this story has more than enough sex appeal to turn over his particular rock."

"Amen to that," Jay said. Amen to anything that would bring justice for his uncle, as well as Dana's wayward sister. And if the program motivated more Americans to volunteer as marrow donors, maybe a match would turn up to save Nikki Harrison.

Though he knew it was a long shot, he fervently hoped so, not only for the child's sake, but for Dana's. With all the losses she had suffered, he couldn't imagine how she'd shoulder the death of Angie's daughter, too. Once more he found himself wondering how Dana was doing, where she was this minute, and what she was thinking. A craving to call her nearly bowled him over, though he knew damned well that hearing her voice would only inflame his need to have her for his own.

And even if she didn't turn him down flat, the last thing

she needed in her life was a wreck of a West Texas sheriff—even one who loved her beyond all reason.

The thought blindsided him, but he couldn't deny it. Like a damned fool he'd gone and fallen for a woman he could never have. The thought deepened the shadow threatening to overwhelm him—a darkness he was no longer certain he wanted to keep fighting.

"Still there, Eversole?" asked Petit.

Jay apologized and told him, "Too much on my mind, I guess." And with the lack of sleep, his focus was unraveling more quickly by the minute.

As they ended the call, Jay tried Wallace's cell number. Though the deputy should have been available, his number rang a few times before going to voice mail.

"I need a word with you." Jay wondered if he was crazy to trust his deputy to choose duty over his own father. Despite Petit's assurance that he and his partner believed Wallace to be clean, Jay relied on the same instinct he'd once used to tell whether the men and women of his unit could be trusted and how far they might be pushed. But if he was wrong, the consequences could be disastrous, maybe even fatal. "Tonight, if possible. Had some trouble earlier that I need to get your take on. Could be something ugly brewing—and you might want to check on your aunt Dorothy tonight. Just drive by her place and keep an eye out for anything suspicious."

*You mean* Uncle *Dorothy?* Jay could almost hear his deputy asking with a wicked grin on his face.

If there had been a call he needed Wallace to take, Jay would have tried the Hooks's house phone number, too. But since either Abe or Estelle might answer, Jay decided he could wait for Wallace to check his messages, something he was normally conscientious about doing.

Jay laid his phone down on the kitchen counter and took out a filter before making a fresh pot of coffee to help him stay alert for any signs of trouble. He sat, intending only to wait out its gurgling cycle, but before he knew what hit him his head nodded toward his chest.

He wasn't sure how much time had passed when he jerked back to wakefulness at the sound of Max's toenails clicking on the tiled floor. Rising from the bar stool, Jay followed the shepherd into the living room, where the animal growled softly, as if he heard something—or someone—outside.

Jay felt the rise of his own hackles. Could Petit have been right about the threat to him? Were Hooks, Navarro, and Schlitz out there, skulking around with guns and gasoline cans in the hope of getting to him before he mentioned their names to outsiders?

With a muscle twitching at the side of his mouth, Jay switched off the lights and drew his handgun. He moved through the house with deliberate stealth, his senses straining for an unfamiliar sound, a smell, a flicker or vibration. . . .

For anything to warn him that the enemy he and his troops had come to ferret out of this apartment complex awaited him with their machine guns and their homemade bombs, with the Molotov cocktails that cooked men alive inside their body armor.

*That isn't right*, some distant recess of his tired brain whispered. But adrenaline overrode the warning as he heard an engine rumble to a stop outside.

That would be the hajjis, pulling their bomb-rigged vehicle close to the building's base—where they meant to detonate it while Jay's men searched the floors above.

If he didn't somehow stop the bombers they'd bring down the building, killing not only U.S. soldiers but innocent civilians. And hadn't he seen children playing in the streets around this building—those beautiful Baghdad children with their dark eyes and mischievous laughter?

No way could he let them die. He refused to be too late again.

Jay crept to the back door and pushed past the K-9, who was wagging his docked tail and whining to get outside.

"Stay in here," Jay whispered to him as he heard the vehicle door shut. "Stay."

If the enemy heard barking he would set off the car bomb for certain. Jay's only chance was to slip up on the combatant holding the remote detonator and take him out before he could accomplish his murderous mission. The enemy was probably moving a safe distance from the blast zone, but Jay knew from hard experience that such terrorists were willing to die to carry out their missions—not only willing, but eager, thanks to the martyrs' glories they believed awaited them in heaven.

*This* isn't *right*. More adamant this time, the warning shook him. But when Jay caught sight of the silhouetted figure, he crept forward, propelled by the fearful power of his waking dream.

The house had gone dark, though Dana was almost certain she had seen a window lit as she'd pulled in. Had he already gone to bed?

She walked a few steps from her vehicle, her hunger to see him—to touch him, if she were being honest with herself—warring with the oppressive blackness closing in around her. With no sign of the moon, the only illumination was the ancient star shine from ten million distant suns.

Far too distant for her eyes to make out anything but a few deeper patches of shadow around her. It was too dark, in fact, to move any farther from her vehicle for fear of tripping on a rock or catching a leg on yet another spiny plant.

A distant yowl shattered the stillness, what sounded like a woman in excruciating pain. With a yelp catching in her throat, Dana lurched back toward the safety of her rental before recalling something she'd read about the area's mountain lions—how their cries were often mistaken for the sounds of women screaming.

But coupled with the darkness, the eerie sound had left her shaken, reminded her that the desert held a host of creatures at home with the night. Unnerved, she decided to make the drive to Pecos and hole up in her brightly lit motel room. Tomorrow she would come back—by the light of day.

Resolved, she reached for the SUV's door handle. But a split second before she could retreat to safety something slammed against her, cracking both her head and shoulder hard against unyielding glass and metal.

# *Chapter Twenty-seven*

*Out here, so many forgotten lives have withered and died quietly
beneath the burning sun.
People ought to take time to remember, to pay tribute.
They should decorate the grave sites and stand at attention
in the kind of old-fashioned yearly ceremonies that bore the hell
out of the living.*

*Because it's the ones who came before who got us where we are
now.
Not the cheap flash and empty promises of modern charlatans.
That's the shit that should be buried and forgotten
before it destroys the last traces of people who got by on sweat
and tears
and even more grit than came flying at them on the desert wind.*
—Undated entry
Angie's sobriety journal
(recovered July 10, interior wall, Webb adobe)

Dana dropped onto her hands and knees and screamed as a
hard kick glanced off her rib cage. Desperate to escape the
onslaught, she rolled beneath the SUV and fought to draw
breath.

Pain exploded in her left side, outstripping the throbbing
of her right shoulder and her skull where she had struck the
rental. Bruised ribs at least, maybe even cracked, she thought
as she struggled to piece together what was happening.

The mountain lion she'd heard—could it have been
closer than she'd realized? Terror—the primal fear of being
torn apart and eaten—had her curling into a fetal ball,
whimpering and shaking. But it was no lion that grasped her
ankle in an iron grip and started pulling, no lion shouting
foreign words in a hoarse voice.

Kicking out, she screamed again, despite the agony it cost her. She dug her nails into the gravel, frantic to keep from being dragged out into the open, where she surely would be murdered.

Yet she was losing ground, inch by hard-fought inch.

"Jay," she shouted, praying he would hear her from the house. "*Jay!* Help me. Please, Jay."

From inside she heard Max's desperate barking. Surely Jay would hear that—surely he would come to save her.

A second hand grasped her belt, above her backside, and just that quickly she was yanked out and flipped over. Strong legs straddled her, and before she could react something hard and metal was jammed beneath her chin.

"Don't move—don't you fucking move or I'll blow your goddamned head off," her attacker snarled before saying something else she couldn't understand.

But Dana had already gone limp in her terror—stunned to recognize the voice of the man who meant to kill her.

"Jay, Jay, please stop," the terrorist begged him.

Urgent as it was that he should keep his focus, it threw him how she kept repeating his first name in the most American of accents. Maybe she'd been educated in the States, as rare as that was in a woman. But how could she know who he was? Had some traitor hajji, an informant in the U.S. Army's employ, passed on such intelligence to enemy combatants?

"It's me, Jay. Me—it's *Dana*," she wept.

Her last word sliced through to the bone, shattering the nightmare that had gripped him. But instead of waking tangled in his sweat-soaked sheets, he found himself straddling a sobbing female, his hand clenching a gun jammed into the tender flesh beneath her jaw.

"*Dana.*" With a shout of horror, he jumped off her and tossed aside his weapon as if it burned his hand. "I thought you were a—"

As he leaned forward to scoop her into his arms, she shrank away and cried out, "Don't. Don't touch me. Don't . . . you . . . ever, ever touch me."

"Dana, I'm so sorry. I never meant to—"

"You're insane—you know that?" Her voice receded as she crawled away. "You could've . . . you would have killed me."

"I never would have hurt—" He stopped himself, confusion spinning through him. He might never have lifted a finger to harm Dana, but it had not been Dana he'd been fighting. Not in his mind. The same mind that had betrayed him back in a suburban theater.

The VA doctors and the Dallas PD shrink, his superiors and Special Agent Tomlin—even Abe Hooks—were all right: Jay *wasn't* fit for duty. Wasn't safe to have a weapon. Or to be near a woman, either.

"I was back at the house sleeping. And I heard . . . I thought you were . . . God, Dana, I'm so sorry. Please believe me." He pressed both hands to his temples, his back bent against the weight of his regret. He never should have come back from his tour. Never should have come home, unharmed, when family men—*his* men—had not. Tears streaming down his face, he understood he had to stop this. But first he had to see to Dana, had to make her understand.

She stood and opened the door of the SUV, and for the first time he could see her, hunched, with her left hand holding her ribs. "You . . . you've *got* to get help."

He stood to face her, raising his palms in supplication. "I know I do. I *know*. But we have to take care of you now. You're hurt. I . . . I *hurt* you, Dana."

It echoed through his mind, her body thumping hard against the SUV, and he felt himself kicking her and dragging her screaming from beneath the vehicle. "I'm so, so sorry. . . ."

"I know, Jay. You don't have to keep saying it."

He heard her terror give way to something more like sorrow: the pity a veterinarian felt for a crazed animal that needed to be put down. A landslide of shame and horror buried him.

"You need . . . you're going to need a doctor. Or a hospital more likely." She reached out as if to touch him, but at the last moment she shook her head and let her hand drop. "I'm sorry. I can't do this. But I-I wish you all the best."

"Dana. Please. Please don't leave like this. I'm awake now. I know you; I swear it."

When he moved closer she tried to pull the door closed. But he caught it first, prevented it from shutting.

"I'd do anything to make this up to you," he said. "Please let me. I-I love you, Dana."

She pulled her key out of her purse, then tried three times before jamming it into the ignition and starting the engine. "I'm sorry, Jay. I really am. But please don't make this any harder."

The hopelessness in her expression forced him to look away.

"I know this is it for us," he told her. "I-I understand what I've done. But could I call you anyway? To make sure you're all right? And to try to explain what happened?"

"I know what happened, Jay. And . . . I think I understand it. I'll . . . I'll be all right, I promise. Just as soon as I get clear of Devil's Claw."

Jay wanted to beg, to drop down on his knees and plead for real forgiveness. But he knew it wouldn't make a difference. Besides, it would be wrong to attempt to bind her to him with pity.

"I'm sorry, Dana," he repeated.

She looked him in the eyes, her own still damp and red. "I believe you," she said, just before he closed the door.

He stepped back from her SUV and watched her leave. Then he turned away and headed for his kitchen, where he hurled a full pot of hot coffee against the freshly painted wall.

\*     \*     \*

Making his own spike strip hadn't been that difficult. The Hunter had merely pounded some nails he'd found through an old fence rail.

He hadn't known for certain he would need it, especially after seeing Dana's vehicle turn into Eversole's driveway. But as he'd settled in to watch he'd been reassured that he had one more contingency covered.

Later would come the call guaranteed to draw the sheriff from his home. Leaving Dana Vanover alone, his for the taking.

Except something had gone badly wrong between the lovers. The Hunter heard the ruckus from the place where he'd pulled off the road outside the ranch gate. First the hunting cat's cry, and then—in the direction of the ranch house—the authentic screams of a woman, followed by a man's voice that rolled like thunder through the darkness.

The Hunter had no clue what could have happened, but for his part he was grateful for the warning the noise gave him. Warning enough to drag the strip of nails across the drive's end just moments before Dana Vanover's SUV rolled across it.

# *Chapter Twenty-eight*

Hey, sis,

Sorry I didn't call you back. Haven't felt too much like talking lately.

John packed up his things and moved out—went to stay at his brother's place (you remember Kyle, the divorced jerk who thinks he's the second coming of Hugh Hefner?) in Midtown. John said this has been coming for a long time, that he's just been waiting for things to "run their course with Nikki" so he could get away from all this and re-member what it was to laugh and live and maybe even have a sex life. He sounded as shallow and selfish as Kyle when he said it, but in spite of that I could see the pain and desperation in my husband's eyes. And I could see I've lost him—even though when this all started, we swore to each other we wouldn't be one of those couples who let a child's ill-ness wreck them.

I swear, every time I think my heart has shattered, something like this comes along to grind the broken pieces underfoot. But I can't run away like he has. I can't do anything except be here for my daughter—because I'm all that she has left.

And she's everything that I have, too. God help us both.
> —E-mail message from Laurie Harrison

As she approached the gate, Dana felt a hard bump, fol-lowed by the *flump-flump* of a flat tire, probably the left front. *Not now*, she wanted to scream.

With her body shaking and every breath an agony, she decided to continue. Who cared if she wrecked the rental's wheel?

But it quickly became apparent that whatever she had hit had taken out not one tire but two. There was no way she could make Pecos driving with that kind of damage.

And even if she had two spares, there was no way she could change a tire in her present condition. Closing her eyes, she swore at the realization that the only sensible thing to do would be to walk back to Jay's. But this time she'd be sure to warn him by phone that she was coming.

She grimaced as their shouted conversation replayed itself through her mind. She could still feel the muzzle of the pistol jammed beneath her jaw and her terror as he'd kicked her while shouting in what might have been Arabic.

Almost as disturbing was the memory of her reaction. When he'd awakened from whatever madness gripped him, there had been no mistaking the regret in his voice or the depth of his despair. Yet she had rejected his attempts to help her, had virtually ignored his explanation. Worse still, she'd called him insane, when she knew that was the one thing he feared most.

"Oh, Jay," she whispered to the darkness.

After putting the SUV in park, she climbed down from the vehicle with the intention of checking out the damage and seeing what she'd hit before she phoned him. She moved forward, her head bent to take a look.

This time there was an instant's warning in the crunch of stone beneath a heavy foot, a noisy exhalation, rough and hot where it fell against her ear. She leaped forward, reacting on pure instinct, turned to protect her injured left side, and ran blindly past the rear quarter panel toward the safety of the darkness.

How could Jay have possibly gotten here so quickly, unless he'd run after her when she'd left? And how could she have been so wrong in believing his violent episode was over?

She tried to scream his name, thinking she might once more jar him out of his hallucination. But it was all she could do to keep moving as agony pulsed across her left side and set off fireworks in her vision.

She wanted to throw herself to the ground, to collapse and fold her arms around her throbbing rib cage. But she heard him closing in behind her, knew instinctively that if she went down he'd be on her, and that this time she couldn't find the breath to stop him.

But neither could she find breath to keep moving. The fireworks intensified, exploding across her vision as pain and lack of oxygen sent her stumbling to her knees.

Hard on her heels, Jay's shin caught her hip. When she dropped he went flying over the top of her, smacking the ground with a grunt that sent a sick chill arcing through her.

Because it *wasn't* Jay. She wasn't certain how she knew, whether it was the size of the body that brushed past her or the timbre of his exclamation, but she knew to her marrow that this was no lover she might waken with a word.

Fresh adrenaline ripped through her, giving her strength to clamber to her feet—and tearing a scream from her when she was tackled from behind.

Jay had brought a flashlight outside to find his discarded weapon, with defeat slowing his steps and Max following close beside him, nervous in the way that dogs got after an owner's outburst.

Jay scratched the dog behind the ears and said, "It's nothing you did, buddy. Maybe your next owner will be less screwed up."

He would have to see to it. Maybe talk Dennis into giving Max a home. The man could use a good dog since that big golden hound he used to ride around with—Annie, Jay remembered—had died years before and Dennis hadn't been able to bring himself to replace her.

But if not Dennis, Jay would find someone. Someone good with animals. His heart spasmed as he thought of Dana. Dana, whom he loved but hadn't been able to keep himself from hurting.

"You . . . you've got to get help," she had told him. As if what he had could be cured with drugs or therapy. As if his life could be reshaped into something safe and useful. Something worth a damn to him or anyone around him.

Maybe Weevil Jenkins would give the dog a good home. Jay could tell him Max was trained to guard stock against aliens. Jay chuffed a laugh as joyless as his mood.

Something banged from the direction of the road. Max barked, his body stiffening as he bounced on his front legs. Jay grabbed the shepherd's collar, not wanting him to run off and tangle with some animal—or maybe the three men Jay had been expecting.

He shushed the dog and stood there, straining his ears for any other noise as Max pulled, hackles raised, and growled deep in his chest.

Jay had just about convinced himself that it was nothing— or more likely a band of foraging javelinas rattling the gate—when another sound carried on the night air: the sound of a car or truck door opening.

Wild pigs didn't show up in pickups, but Hooks and his friends might have.

"You sons of bitches," he muttered under his breath, and resumed his hunt for his weapon. This time he moved with far more determination than he had earlier, slowed only by Max's struggle to escape.

"It's okay," Jay whispered to the shepherd—then turned to where his light's beam caught the brushed-stainless-steel finish of his .45. The same gun that had come damn close to killing Dana.

He froze midreach, his stomach knotting at the thought of touching it. And then he heard a scream of terror—a scream that could only be a woman's.

His thoughts flew to Dana, so determined to get away from him and on to Pecos. Something must have stopped her—or *someone* who'd been caught on his way to burn Jay out.

Max tore free to disappear into the darkness. All hesitation vanished, Jay grabbed his gun and did the same.

He might not be so certain that his own life was worth saving, but he had no such doubts when it came to Dana's.

His beam bobbed and jerked as he ran. Though the light might alert whoever was out there that he was coming, his instincts roared the message that speed counted for far more than stealth. Besides that, Max, who had pulled far ahead of him, was barking furiously, providing one hell of a diversion.

Soon Jay spotted lights ahead: headlights pointed toward the road, taillights gleaming like a pair of red eyes, and the dimmer illumination from the dome light, where the SUV's driver's-side door had been left open. The same SUV that Dana had been driving, but he couldn't see her inside or anywhere around.

He slowed, listening for something beyond his own panting progress, trying to discern which direction Max had taken. The dog's barking, off somewhere to his left, had turned to an aggressive snarl, and he heard someone—he was certain it was Dana—shrieking, "No, don't!"

And then a crack that split the darkness, the ringing thunder of a gunshot, followed by a feminine cry of pain and a furious, "You *bastard!*"

But Max had abruptly fallen silent, leaving only what sounded like a human struggle from the direction of the road.

Jay shunted aside the wave of emotion bearing down on him, switched off his light, and barreled forward. He had nearly reached the road when he heard a vehicle's door slam shut, followed by the sound of an engine as it cranked to life. Panic blasted through him—was Dana's attacker taking her away?

Horrified, Jay burst out into the road, gun raised in the direction of the unseen engine. He was blinded as the driver flipped on the high-beam headlights, but he heard the growl of the fast-approaching motor bearing down on him.

Leaping out of its path he twisted his body, desperate to

take out the driver. But before he could pull the trigger he was struck by two things.

The first was a terrifying recognition.

And the second was the bumper as it caught his left leg and sent him spinning through the air.

# *Chapter Twenty-nine*

*For he shall be like the heath in the desert, and shall not see when good cometh; but shall inhabit the parched places in the wilderness, in a salt land and not inhabited.*

—Jeremiah 17:6
The Holy Bible (King James version)

The Hunter backed the truck a few feet so he could pull around the writhing form instead of running over it. He wasn't certain why he did this, since Jay had never been anything but an unwelcome complication in his life, one last burden dumped on him by his useless younger brother—the brother who had somehow pushed past him and claimed every opportunity . . . including the one woman R.C. Eversole had wanted for his own.

"No—no. We can't just *leave* him," Dana cried.

The Hunter turned a fierce gaze on her, but she didn't shrink back, despite the way he'd bloodied her face. Tougher than she looked, this one—maybe even tougher than her sister.

And she was right as well. He couldn't leave the new sheriff. Better to disarm and take him instead of leaving him to recover and shoot after them or call for help.

Besides, despite their argument Dana clearly cared for Jay. The Hunter reasoned that he could use that to his advantage.

He pointed his handgun at her chest. "You move from that spot, I'll kill him. And then I'll flay the flesh off that body of yours inch by fucking inch. You hear me?"

She nodded, eyes glazing over with fresh terror, so he bailed out and walked around to where Jay was already crawling toward the pistol knocked from his hand.

The Hunter kicked it out of range and said, "On your feet. Now."

Jay didn't rise, but he looked up, his face a mask of horror. Head shaking, he squinted against the headlights' glare and said, "No, this . . . this can't be right. This *can't be*. You aren't—"

"You never should've come back here. Can't imagine what the hell you were thinking." A sign of weakness that the boy had taken the chance for escape he'd been given and had blown it. A sign that, like a sick bull or an injured buck, his nephew—*her* son—needed culling. Before, he wouldn't have allowed himself to see it. But the desert and the long hunt for Angie had burned away all sentiment to leave behind only the stark truth.

"What's . . . what's *wrong* with you?" Pushing himself onto hands and knees, Jay asked, "What in God's name *happened* to make you—"

"Something that should've damned well happened years ago. Something I should have goddamned well *demanded*, except I was always taking care of someone else's messes—"

As Jay grabbed for his ankles, the Hunter stepped back out of range and kicked the sheriff sharply in the temple.

He felt only the dimmest echo of remorse as his nephew dropped face-first into the dust.

Dana flew at the stranger, her raised hands clutching the metal flashlight she had found behind the pickup's front seat. Though she ran at him from behind, some sound must have given her away, for he whirled to face her, his pistol at the ready.

"The last thing you want," he warned her, "is to get to be more trouble than you're worth."

She froze, as chilled by his deadly calm as his untroubled expression. He was a tall man, strongly built for all that he was past his prime. Early sixties, she guessed, judging from the lines that creased his weathered face and the heavy, silvered stubble, but as filthy as he was she could be off as much as ten years in her guess. From his long-sleeved work shirt to his hat, boots, and trousers to his skin, the man was caked with thick dust, and he was rank with body odor, as if he'd gone a long while without bathing. As if he had been living rough, the way Angie had been when Dana found her.

But one item that he carried stood out: a pair of small black binoculars, relatively clean and unscratched, dangled from a strap around his neck. Strange-looking binoculars. But it was his thin face that drew most of her attention.

She had never seen him before in her life, though something about him was sickeningly familiar. Some resemblance . . . or had she caught a glimpse of him on that terrible night when he'd pursued her in the desert darkness, the night he'd shot her sister? Seen him and forgotten, after everything that happened?

"Put the flashlight down," he ordered.

When she did not move fast enough to suit him, he turned his gun to aim at Jay's back, which slowly rose and fell. Or did she only imagine he was breathing?

"Putting it down," she assured her captor as she squatted to set the flashlight on the ground beside her. But instead of waiting for another order, she dropped to her knees and crawled to Jay, desperate to reassure herself that he was still alive.

"Jay," she whispered as she shook his shoulder. "Jay, please, can you hear me?"

Though he didn't budge, one of his eyes looked up at her before sliding shut again.

Brief as it was, that glimpse of blue eye superimposed itself over the coldly cruel face she had just gazed into.

And in a moment of sickening clarity, she understood why it had seemed familiar. The man who had hurt Jay must be R.C. Eversole, his uncle. The uncle who had supposedly burned to death in his bed months before. The same uncle who had accepted bribes and carried on some sort of sick affair with Angie.

Dana shook with a desire to beat her fists against her sister's killer. But she wanted out of this, too, and good sense warned her that if she went off on him—or gave him any indication that she knew who he was—this maniac would shoot her with the same deliberate calm he'd used to take down the nephew he'd helped raise.

The older man squatted across from her. "Help me get him in the cab, unless you'd rather that we left the body. . . ."

He bared yellowed teeth and added, "Then you and I can continue the festivities all on our own."

His words floated between them, so detached from all emotion that she shuddered, for the first time fearing other possibilities than death.

"I'll help," she said, and did, though the effort made her blink back tears against the pain of her injured side.

With a groan Jay roused enough to stagger to his widely separated feet. Leaning forward, he braced his hands on the fronts of his thighs and vomited.

Wincing, Dana laid her hand on his back and noticed the already purpling lump rising at his temple.

"Come on. Shake it off." His uncle grasped Jay's arm and started pulling. "Now, in the truck, both of you. We're going for a ride."

"R.C.?" Jay grunted. "But how could . . . how can you be alive? Am I . . . seeing . . . ?"

"Just shut up and get in." R.C. opened the pickup's passenger door and hoisted Jay inside, where he immediately pitched sideways and went limp.

Dana reached forward to try to help him, but the older man hooked an arm around her waist and dragged her backward before using his body to pin hers against the truck's side, behind the open door.

"No." Despite the pain it cost her, she fought to free herself, then jerked back an elbow to catch him hard in the midsection.

"Goddammit, I . . . have had . . . enough of your shit."

With every burst of speech he crushed up against her harder, and she felt her arm wrenched backward before she felt something cinch up hard against her wrist. Before she could form the thought *handcuffs*, he'd pulled back the other arm as well and tightened the second plastic zip tie.

Then he spun her roughly toward him and deliberately holstered his pistol. Before she could wonder if that could be good news, he pulled a long and wicked-looking knife to take its place.

Her mouth went talc-dry at the sight.

"Now you're gonna tell me," he said. "Where'd your sister hide the money she took from me?"

Dana was shaking so hard she could barely keep her legs from buckling. She couldn't think—and didn't understand what he was asking.

"Money?"

He pressed the blade's tip beneath the hollow under her throat. "I honed it just for you. It's sharp enough to glide straight to your backbone with just the slightest bit of pressure."

She shook her head. "I don't know."

"I'm very good at cutting. Well practiced, you could say."

This couldn't be happening. Couldn't be real. What did she have to do to wake up from this nightmare? "I don't understand what you want."

"My money," he said as he dragged the knife lower, first one inch, then another.

She felt its cool bite, thin and bright with pain. Felt it catch the neckline of her T-shirt and start to slice it downward.

"My money," he continued. "The money I've had coming all these damned years. The money that bitch took from me and hid someplace in this desert."

"I . . . I heard they found that. Ja . . . no, the FBI did," she amended, not wanting the crazed man to kill his nephew on the spot. "They found it by the house where you lived."

Alarm pulsed through her as she realized her mistake. In her terror she had given away that she knew who he was. He *couldn't* let her live now. The blade slipped several inches lower, scoring not only fabric but the skin beneath it. A high-pitched keening rose from the back of Dana's throat, seemingly disconnected from her will.

"Shut up," he said. "Before I jam this knife so far up between your legs you taste steel."

Her eyes rolled back, and for a moment everything went black. But all too soon he was leaning over her, hauling her roughly to her feet and slapping her.

"Where," he demanded, "did your sister hide the rest?"

"I . . . I don't know! She didn't tell me. Didn't have the chance to say anything before you . . . before she was shot."

"Goddammit, don't you understand? I will slice you to pieces if you don't tell me." He pulled the blade away and ran a thick tongue along the flat of it, closing his eyes as if her blood were some rare vintage. "And I guaran-fuckin'-tee you I'll enjoy it more than you will."

Her stomach lurched in revulsion. "But I *can't*. I don't know anything about it."

Eversole jerked a nod toward the truck's cab. "Or maybe you'd like watching me skin him first."

Dana felt her world shift on its axis, felt the blackness of her terror slide away to be replaced by bloodred fury. This man had murdered Angie, and he meant to kill her even more horribly. Whether he'd been driven insane by months of chasing Angie through the desert or something had snapped in him before that, R.C. Eversole was so far gone he was willing to carve up the only living member of his family in an insane bid to recover the money he'd squeezed out of Haz-Vestment.

All this over money.

She lowered her head and glared up at him. "All right. Then I'll tell you."

An unholy light blazed in his blue eyes. It was the last thing she saw before she dropped her head and rammed it upward, smashing hard against his face.

The Angie shaking Jay awake was the young woman from the old family photos, with full waves cascading over her shoulders. Scented with yucca blossoms, the blond ends tickled his cheek, and he looked up to see that in contrast to her fair hair, her eyes were deep and brown—and brimming with the fiery passion that would ultimately lead to her death.

At the moment, though, they burned with fury. "*So are you just going to lie there like a goddamned lump? Can't you hear him? He's killing her. Get your worthless fuzz-stormtrooper ass out there and do something about it. You know what you have to tell him—I did everything but leave you a fucking road map; can't you see that?*"

He saw now that Angie wore a black abaya, that her finger was poised over the detonator button. Sneering at him, she asked, "*Or are you ready to see someone else you care about get blown away on your watch?*"

When he jerked forward to stop her, the splitting pain of his head jarred him awake. And he *did* hear something outside the truck's open door, a desperate struggle playing out in grunts that sounded more animal than human. Adrenaline flashed through his veins, giving him the strength to push himself upright. Without waiting for the black dots to clear from his vision, Jay slid down from the seat and staggered toward the noise.

When he could see he froze in horror, blinking at the vision of his uncle—his *dead* uncle—over Dana, a hunting knife above her stomach, which he'd bared by slitting her shirt open. A thin line of blood marked where his blade had been drawn across the surface of her skin as well. Dana lay trembling on her back, her eyes flared and her pale lips parted—too scared to budge, or even scream.

"Make another move," R.C. glanced up to tell him, "and I will gladly gut her like a deer."

His words sounded strange, as if he were speaking through a mouthful of marbles, and his jaw hung slightly open.

"I don't," Dana whispered, "have any idea where that money is."

"Then I don't," R.C. told her as he raised the knife, "have the slightest use for you alive."

Just as Angie had had no use for money.

"Wait!" Jay's mind snapped to the last of her recovered journal entries—to the message she *had* left him.

"I *know*," he said. "I know where the rest is. And we can take you there right now. We won't give you any trouble."

R.C. stared at him, considering. "I *deserve* that money. I deserve my chance before it's too late. And I can goddamned well assure you that I'm not gonna waste it."

Jay scarcely recognized the man. It was as if someone had hollowed out his uncle and now looked at him through the empty eyeholes. Someone thoroughly undone by bitterness and greed.

"You won't need the knife," Jay assured him calmly. "We'll help you. I swear it."

He extended his right hand in an offer to pull R.C. to his feet. Anything to get him farther from slicing into Dana— as he had surely sliced up the woman who had bribed him. And Jenkins's heifers—had the animals served as some sick substitute to help ease his frustration while he played a murderous game of cat and mouse with Angie?

R.C. switched the knife to his left hand and pulled his sidearm from its holster. Rising slowly, he kept the SIG-Sauer's muzzle facing Jay.

"Get back inside the truck," R.C. ordered.

Jay reached past him to help Dana.

"Leave her," R.C. told him. "We can't take her. Woman fights like a goddamned hellcat. But we can keep the money between us, in the family."

Jay heard her death sentence in his uncle's voice, so he quickly moved between them. She reached up to take his hand, her gaze latching onto his as comprehension passed between them.

And something more as well, a possibility Jay would die to preserve.

"I'm not going anywhere without her," Jay said. "And before you threaten me, too, you might want to think about the implications of killing the only person with a clue where Angie hid that money. Unless you want to spend the rest of your days stuck right here in Rimrock County, driving that old hunting truck and stewing in your own filth while that money rots where Angie hid it."

As he leveled the threat he heard a sound off in the darkness, a dead woman's disembodied laughter.

Or maybe it was his dog, Max, whimpering in pain.

# Chapter Thirty

*Two nights ago the work was not enough, and neither was the desert—not with everything that's happened racing through my mind.*

*After a while the quiet got to me, along with endless grime and lousy food—and that freaking scorpion I stepped on didn't help things. So I piled into my heap and went looking for a place I'd spotted a while back—found it, too, a bunkhouse where the land's rapists sometimes put up workers. Pried off the lock and broke in, and damned if I didn't find what I most wanted but least needed— a full bottle of mescal stashed under one bunk's mattress.*

*I never really meant to drink it. I thought I'd take it back to my squat and keep it hidden, a little rainy-day insurance in case I ever really bottomed out. A trophy of sorts, the proof (eighty proof!) that I was strong enough to keep my ass on the straight and narrow.*

*But halfway home there was this huge clunk from the engine, and that was all she wrote. . . . For what seemed like seventeen years I sat atop the cooling hood with hooch in hand, the seal unbroken.*

*Then all of a fucking sudden I was introducing myself to the drowned worm on the bottom. I don't remember much about what happened after that.*

—Undated entry (loose page)
Angie's sobriety journal
(recovered July 10, interior wall, Webb adobe)

*Saturday, July 14, 12:37 A.M.*
*84 Degrees Fahrenheit*
*Forecast High: 99 Degrees*

As R.C. came around the front end after putting them both inside the truck's cab, Dana whispered, "Have you really figured out where Angie hid the money?" It had occurred to her that Jay might be lying, trying to buy time, as he'd been when he had fallen to his knees, requiring his uncle's assistance to get back inside the pickup. And Dana also had the queasy feeling that their captor would cut them both to pieces once he figured out he'd been deceived.

Jay looked directly into her eyes. "Maybe I've got no business asking at this point, but will you trust me, Dana? Will you trust me with your life?"

There was an intensity in his gaze that sliced straight through her doubt and terror, a brand of confidence that resurrected her own courage. This was a man who had survived both domestic criminals and terrorists abroad, a man who, she had learned in a follow-up news report, had been decorated for valor on the field of combat. She had to think of that and not the brutality his earlier flashback had unleashed.

"Yes," she told him after only the slightest hesitation.

As the driver's-side door opened, Jay reached across her to the passenger-door handle.

"Then run like hell," he ordered, and gave her a firm push outside.

Unprepared and off balance with her hands bound behind her, Dana nearly tumbled down face-first. But the panic blasting through her somehow kept her on her feet— that and the terrifying cacophony behind her. Male shouts erupted, followed by the crack of gunfire, shot after shot shattering the still night.

She ran despite the pain in her side, ran knowing that death could catch her from behind as it had caught her sister. Dana darted around dark clumps that snatched at the fluttering remnants of her shirt, then staggered when she banged against an old fencepost, but there was no going back now that she'd committed to this course.

Or had been committed by Jay's quick thinking and his

courage. Perhaps his sacrifice as well, for she no longer heard the two men struggling, heard nothing but the echo of the blasts.

*He can't be dead, can't be dead, can't be . . .* The thought repeated endlessly, a prayer cast to the heavens.

A prayer that reverberated with the memory of what Jay had told her when she'd left in tears. *"I'd do anything to make this up to you."*

Even get himself killed in an attempt to save her.

A second round of shots began, and though she'd zig-zagged her way through darkness, she heard a rock crack all too near her, followed by what sounded like a bullet rattling through the scrub brush.

*Shooter's closing in—he sees me,* instinct warned her. Without slowing she turned to look behind her, half expecting to spot a flashlight following her flight.

Instead she glimpsed a second set of headlights on the road. Still about a half mile distant, the other vehicle was fast approaching.

Was help coming, or would it be some accomplice of R.C.'s? Before she could decide whether to head back toward the road or keep running farther from it, she tripped again when her foot hooked beneath a stick of some sort.

Without her hands to break her fall, Dana came down fast, her head and upper body slamming against soil as hard as concrete. With the impact, the desert's blackness rose up to hood her like an executioner.

Jay first felt the vibration of the engine and the bumping of the pickup as it jounced along the rough road. Pain followed, an agony that threatened to split his head wide-open. When he lifted his fingers to wipe blood from his eyes, the effort left him groaning, and each bump made him want to vomit.

The urge subsided as the pickup slowed, then stopped.

"I think we lost 'em—whoever the hell that was."

Jay looked up toward the sound. Only then did he realize his lower body was crumpled awkwardly on the passenger-side floorboards, while his arms, head, and shoulders leaned atop the truck's seat.

His uncle sneered down in his direction. "You're god-damned lucky you're alive after that stunt you pulled. Didn't mean to hit you so hard—sure as hell didn't want to kill you before we get my money—but there's no way in the world I was lettin' you get hold of my gun."

That was it, Jay realized. The barrel of the gun had struck the side of his head not far from the spot where he'd been kicked. He'd been fighting to give Dana a chance to get away. But what had happened? Had she made it, or had he simply gotten her . . . ?

"I'm sorry about your woman. She *was* your woman, wasn't she?"

Jay's heart stuttered. He couldn't answer, couldn't even speak.

"It wasn't a half-bad plan," R.C. conceded. "Probably would've worked except for these."

He touched the binoculars hanging from a strap around his neck. "After last time I got myself a pair with night vision."

Jay wondered how, since R.C. was presumed dead. Had he risked driving somewhere, or was someone helping him? But what did it matter if R.C. had shot Dana? What did anything matter now that she was dead?

"*Why?*" It was the only question he could manage without completely breaking down. And even that one syllable reverberated with his anguish.

"Why what? Why'd I go for the brass ring after all these years of living on the straight and narrow?" The older man's laugh turned to a dry cough. "After I found out what those assholes were up to I was out to help myself, that's all, to squeeze out every drop I could. Everything I've been missing out on all these years. Good times with a gorgeous woman—

maybe a little hula girl of my own, once that money set me up to retire in paradise."

*Hell's the closest you'll get, old man.* Because Jay was going to kill him, one way or another, for what he'd done to Dana.

As if he'd read Jay's mind, R.C.'s voice softened as he said, "You did her a favor, son. It ended a lot quicker this way. I just walked straight up behind her after she had fallen and *bam*, it was all over. She never even saw it coming."

Jay's eyes squeezed shut, and he burst out, "*Jesus*," without knowing if he meant it as a prayer for her soul or a curse. If he hadn't shoved her out the door, if he hadn't taken the decision from her, maybe he could have bought a better chance for her somewhere down the line. Maybe . . .

"Even if I'd held her for ransom, like I thought I might," R.C. said, "well . . . there's no way I could've ever let her go."

Some measure of Jay's soul crumbled into ash, one last, resilient stronghold still untouched by either crime or war. That *bastard*—did R.C. think he was *consoling* him?

"So where's that money?" His uncle's voice went hard and flat.

Jay hesitated before saying, "It's at the old Webb place out by Lost Lake."

The place where he would make R.C. pay for Dana, for all the pain he'd caused.

"The Webb place?" his uncle asked. "Angelina's squat? But I've searched high and low through that adobe."

"You had to know exactly where to look."

"Where?"

"You think I'm going to tell you so you can cut my throat and dump my body?" Jay figured that was what R.C. planned for later anyway. But things weren't going to happen the way his uncle intended.

As R.C. continued driving, Jay envisioned himself over-powering the older man, caving in his head with a rock, then jumping back inside the truck and returning to his ranch to find Dana. She would be alive, unhurt—would tell him she'd simply dropped down and played possum, that his uncle had only grazed her slightly or, better yet, had missed her altogether.

She would look into his eyes and say that she loved him, that she had since they'd first met. And he'd wrap both arms around her and beg her to let him stay with her forever.

And when she told him yes, *yes*, her answer would drive the darkness from him and leave him worthy of the gift.

# *Chapter Thirty-one*

*"How far would you go?" I used to ask my little sister.*

*She was annoying sometimes but basically a good kid. A kid who saw the limits and understood the consequences if she pushed too far past them.*

*However far she dared to go, I always had to take it two steps past that. Because the things I cared about mattered so much to me, I was willing to do anything. Even to die for them, if that was what it took.*

*—Entry seven, March 12*
*Angie's sobriety journal*

From her hiding place in the brush, Dana watched the driver climb down from his pickup. Though R.C. Eversole appeared to have been scared off by this truck's approaching headlights, she leaned her face against Max's fur and trembled, waiting like some feral, wounded creature who would bolt if she could only find the strength.

An image of Angie flickered like a hologram through her mind. Angie, who had somehow been driven to this same desperate position—or had chosen it in an attempt to make a difference. Perhaps all the time she'd spent as a troubled teen in wilderness programs had convinced her she could survive the desert long-term. Or maybe she'd started with the thought of hiding only a short time before getting out and finding help, but exposure, injury, or illness had left her too weak or confused to do much more than run from place to place.

Dana knew she would never last as long. She had to risk asking for help, not only for herself but for Jay—if he remained alive to save. Which was why she crept in closer, anxious to identify the man opening the ranch gate, praying she would recognize someone she could trust.

His height marked him as a Hooks, and the dark hair narrowed it down to Wallace. Heart pounding, she decided she had no other choice except to put her faith in him. She crept forward with Max limping close beside her, hobbling on three good legs. "Deputy? Deputy, please help me—"

Her voice rose to a shrill cry as Wallace drew his gun on her and shouted, "Hands up. Keep 'em high."

"I can't," she called. "They're tied behind me."

"Don't you take one step closer. Just turn around so I can see those hands."

She did as he asked and said, "It's me—Dana Vanover. Please don't shoot."

"Dr. Vanover?" Gravel crunched as he approached her. "Who did this to you? You're hurt—God."

"Forget that—I'll be all right." She turned to face him, unwilling to waste time. "Jay needs your help, *now*."

If his uncle hadn't already murdered him for daring to help her . . . Panic shafted through her at the thought.

"The sheriff? Where is he? What happened?"

"It was his uncle. He attacked us. Or attacked me, and Jay tried to interve—"

"His *uncle*? How could . . . *Where*? Where is this person?"

"I don't know," she cried. "He took off with Jay in an old pickup when he saw your lights coming. We have to catch up to them."

"But R.C.'s *dead*. I . . . I was there when we pulled the body out of his bed. And the medical examiner said . . . Look, there's no way it could've been him. Jay called me earlier, left a message that he needed to talk. He sounded worried, and I overheard something at ho— Well, I overheard some stuff I wasn't meant to, and I thought there might be trouble, so I headed straight on over. Maybe I'm too late—"

"That body wasn't the sheriff's. Jay recognized his uncle.

I'm sure of it." She couldn't bear to spend another moment arguing. "We have to go. Before it's too late."

"All right, but let me cut your hands free so you can get up in the truck." He pulled some kind of utility tool from a pouch attached to his uniform belt.

She felt a hard tug and heard plastic snap before her shoulders loosened. "Thanks."

She opened the truck door and coaxed Max into jumping onto the passenger-side floor area before she climbed inside. By the time she fastened her seat belt, Wallace was behind the wheel.

He put the truck in gear, but hesitated. "If it wasn't R.C. in that bed, then who—"

She wanted to rage at him, *Who the hell cares?* But apparently the deputy needed answers to convince him she wasn't leading him astray. "Isn't the FBI looking for the husband of the woman we found in the salt cavern? What's his name? Goldsmith, wasn't it?"

The old sheriff must have killed him, then used the body to stage his own death. Probably it had happened the same day R.C. had murdered the man's wife. Had Eversole gotten greedy and tried to squeeze too much out of the couple? Considering how obsessed the man was with the money Angie had supposedly stolen from him, it made sense.

"Christ on a crutch . . ." Wallace muttered. "Then . . . well, if that's right, where would R.C. be taking Jay?"

She nodded, tears burning her eyes and pointed out the direction in which she'd seen the taillights disappear. "All I know is they went that way. I don't know where they were headed. The old sheriff was half-crazy, ranting about finding the rest of his money."

Wallace's head jerked back and his eyes widened.

"He thought I knew where it was," Dana went on, "thought Angie must've told me before he killed her. He . . . he'd do anything to get it back—probably so he can get clear of the area. He'd kill anybody—right down to his own nephew. Jay told him he knew where the money was, but Angie never said a word to me about it."

Wallace nodded and put his truck in gear. "Then we'd better catch up with them."

"Do you have some idea where they went?"

"Better than that," he said grimly. "I know exactly where they're going."

The shovel Jay had been given bit into the gravel, then rattled an addition to the growing pile at his right. The repeated *scriiitch-rattle* of the work formed a rhythm as surreal as the headlight-lit excavation of the double grave.

While his uncle kept his gun on him from a safe distance, Jay was seized with the notion that this was something from a horror movie . . . or a Middle Eastern desert.

The pistol trained on him became a machine gun; the darkness cloaking the man who held it morphed into the black robe and headdress of a mujahideen guerrilla. They were forcing him to dig his own grave before they tried to make him renounce his government and beheaded him on a videotape they planned to send to the Al Jazeera network.

They . . . no . . . he . . . There was only one, not many. And the night smelled of West Texas and . . .

It was the pain that brought Jay to himself: the soreness of his muscles, the sweat-spawned blisters on his palms, and the sick throb of his head. They combined to ground him in a present even more distressing than his past.

His uncle had shot Dana and had him digging beneath the petals, bones, and pebbles Angie had used to mark the old Webb graves. The same sort of decoration that had marked the site where the body he suspected would prove to be Roman Goldsmith's had been found, where Angie had interred the first fifty thousand.

In the final recovered pages of her journal, she had written of her desire to honor *the ones who came before, who got us where we are now. Not the cheap flash and empty promises of modern charlatans. That's the shit that should be buried and forgotten.*

Those words, along with the prompting of his subconscious—since he refused to believe he had actually been visited by Angie's spirit—had convinced him that the money had been split up and moved to at least two other sites, including this one and the salt cavern where Miriam Piper-Gold's body had been hidden.

If he had guessed wrong, the man standing some six feet away pointing his pistol would surely use the weapon. But come to think of it, he would probably do the same if Jay were right—unless Jay found some way to distract and over-power R.C. first.

Jay *had* to, not for his own sake, but for Dana's. If there was any chance—any chance at all—that she had survived a gunshot wound to her head, he had to get back to her quickly.

He dug deep into his reserves of strength to summon up an attempt at conversation. "So who's been helping you?"

The stony soil rattled as it slid down from his shovel. When his uncle didn't answer, he added, "Somebody had to've. That old truck's not yours, is it? And someone's picked up supplies and stuff for you."

"Is this the part where you try to draw me into conversation to lull me off my guard?" R.C. asked him. With a nod, he added, "Guess you *have* learned something since you left here. I would've tried the same thing."

"I learned a lot from watching you," Jay said, trying not to let his uncle's comment get to him. "It's what made me switch my major to criminal justice while I was putting myself through school. I wanted to be like the first man I respected."

At the moment Jay wanted nothing more than to split the bastard's skull with the shovel he'd been handed. But with his uncle out of range, he used his foot to drive the blade in deeper.

"Flattery now, huh? They teach you that in Dallas? Or did

they have you ass-kiss ayatollahs while you were over there in I-raq?"

"Maybe you could give me a few pointers on sucking up," Jay countered. "The way you've let Abe Hooks run your office all these years. I know about the way y'all 'persuaded' folks you didn't want around to leave Rimrock."

Maybe if he pissed off the man sufficiently, his uncle would grow careless enough to drop his guard. Since Jay was standing in the hole he'd dug, the chances of gaining control were worse than slim, so he'd have to act fast to seize on the slightest opening.

But R.C. simply shrugged. "Hell, boy. That's not Hooks runnin' me. That's just the way things are done out here. The way they've always been done since back before your granddad and great-granddad did their stints as sheriff."

"Things were done that way in a lot of departments for a lot of years. But that doesn't make it right—especially not when people end up dead."

Jay's uncle spit. "I've heard about that pussification training they make cops take now. All that diversity awareness and such shit. And that might be well and good in those fancy college classes they got the ACLU teachin'. But out here we hold with what works—and that's still a strong sheriff givin' bad men till sundown to get the hell out of Dodge."

Something he'd said rang a bell. His reference to the American Civil Liberties Union, maybe. But Jay was far too distracted to focus on it at the moment. "That hippie squatter you and your buddies burned to death back when I was a kid? I still remember him and his woman wearing those tie-dyed T-shirts from the sixties and making candles and wind chimes to sell at craft fairs. Do you really expect me to believe people like that were threatening the peace? Or maybe they were just a little too different for the people here in Devil's Claw?"

"Everybody knew those two were illegally harvesting peyote buttons. You let that sort of business get a toehold, and before you know it all sorts of—"

Interrupting himself, R.C. frowned and pointed to Jay's right. "Should have found something by now. Little thing like her couldn't have dug too deep. Maybe you ought to try a bit farther over that way."

But Jay's shovel had already struck something that felt different. Unlike the noisy, pebbled sand he had been digging, the sound was deadened and the steel blade's bite felt soft.

Far too soft to be explained by the banded packs of cash that he'd expected. As the pungent odor filled his nostrils, dread breached Jay's levees.

Dread mingled with the bittersweet anticipation of his own impending death.

# *Chapter Thirty-two*

*Behold, from the land of the farther suns*
*I returned.*
*And I was in a reptile-swarming place,*
*Peopled, otherwise, with grimaces,*
*Shrouded above in black impenetrableness.*
*I shrank, loathing,*
*Sick with it.*
*And I said to him,*
*"What is this?"*
*He made answer slowly,*
*"Spirit, this is a world;*
*This was your home."*

—Stephen Crane,
"The Black Riders and Other Lines"

As Wallace raced along dark roads, Dana checked Max's leg wound, in part because she couldn't stand the thought of the dog suffering and in part because she had to do something—anything—to keep from going utterly to pieces in her worry over Jay.

"It's not so bad, boy. Not so bad," she reassured the quivering dog as she stroked his short hair. To her relief she found no injuries other than a single slash across Max's upper foreleg, which had nearly finished bleeding. Grazed by the shot, the shepherd had gone into hiding. Dana quickly guessed the reason as she touched the knotty, healed wounds along his side, which she remembered feeling earlier. Someone had hurt the animal before he'd come into Jay's keeping. Some cruel jackass with a gun.

"Never again," she promised Max. Even if Jay didn't make it, she wouldn't let—

Shredded by the thought, she forced herself to ask Wallace a question. "How . . . how did you know her? How did you know Angie?"

"What?" he asked her from the driver's seat, where he had clearly been lost in his own thoughts.

Once she repeated the question, his ring finger tapped a fitful beat against the wheel.

"I didn't know your sister." He noisily cleared his throat. "Not really. Just bumped into her a few times around town."

"Jay said you picked her up when she was drunk. Not long before she vanished."

His gaze flashed sideways. "What the hell are you accusing me of? Because I'm trying to do my job. I'm trying—"

"She told you where she hid the money." Dana's heart pounded with the suspicion that so much hinged on this conversation, even more than Jay's life. "Drunk or not, she told you because she knew you once. Because you'd been together."

Dana wanted to add, *When you were both in rehab*, but intuition warned her not to push him any harder.

"What the . . ." He shook his head emphatically, tapping his ring finger even harder. "You think I'd take up with a woman like that? No offense, but your sister spent so much of her life hammered, she was wrecked. Whatever the bizarro cause, she jumped all over it. Whoever the man, she jumped him, too, as long as he could help her get her next good buzz on—"

"She wasn't always that way."

"I wouldn't know about that," he said as the truck rolled to a standstill in front of the access gate that led to the salt dome. "Now stay put. I need to check this."

He ran out and fiddled with the gate's chain before returning to the pickup and climbing back inside. "I guessed wrong. They didn't come here, so they must've gone over to the Webb place."

"The old adobe? But it's already been searched. And anyway, why would Angie hide the money there—"

"God alone knows why that woman did anything she did."

"Including having your child?"

"What the hell? *No.*" He ignored her and turned the truck around. But as he started back the way they'd come, he finally added, "Look, I've tried my hand at city living. Gave it a damned good shot. From acting, to odd jobs, to private security, which was the only damned thing I was even halfway good at, until . . . Nothing ever really came together for me until this job. Doesn't pay hardly enough to feed a coyote, but if I keep at it, someday I'll be sheriff—if you don't go stirrin' up shit. Like insinuatin' I had something going with some glue-sniffin' lush."

She heard the truth in his voice, as well as the fear that kept him from admitting it. *You're Nikki's father, aren't you? You're just too scared to say so.*

The pickup surged forward as he stomped down on the accelerator.

Dana braced herself as they careened around a curve that returned them to the main road. "She'll die, Wallace. That little girl will die if you don't—"

Wallace jammed the brakes, flinging Dana painfully against her seat belt and making Max yip as his head banged against the dash.

Alarm ripping through her, Dana grasped the door handle. But with breath-catching agony coiling like a constrictor around her side, she couldn't get out, couldn't run. Could barely manage to pull in enough oxygen to keep herself conscious.

"You've got a choice. We can sit and hash this out now," Wallace said, "or we can put an end to this discussion and find Jay. So which is it gonna be, *Doctor?*"

Dana fought to hold back the dizzying swirl of darkness pressing in on her. Biting her inner lip helped; the sharp pinch and the copper-tart blood taste pulled her back from the pain.

She forced herself to focus on the deputy's face. To see

the warring of ambitions. The desire to do right, to be a decent man and a loyal deputy, against the need to prove himself in this place, to these people. And most especially to his father. Had that struggle been what had kept him from either reporting the location of the missing money or making off with it? And by forcing him to make a choice of which man he was going to be, had she pushed him too far?

"*Careful, Dana,*" Angie's voice warned. "*That little shit's a lot more like those bastards than he wants to believe.*"

"Please," Dana pleaded. "We have to help him. We have to get to him before his uncle—"

"Then not one more word about your sister, ever. Swear it."

"I do," she said, mentally begging forgiveness for a choice that was no choice at all. "Just . . . please hurry. *Hurry,* and I swear I'll never mention her again."

As the meaning of the charred smell sank in, a realization struck Jay: that Angie Vanover had gotten the last laugh after all. Too bad she wasn't around to appreciate the moment.

Desperate to avoid joining her, he mentally scrambled for the words that might keep his uncle from pulling the trigger when he discovered that the money he had killed for was beyond reach. For anything that might throw the older man off his guard. But when he looked up at R.C., Jay could come up with nothing better than, "Oh, shit. You're gonna want to see this."

Apparently his uncle misunderstood his tone. Either that, or avarice rose up like the bitter reek to overwhelm his better judgment. With a triumphant grin splitting his sun-creased face, R.C. brought the flashlight closer, his blue eyes avid as he peered down at the money that had so long fed his obsession.

And in that single, careless moment, Jay used the shovel to fling the ashes of his greed full in his face.

"Son of a bitch," R.C. yelled, and wasted a precious instant bringing up his free arm to wipe his eyes.

Seizing his opportunity, Jay swung the shovel, scythelike, his assault aimed for the most vulnerable spot within reach. R.C. bellowed as the blade's edge jolted off both his shins, and he went down hard, squeezing off one shot as he fell. In quick succession three more followed, loud cracks that sounded like the night sky shattering around them. As Jay leaped from the hole his left leg collapsed. He went to his knees, falling in such a way that his sweat-slick palms lost their grip on the shovel's handle.

R.C. still had the gun—Jay caught its gleam in the approaching headlights—and the two Eversoles grappled wildly for it. Slightly taller, younger, and stronger, Jay should have wrested it away in time. Should have found some way to pull free the finger R.C. had threaded through the trigger guard.

Instead he struggled to control his uncle's right wrist, to push the armed hand high enough to keep R.C. from blowing off his head. When Jay tried to use his legs for leverage, he shouted with the pain that detonated in his left thigh, an explosion that splashed across his vision in bright crimson.

In the wake of it he heard Dana calling his name. . . . Dana, who must be dead already. Who would be there waiting for him when his uncle finished him.

"Drop it, R.C. Drop it, or I'll shoot," shouted a male voice.

Was it Wallace? But if Wallace was here, did that mean Dana, too, was—

R.C.'s right hand jerked as he got off two more shots and then a third. But before Jay could wonder how many rounds the pistol's magazine held, Dana's scream penetrated his awareness, a high, clipped cry that followed the last shot.

# *Chapter Thirty-three*

*And that the whole land thereof is brimstone, and salt, and burning, that it is not sown, nor beareth, nor any grass groweth therein, like the overthrow of Sodom, and Gomorrah . . .*

—Deuteronomy 29:23
The Holy Bible (King James Version)

As Dana dropped to her knees, the dog sprang forward, snarling at the man who struggled with his master. A haze of acrid gunsmoke hung before the headlights in striated layers.

Beside her Wallace flailed on his back, his choked screams rising from behind a dark, wet mask. It was a mask of blood, she realized as she spotted a small hole in the left side of his upper jaw. His head jerked, and her heart spasmed as she saw the right cheek, blown out by an exit wound.

A man could die from so much bleeding—die the way her sister had.

Dana ripped off the remains of her shirt and wadded up the cotton. Dressed only in her bra and shorts, she shouted at the fallen deputy, "Lie still, and hold this to your cheek. You've got to apply pressure."

His cries stopped, too abruptly, and his limbs jerked uncontrollably. She was losing him, she realized—losing her last link to Nikki. But she had to help Jay, too, had to do something to save him—

"Dana!"

Her head jerked toward his voice, and she saw him holding his uncle at gunpoint. *Thank God.*

"We have to get your deputy help." She leaned over Wallace to press the cloth against the open wound. "He . . . he's choking."

Heaven only knew what devastation the bullet had wrought before its exit. She had performed enough surgery on animals injured by gunshots to know the throat or upper palate could have been hit. Enough to realize that an emergency tracheotomy might be Wallace's best chance, in spite of the terrible conditions.

Unless . . .

"Help me hold him," she told Jay. "I have to keep him still so I can—"

Grasping the distraction, R.C. swung around with one fist—but too slowly to avoid Jay's clout to the head with his own pistol. Knees collapsing, the older Eversole tumbled to the ground, twitched twice, and went still.

"Can't say I'm sorry I had to do that." Jay squatted with a pained grunt and grasped Wallace by the shoulders.

Dana tried to pull his head back, but the deputy thrashed wildly.

"Quit fighting," Jay ordered. "We're trying to help you."

Wallace did, and all too suddenly, as he lost consciousness. Dana tilted back his head and opened the jaw, then swept her fingers across the back of his tongue to check the airway. She had to work quickly. If Wallace needed a tracheotomy she had only minutes to perform it before his brain was damaged and his system failed.

She moved so quickly that she nearly missed it—the small, hard object in the back of his throat. Repositioning herself for a better angle, she dug deeper—and swept free a clot of tissue that included several of his teeth.

Almost instantly she felt a puff as he expelled the stale air from his lungs before sucking in another breath.

With a silent prayer of thanks, she said, "He's breathing."

She felt around for the remnants of her shirt and held the less-than-ideal bandage to the wreckage of Wallace's cheek. Only then did she notice Jay staring at her, moisture gleaming in his eyes.

"That son of a bitch lied to me. He told me that he'd

killed you—shot you in the head. I was sure I'd never see you again."

Shaking her head, she said, "Wallace's headlights scared him off, I think. I'll be all right, Jay. Help me get him on his side, please. We don't want more blood choking him."

Once they moved Wallace into a better position, Dana added, "We're going to need help. Is there a radio in the truck, or do you or Wallace have a phone?"

"I don't have mine, but let me check him," Jay said. A moment later he added, "No phone here, but I'll need these."

He took a set of cuffs from Wallace's belt and then went to R.C., who had started groaning. Jay snapped a manacle on one of his uncle's wrists.

"Look, I'll split the money with you," R.C. mumbled. As he glanced back over one shoulder, his gaze was wide and empty as a dead man's. "We can still make this right. And I can still get out of Devil's Claw—"

"One more word and you'll die here—right now," Jay told him before he finished applying the restraints.

He picked up the gun Wallace had dropped and laid it beside the spot where Dana squatted. Nodding toward his uncle, he told her, "Shoot him if he moves. I'll be right back."

Dana looked after him as he went to Wallace's truck. He was limping heavily, and she already knew that he'd been knocked unconscious earlier. But in spite of his wounds, she sensed a core of strength she could rely on . . . at least for the moment.

Though he had nearly killed her earlier, she knew that without hesitation he would give his life for hers. Just as she'd been willing to risk everything for him tonight . . . and she could not regret it.

That was the final thought that flitted through her mind before she heard a new voice by the truck.

"How the hell . . . ?" Jay started. But at the sight of the rifle he lost his curiosity about how she'd found him. With his own weapon holstered as he reached across the seat for Wallace's cell phone, Jay knew Suzanne Riggins could shoot him before he had the chance to draw.

But *would* the wife of his uncle's best friend? With her white hair frizzed around her, she looked both pale and sickly. But her gray eyes were inscrutable.

"Wallace called the house earlier," she said in her deep, West Texas accent. "Left a message that you might need someone to watch your back tonight. Dennis . . . Dennis drank himself to sleep again. He's been doing that for days now. Busted up about losing all our money on Haz-Vestment."

"So he told you?"

She shook her head. "I knew. I knew it from the first—why he thought he needed to risk everything. Damned foolish man I married. If he'd asked me, I'd have told him not to take the chance."

"So you came. To help me."

"By the time I got to your place, all I could see were taillights leaving. I was way behind, so I just caught up."

It surprised Jay that Wallace Hooks would ask a Riggins for assistance—unless he knew his father and his friends could not be trusted. "I have to call for help, so how about lowering that muzzle?"

Uncertainty flickered through her eyes, but Suzanne didn't move to comply. And like every man and woman raised in these parts, she knew enough about a rifle to put another hole in him. "We need that money, Jay. Two years ago we lost our health insurance, and . . . and whether or not I make it through this heart surgery, Dennis will lose everything. Everything his daddy and his grandpa worked for."

So that was the lever R.C. had used to convince his friend to help him continue concealing his death. To convince both Dennis and Suzanne.

"Wallace has been shot," Jay said. "If I don't get him help, he'll die."

The tip of the rifle dropped down slightly, as if it were too heavy for Suzanne to hold up. "I'm sorry about that—sorry for what it'll do to Estelle. But Wallace can't be my concern now. Dennis—"

"Don't let your husband's idiotic grudge with Abe push you into making the biggest mistake of your life. I have every reason to believe that Wallace turned his back on his own daddy to save my ass tonight. And if you think I'm about to let my deputy die . . . Hell, Suzanne. The money isn't even here. It's gone. Forever."

Suzanne shook her head, blanching to a color as pale as starlight. "That can't be right. R.C. told us Angelina hid it. We just have to find where—"

"She burned every bit of it," Jay said, though he had no idea whether undamaged bills remained hidden near the cavern where the salt mummy had been found. "She didn't want anyone to profit from—"

"No," Suzanne cried, letting the rifle fall as she covered her face with her hands. "That money—it was our life. My life, and Dennis's if I die. *How* can I die, knowing he'll be . . ."

Jay didn't tell her that his uncle had convinced himself that *he* deserved that million dollars—enough to kill to keep it. Jay was too busy calling the air-ambulance service and struggling to remain upright despite his dizziness and the pain in his own leg. Though his wound was nowhere near as threatening as the one that had brought down Wallace, Jay suspected a bullet had passed through the meaty part of his left thigh.

Once the call had ended, all he had to do was take up the rifle before the woman did something desperate. But a wave of fatigue broke over Jay, leaving him too weak to rise from the truck's seat.

At the sound of voices to his left, he managed to glance over . . . only to see Dana holding the taller, frailer woman at gunpoint.

She had come to cover Jay's back, in spite of all she'd been through.

He stared at her in wonder, more amazed than ever at the miracle of Dana's courage. A miracle that unraveled before his eyes as he lost his grip on consciousness and slipped into the void.

Dana insisted upon being there in the recovery room of the El Paso hospital where she and Jay had both been taken, along with Wallace Hooks. With her ribs taped and her strength buoyed by mild painkillers and a few hours' sleep, she sat in a wheelchair, waiting impatiently for the first flicker beneath his eyelids. Finally she caught the movement of his hand, heard a half-coherent mumble as he came around from under the influence of the anesthesia.

In defiance of the nurse's admonishments that she remain seated, Dana stood at that first stirring and ran her hand along his sculpted jawline, now scratchy with stubble. Next she gently brushed back his mussed hair from the dark bruise at his temple, her breath hitching at the thought of how close she had come to losing this man, this handsome, broken warrior, just as she'd lost Angie.

She couldn't keep from crying, couldn't stop the tears that dripped onto his hand. His eyes cracked open to peer up at her, and relief sang through her at the way recognition warmed them.

At the way he smiled at her, a smile that made her think of locked bedroom doors and soft caresses, of whispers that melted into sighs.

Unable to speak, she leaned forward—wincing only a little at the flare of pain in her ribs—to touch her lips to his, then to kiss him fully, deeply, infusing that small act with all the feeling trapped behind the lump in her throat.

When she finally pulled away, he blinked, then asked, "Where is . . . Where are we?"

"In the recovery room of Thomason Hospital in El Paso," she managed. "You've just come out of surgery to repair the damage to your leg. You don't remember any of it?"

He grimaced after shaking his head. "Damn. Remind me not to try that again anytime soon. . . ."

"You probably have a mild concussion, and you lost quite a bit of blood. Bullet passed right through your thigh, and you didn't say a word about it. Didn't hit the bone, but still—"

"I had bigger worries at the moment. I thought you were dead. I thought I'd never get the chance to tell you . . . I love you. I've been in love with you almost since that first day you showed up in Devil's Claw. I've never known a woman like you—a woman who'd go so far to help the people she loves—and even for a little kid she barely knows. But you're better than just brave, Dana. You're smart and you're a smart-ass, and you make me harder than a diamond drill bit every time I think about you."

"Well, isn't *that* romantic?" She laughed—and regretted it immediately at the renewed pain in her ribs. *A diamond drill bit . . .*

But he loved her, and the warmth of that knowledge spread over her like heated nectar. She swallowed back tears, allowing his words to sink in.

Before she could say anything, he blinked hard, and worry flashed across his features. "I remember now. How you saved Wallace. He'd been shot, and he was choking. Is he . . . is he here?"

"They've got him stabilized. He'll need some reconstructive surgery to repair the damage to his jaw and face, but—"

"Poor Estelle," he said. "She'll be beside herself. Has anyone called—"

"I understand that she and Abe are on their way. But he'll be fine, Jay. And so will you, and—"

"But what happened to R.C.? With both Wallace and me out of commission . . . tell me that bastard didn't get away."

"Not a chance. Apparently the FBI agent you spoke to last night was so concerned he called in a favor—phoned the sheriff over in . . . is it Monahans?"

Jay nodded. "That'd be the Ward County sheriff. About an hour out of Rimrock County. Where Agent Petit's from."

"Anyway, he arrived around the same time as the helicopter. You were sort of in and out of it when he took both your uncle and that woman into custody. He's taking care of Max for you, too—"

"Suzanne—I remember. That was Suzanne Riggins. Hell, she can't go to prison—it'll kill Dennis if she's charged with . . . And it might kill Suzanne, too."

"There'll be time to straighten all that out, Jay. For now, you need to concentrate on getting better. Because . . ." She gave his hand a squeeze and touched his face again, as if to reassure herself that he was warm and solid. Breathing. "Because I was afraid, too. Scared half to death your uncle would kill you. And I couldn't stand that, couldn't bear the thought of never making things right after . . . after what happened earlier."

Jay's face fell, and his eyes went hollow, as if the memory of attacking her had rushed in on him from the darkness. "There's no making up for injuring a woman, for . . . for nearly killing her. A man doesn't—"

She shook her head. "No, Jay. You can't give up on yourself. I won't. Ever. Because I love you. And I love you more this morning than I've ever—"

"You deserve a hell of a lot better than an unemployed head case, Dana, a man who was sent home because—"

"I don't care about that, Jay. I only care about you. We'll get you help. Counseling. Medication. I don't care what it takes. Because I want you. I need you with me."

Muscles tensed in his jaw. "I can't."

"I have the money, Jay—or I can get it. We'll get you the best of help. The best of everything—I swear it." She heard herself pleading with him, even in the face of the leaden shield that slammed down over his expression. She knew how badly she'd just screwed up—knew that reminding him of her family's money had been exactly the wrong thing. "Please. We can do this together."

"I won't be your pet charity project, something broken you can fix. It didn't work for Angie, and it sure as hell won't work for—"

"You're being stupid. Stubborn. Too damned proud to let a woman help you. To let anyone—"

"I won't take the chance of hurting you again. I can't . . . I couldn't live with myself if something happened."

By this time her tears were falling freely. The pain inside her was so wrenching, she didn't even bother to try to hold them back. "But I love you. Please—"

"Don't do this, Dana. It's too hard to see you like this."

She smiled sadly. "Harder than a diamond drill bit?"

But no matter how she tried, she couldn't tease a smile from him. Nor anything but the same ironclad insistence that her time with him was over.

# Chapter Thirty-four

*Content can soothe where'er by fortune placed,*
*Can rear a garden in the desert waste.*

—Henry Kirk White,
from "Clifton Grove: A Sketch"

*Eight months later . . .*

Jay shook his head, darkness clouding his expression. "But you were right earlier; you know that. I've got to get straight before I can trust myself again—and especially before I'm deserving of your faith, or anybody's."

Dana wiped her leaking eyes with a handful of crumpled tissue. But when she looked up to argue with him, the Salt Maiden lay beneath the crisp white sheets and stared out of a mummified face with Angie's deep brown eye set in its sole remaining socket.

When she tried to speak, the corpse's jaw broke loose on one side and dangled askew from a sinew, but it didn't stop her from reaching forward and laying a withered hand on Dana's arm.

At death's touch Dana woke up screaming and found herself trembling, sweat-soaked, with an afghan coiled tight around her as she lay curled on the sofa. Ben and Jerry whined beside her before Ben got up the nerve to place his stubby legs against the cushion and lick her face.

Sitting up, she stroked his head, then reached down to pat her other corgi. But Jerry, always the less confident of the brothers, slid away from her hand with his tail tucked between his legs. Though he had been reliably housebroken for two years, he had recently started having accidents—because her night terrors caused him so much stress.

How could she continue to terrify the animals she claimed to love? And how could she allow herself to continue suffering this way?

The nightmares weren't getting any better. For months she'd told herself—and her mother, who had witnessed more than one such episode—that she was merely worried about Nikki, whom she'd come to love like the daughter she would never have. But since Wallace had allowed himself to be tested, then proved a match and donated the marrow Nikki needed, her doctors claimed she had an excellent chance of achieving long-term survivorship. And now that her parents were finally talking out their differences, the little girl's future seemed assured.

It was high time, Dana decided, to stop moping and start thinking about her own future. Her mother had highly recommended the same counselor-led group meetings that had helped her confront the trauma of her own past. Dana had seen for herself Isabel's transformation, the way her rare, stiff touches had blossomed into hugs these past few months.

"*Please, Dana,*" she had urged. "*I think you'd find it helpful— and heaven only knows I've wasted enough time for both of us. Besides*"—here a certain shrewdness had come into her voice—"*there's a man there I think might be wonderful for you.*"

At the thought, Dana rolled her eyes. After Alex, whom her mother had considered perfection on a platter, she had no intention of trusting Isabel's judgment anytime soon. Especially not with the sticky strands of hope still connecting her heart to a man she hadn't spoken to in months.

But as far as the nightmares went, something had to give. Even if it meant checking out the post-traumatic stress support group she had so long been resisting.

"If my mom can do it," Dana told the corgis, "so can I."

Still, she waited until an evening the following week, for a night she knew her mother would be unable to attend. She arrived late—she'd been tied up in the clinic tending the results of a Yorkshire terrier-versus-raccoon battle—

and stood nervously outside the open door of one of the wellness center's meeting rooms. She felt awkward going in late, walking in among a bunch of strangers and announcing, "Hi, I'm Dana, and I'm a total loser."

But even as she thought it, she knew she was wrong, as wrong as Jay had been when he'd refused to forgive himself for attacking her. The thought swamped her with the same sadness she always felt when thinking of the way he had vanished from Devil's Claw as soon as his deputy had recovered sufficiently to take over his position and the charges against both Suzanne and Dennis Riggins had been dropped.

Jay had vanished from her life as well, without leaving her any way to reach him. She prayed that he had done as he had promised, had gone somewhere to get treatment for the same problem she now faced. But he'd been so despondent, so shattered by what he'd called his weakness and the murder charges against his last surviving relative, that in her heart Dana wondered if Jay Eversole had made it.

Sometimes in her dreams she found his body. Dangling from a shower rod. Shot clean through the head. Encrusted with salt crystals in a white grotto hidden far beneath the desert surface.

Still outside the room, she bowed her head. She couldn't talk about this right now—couldn't open herself to a group of total strangers. It would be like stripping naked, would be like—

A voice drifted out to her, a voice she knew as well as her own, though it had been far too long since she had heard it.

"I started a new job today. I'm working at the University of Houston, in their Veterans Services Office. Seems they went and got themselves the idea I'm some kind of success story. They think maybe I could be of use talking to other returning vets about the things I've been through. I'll be some kind of glorified red-tape warrior, assisting them with college and grant applications and letting them know it won't kill 'em to get themselves whatever kind of help they need to move on with their lives. But it could kill 'em if they don't—or at least kill their chances for a decent future. For damned sure it cost me the one thing I wanted most in this world, the one woman I've been working my ass off to have another chance with, if it's not already too late. I only wish I'd gotten my act together a hell of a lot sooner—"

"Well, you've certainly gotten yourself together now," an older woman interrupted before the sounds of clapping overwhelmed her words.

"Oh, my . . . Oh, Jay." Moving like a sleepwalker Dana stepped inside, breathless and dizzy with relief. With a joy that ignited inside her and lit her like the full moon.

For the rest of her life she would remember the moment when he looked up, the way his vibrant blue eyes flared with hope. For the rest of their lives—his and hers together— they would speak of it, boring their adopted children to distraction with the story of the way they came together in a flurry of sweet kisses. The way they came together, stayed together, and at long last healed each other's wounds.